About the Author

Maximilian Hawker works in frontline children's social care supporting looked-after children and care leavers. He does advocacy work for the charity OCD Action as and when he can, and has been a sufferer of obsessive compulsive disorder (OCD) since he was a child. In 2018, his debut novel, *Breaking the Foals*, was published by Unbound. He lives in Croydon with his wife and two children and a pair of rubbish cats.

PRAISE FOR *RORY HOBBLE AND THE VOYAGE TO HALIGOGEN* FROM CHILDREN

'This is an AMAZING book. It's very exciting and a bit sad at times. Also, I want a little "Gary" to take home.'
– Meredith (10)

'I loved the story so much because it has a lot of drama throughout. I would recommend this book to a friend and I rate it 10/10.' – Ashlee (11)

'This is the strangest book I've ever read… in a good way!'
– Jasper (10)

'I enjoyed the book and found it very relatable. Rory is a nuanced character in a juxtaposed and intricately-woven storyline!' – Ben (14)

'One of the most unique children's novels I'll ever read. Seeing yourself represented in books is so rare and there are a lot of people and children who would benefit from reading this.' – Freya (13)

'Really good detailed book and I like how it's about real-life problems.' – Mmesoma (13)

For every child who has ever whispered, 'What if?'
into the dark.

Contents

Super Patrons

Mohammed Adam
Eli Allison
Karen Attwood
Jamie Baker
Fern Barber
Debby Bentley-Ross
Mark Bowsher
Hollie Burton
Martyn Campbell
Siobhán Campbell
Anne Cater
Chris Chantrey
Jonathan Chin
Gary Clark
Elvis Coimbra Gomes
Stevyn Colgan
Jude Cook
Peter Cook
Harry Cooke
Robert Cox

Garret Coy
Kerry Crichlow
Sheila Dobbs
Sheila Dunn
Jo Edge
Michael Evans
Martin Fernandes
Shira Folberg
Dan Furlong
Rory Geoghegan
James Gill
Daniel Goldsmith
Mr Grace
Emma Grae
Anna Hammond
Evie Hawker
Mark Hawker
Simon Hawker
Nicola Haynes
Giles Heron
Nik Hurrell
Matthew Jarvis
Becca Jiggens
Christina Kennedy
Jacqui Knighton
Pete Langman
Sean Lawrence
Joseph Lee-Overton
Charmaine Lewis
Amy Lord

Fiona Mackirdy
Maris like Paris
Claire Marris
Kate Mason
Edward McGurran
Charmaine McGusty Khoumeri
Erinna Mettler
Adam Mitchell
John Mitchinson
Virginia Moffatt
Jenny Molloy
Mutley Moss
Eva O'Connor
Anita Okoeguale
Esme Pears
Vincent Peart
Jennifer Pierce
Hannah Poole
Jason Preece
Janet Pretty
Stuart Ralph
Andrew Randall
Onjali Rauf
Errol Roberts
Orna Ross
Peter Salter
Ste Sharp
Frankie Slee
Keith Sleight
Allison Strachan

Frankie Sullivan Brown
Richard Taylor
Gail Thibert
Janet Toner
Niamh Toner
Peter Toner
Simon Townend
Victoria Towobola
Alexandra Turney
James Vella-Bardon
Mark Vent
Serge Vincent
John Warren and Michele Dominique
Julie Warren
Roy Warren
Phoebe White
Suzie Wilde
Rachel Willie
Priya Wilson
Mohammed Yassin
Helen Youngs

Before we launch...

Every single day, all around the world, children face challenges that would be difficult and upsetting even for grown-ups to deal with.

I believe that books for children should be filled with love, laughter and adventure, yes – but they should also reflect those challenges that children face, especially the ones that are particularly scary. I wrote *Rory Hobble and the Voyage to Haligogen* because, when I was a child, I had a lot of very frightening things happen to me and I think reading is a powerful comfort and a reminder that the biggest heroes are often the littlest people.

Just because you're a child, it doesn't mean that you can't have grown-up thoughts and experiences because, sometimes, life won't wait for you to not be a child anymore. So, although this book may be scary and upsetting, at times, it is driven by something very special indeed: bravery, friendship and hope.

Welcome to the world of Rory Hobble...

1

The Intruders

It was a sharp November night in South London when eleven-year-old Rory Hobble spotted something impossible in the sky.

He dropped his binoculars, glancing at the bedside digital clock, which projected an eerie, red **23:38**. The only sound was the occasional yell of his mum on the other side of the bedroom they were forced to share in their tiny flat, as she struggled through yet another bad dream. Shuffling over the bed, he leaned his arms into the chill windowsill. Far, far below was what seemed such a little world, barbed in shadow. Unfastening the latch, Rory pushed the window open, the bedroom warmth depressurised into the night and replaced with the wind's bitter breath. Goosebumps assembled over his skin like inverted meteor craters. This always woke him, when the cold snapped at his cheeks, clawing the sleep from sore eyes. But more than anything, he adored craning his neck towards the clouds, hungering for all the wonders that he imagined to await beyond the sky.

Rory glanced at his mum, whose face was twisted and sweaty. She didn't wake.

Then it came... that voice, that doubt which sickened his mind:

Rooory, Rooory. Mum might get cold. Then she might get ill. Then she might –

No, Rory. Deep breath, he told himself. *The thought will go.*

But an image flickered into his mind: his mum, pale and lifeless in an Arctic bedroom. He closed his eyes, shook his head.

After several controlled breaths, the thought – the voice – faded into the background. Nonetheless, he hopped off his bed and stepped over to his mum. But her chest still lifted and dropped. She was fine. He knew that, deep down. In sleep though, she looked vulnerable – a far cry from the daytime carnivore he knew her to be.

He crept back across the floor, careful not to stand on the creaky bits he'd memorised, and avoiding the wire of the tatty, oil-heated radiator.

From under his bed, he dragged out the *Thought Diary*, where he jotted down all those peculiar thoughts that filled his head. All those thoughts that *he* got and 'normal' people – or so he saw them – didn't. He had been advised by his last head doctor to write out every fear and every doubt that filled his mind, assured that it would help him to see them for what they really were: farce. It was a nice diary too, leather.

So, he opened the pages. Moonlight helped him guide a biro through the dark:

I was scared mum would die off hyperthermia cos I opened the window at night.

Okay, it was only a four out of ten on the anxiety scale – the thoughts were always weaker when he was tired – and Rory was able to offer at least three rational responses to counter the discomfort:

1. we dont live in antartica so its not that cold
2. mum is sweating so she must be feeling warm
3. even if she did die tonight it wouldn't nesesarily be cos of the cold

It helped, a little.

Before long, he was back at the window. But the voice would not be quiet.

Rooory, Rooory. Mum might get cold. Then she might get ill. Then she might –

Nope, I'm keeping it open, Rory resolved.

Rooory, Rooory.

And as the voice finally faded, Rory once more turned his attention to astronomical matters.

Above the *ruffing* dogs and mechanical tide of distant cars, there was the sky – *his* sky. It was the same sky that covered all the world and all its people, whether they were of sound mind or not. Of course, living in South London, lights-beyond-count threw up an obstructive pink glow, which made it hard to see the stars. But if he stared long enough his eyes adapted and he could still find them. And name the constellations.

He lifted a finger, tracing the little salt-granule lights.

Right, right, right, his finger moved. Orion's Belt.

Right, down, down, right, down, left, up, this time. The Plough.

Sometimes, Rory took a piece of black card, popped out his medication from those little foil blisters, and lined the pills up in the shape of Cetus or Ursa Major or some such other arrangement of stars. But the Plough he'd made earlier that night, still sitting there atop the up-ended bin that served as a bedside cabinet, looked more like a saucepan. For one absurd moment now, Rory wondered if supernovas and black holes boiled and bubbled inside the real Plough all those light years away.

Occasionally, he would find a ruddy, dusty dot in the sky that didn't shimmer, and he knew that to be Venus or Mars. Maybe even Jupiter. Other than the pilgrimage of the planets, the sky had never failed him in its sameness. The only changeless thing he had in his life – and with that voice in his head making him doubt himself, he'd always relied on this solid sky. Until that night.

Rooory, Rooory.

Okay, I'll check her breathing, Rory conceded to the voice – the doubt.

He tiptoed over to his mum, as though approaching a wild and unpredictable animal, and hovered above her contorted face, listening. Her breath came jagged, but it *did* come.

… Mum's fine, Rory assured himself.

Returning to the window, he snatched up his binoculars again and brought the sky back into focus.

It was still there. *The Intruder.*

He rubbed his eyes and looked once more, this time using

4

only his eyes. Yes, there it was. Brazen. A brightness hanging in the north. It was not a plane. Planes moved and flashed with red and green, and whatever this was, it did not move and it was not red or green. *And* it was brighter than Sirius, the brightest star in the sky – so it couldn't be a star either.

And then Rory sucked in his breath as... another *two* lights appeared, very close to the first! Then another! And another! Now there were five lights, all faintly purple – bold as you like. Not an intruder, but intrud*ers*.

This might be something quite special, Rory decided. *But... it isn't right. These lights shouldn't be here.*

He knew the sky and these lights were... well... intruders!

He knew he wouldn't be the only one seeing this. Astronomers all over England would be aiming their equipment at the sky, surely. And what might they be saying? What might they be making of this strange, new appearance? Stars may burst into life, Rory knew, but whole constellations don't just appear. No. This was something else.

He shifted his weight towards the upended bin that served as a bedside cabinet, snatched a chip of white chalk and hovered over a black leaf of paper, sweeping his Plough-shaped medication aside. He *had* to draw this.

Yeah, he decided, that was near enough what he was seeing.

But it was late and he thought he'd really better get some sleep. He had school in the morning, plus Mum would be awake and angry soon enough.

'Nuh-night, Mum,' Rory whispered into the dark.

Goodnight, stars, he breathed towards the sky. *As for you, Intruders, you better be gone by tomorrow night...*

'Little Grief! Outta bed. *Now!*'

Rory covered his head with a pillow and waited until Mum had stopped shouting before he dared make a move.

Waking up was like having his brain dunked in ice. Rory tried to linger in the cosiness of his duvet, but his mum's jagged voice – addressing him by that unkind pet name – meant he woke clear and clean. The feeling was always temporary, however, as the intrusive thoughts returned immediately, along with the fear and anxiety, which fogged his mind like octopus ink.

After dressing in his school clothes – white shirt, fraying tie, grey trousers and scuffed, black shoes – he left the bedroom, taking with him a *Dorling Kindersley* book on the Solar System to read at breakfast so he could ignore his mum. In the kitchen, the TV was on but he took little notice of it. Mum's yellowing hands shook as she emptied some cornflakes into a chipped, partially-washed bowl. Rory hopped up onto one of the stools at the work-surface, pushing aside a can of beer with stubbed cigarettes sticking out of it like weeds.

'Here yer go,' said Mum, voice impatient, practically flinging the breakfast bowl at Rory.

'Thanks,' Rory mumbled, slouching over his cereal. It wasn't always that she remembered to do him breakfast – not that he was a little kid now anyway. Perhaps when they got somewhere permanent to live he might even get his own bedroom.

He lifted a spoon overflowing with cornflakes and... yeah, that was orange juice. Glancing over his shoulder, he found his mum, in her stained dressing gown, lighting a fresh cigarette with unpredictable hands. She caught his eye, her absent expression sharpening.

'*What?*' she barked, her voice urgent, defensive.

Rory turned back to his bowl, shaking his head and mumbling, 'Nothin''.

He heard Mum's slippers *schwipping* along the torn linoleum floor out into the modest living area, the sound giving way to the *twang* of sofa springs under her meagre weight. He pushed his breakfast bowl aside and opened up his book on the Solar System, scanning over information about planets.

Nothing that explains those weird lights though… Rory sighed.

He dragged himself to his feet and ran water into a glass before taking a seat again at the breakfast area. Half-buried under several unopened letters piled on the work surface – **FINAL DEMAND** this, **URGENT** that and **BUY 1 GET 1 FREE PIZZA** – a scrap of paper caught his eye, bearing the logo of the local council. He glanced at Mum – who was busy smoking and staring at a patch of wall where the damp paper was peeling in great scabbing folds – and snatched at the letter. He read it.

Dear Ms Joyce Hobble,

I am writing to inform you that I am the newly allocated social worker for your family.

I would very much like to visit you and your son, Rory, on the afternoon of Wednesday 3rd November, at around 4pm. Perhaps we can take the opportunity to discuss and review your progress since the last conference, as I can see that there continue to be a number of concerns. I'm also concerned about the lack of progress in getting you both moved from temporary accommodation to a more suitable two-bed property.

I do look forward to meeting you and if you are unable to make the suggested date and time, then please do ring my work mobile (at the top of the page) so we can rearrange.

Yours sincerely,

Limmy Oshunwale

Social Worker

———

'Mum?' Rory said, looking up from the letter and turning his head. 'Y'know it's Wednesday today. Is the new social worker still coming over after school?'

Mum drew a final puff of her cigarette, stubbed it out on a dirty plate on the coffee table, and raised herself with some difficulty, *schwipping* back into the kitchen.

'What?'

Rory held the letter up, a little hesitantly.

Mum tightened the cord around her dressing gown. When she spoke, her voice was hard. 'Yeah. She's comin' over. Expect she'll be like the last. "Oh, Ms Hobble, yer really *must* clean up – keep yer flat tidy. This *really* won't do." Interfering busybodies, think their farts don't stink.'

Mum lit another cigarette. Rory's eyes followed a trail of unwashed plates, cooking utensils and baked-bean cans furred with mould – all filling the kitchen. The living area wasn't much better. No sign of any recent activity with a vacuum cleaner, walls peppered with damp and spiderwebs – which themselves had gathered dust – clinging to the ceiling corners.

'And *you*,' Mum continued, narrowing her eyes and pointing the burning end of her cigarette at Rory, 'can keep yer trap shut about yer *weirdness* this time. Them social work do-gooders say terrible things about me, and I know what they're thinking – they're thinking, "Oh, she can't look after 'er boy. Look at how messed up she made 'im." I don't want any of that when this new woman comes round later. Clear? You know what 'appens if you don't do what I say.'

Rory nodded, feeling a flush of panic and instinctively lifting a hand to his cheek.

Rooory, Rooory…

Nothing ever seemed to change for Rory with his thoughts; he just gritted his teeth and slogged through the day, heart scalding and lungs aching with anxiety. At least evening brought some relief, but only because he was so tired by then that his mind shut down. Waiting for dark… he could have been a vampire.

Rory looked nervously at the bottom corner of the TV screen. Nearly eight o'clock already.

I'll have to leave for school soon, he decided.

'Mum, is there any bread? I want some toast.'

'Toast? What's wrong with the cereal I gave yer?'

Rory glanced at the cornflakes, soggy in their small, bright lake of vitamin C. '… Nothin'. I just – I was just… still a bit hungry.'

'Well, there ain't no bread so you'll have to do without,' Mum said, *schwipping* back towards the sofa. 'Universal Credit don't come through till the eighth.'

Rory sighed, stomach grumbling, but his attention was again drawn to the TV, where several people were jabbering away excitedly in a newsroom. Across the bottom of the screen, a **BREAKING NEWS** ribbon raced along with:

MAYOR OF LONDON TO MAKE FORMAL ADDRESS IN THE NEXT FEW MINUTES

On the TV, the picture cut in half: on the left-hand side, a wide-eyed woman – her mouth running away with her and, on the right... the lights! Those intruders from last night!

'Look, there they are again!' Rory yelled, jabbing his finger theatrically at the screen.

'There are *what*?' Mum snapped.

Rory couldn't believe it. There they were, the lights he had watched switching on in the sky, one by one, the night before, on TV now. Part of him had hoped they'd just go and leave him in peace with his stars – his night sky. But another part of him, he had to admit, had wanted them to stay, curious at the spectacle and the wonder of what they might be.

We return now to the story we brought you earlier about those incredible lights that appeared above South London last night. We understand the Mayor of London is to issue a statement and we cross over to him live.

The picture changed and a man appeared, stepping out of a very important-looking building. His path was blocked by a small armada of microphones and those furry things that look like the hats on members of the Queen's Guard.

'What are the lights?' a voice asked, amidst a babble of other questions.

'At this present moment,' the Mayor began, 'we cannot say with any certainty what the lights were last night. I do urge that no one panics and be assured that we are investigating the matter.'

'There is a suggestion that the lights are still there – but the daylight hides them – is that true?'

'As I said, we are investigating but are unable to give any concrete answers at this moment. That is all I have time for.'

The Mayor marched off, hounded by reporters asking a dozen questions at once.

Rory glanced at the clock at the bottom of the screen again, jumped up and grabbed his worn, black rucksack and blue blazer, both dumped unceremoniously by the door the afternoon before.

'Make sure yer back for this woman later – I'll be in trouble if yer not 'ere,' Mum warned.

'Mm-hmm,' Rory mumbled, slamming the front door shut behind him, mind focused only on the lights.

Number 426, at the top of a block of flats on the Mirth Rises estate, one of two blocks standing side-by-side, glowering over the London Borough of Croydon from the summit of a hill, was where Rory and his mum lived. Up here, a biting wind inhaled the scent of the town far below: petrol, a local refuse centre, fried chicken. The blocks of flats were fifty years old – so Rory had heard residents tell – and multi-coloured cladding had been added in recent times, as though to add a sense of warmth and fun. However, the original grey could still be seen breaking through like an insect shedding its carapace. Up here, the temperature was always a few degrees lower than in the rest of Croydon, as though the cold was more at home.

Out on the shared balcony up on the eleventh floor, Rory drew his blazer close about his body and looked over the railing to the ground below. A graffitied playground sat in between the two buildings that made up the estate and Rory knew there to be needles and energy drink cans jammed into the coils of the animal springers. The chains on one of the swings were knotted so it could not be used. Clumps of crabgrass spewed through asphalt cracks like armpit hair.

Descending in the clanking aluminium lift, Rory heard the bark of arguing grown-ups and the chuckle-chatter of hooded teens racing about like hyenas. The lift's metal panels reverberated with the seismic bass of someone's boombox. With a ping, the lift doors shuddered apart and Rory stepped out into the ground floor entrance. Broken bottles cluttered grotty stairwell corners. An abandoned trike sat stained with dirt punctuated by rivulets of recent rainfall; the colour of the plastic was faded.

Rory's school, Hurling Academy, was a twenty-minute walk away, but he was late this morning and so hopped on the 303 bus that would typically reduce the journey to six minutes; today though, roadworks disrupted normality.

At the back of the bus, Rory slipped and slid on his seat from one side to the other, knocking his forehead against the cold, rattling window, looking out at the mass of grey which was the sky and everything beneath the sky tangled into dreariness.

No, the lights aren't there now, Rory said to himself, gazing up.

Those five lights. They may have made the news, but no one on the bus was talking about them. A few other straggling kids made gossip about people, while the pensioners huddled up beneath grey coats, hands clamped over grey hair. 'The youth today,' Rory heard one complaining.

When he reached school, Rory found the playground deserted, chocolate wrappers whirling through the air. By now, Science would have started. So, he ran past the Art block and through the corridors in the Music building until he reached the labs.

He composed himself outside the classroom, ensuring his hair wasn't too mussed up. Inside, the class turned as one to look at him. Mrs El-Khalil, the teacher – whose name Rory always confused with 'Mrs Alkali' by virtue of her subject – smiled.

Without warning, Rory's mind filled with a single, horrible image: him holding his teacher's hand over a lit Bunsen burner.

It's just my weirdness, like Mum said, Rory reassured himself, controlling his breathing.

'Good morning, Mr Hobble. Please take a seat. We're concentrating on your favourite topic; I'm sure you'll be interested.'

Rory managed a weak smile in response; Mrs El-Khalil knew him to have a passion for all things astronomical. At parents' evening he'd gone off on quite a tangent, discussing the stars, the planets and their various movements. That had been the night his mum swore at one of the other teachers after drinking too much and was asked to leave.

Rory took his usual seat but not before catching the eye of Curtis Varley, who sat behind him.

'Too busy crying into your pillow, freak – that why yer late?' Curtis sneered under his breath, while Mrs El-Khalil went about writing something on the whiteboard.

'Mmm. Right. We'll be picking up with the Solar System again, which is quite fitting considering all the hoo-ha in the news this morning,' Mrs El-Khalil continued in a tremulous voice, clutching small hands together in front of her. Clumps of hair surged from her head as though compelled by some unseen force. It was quite possible, Rory decided, that she had not brushed her hair that morning.

'Mmm. Yes. Now, do we all know the rhyme for remembering the… planets? Quite easy – everyone, look at Curtis, please.'

With a scraping of chair legs, everyone turned uniformly to Curtis, who growled behind a reddening face.

'Mmm. Excellent,' Mrs El-Khalil continued. 'Now, let's run through it again.' She lifted her hands and the whole class slowly found its voice. '"Mr… Varley… Exploded Messily… Juggling Salty Unicorn Nuggets".'

The class chuckled, collectively. Rory grinned, the tone of Curtis's face deepening to scarlet.

'Mmm. Okay. Now, let's do a bit of revision. Who can name the first man in space?'

Several hands shot up, Rory's first and foremost.

'Yes, Rory,' Mrs El-Khalil smiled, pointing at him.

'I-It was Yuri Gagarin, miss. In 1961, April 12th.'

'Very good!'

Rory smiled sheepishly, his heart full of praise. This was basic stuff for him though. He could answer far harder questions about space.

Rooory, Rooory.

Shut up, you, Rory hissed.

'Mmm. Next, what were Neil Armstrong's words as – Yes, Rory?'

Rory kept his arm high in the air, inviting the attention of the whole class. 'He said, "That's one small step for man, one giant leap for mankind."'

'Very good! Our resident astrophile strikes again! Okay, can someone – other than Rory this time! – describe for me how gravity works?'

Rory rested back in his seat, still smiling at his ability, wondering whether others in the class were in awe of his knowledge. As Stevie Falken commenced a mazy definition of gravity, a voice carried to Rory's ear.

'Fffreak!' It was Curtis. 'How you doing, freak? Still a weirdo?'

It was Rory's turn to redden, his smile instantly dissolving. He could hear Sean Ruddock, sitting next to Curtis, sniggering.

'Still being screamed at by your mummy? Don't she like 'er little weirdo?' Curtis hissed.

Sean sniggered all the more. Rory clenched his fists and felt his heart skip a beat.

Ignore him – he doesn't know what he's saying, Rory told himself, finding it hard to control his temper.

'Mmm. Thank you for that… effort, Stevie,' Mrs El-Khalil said. 'I'm sure that, wherever Sir Isaac Newton is right now, he will have managed to turn a little on his side. Now, we're going to crack on with today's work, which is to run through the tasks on page forty-three of our textbooks. Can you all turn to the chapter on "The Sun and Other Stars", please? Quietly, if at all possible!' she added as the class broke into chatter.

'Hey, how's your mum doing?' Curtis's drawl came again, disguised from Mrs El-Khalil under the din of everyone else talking. 'She still mental? Your mum don't love you, does she? That why she drinks all the time?'

Rory gritted his teeth, rifling through his textbook with trembling hands. He could feel the blood coursing through his arms, pumping in his palms and tears filling his eyes. The kid next to him, Richie Adam, was looking at him now too, saying, 'Aww, you gonna take that, Rory? Don't take that from 'im.' Rory didn't care. He wiped a tear from the corner of his eye.

Rooory, Rooory.

Another image flashed into mind: his hands around Curtis's throat.

Go away! Rory growled inside his head. *That en't me!*

He could hear Sean whispering something to Curtis that seemed to amuse him, as Curtis was snorting like a pig.

'Hey, freak, did your mum' – he guffawed, quieter now as the class settled down – 'did your mum drop you on your head to make you all messed –'

Rory span around in his chair, tears running down his cheeks, teeth clamped and eyes piercing.

'Aww, look he's crying! He's actually crying!' Curtis managed through a splutter of laughter.

Rory imagined himself leaping on them both, punching

them about the face until they were all bloody. But he couldn't move, couldn't say anything.

Rooory, Rooory. If you hurt him, he'll get blood on his brain and he'll die, Rooory. You are a bad person who wants to hurt people. I told you so!

Rory unclenched his fists, jumped up and scurried off out of the classroom, right past a startled Mrs El-Khalil. He tore down the hall, past a few more teachers – 'Hey! No running inside!' – and burst through the double doors – out into the playground, breathing hard. He collapsed on a patch of grass, wiping tears and snot from his face, his head swimming.

How dare they say those things?

Curtis and Sean had been picking on him for weeks now – ever since the new school year started. They had been doing the same last year in primary school and he had hoped the summer might have drawn some of the poison from them. But a bully is a wretched creature, though a predator nonetheless.

Finally calming, Rory became suddenly aware of how unnaturally quiet it was out in the playground. No bird calls. No wind. No cars on the road. He felt a strange tingling sensation in his fingers, a crackle in his hair and a whining in his ears. The world seemed momentarily brighter, before fading again to its familiar grey. And then the ground itself was alive. Through the mud and beheaded blades of grass, worms started to wriggle free – first one, then five, then ten, then dozens. Rory watched, stunned, as they performed slimy gymnastics over his feet, around his backside and across his hands: a seething, gelatinous mass. Some of them even seemed to have little flickers of electricity dancing across their pink flesh.

That can't be… he thought and scrabbled away from them, repulsed.

Stealing his attention from the worms, two fighter jet-planes ripped through the sky, rending the silence with a thunderous roar.

Are those military? Rory wondered, as he watched them ascend through a bank of cloud, only to be lost in the slushy atmosphere. *What are they doing here? I wonder if it's anything to do with the lights.*

A gust of wind drew the hairs up on Rory's neck and, for a moment, he felt uncomfortable, as though someone – or some*thing* – was watching him. The feeling intensified into an urge to look up… He did so, gaze falling over a small clump of trees beyond the fence boundary of the playground and, slowly and quietly at first – but then louder – he heard a sound like moaning – hideous, desperate and mournful. His pulse quickened, the sound shooting a sharp note of fear down his spine. Then, the snapping of branches. Beside one of the trees, the undergrowth rustled, as though displaced by something that had now disappeared. The wind whipped around his neck again like a chokehold and, looking back at the ground to find the worms gone, Rory jumped up – spooked – and dashed back into school.

2

Gary

The rest of the day passed without incident and, as the afternoon unravelled, the overcast sky opened and torrential rain set in. When school finally ended, Rory set off home, using his Maths book to cover his head, water sliding off the laminate in great streams.

I wish I *was laminated*, Rory grumbled, inwardly.

He missed the 303 by a matter of seconds, and the display at the shelter-free bus stop flashed a red **13 minutes** indicating what seemed an eternity until the next one was due to arrive, so he decided to walk home as briskly as he could instead.

Alone with his thoughts, Rory tried to imagine what the new social worker would be like. The last one had been quite a forgetful person and, though infrequent, her visits had always brought the worst out in his mum. It'd been years since the first worker, and since then there had been – what was it now? – seven separate people come into his life. And this Lemon... Lily... whatever... was to be the eighth. He looked up at the glowering sky and pressed on a little quicker, not wishing to upset his mum by being late. The consequences were not worth thinking about.

Turning a corner and hurrying past a group of hooded youths, Rory caught a glimpse down an alleyway of flashing ginger shapes, aggressive yaps accompanying their movement. Curious, he stopped and focused. In the shadow of a house, in a semi-circle of wheelie bins and dumpsters, stood at least twelve foxes of various size snapping and swiping at each other in their attempts to reach… *something* on the ground. Rory took a few steps down the alleyway, school shoes squelching in a gruel of gravel and mud. The *something* on the ground seemed as though it was trying to move.

'H-Hey! Get out of there! Go on!' Rory yelled at the foxes, realising that they must be attacking some kind of animal.

One or two of their number looked dimly up at him but, peculiarly, they all remained where they were, sticky snouts sniffling and snuffling for their quarry, slick teeth glinting.

'I said get *out* of it!' Rory yelled again, this time running at the foxes, the scavengers finally scattering.

As the last of the foxes scrambled up a garden fence, Rory reached the bins and looked down at the something on the ground. At first, he thought it must be a sort of rugby ball tied up in a blue bin bag, but no, he hadn't been imagining things a moment ago – it was definitely moving.

Kneeling down, tossing his Maths book to one side and rubbing some of the rain from his eyes, he took a closer look. Whatever it was, it looked like a miniature whale, but its gleaming, rubbery hide was a palette of swirling purples, blues and greys. It seemed to be lying on its side. Along its back were what looked to be crystals – lilac in colour – sticking out like the unruly hair of an anime character. Four great black beads of varying size near the front might have been eyes. And, under its neck and on its belly, triplet bubbles tried pathetically to expand; the bubbles reminded Rory of a frog's throat as it *ribbits*. Whatever this thing was, it clearly didn't belong in the mud outside a semi-detached house in South London.

'Hey, wh-what are you?' Rory mumbled, reaching out with a tentative hand.

The creature responded with the strangest noise: a mournful high-pitched song tinged with a bass that seemed to have been summoned from a depth it did not possess. Rory touched his head, rubbed at his temple – for one moment, it seemed as though there was a flare of imagery in his mind, but it was gone as quickly as it came.

For the first time, Rory noticed a dark substance ebbing out from under the creature.

'A-Are you hurt?'

The creature rumbled and tried to inflate its little bubbles again but then, with a rattle, deflated one final time. It went completely still and quiet. Rory looked it up and down, panic sweeping over him.

No… don't be dead, little guy, he willed.

Hesitantly, he laid hands on the creature's belly. Cold and wet, the texture of rubber. The darkness still flowed out from under it, so he turned the animal over to find a single bite wound. Gritting his teeth, he pulled his school blazer off and pressed it against the wound, holding it for several minutes. The creature did not stir in that time. Rory became aware of hungry eyes at the periphery of his vision. The foxes had smelled blood and returned.

'Come on, you ridiculous thing. Wake up!' Rory hissed, shaking the creature.

Still, it didn't move.

Rory recalled a first aid video he once saw in which someone had stopped breathing, with a paramedic pressing down on his chest and counting. Holding his hands in the way he remembered, Rory pressed them into the belly of the creature and began compressions.

'One, two, three, four,' he puffed, aloud.

Nothing.

'One, two, three, four.'

Still nothing.

Rory ran a hand through his sodden hair, white shirt clinging to his body like damp kitchen roll. He lifted a hand, clenched it into a fist and brought it down hard on the creature's belly. The crystals on its back flickered with light, surely – just for a moment. He hit the creature again. Definitely light! A pinkish glow channelling through the crystals. He lifted both fists and brought them down with all his might – *whack!* – into the belly. The crystals lit up again and remained lit. The bubbles inflated. The creature shook and released gas from several orifices under its tail so violently that it launched like a rocket all of two metres, straight into a wheelie bin, which it hit with a *dunk* before dropping pitifully back into the mud. Rory leapt back in surprise. The foxes scattered once more.

'Ha! You did it!' Rory chuckled – both to himself and the creature, which wriggled about like a fish out of water.

Perhaps it is *a fish out of water,* Rory theorised. Looking up at the sky, he momentarily considered the possibility that more of these creatures might start to rain down.

Suddenly, he realised how long he had been down this alley, how much darker the sky was. He couldn't leave this thing behind though... Ripping open his school bag, he chucked in his Maths book, then picked up the creature – pressing his blazer into its wound once again – and stuffed it into the bag as well. It was surprisingly light, considering it looked to be a shrunken version of the heaviest animal to have ever lived. It gazed up at him from the bag, each of its eyes – four on the left and four on the right of what must be its face – shiny with apparent emotion and gratitude. Rory looked down at it.

'Oh, don't look at me like that. I'm gonna be in enough trouble as it is.'

But the creature simply nodded, emitting a contented rumbling noise, from deep within its belly.

☆

Rory opened the front door. Mum looked distinctly unimpressed, arms folded across her dressing gown, out of which she did not look to have changed all day.

'Just *where* have yer been?' she spat, before grabbing him roughly by the arm and dragging him inside. 'Look at the state of yer.'

'I-I'm sorry, Mum. I got side-tracked. Is... *she* here?'

'Of *course* she's here! More of an oddball than the last. God only knows what she thought I'd done with yer. What will she say when she sees yer?'

'The oddball would say that Rory could do with a towel and some hot chocolate.'

Rory shook some of the wet from his sleeves and turned in the direction of the voice – his mouth dropped open. The woman he found standing in the flat was young – perhaps in her early twenties – and quite unlike anyone he'd ever seen before. She had smooth, dark skin with bronze hair fizzing off her head in every direction like a series of firecracker explosions. Her eyes were honeyed with the glint of a private joke, and her green lipstick gave her an amphibious quality. Her waistcoat was a peculiar patchwork of rusty leather and tartan suede, and she sported a velvety cravat resplendent with stars and comets that half concealed a lanyard with her local authority ID badge. A leather skirt cut off at her knees, giving way to purple-and-black hooped tights that ended in big-buckled boots.

She held out a hand, a smile lifting her lime lips. 'My name is Limmy and I'm startled that it is customary for you to *swim* home from school.'

Her accent was unusual. There was a slight hint of *quelque chose comme le français* as well as something else.

Rory snapped out of his trance and extended one dripping hand. 'O-Oh no, I didn't swim. It's raining, you see. So, I-I got wet.'

Coolly done, you absolute muppet, he scolded himself.

Mum grabbed Rory by the shoulders and frogmarched him towards the bedroom. 'Thank you for that. Now, let me and 'er continue our chat –'

'Actually,' Limmy spoke up, 'I should very much like to

speak to Rory a little. Ms Hobble, perhaps a towel and – you must be hungry, Rory.'

Rory's belly grumbled. 'O-Oh no, I'm good.'

'He knows where the freezer is if he wants anythin',' Mum piped up, her mouth twisted in apparent irritation.

'Is that so?' Limmy replied, one wild eyebrow lifting. 'Do you prepare meals and freeze them down for him?'

'Nah,' Mum's voice shot from the bathroom – it sounded as though she must be fumbling through the airing cupboard for a towel. 'Who's got time for that? We got chicken nuggets from the local. Fish fingers. Waffles.'

'A balanced diet then,' Limmy called through to her.

Mum plodded out, holding a towel, slippers scuffing the linoleum. 'Well we got baked beans too if that's what yer mean.' She turned to Rory, chucked the towel at his head. '*Don't* make any more of a mess than you already 'ave.'

Rory removed the towel from his face, slipped his rucksack from his back, being particularly gentle with it, and – watching Limmy's inviting expression with curiosity – sank into the sofa, more because it was falling apart than because it was in any way comfortable.

'May I?' Limmy asked, indicating that she wished to sit next to him.

Rory nodded, glancing down at his bag.

I hope that thing *is okay in there*, he worried.

The mysterious creature had been quiet all the way home, which unnerved Rory so much so that he had had to keep checking to make sure it wasn't dead. Every few minutes, the voice in his head had hissed, *Rooory, Rooory. The creature is so quiet. Perhaps it's dead. You let it die!* But each time he was compelled to check, it had just gazed back up at him with such apparent devotion as to suggest Rory were the herald of a new religion.

Rory took a few moments to dry himself, gulping down the lukewarm chocolate Mum prepared in the microwave.

'So, Rory, I know you've just gotten in from school and all you want to do is relax, but I'd hoped to run over a few things with you' – Limmy opened a hand towards him – 'and with your mum' – she opened a hand towards his mum, who was busy lighting a cigarette with a mischievous lighter. 'How does that sound?'

'Okay, I guess,' Rory mumbled.

Mum crossed one arm over her belly, took a drag of her cigarette and shrugged. 'Whatever.'

Rory picked at his knees.

I s'pose she wants to talk about my weirdness, Rory thought to himself.

He had spoken about his condition countless times with social workers over the past eighteen months and then all over again once he'd waited thirteen months for the head doctor. The social workers would come in with their notepad and biro, asking him things like, 'Do you ever feel like hurting yourself?' or 'Why do you think something bad is going to happen?' One had even asked him once if he was making it up because he wasn't getting enough attention.

Mum says that sometimes too, Rory reflected.

A few years ago he could barely get his mouth around the term 'obsessive compulsive disorder', let alone understand what it meant, but now he felt like he could go on a TV show and use it as his special talent.

Next up: Rory and his amazing, messed-up mind!

'Now then,' Limmy began, smiling at him. Rory looked for a notepad but one was not forthcoming. 'I know you've been diagnosed with OCD. But – and I don't know about you –' she leaned in, lifting a hand to the side of her mouth, conspiratorially, 'I never really understood all those fiddly things doctors say; they don't help you understand what's going on much, do they?' She pulled away, a smile still playing on her lips.

'I... I guess not,' Rory replied, positioning his hands on his knees, each identically placed. 'I don't think anyone *really* understands it.'

Limmy clapped her hands. 'And how could they when you're the one experiencing it? I bet you always get asked to score things out of ten on how difficult your thoughts are. Am I right?'

Rory pictured the *Thought Diary* under his bed and nodded, a stray smile slipping briefly onto his face.

'People like me are good at sticking labels on others,' Limmy continued, her smile a little sadder now.

'Damn right!' Mum interrupted.

'*But*,' Limmy persevered, '*I* don't like to do that. And we don't have to talk about it if you don't want.'

Rory lifted his head. 'It's... okay. I'm used to it by now. The thoughts I get – I don't want them.' An image flashed into mind of him throwing Limmy to the floor, and the guilt made him wince. 'I get these thoughts of hurting people but I'd never, *never* do that – I swear!'

'I know, I know,' Limmy said, raising her hands. 'I imagine it's like having a parasite burrowing through your brain. And

27

all you want to do is to stop it getting into every little corner by ripping it out.'

That's exactly what it feels like… , Rory thought to himself.

'Let's not give the boy nightmares,' Mum said loudly, lighting another cigarette. 'He's already messed up as it is. Don't want him thinkin' insects are gonna start eatin' 'im as well.' A small glow seemed to fade from Limmy's eyes. 'You don't have to put up with him every day. All his blubbin' about nonsense things,' Mum continued, one shaky hand scratching her greasy hair. 'It don't make no sense. Swear he puts it on. Just for show.'

'And do *you* put on a show, Ms Hobble?' Limmy responded, quite calmly – not a hint of anger in her voice; curiosity, if anything.

Mum took a deep puff of her cigarette, chapped lips tightening around the soggy, searing stem.

'What d'yer mean by that?' She swore quite profanely, mumbling something about social workers always making accusations.

'Well, you told your last worker that you would keep your home clean, stop swearing in front of Rory and try to be a little more understanding of him. Was *that* a show or was it a genuine commitment?'

'Yeah, I'm gonna do that. But, you know, it's hard, innit?' Mum said, her hands shaking again. 'It's hard for me.'

Rory looked down at his knees again.

Limmy made eye contact with Mum, her expression softening. 'Nothing good and lasting is achieved overnight, Ms Hobble.' A pause. 'How's the new medication working out?'

'She don't always take it,' Rory said, instinctively, and immediately regretting it.

Mum swore again. 'Why'd yer go and say that, Little Grief!?'

Rory looked up at his mother, who was shaking. 'I'm sorry, I didn't –'

'Yes, yer *did*! Yer want *'er*' – she flung a hand in Limmy's direction – 'to snatch yer away from me? Put yer in a stranger's 'ome, or *worse*.'

'Ms Hobble,' Limmy said, firmly, standing up as she did so. 'If you don't at least try the medication then you'll never know what might be. And having a go at Rory – who's only concerned for you – isn't helping matters either. And what was that you called him? Little Grief?'

Mum sniffed, running a hand through her hair again. 'Yeah? It's my name for 'im. He's my Little Grief 'cos he does my 'ead in.'

Rory looked again at his knees, lining his hands up precisely.

'And how does that make you feel, Rory?' Limmy asked, quietly.

Rory focused on his knees and shrugged his shoulders.

'He does my 'ead in 'cos I love 'im!' Mum snapped, pointing one shaky finger at the social worker. 'Don't you go thinkin' otherwise!'

Rory made to say something to his mum, but thought better of it. A brief smile flickered at his lips though.

Mum doesn't usually say she loves me… he reflected.

'Well, I'd better be going,' Limmy declared, after an uncomfortable silence. Her tone was reluctant. 'I'd like to pop in again in a few days, just to see how things are going.'

'Do what yer like,' Mum replied, making a point of looking

away from Limmy, her voice unemotional now. She *schwipped* into the kitchen and leaned over the sink.

'Walk me to the door, would you?' Limmy asked Rory, giving him a wink.

Rory looked at Limmy, then at the door, only six feet away. 'Umm, sure.'

Rory pulled himself up, careful not to kick his rucksack in any way and thankful for the creature's mercy in not making any high-pitched noises or, worse still, erupting gas again. He followed in Limmy's wake and watched as she gathered up a green umbrella and opened the front door. She stepped into the night, not putting her umbrella up just yet, as the balcony outside was sheltered from the rain – though not from the blustery wind trying to scoop up the social worker in its furious fist.

'Rory,' Limmy began. 'It was a pleasure meeting you. Here's my number.'

She handed Rory a slip of paper with a mobile contact on it.

'Your mother... You know she is unwell, and it's not her fault. You are in a difficult position, I know. I was once in a difficult position myself... Try and tolerate her moods where you can, but if you ever feel worried, or in danger, then call me.'

Rory looked down at the phone number, nodding once.

Limmy made to move away, but stopped as she did so, turned back, leaned in towards Rory and placed a hand on the door knob. 'Oh, and at school today, you were alone outside the building. Not a good idea to be on your own at the moment – what with those lights in the sky.' She looked up into the clouded sky, as though checking to see if the lights were still there. '*Something* was watching you from the trees. Keep your door locked and your windows fastened at night, Rory, *especially* at night – that's when they will start looking for your mother.'

Before Rory had a chance to recover from the shock, Limmy had closed the front door, leaving him standing again in the quiet of the flat.

Later that evening, Rory sat in bed, trying to ignore his mother's cries and thrashing as she endured yet another nightmare. In the dark, as the Moon's milky beam streamed through the navy curtain, his hands looked blue. The intruders were still in the sky and had been since the clouds cleared and he'd gone to bed straight after Limmy left. His stomach grumbled reproachfully for having missed another meal, as the electric meter had ran out of money and prevented the use of any cooking appliances.

It doesn't happen often… , he tried to reassure himself.

Rory peered under the duvet, finding the peculiar whale creature at the foot of his bed, gazing up at him and making little cooing noises, like a ferret. It would almost be cute, Rory decided, if it wasn't for its gas problem: a long, steady stream of quiet-yet-clear emissions that one might expect from someone who lived solely on baked beans. Making this connection earlier, Rory had tried to give it some cold beans after Mum had fallen asleep, but it hadn't wanted any.

Probably stuffed its face with beans out of the bins this afternoon, he imagined.

Instead, it had enjoyed a bowlful of milk, nodding cheerily as its lips – what else could he call them? – had become ever more plastered with a white moustache and goatee. A rub down with a towel had cleaned it right up and the contents of an old first aid kit had served to patch its wound. It now had a slightly yellowed bandage tied around its middle and knotted about one of its curious purple crystals.

'What are you? And where did you come from? Did the lights send you?' Rory whispered into the dark under the duvet, the creature's crystals now emitting a faint pink glow – almost like a nightlight.

It rumbled by way of response and let out another hissing cloud of gas.

More important than where it came from, Rory decided, *is to think of a name.*

'I can't keep calling you "you", after all.'

He didn't want it to be anything silly, as he felt the creature looked silly enough without being called something like Zarp or Zuggerwoon. He briefly considered calling it something that honoured its gaseousness, such as Novabum or Fantastic Mr Fart. But that idea was also silly. He thought of all the sci-fi films he'd seen and loved from the eighties and the nineties, and remembered one with flying cars, weird aliens and one of his favourite characters played by the actor, Gary Oldman... Gary, Gary, Gary. Suddenly the name 'Gary' seemed a respectable and dignified choice. Besides, the creature kind of looked like a Gary.

'I dub thee Gary of South London,' Rory whispered, patting the creature first on one cheek and then on the other. 'I'll watch over you and we'll be best friends.'

Settling into his pillow, Rory stared across the room at his mother. She looked so distressed in her sleep. He'd used to wake her up when she had nightmares, but they would return just as soon as she fell asleep again, so he had long since stopped bothering. On her bedside cabinet, the blister pack of her medication had two tablets missing, which made Rory very happy.

Perhaps she actually listened to Limmy, he hoped.

But just as quickly, his happiness faded as an intrusive thought buzzed into his head.

Rooory, Rooory. Just what did Limmy mean earlier? Something is watching Mum and it was watching you earlier. You will lead it to her and she will die!

He tightened the duvet around his body as the wind came to the window with a whistle and a rattle.

Just what did Limmy mean though? Something is watching? What if whatever it was that was watching me at school followed me and knows where Mum is? She's going to die and it's all my fault! Rory worried.

He felt the tears in his eyes and practised deep breaths to calm his nerves. Slowly, the worry lost its intensity and a yawn pushed it from his mind almost altogether.

Gary wiggled his (Rory had decided to think of it as a 'he') way up from the foot of the bed and soon emerged from under the duvet, like a mole from the earth. He looked at Rory and even *its* eyes looked tearful. Rory sniffed hard and wrapped his arms around the creature, which started to inflate all three of its frog-throat pouches.

Eventually, Rory fell asleep and, that night, if any intruders *had* been peering through the cracks in the curtain of the bedroom window, they would have seen a woman tossing and turning in one bed, which in itself would not have been peculiar. But if they had turned to face the other bed, they would have seen a boy wrapped around a slowly-expanding, and intermittently farting creature, floating towards the ceiling, a duvet covering them both. And *that* would have been a peculiar sight indeed.

3

Under Intelligent Control

The next morning, Rory enjoyed the strange sensation of waking without Mum's shouts ringing in his ears. Sunlight lasered its way through the curtains, catching dust motes as they glided about like tiny astronauts adrift in a vacuum. On the opposite side of the room, above Mum's empty bed, Gary bobbed about like a balloon, butting into a cupboard with louvre doors; he changed direction here and there with tiny gaseous emissions that seemed to provide a means of propulsion.

Rory glanced at his bedside clock. It already read **08:20**.

'Oh no! I'm gonna be late!' Rory cried, feeling a familiar anxiety trickling through his guts.

He jumped out of bed and hurriedly dressed, weighing up a decision on what to do with Gary. If he took the creature to school, it would have to be stuffed in his bag all day, but it should at least remain hidden. If he left it at home, it would be free to float and fart to its heart's content. He pictured his mother sitting on the sofa, suddenly confronted with Gary and the outcome in his mind was not pretty.

'Gary, you're coming with me,' Rory commanded, holding his rucksack open.

Out in the living area of the flat, Rory found his mum slumped in the sofa and watching TV, drawing on the cindery end of a cigarette; on the coffee table, a number of butt-ends floated in a half-finished cup of tea like flotsam from a shipwreck. However, at the breakfast area, a wonderful aroma drew his attention to a small plate of cooked food.

Rory cleared his throat, nervously. 'M-Morning, Mum. How long you been up?'

His mum turned to him, actually smiling, and pulled herself up – with apparent effort. 'Mornin', Litt– … Rory. Not long. I… well, I made yer breakfast.' She pointed at the plate of food in the kitchen.

Rory looked at the plate, frowned, and walked slowly over to it. By Hobble family standards, it was a feast: an egg (poached), one hash brown, one rasher of bacon, one sausage and some fried (well, slightly burnt) mushrooms with a cup of tea beside it. He looked back at his mum, who smiled again and stretched out her hand, inviting him to sit. Rory could feel his stomach cramping. He gently lowered his rucksack to the floor and threw himself on the breakfast. It tasted wonderful. Greasy, salty goodness. He slurped at his tea – hot as opposed to lukewarm – and looked up as his mum settled into a stool beside him. Mother and son made eye contact and each smiled a genuine, cosy smile.

At once, Rory's chest relaxed and the voice that was always in his head quietened, like the volume being turned down on a TV. He remembered the time, but there was nothing he'd rather be late to school for.

'Y'know, I remember when that psych first told me 'bout what was goin' on in yer 'ead, Rory. I'd never bin so scared. I didn't understand it. All I wanted ter do was 'old yer and not let them thoughts 'urt yer. But I couldn't do that.'

Mum pulled a lighter from her dressing gown pocket and fired up another cigarette. Rory continued to work his way through the breakfast, occasionally glancing up at his mum.

'Y'know...' Mum began again. 'I *do* call yer Little Grief 'cos yer do my 'ead in, but... Not like that. It does my 'ead in to see yer grief – to see the grief this Obsessional Complaining whatchamacallit does ter yer. I can't stand ter see yer un'appy.'

Rory was alarmed to see his mum actually start to cry.

'Don't cry, Mum. I-It's okay. I've got my *Thought Diary*. A-And I've got my pil–'

But enough of the word had escaped his lips and he watched his mum as her crying stopped, instantly, and all the warmth evaporated from her face like water from a living world.

'Pleased with yerself, I bet,' Mum said, in her more familiar, flat tone.

Rory carefully stood up from the stool, picked up his rucksack and made towards the front door – one eye on his mum – muttering, 'I-I should get to school.'

Mum stubbed her cigarette out in the middle of Rory's uneaten egg yolk. She turned to face her son, eyes keenly peering at him with clawed, jaundiced hands gripping either side of her stool. Her eyes were swollen and teary; lips, chapped; nose, red raw.

'Your performance last night,' Mum spat. 'Tellin' *that woman*

I don't take my pills. Sometimes I forget, Little Grief, but she'll just use tha' against me. All them social workers want to do is get me locked away. They think I'm mad but they don't realise that *I know*' – she tapped her head furiously – '*what they're up to.*'

'W–What are they up to, Mum? … She seemed nice enough to me.'

Mum hopped up and strode towards her son, taking Rory by the shoulders. She leaned in so close that Rory could practically taste the smoke on her breath, hear the wheeze in her throat.

'That's what they're all like at first. Don't you remember the last one? She was all sweetness and light before all those *conferences* and *plans*. This one will be the same. All they want to do is separate us.'

'Wouldn't they have done that already then?' Rory ventured.

Mum laughed a forced, shallow laugh. 'Yer silly boy. They have to grind us down first. Get us weak. So that everyone else sees what they see. *That's* when they'll lock me away and take yer to live with some stranger. Yer want that, huh?'

'N–No, Mum,' Rory replied, trying to shake free of the hands on his shoulders.

'But yer *must*, Little Grief. Yer *must*,' Mum yelled. 'Because yer never stop with all this rubbish! All them weird thoughts. Those social workers think *I* did this to yer. That I've *messed* yer up somehow. But yer were messed up from the start!'

It all happened so suddenly. Rory managed to rip Mum's hands from his shoulders and, as he did so, she fell over backwards and smacked her head with a sickening *dunk* against the bottom of the kitchen counter. Momentarily, her eyes glassed over and her mouth became a thin, formless line. But she was soon aware again, one hand propping her body up, the other feeling the back of her head.

Rooory, Rooory. That was attempted murder. You tried to kill her. She'll have bleeding on the brain!

'Mum,' Rory mumbled, sniffing as he stepped tentatively forward, veins turning chilly. 'I-I'm sorry. I didn't mean to… A-Are you okay?'

Mum looked up at him, eyes filled with a poison that made Rory flinch.

'Get out. Get out. Get out. Get out. Get out.' Her voice was louder every time she said it. 'Get out. Get out. Get out. Get out.'

Rory retreated, the words filling his head – filling the entire flat. He fumbled with the front door, fell through and slammed it behind him.

At school, in lunchtime detention, Rory did not focus on the irritating ticking of the clock or the dreary voice of Mr Winters as he marked Maths homework out loud; instead, chin supported by hand, he stared out of the window at the other boys on the school grounds cloaked in fog. He had been very late to school and this was his punishment: the withdrawal of break-time privileges and limited opportunity to get lunch from the cafeteria, ten minutes before afternoon lessons were due to commence. Right then, the dinner ladies would be dishing out soggy chips and pizza on Styrofoam plates, ready to be washed down with Rubicon, Coca Cola or something equally tasty.

I'm so hungry I'd settle for an apple, Rory sighed.

There were only five boys in detention, including himself. Behind him, Sean Ruddock and Curtis Varley whispered and sniggered together.

Rooory, Rooory. I hope Mum is okay. She might be dead. And you did it!

Rory looked down at his desk, running hands over the back of his head, as though to tease the thoughts through his scalp and flick them away. His chest was so tight, like knotted rope on an old sailing ship. And it hardly ever went away – perhaps it did when he was particularly tired and he had gone past caring whether his fears would come true or not, but other than that it was as much a part of him as the flesh on his bones.

The classroom door flew open, whacking a table so hard it made everyone in the room jump.

'Jeff, you've got to turn on the tele – look at the news!' The speaker was Mrs El-Khalil, the Science teacher. 'Oh, hello,' she said, noticing Rory.

Rory smiled, sheepishly.

Mr Winters, perhaps glad to be offered an escape from marking Maths homework, did not reply to Mrs El-Khalil, but simply scrabbled about for a remote in his desk drawer before turning on the small TV, fastened to the wall.

'What is it?' Mr Winters finally asked, as he waited for the TV screen to flash into a channel.

'The lights again – I know you're the only other person interested,' Mrs El-Khalil replied, one arm folded across her chest while she chewed on a fingernail. 'Apart from Rory, that is.'

Rory returned Mrs El-Khalil's nervous smile.

The TV screen materialised on a channel with a fancy studio

and **BREAKING NEWS** flashing across the screen in red and white, much as it had at home yesterday. The caption, this time, read:

PRIME MINISTER TO ADDRESS NATION ON UNIDENTIFIED LIGHTS

Rory's worries disappeared as his mind re-attuned to events unfolding before him. He did not pay much attention to what the presenter said, but watched as the screen transitioned to a camera view of a podium set up in front of a big black door with a silver 10 on it. Rory recognised this as Downing Street, specifically the home of the Prime Minister, as he had seen it on TV before. Before long, a woman came out of the door to a flurry of questions and camera flashes. She stepped up to the podium, holding on to some documentation. As the various journalists, cameramen and reporters settled down, the Prime Minister began her address in a strong Birmingham accent.

I've just chaired a session of the government's emergency committee "Icebreaker" following the sudden appearance of unidentified lights in the skies above South London –

'Icebreaker? What's Icebreaker?' Mr Winters hissed to Mrs. El-Khalil, who shrugged, eyebrows knitted in concentration as she continued to chew her fingers.

– and have spoken jointly with security and military officials, as well as a number of prominent academics in the scientific community. This government has also liaised with officials at NASA, the European Space Agency, Roscosmos, the China National Space Administration, the Japan Aerospace

Exploration Agency and the Indian Space Research Organisation. On the back of our communiques and intelligence, I can now give the nation fresh information on the phenomenon.

Rory leaned in, hardly daring to breathe. All around him, the other boys in detention did likewise – even Curtis and Sean seemed interested. Mr Winters and Mrs El-Khalil were transfixed.

It is important first to note that there should be no cause for alarm, but the Home Secretary has been given special powers to order a constant police street presence wherever a local authority deems it necessary. The Justice Secretary has been granted similar powers should a military presence be required on the streets and, as we speak, barracks up and down the country are being placed on alert.

I can now confirm that the lights above South London cannot be explained as any known natural phenomenon – terrestrial or astronomical – or as any man-made craft of which we are aware. We have no cause to believe there is any immediate danger posed by the lights. However, we are treating the lights as being under intelligent *control, and are currently working across international borders to establish lines of communication.*

'I knew it!' Mr Winters yelled, clapping his hands violently. He looked excitedly around the classroom, and Rory felt genuine concern for the man's state of mind, so deranged were his eyes. 'Did you hear what she said?' he continued, jabbing his finger excitedly at the TV. '*Under intelligent control.*'

Sean was the first to pipe up. 'Yeah, what does that mean though?'

Mr Winters tutted, throwing his head back with such exaggeration that it was a wonder it did not fall off his neck altogether.

'It's clear Ruddock's mouth, at the very least, *isn't* under intelligent control,' Mr Winters barked.

Rory made eye contact with Mrs El-Khalil, who smiled encouragingly.

'I think Rory knows,' she said.

'Umm,' Rory began, twisting in his seat to look at the other boys. 'It means they – the lights – are… well, they might be… *aliens*.'

One of the boys, Mandeep Chander, looked horrified. Another, Jamie Baker, scratched his nose.

'They come to take you home, Hobble?' Curtis hissed, making Sean cackle.

Rory frowned, turning back to the front of the class where Mr Winters was rooting through one of his desk drawers.

'Jeff, what are you doing?' Mrs El-Khalil asked, her face the very picture of concern.

'I'm getting out of here,' he replied, head and arms buried in paperwork, stationery and confiscated mobile phones. 'This is it! The end is nigh! I for one will not be abducted, studied, *probed*. I have a supply of tinned foods in my larder that would put Tesco to shame and I am going into the country – to escape the invasion.'

Mrs El-Khalil looked down at Mr. Winters with an expression of pity. Rory caught her eye and she inclined her head, as though pleading for the sanity of his input.

'S-Sir,' Rory began. 'If they *are* aliens and they wanted to invade, wouldn't there be more lights? If those are their ships...'

Mr Winters' head popped up above the desk, his moustache giving him the appearance of a discombobulated squirrel. '*These* lights are probably scouts!' His head disappeared. 'A-ha! Found them!' He emerged once more, holding a set of car keys in between thumb and forefinger, jangling them victoriously for all to see. With a sweep of his chair, he was up and grabbing his coat. He strode to the door, paused, then returned and took Mrs El-Khalil's hands in his own.

'Come with me, Tabatha,' Mr Winters urged. 'Come with me and perhaps we two can rebuild civilisation once the aliens have destroyed our cities and incinerated our species.'

Mrs El-Khalil snatched her hands away. 'I'm not sure my husband would be comfortable with that, Jeff.'

Mr Winters nodded, a look of disappointment in his eyes. He turned to Rory and the other boys. 'Stock supplies, lads. Build a bunker and grab what weapons you can. Trust no one!' He ran off.

'I'm sorry about that, boys,' Mrs El-Khalil said. 'I'm sure there is really nothing to worry abo– What's the matter, Mandeep?'

Mandeep snivelled into his blazer sleeve. 'Will my mum be incinerated by the aliens?'

Mr. El-Khalil sighed, covering her face with her hand.

Rory looked back up at the TV as the Prime Minister concluded her speech.

We will provide regular updates on fresh developments as and when they occur. But I ask that you remain calm and show that British pluck we all possess. Take comfort when I say that there is no reason to think they are hostile.

The afternoon pushed forward, darkness seeping into the pallid daylight like an incursive force. The fog over the school grounds was still thick but that was not reason enough for PE to be cancelled, so Rory and his twenty-eight other classmates were screamed onto the fields by Mr Chin, the balding sports teacher who, much like every sports teacher in the country, considered his subject to be unmatched in its importance. Rory shivered in his blue shorts and white top, the damp fog pressing his skin like chilly papier-mâché. However, he was thankful for the fog too, as it allowed him to sneak his rucksack out onto the field without Mr Chin noticing. He dared not let Gary out, despite the creature's occasional whimpers, though his proximity seemed to have a soothing effect. He had managed to buy it some milk from the canteen after detention (he had bought himself the last corner of a fish pie and the taste of haddock kept repeating on his breath), and it had lapped that up as greedily as a puppy. With people like Curtis and Sean doing PE as well, he could not let his bag out of sight, as they had, in the past, been known to take it from him and kick it about the playground.

And Gary would not appreciate that one bit, he thought to himself.

As was the lot of many a non-sporty boy, Rory was invariably picked for goalkeeping duties which, on that day and on every other, tended to involve a whole lot of standing around watching other boys running about, shouting and occasionally collapsing under what, professionally, might have been classed as a career-ending tackle. He was thankful for his goalie gloves, which kept his hands protected from both the elements and the muddy splatter of the football when someone took a shot, and he tried to keep the rest of his body warm by jogging on the spot. The one saving grace today was that he had been picked for the team with the better players, and so the majority of the action saw his teammates camped in the opposition's final third.

Rory hadn't quite taken in the full ramifications of the history-making speech made by the Prime Minister less than forty minutes earlier. He gazed skyward as though expecting to see a spacecraft descending towards the football pitch, first contact to be made in a particularly rough part of South London. But there was nothing – only a uniform bank of pale cloud hanging over Croydon like a threat.

The ball whistled past him and a cheer from several boys alerted Rory to the fact that he had conceded a goal. He looked behind him and watched the ball escape through a hole in the net and roll out of sight into the fog. Turning back, he was confronted by his teammates.

'What you doing, weirdo!' Curtis yelled, shoving him in the shoulder. 'Why didn't you move?'

'S-Sorry,' Rory replied, bowing his head. 'I was distracted.'

Curtis swore spectacularly and jogged off back up the pitch.

'Go and get the ball then, div,' Sean shouted at him from near the halfway line.

Rory sighed, turned and ran off into the fog. He soon reached the steep bank at the end of the field that fell away to a tall mesh fence separating the school grounds from a railway line. At the bottom of the bank, Rory saw the ball. Swearing under his breath, he inched down the bank, overgrown grass concealing treacherous pockets of mud. As a train thundered past, the slipstream caught Rory and he lost his balance, tumbling down the bank and crashing into the fence with a painful smack. He groaned and pulled himself up, using the fence to do so – rust rubbing off on his hand and mixing with sweat in bronze pools. He was covered in mud and fresh cuts grazed his knees and forearms. Other than that, he thought he was unhurt, so he scooped up the football and made to climb back up the bank again.

That's when he heard it.

From across the train tracks, among the trees that constituted the vanguard of the Croydon Woods, came a sound that gnawed into Rory's bones and spread a chill. It was like the agonised wail of a mother burying her child mixed with the sore rattle of a man being strangled. It was a noise that, in every conceivable way, lit the senses with distress.

Rory backed up against the bank and looked into the trees, heart hammering a plea in competition with a primal need to know what the noise was. It was like the noise he had heard in the playground yesterday, when he ran out of Science class, only more intense. Nearer.

His eyes travelled over tree branch, trunk and bush for what seemed an age, but he saw nothing... at first. Then – there! Something chalky-grey in colour. No defined shape. Just a flash in among the leaves. He hardly dared look again and cried out as another train hurtled past.

'Rory!' The voice came from the top of the bank. It was one of his teammates. 'Got the ball?'

Rory looked up at a kid called Tyrell and, slowly, the reality of the situation pressed back in upon him. As the train passed, he looked away over the track into the trees. There was now only silence. And no sign of that chalky-grey colour… whatever it was.

'Rory! C'mon!'

Tearing his attention from the woods, Rory dragged himself up the bank.

Back on the football pitch, he held a hand up in apology at the sound of indignant yells and boos, hoofing the ball up towards Curtis and Sean both standing in the centre of the pitch, hands on hips, scowls on lips. Curtis brought the ball to a stop, spat, and got the game underway again. Rory half kept his attention on proceedings up the pitch, but was distracted also by his rucksack, to the side of the goal, which was now shaking and rolling about.

No, no, no… Not here, not now, Rory pleaded.

Rory checked the play (Sean was holding off an opposition defender on the edge of the opposing team's box) and jogged over to his bag, holding it down and opening the zip a little, ensuring his back was to the pitch and any wandering eyes.

'Gary, what is it?'

Gary's crystals flashed in an array of deep purples, his eyes moist and – had he had them – eyebrows moving up and down. The creature was clearly not happy and trying to communicate its unease. Instinctively, Rory looked back into the fog towards the bank leading down to the trainline, but he could see nothing. He stroked Gary's head, his hand rising and falling over the creature's damp, obdurate hide. Gradually, it calmed.

'Rory! Man on!'

Rory looked over his shoulder to find an opposition player bearing down on goal. Swearing, he zipped his rucksack, jumped up and dashed out towards the player, who drew back his foot – ready to pull the trigger. Rory slid in and his boot connected with the ball, taking it away from the attacker and straight up into the face of the onrushing Curtis, who had tracked back to help defend.

There was a sickening crack and time itself seemed to pause.

'You split my lip!' Curtis screamed, clutching at his face, a palette of mud and blood. Teammates and opposition players alike crowded around him, some to ask if he was okay, others to review the damage.

Curtis locked eyes with Rory, the hatred and a promise of violence all too present.

Oh, dear God, no…, Rory begged, wordlessly.

He pulled himself up, smartly, just as Curtis grabbed him by the shirt and punched him square in the jaw. He hit the ground with a ringing in his head and Curtis kicked him several times in the legs and stomach for good measure. The only sound in his ears was the *thunk thunk* of his pulse and the chorus of, 'Fight, fight, fight!' from the other boys.

'You stupid freak!' Curtis yelled with each kick, his voice growing hoarser. 'You and your weirdo mum – you're freaks!'

Rory curled up as much as he could to escape the punishment, hardly able to keep the tears from his eyes and wholly unable to defend himself against the bigger, rougher boy. And that is when the chants from the other boys turned to gasps. Even Curtis stopped his kicking. Rory looked up at them all to find their eyes locked on to something at about chest height behind him. He turned his head to see his rucksack *levitating*.

'Gary...' he whispered.

The rucksack started to squeal: an angry, indignant sound building towards a crescendo. Then, with an almighty hiss of escaping gas, the rucksack rocketed through the air straight into Curtis's face, knocking the boy clean off his feet and into a satisfyingly large puddle of mud. The rucksack then swung around and fell at Rory's feet.

Gary, what have you done? he said to himself, panicked that the creature might have hurt itself in its noble effort to defend him.

He picked himself up and surveyed the vast ruin of Curtis before him.

'What the *hell* is going on here!' Mr Chin barked, shoving several boys aside and stomping over to Rory and Curtis. He looked down at Curtis, groaning and clutching his face. 'Get up, lad!'

'He broke my nose!' Curtis whimpered, pointing an accusative finger at Rory as Mr Chin hoisted him up. 'He's a maniac! He hit me in the face with his bag!'

Mr Chin turned to Rory. 'Is this true?'

Rory was too stunned to respond, his throat suddenly dry. 'I-I...'

'You all saw it!' Curtis yelled, looking back at the other boys. 'You saw him throw his bag at me!'

It wasn't a question; Curtis was demanding support.

Sean was the first to respond, looking at Mr Chin. 'Yeah, he did, sir. Got his bag and smacked Curtis right in the face. He's mad!'

Sean's testimony encouraged a general assent from many of the other boys, who were apparently ready to dismiss the reality of what they *had* witnessed as having been too bizarre to have actually occurred.

Rory started to find his voice, face reddening at the injustice unfolding. 'No, sir, I–I didn't… I didn't… Look at my mouth! *He* hit *me!*'

Mr Chin gave him a baleful glare, as though about to pass sentence on a murderer. 'Rory, get showered, get dressed and get to the headmaster's office. I do *not* tolerate assault in my lessons. You could be expelled for this.'

Behind Mr Chin, Curtis snapped his fingers and mouthed, 'Shame!' with a twinkle in his eye.

Rory made no effort to hide the tears and felt a familiar pang of anxiety flood his mind.

Rooory, Rooory. You're going to be expelled. No more education for you. You've ruined everything!

The headmaster's office appeared to be in a state of civil war. At once, it was a creaky throwback to a time when all headmasters' offices were stately: bookcases with leather-bound manuscripts flanked each wall; a glass cabinet at the back displayed medals several decades old; and the desk behind which Mr MacSteward sat might very well have predated the Battle of Agincourt. But since the Hurling Federation had taken over the school and made it an academy, evidence of modernity was now also to be found in the office: local newspaper articles on the wall reported the attendance of a peripheral member of the royal family at Hurling Academy's opening; a hi-tech coffee machine sat in one corner; and a curved-screen monitor stood pride of place on the desk, currently tilted to display a CCTV view of the corridor along which were situated all the senior teachers' offices (rumour had it that Mr MacSteward had requested CCTV be positioned there so as to watch for the approach of Mr Winters, whom he detested, though with the latter having now gone to live the life of a hermit with his baked beans in the country, perhaps the camera too would be consigned to the past).

'Mm-hmm. Mm-hmm. Aye,' the headmaster said, speaking gravely into his walkie-talkie. 'No... No... Well, ah'll have a wee word wi' the lad now, see whit he has tae say fer himself. Thank you, Graham.'

Mr MacSteward replaced the walkie-talkie on the desk and looked across at Rory.

'That was Mr Chin, in the nurse's room. Y'know, ye gave that Varley lad a batterin'.'

The words hung in the air and Rory fought back the tears, staring down at his hands splayed out on his knees, symmetrically.

The headmaster sighed with exaggeration. 'Whit's the matter? Ah ne'er had ye doon for the violent type.'

Rory shook his head and the tears rushed down his cheeks.

'Here, grab a tissue,' Mr MacSteward said, offering Rory a box of them. 'How're things at hame?'

At the mention of home, Rory's vivid imagination twisted into another unsettling image: Mum lying unconscious, head propped slightly against the bottom of the kitchen counter. But… that's not how he had left her earlier… or was it?

Rooory, Rooory. You knocked her out. She's been lying there all day, waiting for help. And now she's dead!

His breathing came faster as his lungs constricted.

She was awake when I left, wasn't she? She was telling me to get out… Or did I imagine that? What if she's unconscious and she needs a doctor? Rory argued with himself.

'Rory! We'll talk agen the morn. Let me jes' call yer maw, let her know whit's bin goin' on. School finished a wee while ago now, so she'll as like be wonderin' where ye are.'

The headmaster awkwardly tapped at a keyboard, mumbling, 'Reindeer flotilla' – perhaps his password – and then peered into the computer monitor for a good thirty seconds, talking to himself. He seemed to find what he was looking for, picked up a mobile phone and dialled in a number, referring to the screen every third digit. He held the mobile to his ear and winked at Rory.

What if she doesn't pick up? Rory worried.

'Oh hello, Ms Hobble. I've got yer lad in my office wi' me. He's had a wee bit of a scuffle here today, so I'm just going tae send him hame on the bus. Gi' us a call when ye get this though. Bye fer noo.' He disconnected the call and tapped away at his mobile. 'Rory, there was nae answer, so when yer maw gets my message –'

But Rory was on his feet, snatching up his bag and dashing straight out of the headmaster's door – a 'Where ye goin', son?' ringing in his ears. He swiped away at the tears on his cheek, trying to convince himself his mother wasn't dead, but the voice would not go away.

Rooory, Rooory. Rooory, Rooory. Rooory, Rooory. Rooory, Rooory!

4

Missing

Outside school, the fog was still heavy and the mid-afternoon sky darkened. Rory ran past the playing fields and over the bridge that hung above the railway, bringing him level with Croydon Woods. So fixed were his thoughts on getting home that he did not pay attention to the treeline or dwell on the unsettling noises he had heard earlier. However, his attention was dragged to the trees once again when he heard a sound like a howl of anguish. He stopped dead in his tracks, eyes searching the woodland, heavy canopies shadowing the forest floor as all the darker and harder to pierce.

Again, another sound came, only this one was not so anguished – instead, it was a gentler moan.

Rory felt the hairs stand on end all over the back of his neck, and Gary shook in the rucksack. PE was the last class of the day and he had been waiting to speak to Mr MacSteward for over half an hour, as the headmaster had been in a meeting with some governors when Rory first reached the office.

Consequently, the roads were nearly empty and only a few straggling students could be heard here and there in the distance; other than that, Rory was quite alone.

He needed to get home to check on Mum, but at the same time, just as earlier, there was a deeper persuasion, urging him to find out just what was going on in those woods.

'Sorry, Gary – I know you don't like it. But I gotta know.'

Gary whined in response, but made no further show of reproach.

Rory stepped off the pavement and onto the slope, which led down into the woods. The ground was sodden, so the grass squelched underfoot, but a few misplaced steps left snapped twigs in his wake. Reaching the trees, Rory paused. The fog carried into the woods as well, though there it was not as thick. The trees were tightly packed, like matchsticks in a box, and bushes, weeds and moss consumed much of the floor.

Rory moved in among the trees, and was surprised just how dark it was away from open sky. His awareness of sound changed as well, and every scuttling animal, rustling leaf and whisper of wind was a nervous moment for him. He walked about for a while, straining his ears to identify any other sound that might be considered out of the ordinary, but nothing came. Then, just as he decided to carry on back home, he heard it...

Urrr-ruuuh-uuuuh-uuuh...

It was close by, and this time the noise was different – in some indefinable way, it sounded like language.

'Hello?' Rory said, but there was no response.

He looked around: behind this tree, over that bush... but nothing. The Prime Minister's words from her press conference came to mind: *there is no reason to think they are hostile.* But Rory took a few steps back anyway, hushing Gary, who was whining once more.

This is ridiculous. Utterly ridiculous, Rory thought to himself, shaking his head.

As he started to head back towards the road, he heard it again, closer this time.

Urrr-ruuuh-uuuuh-uuuh…

He sucked in a sharp, fog-moistened breath and darted his head about, looking anywhere his eyes could penetrate in the gloom.

'I-I know you're out there!' Rory yelled, finding the courage to broadcast himself. 'I saw you earlier. You might as well show your face and stop hiding.'

He let the words echo out of existence, but still there was nothing – only the wind shuffling leaves like a pack of cards. After a good minute, Rory turned around and began walking back to the road yet again. Gary was silent, which Rory found more uncomfortable than his whining. Walking past a large oak, he came level with a bush far bigger than he and he heard the noise again, level with his ear.

Urrr-ruuuh-uuuuh-uuuh…

Rory whipped his head round with a yelp, slipped over a rock and landed heavily on his backside. Staring into the bush though, he saw absolutely nothing.

Okay, I'm done. This is silly, he decided, with more conviction this time.

He pulled himself up, annoyed with himself for, as he saw it, overreacting. As he did so, he cast a casual glance back in the direction from which he came, and only then did he see it: a thin, pale arm with four nail-less fingers disappearing behind a tree not twelve feet away, gone before he even realised what he was seeing. In that hideous moment, the wind caught his hair and he staggered back, heart drumming with terror. Gary whined and Rory broke into a run, flying through the trees, tearing through the bushes, desperate to reach the road and civilisation again.

Coming up to the pavement, Rory was more interested in looking over his shoulder to check if he was being chased and so dashed onto the road into the path of an oncoming vehicle, which swerved wildly to avoid him, coming to a stop amidst a beeping of horns and screeching of tyres.

'Stupid kid!' the driver barked at him through an open window.

But Rory was already running off into the distance towards home, mindful only of the need to get away from Croydon Woods as quickly as he could. He finally came to a stop a quarter of a mile up the road, where he could see the Mirth Rises estate hanging above a break in the fog. Doubled up and catching his breath, he heard a car pulling up behind him, its dipped headlights painting his shadow weakly across the pavement. The car came to a stop and a door opened.

'Rory? I thought that was you,' came a woman's voice, familiar.

Rory turned around. 'Limmy?'

It was the new social worker.

'Come on, get in. You look like you've seen a ghost.'

A few moments later and Rory was in the passenger seat of Limmy's purple Mazda, the cranky old car winding its way up towards the estate. In his lap, he clasped his rucksack tight to his belly and glanced – as subtly as he could – to his right. Limmy was still wearing that same leather and suede outfit from yesterday and there was a stern expression on her face.

'What happened to you today?' she asked, her tone unsettled.

'At school?' He looked down at his bag. 'Nothin'. Just a… a bit of a fight with another boy.' For the first time, he was aware of the pain in his stomach and legs where he had been kicked by Curtis.

'Hmm. Apparently, your headmaster sounded worried on the phone.'

Rory looked at Limmy. 'You spoke to him?'

'Not me personally. But why else do you think you're in my car right now? Hmm? You think I spend all day stalking you?' Limmy's tone was indignant, but tempered with a hint of humour in it too. She turned briefly to him and winked, as though to suggest she *had* been stalking him all day.

Rory smiled, despite himself. 'No, miss.'

'"No, miss" is correct. He rang my office after you ran out of his. I got a call from my manager and, well… luckily, I was already out and about, so I thought I'd drive along the route from your school to home. See if you were – Watch where you're going, you *madman*!' Limmy huffed, beeping her car horn and yelling out of her open window. 'Honestly, you take your life in your hands on the road…'

Rory sighed, knocking his head against the cool glass of his own window.

'Hey kid, I wasn't joking when I said you look like you've

seen a ghost. Hot chocolate will sort you right out. Then you can tell me all about what's... going on.'

Rory nodded, meekly.

I'm too tired to fight her as well, he thought.

'Yes, miss.'

The car drove past the turning for Mirth Rises, but Rory didn't even register it. His fears for Mum had been supplanted by a single image: the arm on that tree. Soon, the lights would be present in the sky again. He recalled what Mr Winters had said about an alien invasion. About the lights being scouts. The thought of just what exactly *had* been in the woods with him not fifteen minutes earlier made him shudder.

Maybe I could tell Limmy..., he deliberated.

Before long, Rory and Limmy had parked up outside a little café specialising in African food called Caffrica ('The owner thinks he is so witty,' Limmy told Rory, rolling her eyes), which they entered, grabbing a table. The café was empty, save for one enormous man working behind the counter, singing what Rory took to be a hymn rather loudly and badly.

I will glory in my Redeemer,
Whose priceless blood has ransomed me.

Rory slipped into a seat at a table while Limmy turned the **OPEN** sign on the door around so it said **CLOSED** before going to the counter and ordering two hot chocolates. Soon enough, she was sitting with Rory and handed him his drink, the steam rising up in tendrils.

'In Aztec mythology,' Limmy began, 'the god Quetzalcoatl

stole cocoa from the gods and gave it as a gift to humanity. So, whenever you drink chocolate, you must remember that you are drinking something stolen from the lips of gods themselves!'

Rory managed a weak smile, which Limmy returned.

'You must be pretty fed up with all these strange people coming into your life. And here you are in an African café having hot drinks with yet another strange person whose hair looks like an explosion in a firework factory! Dearie me.'

Rory smiled, more warmly this time.

'So – and I promise I will not judge you –' Limmy continued, pressing a hand to her heart in a gesture of solemnity, 'why don't you tell me what's been going on?'

Rory swirled his cup around and looked into Limmy's expectant face. In her eyes he could find no sign of the undisguised, hard professionalism he had seen in previous social workers; sometimes there had been a business-like sternness that put him off talking. Instead, there was a glitter of humour and a secret-keeper's promise of sanctity.

Perhaps it would be good to talk to someone..., he decided.

Rory began by relating the events of two nights ago when he'd first seen the lights in the sky. He then described the bullying at school and the first encounter with something unseen in the playground. Pausing only briefly, he also talked about his argument with Mum and how she'd fallen to the floor (feeling a momentary pang of remorse and a need, once again, to get home), then the fight on the football pitch. He also briefly mentioned his encounter in the woods, but tried to pass it off as something altogether too silly even for consideration.

There was no room in his story for Gary, who he still regarded as something too precious to risk discovery.

When he finished, Limmy leaned back in her chair, taking several quick sips of her chocolate, leaving an impression of green lipstick on the china mug. She '*hmm*-ed' and pressed several fingers to her mouth, looking slantways into the air as though deep in reflection.

'A fine series of events, Rory,' she eventually said. 'But...' – she rooted around in one of her jacket pockets, discarding an old apple core, an empty packet of crisps and a half-eaten chocolate bar – 'I think there is still more to your story that you are afraid to let on.'

Rory panicked under her words, instinctively lowering a protective hand over his rucksack. 'N–No.'

Finally, Limmy pulled out a flute-like object from her pocket and held it victoriously in front of Rory. '*This* is a syrinx. Do you know what animal absolutely *loves* the syrinx?'

Rory shook his head, sipped his drink and momentarily felt guilty that an Aztec god had been robbed of it.

Limmy leaned towards him, grinning. 'A muktuk!'

'What's a muktuk?'

'I'll show you.'

Limmy leaned back, raising the syrinx to her lips and closing her eyes. She played a tune so deep and poignant that Rory was instantly lost in its haunting beauty. It brought to mind a surreal image of a group of whales visiting a graveyard and leaving flowers at a tombstone.

It kinda sounds like Gary..., he thought.

Automatically, Rory glanced to his right and then looked back again at Limmy. His eyes widened and he looked to his right again: his rucksack was levitating (not for the first time that day) about half a metre above the table. Checking that Limmy's eyes were still closed, he pushed the bag back down on the seat beside him. But, after a moment, it started to rise again, so Rory pushed it back down once more. Then it rose a third time. Limmy interrupted her playing with a giggle and opened her eyes. Rory looked at her with worry.

'You don't need to hide it from me, kid. I know what you've got in that bag of yours. Why don't you let it out and we can give it some milk?'

Rory managed to close his mouth and, unable to respond in any intelligent way, tentatively unzipped his bag. Gary peered out, making a curious noise as though to say, 'What's going on then?' and wriggled free. He floated across the table to Limmy – gravity being no concern of his, thank you very much – and seemed to purr as the social worker scratched his head.

'*This*, Rory, is a muktuk.'

Rory frowned.

'Kingdom: Exoanamalia. Phylum: Megafauna. Order: Asteracetacea. But, in everyday talk: muktuk. Yours is a pup – just a baby. What's its name?'

'Gary…'

'Are you a baby, Gary, are you a baby? Yes, you *are*! Are you a cute, *cute* muktuk? Yes, you!' Limmy cooed in a baby voice, scratching Gary under his chin, the little creature's pouches inflating and deflating in rapid succession.

Rory simply stared back at Limmy, profoundly confused, brain struggling to process all of the questions he had for his social worker.

'How did you know Gary was in my bag?'

'When you've been around muktuks you attune to that low, bass rumble they make when they're hungry,' Limmy replied, continuing to stroke Gary, who was furiously trying to get into Rory's mug of chocolate, which made Rory guilty for having kept Gary hungry. 'I heard it last night when I first met you and your mum, so I've kept the syrinx with me since – just in case I bumped into you again. Where did you find it?'

Rory, seeing that there was little point in concealing the remainder of his story anymore, told Limmy all about how he'd rescued the muktuk from the foxes and how it had defended him today in PE, which made Limmy laugh.

'Serves that boy right for being so nasty. Muktuks are *fiercely* loyal when they bond with someone. You better get used to Gary, kid, 'cos he ain't going anywhere! Hmm, and that is a complication…'

Rory's smile faded a little. 'Limmy? Yesterday, you said some*thing* comes out at night and starts looking for Mum. Is that what was in the woods earlier?'

Limmy stopped stroking Gary and her smile vanished. 'Maybe so.' She looked up at a clock on the wall. 'It's getting late – and it's almost completely dark outside. Perhaps we should get you home. Your mum will be worried, and… I should make sure she's okay.'

Rory felt the bottom drop out of his stomach. 'You mean… you think I was right to be worried? That maybe I killed her?'

Limmy managed a weak smile. 'No, kid. I just think it's worth checking that she's… alright.'

'But she didn't answer the phone earlier when Mr MacSteward tried her.'

Limmy's eyes narrowed. 'Really? 'Cos I couldn't get through to her either. I just assumed she was asleep or something.'

'You think something's happened?' Rory asked, his voice trembling.

'Stupid, *stupid*!' said Limmy, slapping her forehead. 'Come on, kid – we need to go!'

A few minutes later and the pair were tearing down the road in the Mazda, the engine groaning and creaking under the urgency of Limmy's maverick driving. The fog was still thick and the car's headlights painted it a dull yellow. Above the fog, the sky was far darker, with the cloudbank gorging on the last slivers of daylight and regurgitating a spectrum of purple and grey.

Gary floated contentedly over Rory's lap, the muktuk's crystals pulsing a delicate mauve, the bandage still firm around its middle. Rory had many questions for Limmy but, for the time being, he was just as focused as her on the need to get back home. He didn't quite understand what it was that made Limmy think she was stupid, but as far as he was concerned if she was worried then so was he.

When they arrived, Limmy pulled up in one of the residents' parking bays and they both jumped out, Gary floating along behind them. Looking up, most of the Mirth Rises estate was hidden in fog as well, lights from the many flats puncturing the gloom as did the bass-heavy music booming from different directions.

'Come on, kid, let's get to the top – watch yourself, though.'

Rory nodded, following Limmy at a jog into the stairwell

of the block where he lived. They found the graffitied lift and travelled up to the top floor.

Rooory, Rooory. She'll still be lying there. She was calling for help. But you were not there!

He pictured himself not only pushing his mother to the ground, but grabbing her hair and banging her head against the floor for good measure and feeling shame for thinking such a thing. He gritted his teeth against the impact of the thought, his heart skipping a beat, as he wondered if he had actually hit her when she was on the ground as well.

'You okay, kid?'

'I–I'm fine,' Rory lied.

Limmy tried a reassuring smile.

'What if… what if something's happened to Mum though?' Rory asked, his face creased.

Limmy messed up his hair. 'Then we deal with it to the best of our ability.'

Rory struggled with this answer as it was not the reassurance he sought.

The lift finally reached the top floor and the pair walked out into a stairwell, silent save for the distant music and the wind.

'Stay here,' Limmy whispered.

Rory looked at Gary, who made a mournful noise and watched as Limmy crept to the beginning of the walkway that led to several flats, one being 426. Limmy peeped her head around the corner, paused and waved Rory over.

'I think it's best if you stay here,' Limmy said.

'What? No way!' Rory replied, fiercely.

Limmy held a finger to her lips, sighing. 'Alright, alright. But we need to approach quietly. Just in case.'

'Just in case… what?'

Rory remembered that arm around the trunk of the tree in Croydon Woods and shuddered.

No way can that be up here…, he told himself.

Rory and Limmy walked cautiously past several front doors, Gary floating behind them, gently expelling gas so as to propel himself.

422… 423… 424… 425…

Coming to number 426, Rory sucked in his breath: the door was ajar, the wood around the lock cracked apart. Limmy looked down at him with a frown and nodded, as though checking he was okay. Gently, she pushed the door open – but just a little. Rory looked through the widening gap into the flat, which was almost pitch black. As the door opened more and his eyes adjusted to the dark, he could see that the main living area had been ransacked: the sofa was on its back, the material torn; the coffee table had been knocked aside and all the empty plates, dirty mugs and cigarette butts swept to the floor; and the TV had what looked to be a potato masher sticking out of it.

Rory wrapped his hands about his shoulders, protectively. He drew in a breath, ready to shout out, but Limmy's hand clamped his mouth and she shook her head furiously: a warning. Moving into the living area, Rory looked down at the floor where Mum had fallen. She was not there. He stepped around some cutlery and went into the kitchen. No one was there either. But the stacks of dirty plates had been knocked to the floor and Rory tiptoed around a mess of broken china and day-old, three-day-old, week-old food.

Limmy beckoned to him at the entrance to the little hallway, which led off to the bedroom, bathroom and airing cupboard, so he followed her, Gary still floating about, his crystals pulsing calmly like a steady heartbeat.

If Gary is okay, then I'm okay too, Rory assured himself.

Limmy popped around the bathroom door, paused, then re-emerged and shook her head. Next, they both moved into the bedroom. Again, the room was a mess: shredded duvets and Mum's bedding occupied the floor; the bedside cabinet was overturned; and Rory's action figures were scattered everywhere. A particularly loud gust of wind drew their attention to the window, which had some manner of – *what is that?* – sharpened bone protruding from it, the length of a metre stick, perhaps. And flapping about near where it penetrated the glass was what could only be described as a scroll.

'What *is* that?' Rory asked.

Limmy tapped her fingers over her mouth and gently directed Gary towards the scroll. The muktuk's purple glow illuminated it and, to Rory's astonishment, electric blue words started to appear, as though the writing was being tattooed into the scroll itself.

'As I thought,' Limmy muttered. She snatched the scroll from the bony spear and turned to Rory. 'This scroll is parchment made from the bark of an Ares' tendon and the writing is sap from the fibre of a Martian slipknot; it's fluorescent blue, so any exposure to light will show it up.'

Rory had no idea what Limmy was talking about, but despite the increasingly dreamlike quality of the day's events, he cared only for what the writing said – for any clue it might offer to what had happened here in his home.

Limmy seemed to sense Rory's impatience, scanned the note over once and growled. She swept a hand through her hair and the glow of the words caught the wet in her eyes. 'I'm sorry,' she said. 'I've failed. He's got her.'

'Who's got her?' Rory replied, his pulse racing.

Limmy handed the note to Rory and he read it:

Dear Rory,

I do not like to part you from your mother, but I have need of her and her alone.

*You may be of a courageous mind and tempted to follow – perhaps they will even give you opportunity – but I warn you now and just this once: do **not** follow me, for I am going to a place where you will find only nightmares.*

Whiffetsnatcher

Rory looked up from the note, all the blood drained from his face. 'What is this?'

Limmy opened her mouth to speak but, as she did so, Gary started to whine and the pulse of his lights collapsed out of rhythm. Both Limmy and Rory looked towards the bedroom door, but there was nothing there. They listened. There was no other sound either.

'Silly muktuk!' Limmy said, breathing out. 'You're getting yourself in a flap! Come on, Rory' – she took his hand in hers – 'there may still be time to rescue your mum, but we *must* hurry.'

Limmy led Rory out quickly through the bedroom door and hallway straight into the living area, where she stopped dead in her tracks. Rory cried out. Standing between the TV and the front door was a small, pale figure, whose arm Rory instantly recognised from the woods. The creature was humanoid with blotchy white-grey skin, which sagged in places as though it were once extremely fat but had lost a lot of weight. Its face was not dissimilar to a human's, though its mouth and nose were tiny, as were its sunken eyes, which were coal black. It inclined its head towards Limmy and Rory, seeming to sniff its surroundings, that hideous noise rolling out from its wrinkled throat.

Urrr-ruuuh-uuuuh-uuuh…

Limmy threw a protective arm across Rory. 'No sudden movements.'

The creature, however, disagreed with Limmy and skittered past the coffee table and onto the upturned sofa, reaching a hand out and grabbing hold of Rory. He cried out and staggered back, looking from the icy hand gripping his wrist into the face of the creature. For a moment, their eyes met and Rory was filled with a terrible sadness, as though some unknown tale of pain was playing out in the dark of those irises. But the moment was broken as, with a cry of indignation – and an impressive explosion of gas – Gary powered his crystals to an intensity of white light that illuminated the flat just as surely as would the explosion from an atomic weapon. The creature screamed a strangled crescendo of surprise and agony, snatching its hand from Rory's arm.

'Come on!' Limmy yelled above the cries of the muktuk and the intruder. 'We need to go, *now!*'

They tore out of the flat, Rory risking a quick glance at the creature (it was doubled over, clutching its face) then watching as Gary shot on ahead of him, still pulsing with energy before powering over the ledge of the walkway and plummeting towards the ground.

'Gary!' Rory screamed in horror, almost tumbling over the balcony in pursuit of his little friend – the fog had swallowed him, but he could still see a faint pulse of light far below. Limmy dragged Rory away from the ledge, towards the stairwell and the lift.

'Don't worry, Rory – he'll be fine. But we need to catch up with him. Something's got his attention and it may just lead us to your mum!'

5

Above the Sky

Several minutes later, Rory was once again sitting in the passenger seat of the Mazda, gripping on to his seatbelt, as Limmy wrenched the car through the streets. Up ahead, Gary was illuminated by the purple glow of his crystals, the muktuk careering through the back roads as though trying to escape a maze. Cars swerved to avoid it, leaving drivers gawping at the spectacle.

'Where's he going, Limmy?'

'I don't know, kid. But he's in a mighty big hurry to get there...'

Rory clung on to his seatbelt all the more as Limmy made another wild swing of the car, rear wheels skidding across the road with a screech.

'That *thing* back at the flat... It's what I saw earlier today in the woods.'

Limmy nodded, but kept her eyes firmly on the road. 'They're called "the Pry". Dangerous little buggers.'

'*They?* You mean there's more!?'

Limmy glanced at Rory. 'Many more… I know that this must all be very, very confusing… but weird and wonderful things will happen this night, Rory Hobble,' Limmy said, her voice quiet but with the promise of dangerous magic. 'And you will be at the heart of it.'

Finally, Gary came to a stop outside St. Joseph's Church, farther out from the middle of Croydon. The building was so old that it looked as though it were built in anticipation of the birth of Christ. A graveyard surrounded it like a moat. It was one of the largest churches in South London and sported an impressive bell tower, the top concealed in fog. The stained-glass windows were illuminated with interior candlelight, casting colourful illustrations of bearded men, angels, sheep, robed women and yet more bearded men across tombstones and gnarled oaks. The high, vaulted sound of an organ, accompanied by hymn song, broke through the stone of the building and the cracks in the mighty wooden doors.

Bathe me in Your light, Lord Jesus
Bathe me in Your light.

Jumping out of the car, Rory and Limmy ran into the graveyard, catching up with Gary, who had stopped outside the arched main doors. The muktuk was cooing, as though enchanted by the sound of the singing.

'What are you doing, Gary?' Rory asked, holding his hands out.

Gary turned around in the air, his little frog-like pouches inflating and deflating. The creature's eyes were wet and shiny. He turned around again, and his crystals charged with light.

Rory and Limmy both looked from the muktuk to the church doors and realised what was about to happen.

'Oh no. No, no, no,' Limmy pleaded. 'Don't go in th–'

But it was too late. Gary's coo became a scream of excitement that might have been amusing under any other circumstance, and he battered right through the church doors into the narthex and then through another set of doors into the nave.

Holy, holy, holy
Friend and Saviour from above,
Bathe me in Your light, Lord Jesus.

Limmy growled and dashed in after the muktuk with Rory hot on her heels. She waved apologies to the stunned congregation ('Sorry! Dog on the loose! Lamp caught on its collar! Come here, boy!'), as people jumped up from their pews. Gary seared a path right through the church towards the priest standing in front of the altar, who managed to make the sign of the cross before leaping straight into a choir of children on the other side of the chancel. Gary flew right over the altar, leaving in his wake the afterglow of burning crystal, his scream of excitement and a thoroughly bemused congregation of worshippers.

'This is a holy place!' the priest managed to shout after Rory and Limmy as they rounded the altar and dashed after Gary through another door.

The pair caught their breath and found themselves in a small chamber with dim lighting and a ladder leading to a hole in a wooden ceiling. Higher up, Gary's crystals cast a purple investigation through the dark rafters.

'This… is the… bell tower,' Limmy panted. 'Gary's trying… to get… high up.'

'Then I'm following him!' Rory replied, leaping onto the rickety ladder and beginning his ascent.

Up the first ladder, Rory found himself in a high-ceilinged cylindrical room with several lengths of thick rope hanging down from a large and vicious-looking hook, dangling through a hole in the ceiling. He saw the back half of Gary disappear through this hole, up into the very highest point of the bell tower. Grumbling to himself, Rory surveyed a series of ladders leading up to a hatch in the ceiling. He took a deep breath and commenced his climb again. About halfway up, he heard Gary squealing at something and, fuelled with worry, Rory pushed himself all the harder.

'I'm coming for you, Gary!'

From somewhere far below his feet, he could hear Limmy warning him to be careful. Her voice was joined by another.

'Tell that feral child to get right back down here this instant! This is a place of sanctity!'

'He'll be just a minute, your holiness – he's fetching our dog. Really sorry for the inconvenience,' Limmy replied.

'That *dog* was flying!'

Rory shook his head and carried on climbing. At that precise moment, a noise like an oil tanker's foghorn fired from somewhere outside the building, rattling the stained glass and throttling dust out of every crevice. The congregation seemed to be collectively screaming from back down in the nave, but the din soon settled. He could once more hear only his shoes *knock-knocking* on the ladder rungs and the pulse of blood beating in his ears. He didn't know what was out there, but he didn't sense danger, though he couldn't explain why.

Eventually, he reached the hatch and clambered through it, collapsing beside the church's heavy, bronze bell to try and catch his breath. The bell was surrounded by four colossal circular frames, glassless and filled instead with wooden shutters, which were punctuated with sufficient breaks in a floral design to let in the night air. He looked around, head whipping from one frame to the next. The bell swayed serenely as though shaking its head. He realised that the wood from one of the frames had gone, leaving a massive circular hole and a ludicrously scary fall to the graveyard. He grabbed hold of a wrought-iron handle hammered into the stonework, stood up and stepped towards the chilly night. The hairs on his arms leapt to attention. A shiver played like a theremin down his spine.

'H-Hello?' Rory called, unsuccessful in trying to disguise his nervousness. 'Is anyone there?' His voice echoed.

A squeal pierced the silence and a purple glow broke through the fog, materialising into Gary.

'There you are!'

Gary floated straight into Rory's arms and purred, the creature's movement calmer now. 'What are you doing up here?' Gary continued to purr, his crystals flashing in various shades of purple, pink and, for the first time, turquoise.

Listening through the foggy evening, Rory recognised something that, for all the world, sounded like enormous bellows shooting air onto a blacksmith's fire. The fog rolled around him and then, a distance above, it slipped away revealing a small portion of starless sky. But what sat in that small portion of sky was by no means small. Rory tried his very best not to scream as he staggered back.

It looked like a cross between a whale, a hot air balloon and a mountain floating there in defiance of gravity. He heard a noise like a generator firing up, and the sky beyond this *creature* – for that is what it was – ignited into a glacier of blinding light. Whatever this was, it was alive. Low groans rolled out from what Rory guessed to be a mouth, and a bubble like a frog's throat swelled below it.

Gary seemed utterly delighted and that was when it hit Rory: *that thing is a muktuk as well!*

He reached one tentative hand out towards the creature, looking out on the rolling fog bank below and squinting up at the lights above, feeling like he was standing on the promontory of a dream. Somewhere beyond the lights, he could see some kind of tube coursing up into the sky, disappearing against the night. Higher up in the clouds, to each flank of the muktuk, a series of four lights appeared – two on either side of the creature clearly belonging to *more* of these muktuks – and, again, Rory was struck by the realisation.

Five purple lights… The intruders. The lights in the sky are enormous muktuks! he said to himself.

Gary eased away from Rory and drifted towards the muktuk, which opened its mouth a little. From between teeth like harp strings, a single tentacle extended, translucent and flashing as though an electrical storm was taking place within it. The tentacle pushed out towards Gary and, for one awful moment, Rory thought *his* muktuk was going to be gobbled up. But Gary opened his mouth and extended a similar tentacle; the two tentacles made contact in a spit and fizz of cerulean sparks, and the crystals on each muktuk's back began pulsing in pinks, purples and turquoises, completely in unison.

Rory heard someone climbing the ladder behind him and looked around to see Limmy huffing and puffing.

'There... you are. Did you... find... the muktuk?'

Rory smiled, pointing.

'Oh... my God,' Limmy said, coming to stand beside Rory. 'This is so rare!'

Rory raised an eyebrow. 'You're kidding?'

'No, no, no. Even for me. You hardly ever get to see a muktuk adult and her pup like this.'

Rory looked again at Gary. 'You mean... that's Gary's *mum?*'

Limmy nodded. 'Yes, it seems so. That's why he was in such a hurry – his mum was calling to him.'

After some time, the big muktuk rolled out a series of bass noises that seemed to upset Gary, who withdrew his own tentacle and floated back over to Rory.

'What is it, Gary? What's wrong?'

Gary purred and nuzzled the crook of Rory's elbow.

Rory looked up at the big muktuk and watched as it moved backwards into the fog, the brilliant lights on its back fading into formation with the four other lights in the sky.

'It looks like Gary's lost his mum too,' Rory muttered.

Limmy gripped Rory by the shoulders and knelt down in front of him. 'We won't abandon her, kid. But following her means going up against the Whiffetsnatcher.'

Rory remembered the note in his bedroom. *Do not follow me.* He screwed tight his eyes and shook his head. A flood of questions he had been storing up suddenly exploded from his mouth.

'Who is the Whiffetsnatcher? What are the Pry? Do they *all* look like creepy little grandpas? What are muktuks? Why does the fibre of a Martian slipknot glow? And *who are you?*'

Limmy smiled, standing up once again. 'Listen carefully to me: if you want to see your mum again then you will have to come with me. But that means more than you know. If you come with me, you will leave your life here behind. And you will have to come *now*. You will not be able to bring any toys, a toothbrush, a change of clothes or any fresh underwear. I can show you a world you never knew existed – a world beyond imagination, but a world filled with danger too.'

'Is it somewhere outside London?'

'Yes, kid – it's outside London. Now, will you come with me?'

Rory looked out of the bell tower as the fog began to lift. Croydon seemed such a little world, buried beneath layers of emptiness just waiting to be filled.

'There's nothing left for me here. And I... I have to find my mum.'

Limmy gave him a quick hug, squashing Gary a little, who complained with a squeak of irritation. Rory looked out towards the graveyard below.

'Limmy!'

More of the pale humanoids were approaching the church.

Limmy looked as well. 'No... We're trapped.'

Gary, however, hovered beyond the tower in the open air and, with a concentrated squeal, building in volume, inflated his three pouches until they were bigger than space hoppers. He floated back to the bell tower, bumping into the stone as he did so.

'He wants us to get on,' Rory shouted in realisation. 'Come on, Limmy! Quick!'

Rory took a deep breath, careful not to look at the ground, and jumped out of the bell tower, landing with a bounce on one of Gary's pouches, clinging on despite the miscue.

'C-Come on, Limmy!' Rory yelled, his heart racing. 'It's the only way.'

'Please don't let me die, Gary,' she called, before taking a deep breath, clapping once and leaping out of the bell tower – screaming as she did – and latching on to the pouch on the other side of Gary. The little muktuk squeaked away and then, with a burst of speed that almost dislodged Rory and Limmy both, shot over the graveyard towards the Mazda, parked up on the road. Over the heads of the Pry, Gary accelerated, making a noise much like a deflating balloon, finally bouncing through a wooden fence and into the side of the car. Rory and Limmy picked themselves up, scrambled into the car (Rory grabbing Gary as he did so) and accelerating away from the church just as the Pry reached their parking spot.

Limmy drove them still farther from the more populated parts of Croydon, headlights illuminating great oaks and horse chestnuts twisting out of ivy, mud banks and bushes, glowering over the road with arboreal menace. Rory stroked Gary's head: the little muktuk was bleeding through yesterday's now filthy bandage, the expansion of the pouches on either side of his belly having dislodged it a little.

'Limmy, is he going to be okay?' Rory asked with concern.

Limmy glanced down, then back to the road again. 'Try and

slip the bandage back over the wound; there's a member of my crew who will know what to do.'

Rory puzzled over Limmy's choice of words. 'Crew? You mean... we're going on a ship?'

Limmy chuckled. 'It's a ship, Rory, but not as you know it.'

'Look out!' Rory yelled, pointing at something beyond the windscreen.

Limmy saw it too – a figure in the fog – and dragged the steering wheel so that the car skidded off the road in a squeal of tyres. The car flew over the pavement, towards a copse of trees, and slammed into a knot of roots and bushes. Airbags punched both Rory and Limmy in the face, and bounced Gary off into the back of the car like a beach ball.

At first, Rory's head rung and his eyes spun, but he slowly became aware of Limmy shaking him, asking if he was hurt.

'No... no... I'm okay, I think.'

Limmy breathed out, relief. 'Good. 'Cos we have to get moving, kid.'

Rory thought back to the figure on the road: pale, sagging, black-eyed. The Pry.

Limmy opened her door and stumbled out, Rory doing the same while urging Gary to follow, which the little muktuk did with a series of whines. The trees lit up, just for a moment, as a huge blur of green, white and blue thundered past: a tram. The noise echoed out and, in the ensuing silence, another noise came.

Urrr-ruuuh-uuuuh-uuuh...

Rory and Limmy spun round to find three of the Pry squatting not fifteen feet away.

'Run!' Limmy roared, swinging round and almost tripping over a tree root.

Rory didn't need telling twice and quickly caught up with his social worker, flinging his cumbersome school blazer off as he did so. Gary floated along at head height, trailing half a dark bandage, his crystals flashing purple, though not as brightly as before. Behind the trio, the horrible groaning from the creatures followed, interspersed with clicks and wails that could have been language.

They fell out of the trees towards the tram-tracks and ran along beside the rails.

'If we can... make it... to... the tram stop,' Limmy panted. 'I can... get us... to safety.'

Rory risked a glance over his shoulder and found the three Pry keeping pace and reaching towards him with their long, wrinkly arms.

'Gary!' he yelped.

The little muktuk fell back, in between Rory and the creatures, supercharging his crystals to a burst of white intensity – just as he had done back in the flat. But, this time, Gary dropped to the ground afterwards, pouches deflated. The Pry were also on the ground, rubbing at their eyes, screaming hideously.

'Gary, no!' Rory cried, making to run and grab the muktuk, but Limmy threw a hand across his chest and ran over to grab the creature herself.

'Come... on! He's... bought us some... time,' Limmy managed, face slick – one arm wrapped around Gary, the other waving air in her face.

They reached the tram stop, just as another tram pulled in,

ringing its bell, the driver waving at Rory and Limmy in an attempt to shoo them away from the track. The pair burst onto the tram, its light almost blinding after having run in the dark.

'Everybody off!' Limmy hollered, handing Gary to Rory and clapping her hands. 'Come… on… now!'

Rory counted six passengers, all but one glued to the screens of their phones. A few glanced up, but no one made to move.

'I said: everybody off. Now!' Limmy repeated, louder this time.

'Keep it down, love!' a man with a fade haircut and tattoos yelled.

But in that same moment, the door to the driver's cabin clattered open and the driver staggered out.

'Everybody off – *now!*'

Limmy and Rory exchanged glances, sidestepping the driver whose look of determined panic seemed to motivate the passengers into abandoning the tram.

'Come on,' Limmy instructed, walking up and into the driver's cabin and taking the seat.

Rory followed her, reassuring Gary as he did so, and closed the cabin door behind him, locking it for good measure.

'Look!' Rory said, pointing out of the windscreen.

The three Pry seemed to have recovered from Gary's light and were running down the tracks again.

'Why are we in here, Limmy? We're trapped.'

'No, kid. I told you I can get us to safety. But we need this tram to do that.'

Limmy watched the CCTV feed on a monitor and, as soon as the last passenger was off the tram, she pressed the button to close the doors. Outside, Rory could see the passengers pointing at the Pry and fleeing from the tram stop. With a judder, the tram jolted into movement, Limmy's hand wrapped around a joystick-like device.

'W-What are you doing?' Rory asked, in horror.

Gary also made a noise of reproof.

'No idea, kid! I'm not exactly Transport for London material. But we need to get to my ship; we need the help of the Gammaguild. The car would have been quicker but that's not gonna happen.'

'Gammaguild?' Rory echoed, wondering what his social worker was talking about now.

Limmy flashed him a grin. 'You'll understand, soon enough. Now, let's clear those Pry away.'

Limmy pulled a chain and the tram rang out its warning bell as it accelerated at the three Pry, who dived out of the way, narrowly avoiding been splatted. The tram rattled on its rails, downhill and alongside woodland until it entered a tunnel.

'We should be okay now,' Limmy said with a sigh, flopping back in her seat.

But just as she finished speaking, the lights throughout the tram flickered and then died, plunging the two carriages and the driver's cabin into darkness. Overhead, a *thunk thunk thunk* competed with the clatter of tram wheels on rails.

'Oh... That can't be good,' Limmy muttered, looking up and around.

Rory jumped, yelled and pointed at the cabin window to Limmy's left: the face of one of the Pry – illuminated in orange light – peered in at a horizontal angle before disappearing.

'They must have jumped on after they got out the way,' Limmy said. 'Don't worry though, the doors are locked and I don't think they're strong enough to break the glass. Weedy little buggers, mostly.'

A Pry skittered down the windscreen, spread-eagled against the glass. It looked far from comfortable and Rory met its miserable black eyes.

'Get out of it!' Limmy shouted, waving one arm at the creature as though her instruction might dislodge the determined creature.

Rory clung a little tighter to Gary and looked down at the control panels before him. He found one with the symbol he was looking for and let go of the driver's chair before pressing it. Looking up, he found the huge windscreen wipers waving from side to side, sweeping against the Pry's gnarly extremities. The creature screeched, but managed to reorganise its limbs so as to maintain a grip. Rory searched for another button, found it and held it down. Twin arcs of water shot up from beneath the windscreen, one catching the Pry in its mouth and the other in what might have been its backside. The creature made the mistake of releasing one hand to try and protect itself from the jets and the windscreen wipers swept it away to the right of the tram and out of sight.

'Good work, kid!' Limmy said, excitedly, clapping Rory on the shoulder.

Gary wriggled about and made his own little happy noises.

But the victory was short lived. As the tram left the tunnel, a number of loud thuds on the roof indicated a growing Pry presence. Rory looked out of the window and up into the trees, where he identified little bodies flinging themselves towards the tram.

'How are they avoiding the electric cables?' Rory asked, his heart thumping.

'Keeping to either side of them, probably.'

Outside, a flash of light broke the darkness momentarily and Rory spotted a figure fall from the tram and hit the ground hard.

'Guess not all of them are,' Rory mumbled. 'What now, Limmy?'

The tram crested a hill, shot through another stop and thundered across a road, before levelling out with houses either side.

Limmy reached into her waistcoat, pulled out a device that looked something like a radio and flicked a silver knob on it. 'Xam, this is Limmy. Do you read? Over.'

Limmy's question was met only with static.

'Xam, this is Limmy. Coming in hot. Do you read? Over.'

Still, there was only static.

Limmy sighed and looked at Rory. 'Probably gone to cook himself the egg of a gub-gub bird. I swear, that man's appe–'

A loud voice suddenly cut across the radio. '*Xam is in the house! Well… on the ship. How's it going, Captain? You'll have to excuse me*' – there was the sound of what might have been cutlery on a plate, and when Xam next spoke, he seemed to do so with a full mouth – '*I jus' popped t'the 'itchen t'make mysel' sm' egg, s' I was away for juuus' a min' or so. O'er.*'

'Fine, fine,' Limmy replied, impatient. 'Fire up the Scoob – I'm coming in hot by tram. Approaching East Croydon now. We're leaving. Over.'

'*Leaving?*' came Xam again, coughing as though he'd just choked on something. '*But what about the target? Over.*'

'The Whiffetsnatcher has her, but' – she leaned forward to look at the sky through the top of the windscreen; Rory looked too and saw the five lights still there through the cloud – 'he hasn't left yet and we may still be able to catch him. I have the target's son with me. Over.'

The sound of Xam smacking his lips came through the radio. '*Oh, very good! Hello, Target's Son! I hope you have a better name than that though! Over.*'

Rory leaned towards the radio, unable to keep a smile from his face. '*H–Hello! Yes, it's Rory... Oh! Over.*'

Limmy cut across Xam's response. 'Keep focused, Xam! Get your backside in the air, quick!'

'*Roger that, Captain!*'

Rory gazed out of the windscreen. A little way up ahead, the track curled past a building that looked like a fifty-pence coin – something large and bright torpedoed off from its roof and towards Central Croydon. A thud at the window next to Rory made both him and Limmy jump and they looked out to see another Pry, this one using a foot to kick the glass. It did so once, twice, three times and, on each occasion, the glass cracked a little more.

'It's going to get in!' Rory yelled, retreating from the window.

But, as the creature readied its foot one more time, a blue sign beside the tracks swatted the little monster right off the tram.

'That was a close one,' Limmy said, breathing heavily.

The tram tore past another stop by a train station and shot down a slope – shops and plush high-rise flats revealed in peach lamplight. There was no longer any thumping from the roof of the tram and so Rory relaxed a little, daring to believe that they had lost the Pry. He looked down at Gary and gave the little muktuk an affectionate stroke under what might have been its chin; the creature cooed and his crystals fluttered purple.

Beyond the windscreen, Rory noticed something hanging in the sky above a road lined with shops – a shape, as yet undefinable.

The radio roared into life once more, making both Rory and Limmy jump. '*Whaaargh! Captain, I see you, but…*'

Rory and Limmy exchanged a glance.

'But what?' Limmy prompted.

The radio went quiet for a moment, then… '*Captain, they're everywhere – crawling all over the tram. Pry! There must be dozens of them.*'

Limmy swore. 'Okay, Xam. Just look after the ship. Over.' She tossed the radio to Rory. 'Here. Keep hold of that in case we need it again.'

Suddenly, on that undefinable object in the sky, a series of intense lights fired up – several flickering out of existence in the process. It was too far away for Rory to properly make out what it was precisely that had been lit up, but whatever it was, it looked to be about two or three buses in length.

'*That's* my ship, kid.'

Above them, the thudding on the roof returned and intensified. Rory looked behind him out of the cabin and into the tram carriages. Multiple figures were at the carriage doors and windows, hitting the glass in an attempt to break in.

Gary made a mournful noise.

'I agree, Gary,' Rory whispered. 'But we'll be okay. Right, Limmy?'

'Certainly hope so,' Limmy replied. 'Unless they figure out how to open doors.'

Gripping the joystick that controlled speed and then bending it forward, Limmy accelerated the tram. She sounded the bell, causing people ahead to run out of the way of the oncoming tram. 'Outta the way, pedestrians!'

In the sky, Limmy's ship careered about all over the place, if the movement of its lights was any guide.

'What now?' Rory asked.

Before Limmy had a chance to respond, the radio crackled into life again. '*Captain, I'm ready, but the Pry are all over you,*' Xam reported, his voice full of urgency.

Limmy remained quiet, her face a study in concentration.

However, Rory had something of an epiphany; he looked over his shoulder, back at the Pry whose efforts to get inside were becoming increasingly determined, and clapped his hands.

'Limmy, your ship – how many lights does it have? How powerful are they?'

Limmy looked at him, her brow knitted. 'I don't know. Quite a lot though, and they are pretty strong. What are you–'

Snatching up the radio, he said, '*Xam, this is Rory–*'

'What are you doing, kid?' Limmy demanded.

Rory held up a hand. 'Xam, can you lower the ship and bring it towards us? I think I have a way of getting those Pry off the tram. Over.'

Limmy snatched the radio. '*Zut!* What are you doing?'

Rory smiled and his voice was full of excitement. 'Remember back in my flat and by the tramline? Those things couldn't stand it when Gary lit up. They don't like the light.'

'No…' Limmy replied, then her eyes illuminated. 'Yes! I see what you're thinking! I like it.' She picked up the radio. 'Xam, do as Rory says, but as you approach, keep your lights off. Then, as you reach us, fire up every light on the ship and drop the cargo bay door. Over.'

'… *And the light will blast those little buggers off the tram and you'll drive straight into the ship. Yes! You're making me nervous though*' – he burped, excused himself – '*and I think I ate my egg too quickly. Over.*'

'Pull this off, Xam, and I'll get you an extra-big crate of gub-gub eggs when we resupply. Over.'

Rory watched as the ship's lights blinked out one after the other, leaving it in darkness. He looked at Limmy.

'Y'know, I wasn't going to suggest you drive the tram *into* the ship…'

Limmy pressed the joystick forward again. 'Maybe not… but we're running out of time. This will probably be… bumpy,' she warned.

Rory repositioned his feet with the sudden burst of speed, but he clung on tightly to Gary, watching the vague outline of the ship hurtling towards them above the street: it still jerked from side to side, but not as much as before. Behind him, several panes of glass smashed as the Pry found a way through. Up ahead, the ship loomed like a charging rhinoceros, filling more and more of the windscreen.

'Limmy…'

She pulled the radio to her mouth. 'Now, Xam! Lower the cargo door! Fire the lights!'

Xam's only response was to scream but, sure enough, Rory watched as a ramp juddered out from the underside of the ship

– not all that big, but big enough for them. A series of lights burst into a supernova and the collective screech of the Pry told them the plan was working.

'Maybe this will be more than a little bumpy!' Limmy yelled above the noise.

The ship filled more and more of the windscreen and, soon, it was all Rory could see. He screamed. Limmy screamed. Xam screamed. Gary... well, Gary made a Garyish noise.

The ramp was a huge, metal tongue, lolling out of the mouth of a prehistorically immense beast. Limmy dragged back on the joystick. The tram's metal wheels erupted in agony as the vehicle rolled on, losing speed. The ramp from the ship clipped the ground, sending up a shower of sparks and... the tram slid up and into its belly, spinning into a cargo bay and coming to a complete stop but not before smashing through a dozen crates marked **GUB-GUB EGGS**.

Limmy paused only for a moment before roaring into the radio... 'Raise the ramp, Xam, and get us out of here!'

Rory felt a hideous lurch in his stomach as the ship started its climb. The ramp groaned with the effort of moving, but it didn't seem to close properly. Limmy staggered out of the tram driver's cabin, jumped through a hole that was once a door, and weaved a path against the g-force, over to a huge rivet with a big red light next to it. Rory let Gary out of the driver's cabin and clambered out himself and then through the shattered door, watching Limmy as she kicked the rivet several times before the light next to it turned green and the ramp locked into place.

Limmy looked up with a smile. 'Always does that!' She

swayed over to him and grabbed his hand. 'Come on, kid. Let's get to the Dome.'

When Limmy had originally said 'ship', Rory had not pictured *this*. He could hardly comprehend the corridors as he flew through them in Limmy's grip and, before long, they both came out onto what looked to be some kind of a Bridge; only, what might have been a viewing screen on the *Enterprise* or a starscreen on the *Millennium Falcon* was here, instead, a gargantuan Dome composed of many triangular panes of glass – it gave the impression, in Rory's mind, of the eye of some insect. He was also vaguely aware of other people on this Bridge and a number of control consoles, but his attention was primarily gripped by what he was looking at outside the 'Dome'.

'Limmy?' Rory mumbled. 'Is… is that…?'

Limmy adjusted her cravat and folded her arms. 'Sure is! Space. We are now above the sky.'

She invited Rory to take a seat, striding purposefully forward into the middle of the deck. 'Mira. Status update.'

'We can go,' came a very young-sounding voice, almost bored.

'Good enough for me,' Limmy said, nodding. 'Xam, where is our prey?'

'A bit to the left,' said a very large man occupying an equally large seat in front of a complicated panel.

'Not very technical, Xam, but it'll do. Pursue. Mira, we need starboard thrusters to bring us about.'

'Mm-hmm,' said Mira.

'Captain,' said Xam. 'We can't pursue the *Phaethon* without umbilicking with Rongomai.'

'The *Phaethon* is still in orbit. This is our chance to board. We can't waste time umbilicking,' Limmy replied.

Rory hadn't the faintest idea what these strange people were talking about, but as the view beyond the Dome changed, he stood up, taking in a deep breath. Curving away below them in a dark semi-sphere was Earth and what looked to be Western Europe was a clot of cloud and golden light.

'Beautiful, isn't it?' Limmy said, looking back at him and smiling.

'H-How is this possible?' Rory whispered.

'Buckle up, kid. There'll be time for questions later but, right now, your mum is on *that* ship, the *Phaethon*' – she pointed at something beyond the Dome; Rory followed her finger to see another craft in orbit, attached through various tubes to five glowing muktuks – 'and while it is stationary, we have a chance to get her back.'

Watching as Limmy took a seat – perhaps her captain's chair – Rory did likewise and coordinated a series of belts into a central socket between his legs. He did so just in time, as the Dome shuddered quite disturbingly and they accelerated towards the other ship.

The Phaethon she called it – Fay-uh-thon..., he thought, chewing the name over on his tongue.

'We can do this, guys!' Limmy yelled above a racket of rattling metal.

The *Phaethon* remained motionless as they closed on the ship. The distance became smaller and smaller.

'We're going to do it!' Limmy said again, sounding more surprised than celebratory.

No sooner were the words out of her mouth, however,

than each of the muktuks attached to the *Phaethon* turned their town-sized bodies to face away from the Earth: the whole show was painfully slow to watch, but not so slow that Limmy couldn't start swearing very loudly, evidently frustrated at the prospect of losing her 'prey', as she called it. Rory pictured his mum alone there on that strange ship with who knew what horrors surrounding her, begging to be let go – to return home to her son. He opened his mouth in a silent plea to whatever power was controlling the *Phaethon* not to leave him behind. He felt the tears run down his cheeks as, finally, the *Phaethon* itself turned away, the muktuks' crystals ignited with purple energy and, in a flash, the ship was gone.

'N-No...' Rory muttered, as their ship drifted to a stop. He undid his seatbelt and ran forward, placing a solitary hand on one pane of glass. He was dimly aware of the voices behind him, of hands reaching for him, but the sound of their voices echoed, his vision blurred and, with a searing explosion of vomit, he fell to the deck, unconscious.

6

The World Beyond

Rory awoke in an exquisitely comfortable bed. It was large –
bigger than a double – with a fur-lined mattress and pelts for
a duvet; the pillow, also, was furry and warm, and his head
seemed to sink right into it. On the ceiling was a strange
growth that vaguely resembled a clump of portobello
mushrooms, glowing a dim turquoise, the only source of light.
He looked around the room. The creamy walls seemed
sculpted – the material perhaps not dissimilar to bone – with
luminous blue veins coursing through. Any lingering
possibility that this was all just a weird dream dissolved as Rory
looked to his left out of a porthole set deeply in a wall, to find
stars travelling by like little sodium wayfarers on a pilgrimage.

In all the excitement of recent events, his intrusive thoughts
had been kept at bay, his mind too caught up in all the activity.
Now that he was alone, however, in silence and not in
immediate danger of being taken by pale little monsters or
splattered across the inside of a cargo bay, he could feel the

thoughts moving in again like the vanguard of an unstoppable army. The voice that came with them was not like a *real* voice; instead, he could see words in his head that he only half heard. At once, their power was complete and irrefutable but, at the same time, some deep, rebellious part of him fought on with the firm belief – no, the firm *knowledge* – that the thoughts were ridiculous. Too rarely was this rebellious part of him strong enough to repel the thoughts, though, and consequently he was left with them occupying his mind, twisting his innards and playing on his greatest fears. Such was the power of obsessive compulsive disorder.

Rooory, Rooory. Mum is far away now. And all she remembers of you is that fall. What if the blow to her head made it easier for her to be caught?

The 'what ifs' were the most terrible part. It was not simply enough to have an unpleasant image in his mind. And *this* 'what if' was particularly powerful, as it took the reality of what actually happened and twisted it until the memory itself was distorted.

Rooory, Rooory. She didn't slip. You pushed her over. See, you're a violent, nasty little boy!

The conviction of the thought was devastating and his memory of the last time he saw his mum transformed. He saw it in his mind, just as surely as though he were back there. Mum neared him and neared him before he deliberately pushed her to the floor, her head smacking against the bottom of the kitchen counter. His chest flashed with the memory and tears sprang to his eyes.

I wish I had my Thought Diary… then I could at least write about this and try to fight it, he said to himself, but it was back on

Earth. And then he remembered what else was back on Earth: his medication.

At that moment, an oddly shaped door opened in the wall and Limmy popped her head in like a meerkat. 'Ah! You're awake! Can I come in?'

Rory nodded.

Limmy stepped in and closed the door behind her; she was wearing a leopard-print dressing gown and fluffy slippers. Her hair was even more of a mess than usual and her lips were no longer green. She walked over to the bed, sat down and offered Rory a mug. 'It's not hot chocolate, I'm afraid, but you must be thirsty after everything we've been through.'

Rory gratefully accepted the mug and downed its contents in a few short gulps. It seemed to be water, but it had a strange quality to it – as though it was produced not in a spring or a lake but in something metal.

'You've been knocked out for... oooh, must be three days now,' Limmy informed him. 'We've managed to get water into you, but you've been delirious. Our doctor doesn't know exactly what happened to you in the Dome, but... our doctor doesn't understand people very well, and I suspect the shock of all... *this*' – she spread her arms out – 'has made your body think, "Nope, can't deal with it. I'm done."'

Rory looked away and settled back into his pillow. 'She's really gone... isn't she?'

Limmy lowered her eyes. '...Yes. For now. But Xam and Mira are doing all they can to get this piece of junk up to speed.'

Rory wiped yet another tear away. 'It's all my fault.'

Limmy scooted on up the bed, and gently turned Rory's face

towards her. 'Hey, I know I can't make that thought go away, but… anything you did or didn't do… it had no bearing on what happened to your mum. There is no *way* you could have stopped the Whiffetsnatcher or, indeed, the Pry from taking her.'

Rory felt a familiar panic rising up in him. 'But when I… when she fe–' He paused, the memory twisting in his mind. 'When I *pushed* her, she hit her head. What if she was unconscious when they came for her? Or what if she *was* conscious but unable to defend herself?'

Limmy's face was empathetic. 'Even if she had been one hundred per cent fit and healthy, armed to the teeth and able to run faster than a cheetah, she'd have still been caught. She was up against a very evil man and very unpleasant creatures, all of whom would have hunted her relentlessly.'

Rory considered Limmy's words and felt the reassurance arrest his fears immediately, like a bag of frozen peas over a fresh burn: exquisite relief, if only temporary.

Rory pulled himself up in bed. 'Why did the Whiffetsnatcher take her? Who even *is* the Whiffetsnatcher?'

Limmy's face crumpled. 'The Whiffetsnatcher is something of a legend – beyond the Earth, that is. For decades he's been abducting children and, so the stories go, taking them to the outer reaches of our Solar System, to a planet called Haligogen.'

Rory frowned. 'But I never learned anything about a planet like that at school…'

Limmy chuckled. *'Certainement pas!* You will find that there's a lot they didn't teach you in school, kid. Now, no one's ever seen Haligogen, supposedly – besides the Whiffetsnatcher and his original crew – which is why the planet is something of a myth.'

'Why does he take children there?'

'Well,' Limmy continued, playing with one of the tassels on her dressing gown. 'The story goes that Haligogen is... special. The Whiffetsnatcher always claimed that there was something about it that could *heal* a person – both in mind and body. But, as I've heard it, he never offered any proof. He was laughed at. And that was a mistake. Started abducting children from Widdershins who were born... different – and also from Earth. They were never seen again and the Whiffetsnatcher has been rogue ever since.'

Rory mulled over Limmy's words, hands absently lining up on his knees, while he looked out of the porthole at the emptiness passing by. He wondered where Widdershins was – or, indeed, what it was – as he'd never heard of such a place – but, for the moment at least, he was more interested in the Whiffetsnatcher's intentions. 'S-So... if he was abducting children... why'd he abduct Mum?'

Limmy looked him square in the eye. '*That* I honestly don't know. All I was told was that he had an interest in her and that I was to prevent him from... from taking her.' She turned away and looked at the floor.

Rory nodded, satisfied that he was getting some answers.

But there is still so much more. So much, he thought to himself.

'There's a lot I don't know. I don't even know what to ask first. This is all so... unbelievable.'

At that moment, he felt something nuzzling the small of his back. Alarmed, he looked around and was shocked to find his pillow creep out from behind him and crawl blithely down the bed; under its hairy flanks he could see little legs shuffling along.

Limmy looked up at him, glanced at the pillow, then back at him. 'Hmm. I think I know how to explain this better.'

Now that he was calmer, Rory was able to appreciate the ship as he and Limmy moved through its passages. It was different to all the spaceships he had seen in films. There were no sleek metallic corridors with automatically opening doors. There were no hi-tech control panels or holograms. And, disappointingly, there didn't seem to be any flashy weapons capable of firing particle beams or blasts of energy. Instead, the ship had the feel of a shell, hooked up with dated technology to support questionable functionality. The bone-like walls were, apparently, everywhere, with doors sliding open – by hand! – to reveal additional rooms ('The material is a sort of calcium/protein fusion not native to Earth,' Limmy explained. 'Think of it like a mix of bone and sea sponge – very light but very strong and easy to mould.') The floor was bone-like too, with the same blue veins that Rory had seen in his chamber. In the lower section of the ship, Limmy said, the floor was partially made of glass, allowing you to see outside and into space. Also similar to Rory's chambers were the turquoise mushroom lights, which appeared to be in use all over the ship.

'We call her the *Scuabtuinne* – "Scooby" for short,' Limmy told him. 'She's not the most spectacular ship going, but she's as dependable as a grandma's tea and biscuits on a winter's day.'

'Skoo-ab-thih-nuh,' Rory recited. 'Skoooooo-ab-thih-nuh.'

There *were* some signs of technology, though. Wires linked

devices that resembled little megaphones, which Limmy explained were used for quick communication from one area of the ship to another ('And it lets Xam broadcast his music to us all!' she added). There was also some form of ventilation system in place; at one point Rory could have sworn that he heard something running through it, but Limmy brushed his concerns aside.

The ship itself was not very large – *'cosy' might be the best description*, Rory decided – and it was not long before they reached wherever it was Limmy was taking them.

'Now, Mira probably wouldn't appreciate us doing this,' she whispered, as though disclosing a nefarious plot, 'but, between you and me, she is *very* talented and her work deserves to be seen – not shut away. And besides... this is the quickest way to bring you up to speed.'

Rory watched as Limmy pushed aside a double-panel door to reveal a quite remarkable room. It was about the same size as the chamber he'd woken up in, but with an empty cream-coloured floor. The walls were covered in a wonderful tapestry, however, winding around and around the room before finally tapering off about three-quarters of the way to the floor, and coming to a frayed end on the floor itself in a campsite of needles, threads and little vials of coloured fluids.

'*This* is our secret history, kept hidden from the people of Earth – hmm, mostly – and it depicts over one hundred years of events that have led to... well, led to us standing here on a spaceship, travelling at about, oh, two hundred and thirty thousand miles per hour – give or take – towards the Martian system.'

Rory was transfixed by the beauty of the tapestry.

Everywhere he looked there were little scenes with people – presumably of importance – accompanied by a specific year and a description of what was going on. He was reminded of a History lesson he'd once had where the teacher showed the class something called the Bayeux Tapestry, which brought to life the Norman conquest of England – this tapestry was similar in many ways.

'It's amazing…' Rory whispered, after he had taken it all in. 'Where does it begin?'

Limmy put a hand on Rory's shoulder and directed his attention to an image of the birth of a girl; the sewing was intricate and the infant's clenched eyes and open mouth really evoked a sense of feeling. He could almost hear her crying.

'"1893"', Limmy read. '"The Birth of Beatrix Quidnunc" – *she's* the person who started all this, really.'

'What do you mean?'

Limmy pointed to the next scene, which showed a girl – perhaps in her teens – wearing a frilly dress and bonnet in a field, scooping up what could only have been a muktuk. '"1907 – Discovery of the First Muktuk",' Limmy read. 'From what I remember being told, she was out playing in a meadow near her home in Westerham – not too far from Croydon – and that's when she found it. She was worried it was dying and fed it bread and milk; she can't have realised at the time how much the creatures actually *do* love milk – or anything dairy! Anyway, she and her father looked after it but it grew very big, very quickly, and, allegedly, the villagers of Westerham celebrated it at a festival every year – they were led to believe that it was not a living thing but some ingenious mechanical dirigible.'

Rory reflected on Limmy's words, struck by the fact that his discovery of Gary was not dissimilar to this Beatrix's own encounter, over a century ago.

Seemingly sensing Rory's thoughts, Limmy pointed several scenes along to one that showed a group of hooded individuals meeting in a candlelit semicircle inside a grand house. '"1928 – Formation of the Gammaguild",' explained Limmy. 'This was a crucial moment in our hidden history. By this stage, Beatrix was married and had a child, but her husband died in the First World War. After the War, she and a group of others went into space on the back of a muktuk, trying to leave behind all the misery that the world had witnessed.'

'How could they have gone into space on the *back* of a muktuk? They'd have suffocated…' Rory interrupted.

Limmy smiled though, tucking her hands into her dressing gown pockets. 'Ah! Well, you don't know everything about muktuks – as you yourself said! I assure you: it is easily possible, but you can learn the "how" of that later.

'Anyway, as I was saying, the Gammaguild was a secret society formed after Beatrix and her team returned to Earth and couldn't face the prospect of continuing in their old lives; after all, the things they discovered on their journey!' – Limmy waved a hand as Rory tried to interrupt again – 'I'll come to it! I'll come to it! So, they purchased an estate in Westerham at auction and developed a community, building expertise and stockpiling resources. Oh, and studying the clutch of eggs that Beatrix's muktuk had laid.'

Rory raised his eyebrows and imagined, for one disturbing moment, Gary becoming the size of a city and giving birth to several thousand offspring.

'Of course, it's the male muktuks that carry the babies,' Limmy continued, making Rory sweat a little. She paused, grinning. 'If we...' – she pulled a hand out of her pocket and plotted a course along the tapestry with her forefinger – '... aha! Yes. Here.' She pointed to the image of some kind of submarine embedded in a cliff. "1952 – The Founding of Widdershins".'

Rory recalled Limmy mentioning the name 'Widdershins' earlier.

'Now, this is another crucial event. For some time, the Gammaguild had been developing a ship called the *Aeneas*' – *Ih-nee-ous*, Rory repeated in his head – 'which, pulled by the last two muktuks the group had left to them, carried them to Mars. Well, I should say "Minerva" – one of Mars' moons.'

Rory felt his forehead creasing. '...But Mars only has two moons: Phobos and Deimos.'

'Well, try telling *that* to the people of Widdershins: the settlement was established on Minerva, beside a waterfall, where the *Aeneas* crashed, and has been growing ever since. Minerva is a remarkable world – I've only been there once, mind, but... well, wow!' Limmy continued, her voice excited and quite emotional. 'Any questions so far?'

Rory had a hundred questions. But perhaps the answers to some of them would come in time, he thought. For now, though...

'How has all of this been kept secret? I mean, it's fantastic and... well, I knew nothing about it. No one does!'

Limmy raised a finger again, navigated back down the tapestry and singled out another scene: this one featured a dusty field with bits of metal everywhere. "1947 – Prototype R

Crashes in Roswell, New Mexico",' read Limmy. 'The signs are there to see. All those reports of UFOs, aliens and abductions... well, some of them are plain silly, yes, but others are actual sightings of... *us*. The truth is out there. The accident in Roswell caused a massive political storm. The Gammaguild had been testing out craft for a few years; Prototype R was doing well before it crashed in the United States.'

'People know about this society then?'

'Some, yes. It's been kept hidden for a long time – and for good reason. If everyone knew, then there would be uproar,' Limmy continued, stepping forward and crouching over the frayed end of the tapestry, picking it up and running it through her fingers. 'Just imagine it: you're stuck there on Earth living your life, working your job, and then you learn that there could be a new life for you off the planet on a world you didn't even know existed, yet you've been denied that chance. But it's not just that; there are many interests at stake – not all of them good. Our Society uses technology that would turn the Earth's economy upside down if it were known about – and then think of what the world's religions would say!'

Rory looked up at the tapestry again and reflected on the Prime Minister's address to the nation a few days ago.

'... I think it's wrong to keep this from them; people deserve to know.'

Limmy stood, turning to him. 'And there are rumours that the Cosmic Commission – oh, that's the government in Widdershins – is working with Earth's space agencies to do just that... but I don't know enough about it.'

A voice made the two of them jump. 'What are you *doing*?'

Rory and Limmy turned in the direction of the voice: a girl

stood at the panel doors, hands on hips, face a thunderstorm. It must have been Mira. He didn't get to see her properly in the Dome, but he could see her well enough now. She looked about his age, brown-skinned and black-haired, with blue workman overalls on and a toolbelt to hand – only a lot of the tools she carried were unlike anything he'd ever seen before.

Limmy took a step forward. 'I'm really sorry, Mira. This is my fault. I know you don't like us coming in here, but I thought it would be the best way to show Rory some of our history.'

'Y-Your tapestry is really, really good,' Rory added, feeling guilty.

Mira narrowed her eyes, crossed her arms and stamped her foot. 'It's not good. It's *rubbish*.'

'Okay, Mira. We'll leave you to it. Come on, Rory,' Limmy said, grabbing Rory and dragging him out.

Behind them, the panel doors slammed shut.

'What was that all about?' Rory asked.

'Best never to compliment her – at least not to her face. Come on, let's meet the rest of the crew.'

Limmy led Rory deeper into the ship and it wasn't long before he could hear a strangely mechanical whistling echoing up from further down a corridor. Rounding a corner, they arrived at an open archway – the bony curve of it ornately carved in floral designs – leading into a space about the size of a large newsagent. The inside was a wall-to-wall mess of various bottles, vials, medical instruments and books crammed into cabinets and bookcases; bizarre tentacled plants proliferated, most of them red. Two beds were set against a farther wall underneath another arch, with the option for curtains (heavy-looking, red-and-cream velvet affairs) to be drawn separately around each bed. Little metal lanterns hung from the ceiling at intervals, and seemed to each hold a gloopy mess of those mushrooms, though the rot had apparently adversely affected some of them to the point that the light shone with next to no potency. The walls were mosaicked in images that looked positively Greek. In the middle of the room was an island table of the same bone as the panels everywhere else on the ship, and there were various tatty white drawers set within it.

Standing at the island was the source of the whistling. It was hard to tell whether it was a person, a machine or an alien. It had what could only be described as a plague doctor's mask of a face, complete with huge, pointy nose and glowing eyes, along with a black, hooded poncho. Rory instinctively withdrew, but Limmy simply smiled and encouraged him.

'Hey, Beak!' Limmy called. 'Beak' stopped its whistling, looking up at the pair. Rory stepped forward, giving way to Limmy's encouraging nods. 'This is Rory – our newest crewmember. Rory, this is Beak, ship's doctor.'

Beak moved out from behind the island, rolling on a single wheel towards Rory and stretching out a hand, the motion producing an accompaniment of whirring sounds. 'It is a pleasure to make your acquaintance,' Beak said – it was extremely well-spoken and had a distinctly English tone, though there was something very artificial about it. Rory stared at the proffered hand, too scared to do anything. 'Does my appearance upset you?'

The bluntness of Beak's words shocked Rory back into self-awareness and he found his cheeks warming. 'What? N-No! I just… never saw anything – any*one* – like you before.'

'Rory was completely planet-minded until a few days ago,' Limmy added in a mock whisper.

Beak looked from Limmy back to Rory, its neck movement stilted and accompanied by another whir; it withdrew its offer of a handshake. 'I understand. Perhaps I should explain what I am.' Limmy nodded, smiling. 'I am an artificial intelligence – a prototype medical droid declared a failure by the Cosmic Commission's Chain of Health, Medicine and Exo-botany.'

Rory looked at Limmy. 'A… a failure?'

Limmy tilted her head from side to side, weighing something internally. 'Well… *technically* a failure. It works just fine, though – well, so long as Lancelot keeps going.'

Rory looked back at Beak. '… Lancelot?'

Beak lifted its poncho to reveal a cog-riddled, nutted-and-bolted belly, in the middle of which was a sealed hamster-wheel being ridden by… 'An exo-cricetid, on whom the crew has bestowed the name "Lancelot", though I do not see the resemblance to the Old English figure of mythology.' The exo-cricetid, as Beak called it, stopped its running and turned to face Rory, its little black nose sniffing away with enthusiasm, making Rory laugh despite himself. 'Lancelot serves as my central power unit, generating energy by continually running around in its wheel.' Beak covered its belly again.

'Can't you just use a battery?' Rory asked.

'Exo-cricetids *are* batteries,' Limmy replied. 'When settlers first arrived on Minerva, they had to use the moon's natural resources quite inventively. Exo-cricetids can run at up to fifty miles per hour and take a looong time to tire. They were used in early contraptions to generate power and are still used today – especially off-world. Beak feeds and waters Lancelot, and Lancelot keeps Beak operational. They have a symbiotic relationship.'

Rory frowned, wondering what would happen were Lancelot to suddenly drop dead, but decided against asking. Instead, he looked around the sick bay again and his eyes fell on an incubator towards the back, inside which was...

'Gary!' he yelled, running over to have a better look. The incubator was large and glowed blue, with various wires and tubes protruding from it. Gary appeared to be asleep, his head resting on a little blanket and another blanket covering much of his body. Rory looked over his shoulder at Limmy and Beak as they came to join him. 'Will he be okay?'

'The muktuk calf,' began Beak, 'is not "okay", but it is not so injured that it needs to be destroyed.'

Rory blanched and Limmy held up a hand, as though asking the doctor to be more thoughtful. 'He's fine, kid,' she added. 'Just needs to rest up a little, but he'll be right as rain in no time. Don't mind Beak – it just needs to work on its bedside manner.'

'Can I query, Captain?' chipped in Beak. '*Bedside manner.*'

Limmy leaned against a wall. 'Bedside manner. Y'know – speaking gently to the sick. *Empathising* with them.'

Beak span a little on its wheel. 'Curious. How does that improve one's medical ability?'

'Well, it... doesn't exactly,' Limmy conceded, folding her arms. 'It's just *good practice* – in a doctor.'

'Fascinating, though unnecessary,' Beak responded, quite

chirpily. 'And I cannot empathise, as I lack emotion. I can, however, evaluate the likelihood of a potential respon–'

'Okay, okay, Beak – I get it,' Limmy interrupted, pulling herself back into a standing position. 'Come on, Rory, let's go up to the Dome. Introduce you properly to Xam.'

Rory watched Limmy shuffle away on her fluffy slippers, and looked at Beak, who glanced from its captain back to him. 'I am glad to have met you, Rory.'

Rory smiled, jogging after Limmy. 'I was glad to meet you too!'

The Dome of the *Scuabtuinne* wrapped much of the way around the Bridge, giving a view above, in front and to the sides. Beyond the Dome itself was the infinity of space, rushing by. Over to port, outside the Dome, was a massive tube that apparently came from somewhere on the top of the ship and led off out of sight to somewhere below. Inside, though the technology appeared dated, there were panels everywhere: light flooded in turquoises and pinks from displays, buttons illuminated in moody cerulean. The metal of the workstations and the floor was dark, the seats bulky, padded and torn through use.

This was Rory's second time on the Bridge, half-surrounded by the Dome and, having seen most of the ship now, he concluded that it was by far the closest part of the *Scuabtuinne* in appearance to a 'typical' spaceship.

The Bridge was split over two levels: on the uppermost was what could only be the captain's chair, with a line of monitors set against the wall behind it like old arcade machines. To the left was a semi-circular workstation behind which Mira stood a few days before. On the lower level of the Bridge, Xam sat at his own massive workstation, which seemed to boast gadgetry that embarrassed the technology elsewhere.

'Xam!' shouted Limmy, jumping onto the lower level of the Bridge and slapping the huge navigator on his back. 'You didn't get a chance to say a proper hello to Rory earlier.'

Xam removed something like a headset, span around in his chair and extended a sweaty hand, which engulfed Rory's. 'Yo, what's the story, little Rory? Good to meet you properly. Last time I saw you I was carrying you over my shoulder.' His tone was teasing, but his smile warm and Rory took an instant liking to him.

Xam was dark-skinned – like Limmy – with hair resembling a gorse bush. His size and smooth face suggested a small child that had been inflated to epic proportions. He wore fingerless leather gloves, a long-sleeved black top, waistcoat and cargo shorts.

'I've been showing Rory around, introducing him to everyone. Want to tell him what you do?' Limmy prompted.

'Well, currently I spend most of my time mourning the loss of all our gub-gub eggs,' he replied, affecting a look of extreme tragedy before turning to face the Dome front. 'Out here, in the chill of endless space, in the frost of starlight, a man needs warmth to sustain his soul: gub-gub eggs, alas, were my warmth, snuffed out by the captain's appalling driving.'

Limmy slapped Xam hard on the shoulder and he pretended to have been severely injured.

'Xam is our navigator. He makes us go forwards and backwards, with a little side-to-side for good mea–'

'Oh, that's just my hobby,' Xam interrupted, sweeping around to face Rory once more. 'My main job – my *passion* – is cooking and I make a pretty sweet chef – if I say so myself –'

'What Xam *means* to say,' Limmy interrupted, 'is that he takes the job of navigating very seriously and is an expert cartographer of space and lander of ships. He is also a mathematical genius. Tell Rory how long it will take us to get to Widdershins.'

Xam tapped several fingers on his chin, appearing to concentrate intently. 'I estimate… a month and a bit. Oooh, we'll arrive in time for Christmas – hopefully – weather permitting.'

'Weather… permitting?' Rory repeated.

'Solar flares, meteor showers, Asteragradon attacks… the usual,' Limmy replied, off-handedly.

Rory frowned – not for the first time – and reflected on the prospect of a journey through space. He realised he would have plenty of time to learn how the ship worked, and what life was like beyond Earth. However, one thought niggled…

'But… what happens when we get there, Limmy?' Rory ventured. 'We *are* going to find my mum, right?'

Limmy squeezed his shoulder. 'We'll do our best, kid. I promise. We have to go to Widdershins first though, to report back on our mission.'

Limmy and Xam shared a glance.

'You mean… your mission to stop the Whiffetsnatcher from… from taking Mum,' Rory pressed.

Limmy hung her head. 'That's the one.'

'Limmy is the best – she'd have done everything she could,' Xam added, gently.

Rory thought it over a little more and felt a stab of anger. 'When you first came over to my home… you said you were a social worker. You lied. And you could have taken us away there and then – hidden us. Instead, you told me to be careful and look out for my mum.'

Limmy seemed to struggle with her words, but held a hand up to stop Xam responding for her. 'No, it's okay, Xam. Rory… technically, I didn't lie to you: I *am* a social worker. But obviously I'm more than that.'

'Limmy is a sleeper agent,' Xam said, a note of pride in his voice.

'Xam's right,' Limmy continued. 'I live on Earth, but I work for the Cosmic Commission. I've known about the Society in Widdershins since my foster parents told me – ever since then I've been a sort of… secret agent. I have a life on Earth and a life beyond Earth and I've only ever been to Widdershins once before, like I said.'

'But you're captain of a ship as well?' Rory replied, feeling confused.

Limmy smiled, glancing at Xam. 'Perhaps I'll tell you how *that* happened some other time. But mainly my life is on and around Earth. I did study to be a social worker, found work in Croydon, and so my position was perfect for making contact with you and your mum. But there are *other* sleeper agents too, and if it hadn't been me then it might have been a new doctor, or dentist, or police officer coming into your life, or something.'

'And if all that failed, we could have just abducted you ourselves,' Xam said, brightly.

'Xam's right. I didn't know that the Whiffetsnatcher had

already found your mum, otherwise I would have…' – she hung her head – 'I would have taken action. You see, by revealing myself to you now, I have effectively ended your time on Earth and any chance for you to have a normal life.'

Rory relented, smiled and tapped Limmy's arm. 'It's okay. I know you tried your best and… I didn't have much of a life back on Earth anyway.'

Limmy returned the smile and gave Rory a hug. 'Thank you. To be honest, I think my life on Earth is over now as well. When we reach Widdershins, you'll have to make a claim for asylum.'

Rory looked from Xam – who nodded encouragingly – back to Limmy. 'What does that mean?'

'It means that, when we arrive, you'll have to go before a group of people called the Chain of Migration and explain why you want and *need* Widdershins to be your new home. You'll have to talk about what happened on Earth and why you couldn't stay. Also, you'll need an advocate to vouch for you. I'll be your advocate – Are… you okay?'

Rory turned the colour of porridge. 'That sounds scary and… and what if they say no, no I can't stay?'

Limmy smiled, ruffling his hair. 'It's not so bad, don't worry. And they won't say no. They only say no if you're an "undesirable". I *hate* that word…'

Rory remained a little pale, acknowledging that many people had found him undesirable throughout his life. He stumbled a little, but Xam and Limmy supported him.

'Easy there, Rory!' Xam said, laughing.

'Yes,' Limmy added, clapping her hands. 'Enough excitement for now. You need to rest and *I* need to do some

captaining. I know you've still got lots of questions and…
there's plenty about the ship you don't know yet, but answers
will come. In time.'

Rory nodded, disappointedly, but gave Xam a friendly wave
goodbye. He glanced over his shoulder as he left and, once
again, that huge weird tube outside the Dome came into focus.
He wondered what it might be and where it might lead.

7

Tall-Tongued Henley

Several days later, Rory was in his room, leaning on the sill in front of his porthole, staring out at the stars, much as he had on the night he first spotted the Intruders. He had hardly touched the dinner Xam brought him a while back ('This is belja stuffed with reefnut,' he'd said, presenting Rory with something very steamy and quite vegetable-like in appearance – it had tasted horrible), and he'd struggled with the metallic water too. Worse than that, he was feeling the effects of not having taken his medication for a while now: the tightness in his lungs, his fast-beating heart and the images in his mind that brought tears to his eyes. He saw himself ripping down Mira's tapestry and throwing her to the ground; tying Limmy's dressing gown cord around her neck, tighter, tighter; taking one of the forks Xam delivered with his meal and stabbing it into the big navigator's hand; tearing Beak's pointed nose off and driving it into Lancelot the exo-cricetid. These were thoughts that would upset an adult, but instead had chosen to shelter in Rory's mind and all he could do was to tell himself that they did not reflect who he was and that his distress was a sure sign that they were not the real him. But the pain confined him to his room for the first time since he had been diagnosed with this cruel condition.

He tried to focus his attention elsewhere.

Every now and then, a crew member used the *Scuabtuinne's* megaphone system to communicate with someone else on the ship. So far, Mira had complained a lot about missing tools that she needed to fix the toilets, and Beak had asked Xam several times to restrict his singing to the Dome and not broadcast it ship-wide; Xam seemed to have a penchant for a singer popular in the 1990s called Enya. Occasionally, the creaking of footfall outside his quarters indicated the presence of someone walking or running by, but other than that it had been quiet.

He felt something tickling his ankle and looked down to see his pillow, apparently seeking affection after a good half-hour of exploration. Rory sighed, slid down the bony wall and stroked the pillow, which purred contentedly. The creature was quite docile and extraordinarily trusting, but then again, if its species was used as a headrest then it very much ought to be. Looking down at it, Rory sensed a fresh image coming into his head: it was him, not stroking the pillow but stamping on it, repeatedly. As ever, with his intrusive thoughts, he felt ashamed to have imagined such a thing and upset that even so rare a moment as stroking an alien pillow should still ignite the OCD.

The thought gave way, though, and instead he focused on what Limmy had said a few days ago about claiming asylum in Widdershins. Having been born in England and having lived his entire life there, until now, the idea of asylum was something that had always been as alien to him as his pillow. He took an interest in the news and current affairs, and so was aware of how asylum seekers were portrayed in the media. According to the news, some of them were responsible for bombings; some were involved in gangs or other forms of crime; across the Channel, many of them survived in camps; and, in the Mediterranean, families of them crossed the sea, desperately making for Europe. These were the narratives he had always found to be fear-inspiring, as though the mere presence of these people from strange and exotic countries should be enough for him to strike up his survivor's instinct.

Is that how it'll be in Widdershins? he worried. *Will I be refused and put in a camp or taken back to Earth?*

Outside his door there came the dim noise of gas being expelled. Rory looked up, listening. The sound came again. *Gary.* He picked himself up, gave the pillow one last scratch and stepped over to the sliding door, opening it to find the little muktuk bobbing about outside.

'Gary! You're alright!' Rory said, wrapping his arms around the creature. 'You look okay now.'

Indeed, Gary no longer had the bandage around him and, instead, sported a gauze pad over the bite he had sustained from the fox back on Earth. His crystals pulsed in energetic swirls of purple and pink, and his little inflatable pouches – one under his chin and two either side of him – hissed and wheezed, presumably with the effort required to keep him aloft.

At that moment, Rory's ears popped and there was a noise like static in his head. He slapped his ears a little and yawned to try and unclog the discomfort. But beyond the static, there was a sound much as a neighbour's TV might make through a wall: a dim mumble of communication. Amidst the mumbling, his mind seemed to fill with smoke and two black images appeared: a small, humanoid figure and an even smaller muktuk. The muktuk image drifted away from the humanoid, which then followed. As quickly as it came, the static, the mumbling and the images disappeared entirely, and Gary shot off down the corridor.

'H–Hey, wait!' Rory called, but the muktuk had gone.

Looking around him, as though he had been caught committing some form of minor mischief, Rory jogged off down the corridor too, trying to catch up with Gary.

Although Rory had by no means seen all of the ship, he thought he had seen most of it. However, Gary led him somewhere he certainly hadn't been. It was a part of the ship that felt as though it was on a gradient. The calcium walls and flooring deconstructed and became an assemblage of dark metals. The walls were a rusted, heavy iron that could have passed for trophies from a decades-old shipwreck, and the floor was a latticework of similar metal, damp from a dripping ceiling. Gary's crystals illuminated what would otherwise have been near-perfect darkness. His light eventually wrenched a staircase from the black: a staircase that wove up towards a perfect circle of pale, green light, suspended above Rory in the void. Gary seemed perfectly unconcerned and simply floated on up the staircase. Rory hesitated, momentarily, but reminded himself that Gary had, so far, shown distinct signs of nervousness whenever there was trouble nearby. Confident in the muktuk's judgement, he followed.

Each footstep on the stairs imparted a dull *dook dook dook* to the dark, which did not seem to echo, suggesting that, had this place been lit up, it might not actually have been as large as the staircase implied. Approaching the circle at the top, he could hear what could only be described as breathing: a great, shuddering snort as of a rhinoceros jogging along at a pace it found decidedly uncomfortable. Close enough now to look inside the circle, Rory would have called it the entrance to an underground tunnel – though that would be impossible in the middle of space. He felt a gentle spray on his face, touched his fingers to it and found a green juice on his fingertips. Surprised at his own bravery, he pressed it to his tongue; the taste was of boiled spinach.

'What is this place, Gary?' Rory hissed, not wishing to raise his voice too much.

Gary turned one hundred and eighty degrees, and flashed his crystals again, before turning back and floating into the tunnel. Rory called out to him once, but the muktuk was gone.

S'pose I have no choice now…, he realised.

Rory climbed the last few stairs and took his first steps into the tunnel. There was a light breeze inside and the walls were coated in a fine, faintly luminescent moss. The smell of mint was pungent, and the air was fresh and chill on his face. The tunnel itself was, perhaps, ten feet high and the same again across. Farther down, Gary's expulsions of gas echoed as the muktuk continued on his own determined journey. Rory's feet sank into the ground, the texture sponge-like. *Almost organic…* The tunnel wound away downhill and there was no end in sight; Gary himself was almost out of sight, but his coos that echoed up suggested he was in the mood for adventure.

Rory walked on for some time. Every now and then, the 'breathing' intensified and he was covered in more of the green juice, the tunnel reverberating all around him. Occasionally, it moved more dramatically, lurching quite abruptly to the left or right. Eventually, he came to a section of tunnel that flowed steeply downwards, so much so that the moisture that had simply sat on the floor now trickled down like an angled waterfall. At the bottom, though, there was far more light and the moss opened out onto some kind of lawn. Gary was there, at the bottom, waiting for him, performing loop-the-loops, perhaps to amuse himself.

'Okay, Rory,' Rory said to himself out loud. 'Nothing to it… just a horrendous plummet to your death if you misstep.'

He eased himself down, feeling for a secure footing as he did so. The dampness under his boots made a sucking sound, which clapped off the tunnel walls. His feet slipped a few times, but he managed to grab hold of bony protrusions from the ground when he did feel himself falling. His confidence grew, and he slid in part and stepped where caution was required. About halfway down, the tunnel gave a great shudder and moved again, only this time it lifted up and outward, increasing the gradient of the waterfall. Rory saw what was happening and realised that if he didn't slide to the bottom immediately, he would be left dangling – or worse – when the tunnel became wholly vertical.

'Just like a log flume,' he mumbled. 'You can do it!'

As the tunnel shuddered yet again, he threw himself into the middle where the moisture was heaviest and slid – screaming as he did so. The air became a breeze in his hair and little pocks and lumps in the tunnel bumped into his hands and thighs as he gathered speed. Towards the bottom, Gary cried his strange muktuk cry and disappeared entirely.

'Gary!'

Rory caught his foot awkwardly, performed a forward somersault, and tumbled the final twenty feet, crashing through a series of sticky tendrils at the tunnel's end and landing with a sickening thud in the grass over which Gary had been hovering. Rory groaned with the impact, his vision swirling as though he had been drinking wine. He tried to wiggle his fingers and toes: they worked, so he reasoned he was not paralysed.

Once his vision returned to normal, he pulled himself up gingerly onto his elbows and took stock of what was around him. The grass he sat on was thick and hard – unlike the kind of grass on his playing field at school – and seemed to crunch underneath, oozing out a sticky pink substance. It fell away to the treeline of a tall forest close up ahead, but the trees were not oaks, or pines, or chestnuts – or anything else familiar; they were, instead, monstrous, bendy affairs with bark that looked to have been covered in a camo-green dust. High in the canopies, capillary-like fronds were expelled along gigantic serpentine branches, the shoots of all the trees interlocking in a vast network. The light that fell upon the trees and, indeed, the grass underneath Rory was of a purple hue, shafts of it unfurling from a vast aurora set against a starlit sky. It was so beautiful that Rory even felt the stirring of a tear in his eye.

I thought you could only see things like this in a videogame, he thought.

Snap!

Rory's attention was torn back from the sky and he peered off into the forest at ground level now, eyes scanning past strange vegetation.

That was definitely a noise, he realised.

For a moment, he worried that a pale, grey arm would slither out from behind a tree trunk, but, as the moment passed, nothing happened. Then a bush moved and Gary came floating out and towards Rory.

'Oh, *there* you are. Not feeling so heroic today then?'

But Gary ploughed straight on into Rory, headbutting him in the stomach repeatedly.

'Hey! Knock it off!'

Gary gave up and floated away back up the tunnel, behind Rory.

In that moment, the forest erupted and at least a dozen men came roaring out, brandishing nets full of what looked like fruit and lengthy poles with spikes and hooks. Rory was frozen to the spot – as were the men – and they all looked at each other for what seemed the longest time.

'Stowaway!' one of the men – a particularly hairy individual – bellowed, pointing one accusatory finger at Rory, who mouthed, 'Me?' in bewilderment. The chant was taken up by the rest and, as one, they charged forth, the fruit-laden nets relieved of their content and, instead, thrown over Rory.

'Let me go! Hey! Let me go!'

But the men were indifferent to his protests and soon had him well and truly trussed up, lifted high above their heads. Rory's view of the sky was broken off as he was carried into the forest and, soon, all he could see was a dark mesh of canopy. Below him, the men settled into a rhythm and a song:

Into trees and into dark,
Over thorn and under bark,
Take the interloper far –
Ropes will serve him as a car.

What foul plot he comes to do?
We'll have answers once we're through.
Stretch his arms and draw a tooth.
By this act we'll have the truth.

By now, Rory had come to the conclusion that these strange people meant him no good – the dubious lyrics of their dreadful song confirming this in his mind – and he tried to wriggle free and call out for help, but his bonds were tightened and the closeness of the trees smothered his voice.

To the temple, to the dock,
Down the hill and over rock,
Plucking truth with pincers hot –
He won't dare to tell us rot.

And if our means should not bear fruit,
Or if he does not choose to hoot,
Our Whisperer then surely would –
Old Henley then will wring him good.

The canopy untangled and Rory could once more see the sky – the aurora still wriggling in psychedelic pinks and purples. A shift in his position told him that the men were now carrying him downhill. Lifting his face a little, he could see ahead: a lake, flanked on one side by towering crystals – much like those on Gary's back – lay placid with a stone pyramid on the near shore. Running up to the pyramid and all the way down to the shoreline were ramshackle huts made of wood and scraps of material, opening out into a system of gently bobbing piers on the water. Beside the piers were a number of small boats that looked as though they had been carved out of enormous cinnamon sticks. There was a buzz about the place, with myriad people – male and female – going about their business in the fashion of a seaside market. But above it all, the pyramid was very much the prominent feature. The pyramid itself was relatively small and stepped, as in the Aztec and not the Egyptian style, each step being in itself a robust, rectangular block. A flight of these steps led up to the top where a figure reclined in an ornate chair, apparently comfortable in overseeing the activities of all the people beneath.

As Rory was carried into the little settlement, he found the dwellers throwing him hostile glances – one or two even spitting as the men carrying him shouted, 'Stowaway!' to all who would listen. Which was apparently everyone…

At last, they came to a standstill at the base of the pyramid and flung Rory down quite unceremoniously so that he lay in a knot of ropes, more confused than ever as to how he had ended up in such a strange place, having been on board a spaceship less than half an hour ago.

The men who had transported him kept in a semicircle, shaking their fists and calling up to the figure above. Rory still heard the chant of, 'Stowaway!' from all corners of this hellish little place and sensed that more of the settlement dwellers had gathered to see what all the commotion was about. At last, the figure on the pyramid held up a single hand and the chanting ceased, instantly.

One of the men who had been carrying Rory stepped in front of him; he was heavily tattooed and wore a handkerchief over his head. 'We found 'im at the umbilical. Looks like a stowaway. Dunno what he wants, mind. Want permission to use our' – he grinned – '*methods* to get the truth out of 'im.'

Rory's line of sight was obscured by the tattooed man, which made it difficult for him to see what was going on. There was utter silence, which lasted long enough to give way to muttering among the settlers.

'I think he's asleep!' more than a few people suggested.

Eventually, the man who had initially addressed the recumbent figure shuffled forward with short, nervous steps. He looked back at the crowd, many people nodding encouragement. He climbed the pyramid steps and came to a stop in front of the figure, but there were still no signs of life. Clicking his fingers, he leaned one ear in towards the figure's face.

'I am quite awake!' the figure yelled, leaping up and brandishing a knife.

The tattooed man jumped several feet in the air and tumbled down the steps, coming to a stop in front of Rory; he scrabbled up and dissolved into the crowd.

Rory took stock of the figure on the pyramid. He was a tall man – perhaps in his fifties – with tousled peppercorn hair and a short, greying beard. He sported black eyeliner, a single golden earring and a mischievous glint in his eyes, with the slightest curl of a grin poised in the corners of his mouth. He was dressed in colourful, leathery throws about his shoulder with a bare, hairy chest and an assortment of necklaces, some of which held the skulls of tiny creatures. To protect his modesty, he wore a pair of cargo shorts with a buckled belt hanging limply about his waist. He had no shoes and his feet looked filthy.

'So, a stowaway are yer?' the man barked in a rough, potent voice, pointing with his knife and offering Rory a vicious grin: teeth so white they could be porcelain.

'N-No, sir,' Rory mumbled, by way of response. 'I don't even know how I got here...'

'Hopped on at Widdershins, eh? Catapulted yerself from the Moon, perhaps?' the figure continued, commencing a lazy walk down the pyramid steps.

The crowd behind Rory gave up a collective snigger.

'N-No, sir. I don't know how I ended up here.' He looked around. '... Wherever here is.'

'Yer on *sacred* ground, m'lad. Yer on the back of Rongomai,' the man growled, reaching the bottom of the steps and looming over Rory.

Rory shrank into himself, glancing warily at the knife and struggling to understand what he meant. 'A-And who are all of you?'

'We're devotees of Rongomai; we live here on his back. And I'm Henley – some call me Tall-Tongued Henley – and I'm in charge around here.' He leaned in so close that Rory could smell his putrid breath. 'Now, we don't want things to get ugly: *why* have yer come?'

Rory sensed the crowd behind him moving closer in too.

I'm going to be killed! he realised.

But a familiar squeal punctuated the tense atmosphere and everyone cast a gaze around for its source.

'Look!' one member of the crowd yelled, pointing back up towards the forest.

Rory strained to look past the legs of so many people, but what he did eventually see filled his heart with relief: Gary, puffed up and flashing purple colours through his crystals, brazenly fired down the hill from the forest and into the settlement. The crowd parted as the little muktuk scorched up the main thoroughfare, people leaping out of his way as he did so, and shot right into Rory's arms.

'You came back!' Rory said, smiling and hugging the creature tight to his chest.

Beyond Gary's song, Rory felt a crackling in his ears and the sound of a distant whisper, but he could not make the words out. Gary turned on Henley, puffed out his pouches and flashed brighter, fiercer colours through his crystals.

'What blessing is this,' Henley hissed, 'when a god-child should come before us?'

Rory was surprised at the reaction and even more so when Henley – followed by the crowd – fell to his knees and stretched out his arms along the ground, as though in supplication.

'Oh, divine muktuk! Yer bless us with yer presence. But why do yer come between us and this intruder? Speak yer holy words to me.'

At this, Henley's face became one of concentration and his eyes closed. Gary's crystal colours slowed in their geometric swirls and there was only a dull, bass warble from deep within him. Minutes passed but it felt like hours. Eventually, Henley raised his head, opened his eyes and stared with renewed curiosity at Rory. He leaned in as he did before and Rory prepared himself for the worst. But, instead, Henley pocketed his knife, clasped Rory's shoulders and kissed him once on each cheek.

'Har har! Rare lad! Brilliant lad!'

Rory looked into Henley's face, perplexed by the sudden change of attitude.

'A-Aren't you going to torture me?'

Henley's mouth spread into another wicked grin. 'Torture the companion of a god-child? Never.' He leaned in again. 'Besides, children are too fragile to torture and end up breaking. There was this one time beyond the Asteroid Belt: lad like yerself, split apart in six pieces!'

Rory gulped.

Henley patted Rory on the shoulder and moved past him to address the crowd. 'This boy has come down from the *Scuabtuinne*; he is the Captain's charge and a friend to muktuks. We are to welcome him and he can call us family.' The crowd looked sullen. 'Unless… anyone still wishes to squeeze, scratch or stretch him?' The crowd was silent. 'Hmm, I thought not. Now, back to work!'

As the crowd dispersed amid a series of mumblings, Henley put an arm around Rory and drew him towards the pyramid.

'So, yer still planet-minded. All of this' – he swept his other arm around – 'must be very strange to a lad.'

'H-How did you know I come from the ship? And about Limmy?'

Henley affected a wounded expression, pressing his free hand to his heart. 'Yer mean ter say... Limmy didn't tell yer about *me*?'

Rory wondered whether he had missed something. 'She... took me to meet the crew. And I've seen most of the ship now too.'

Henley pressed Rory's shoulders, forcing him to take a seat on the pyramid steps and then sat down himself. Gary occupied himself by floating in mid-air, spinning around in a circle.

'She didn't show yer everything, m'lad,' Henley growled. 'This here,' he continued, jabbing one finger towards the ground, 'is Rongomai and *I* am a Muktuk Whisperer.'

Henley grinned in what seemed to be a familiar expression for him: brilliant teeth on show and a slight madness in his eyes. Rory recalled the name 'Rongomai' being mentioned before by Xam when the ship first left Earth – something about 'umbilicking'. He had no clue as to what a Muktuk Whisperer might be, though it suggested communication of some kind.

'What is Rongomai?'

'Rongomai is what *he*' – Henley pointed at Gary, who was now doing loop-de-loops again – 'will eventually become: an adult muktuk. Gargantuan. Mighty.'

Realisation hit Rory all at once and he looked around at the pyramid, the forest, the sky, the mountain-sized crystals beyond the lake. 'You... you mean to say –'

'Har har! Yes. You are *on* a muktuk. Rongomai is his name and the umbilical links him to the *Scuabtuinne*. Look!'

Rory followed the direction of Henley's outstretched finger and saw, beyond the forest, the 'umbilical' curving up into the sky attaching itself to the *Scuabtuinme*. The ship was tiny in comparison with the vast muktuk landscape around him.

Henley continued, 'I – and I alone – can speak to Rongomai and *we*' – he flung a hand towards the settlers – 'are Rongomai's custodians. Our lives are dedicated to the care of the muktuk. We sweep his forests, polish his crystals and live here beside the lake, blessed. It is a great honour to serve a muktuk in this way.'

Rory looked up at the pyramid. For the first time, he saw that each of the stone slabs it was made of were etched with carvings: some showed crystals, some planets and one particularly impressive example presented a group of muktuks on a journey of some kind.

'You make it sound like a religion.'

'Har har! Rare lad! I can see why yer'd say that. And, in many ways, it *is* a religion. But it is more than that. I told you I am a Muktuk Whisperer. Well, that means that I am gifted with the ability to *talk* to muktuks. Rongomai's is a great and ancient intellect – a mind that surpasses centuries, millennia… While we humans were on Earth clubbing each other to death and decorating our caves, Rongomai was sailing the stars on his forever-migration – his rhyme keeping secrets that unfold behind the clouds of my knowing, and there over rainbows is the answer to his story. By coming into space, we have stepped onto *his* hallowed ground.'

'How big is Rongomai?'

Henley played with his beard. 'Well now… I en't exactly ever pulled out a ruler… but he's probably the size of a…' – he looked at Rory again – 'well, perhaps the size of one of yer small Earth towns.'

Rory tried to imagine a creature so enormous. 'I-I have so many questions, Henley.'

'Ask away! Ask away! "Knowledge is the only richness worth greed," as a friend of mine used to say.'

Rory looked around again: at the forest, the lake, the crystals, the sky. 'How is it that Rongomai has all… *this* on his back?'

'A question that has been considered ever since Beatrix Quidnunc and her team went up into space on a muktuk almost a hundred years ago. Ever since then they've been studied – the muktuks. Since the Cosmic Commission was created on Widdershins, it's been the Chain of Exo-biology that's continued those studies. We know quite a lot about them. But there are still many mysteries and even Whisperers like me can only fathom so much from muktuks.

'But their ecosystems – so, the life and atmosphere that springs up on their backs – is a common trait of all muktuks, it seems. The "rock" is keratin, like hair or nails on *you*. The atmosphere is a result of waste gases vented from within the muktuk, just as we might sweat.' He paused, sniffed one armpit and grimaced. 'The atmosphere is carbon dioxide, oxygen, methane, nitrogen and other gases, and there is enough oxygen for it ter be breathable – which yer must have realised already else we'd be dead! The auroras yer see are the Sun's charged particles hitting the oxygen and the nitrogen. Water is another waste product, but it's not like water on Earth, though it is drinkable. As fer the trees… they were spores picked up on another planet or a moon. The trees and plants on Rongomai are mostly native to Minerva, which –'

'Is a Martian moon!'

'Har har!' Henley roared, clapping Rory on the back.

132

'Brilliant lad! Yer not completely planet-minded, after all! Now, the crystals are the most interesting thing. They're called *porphuragate* and we don't know enough about them yet – not fer want of trying. Somehow, they... *power* the muktuk, like an engine. And what an engine! A muktuk, I tell yer, can travel faster than' – he closed one eye and counted on his fingers – 'one three-thousandth the speed of light! I think... anyway. Imagine that, m'lad! Which is why the *Scuabtuinne* is hooked to Rongomai. Out here, beyond Earth, muktuks are our steeds: our feeble little spaceships link up with 'em – hitching a lift in the gods' atmosphere, protected from the Sun's radiation – and, by doing so, can travel great distances nice and sharpish.'

'But... how does that work? How does a ship link with a muktuk? And wouldn't the muktuk just take the ship wherever it wanted to go?'

'Muktuks are migratory: they travel from the outer Solar System ter the inner Solar System where it's warm and they use planets like Earth and Venus as breeding sites, leaving their young behind. When each god-child is ready, it leaves the inner Solar System and journeys to the outer Solar System where it meets up with others like it at great feeding grounds around icy worlds like Uranus and Neptune. And before you ask: kuldrevet.'

Rory creased his brow. 'Kul-what?'

'Kuldrevet,' Henley repeated. 'That's what muktuks eat. A bit like krill that whales eat on Earth. Any ship in the atmosphere of a muktuk is still caught in its gravitational pull, but can use its instruments to navigate. The ship sends navigation commands down here and a Muktuk Whisperer –

in this case, yours truly – communicates with the muktuk and suggests a new course.'

'What's it like to talk – to *whisper* to a muktuk?' Rory said, his mind filled with the excitement of being able to actually communicate with an alien creature.

Henley leaned back against the pyramid. 'Har! It's like...' – he looked up, thoughtfully – 'being dunked in honey and having to gently pull on the silk of an asteroid spider's web. Yer tug a little to get Rongomai's attention and when yer have it yer can give 'im basic ideas, requests and warnings. Of course, muktuks don't speak English – or French, Lithuanian or Dari for that matter! – and so what is communicated is more... *ideas*, I s'pose. It's hard ter explain. Some ideas are too unique to us as humans for another species to understand though. A muktuk understands the notion of movement: up, down, left, right – because it moves in three dimensions, like us. But a muktuk doesn't understand something like... tripping over a shoe and falling down a flight of stairs! It will never experience that... and, besides, muktuks are not well known for wearing shoes. A Muktuk Whisperer develops a bond with one muktuk and the two get ter know each other and form an understanding, over time. And, eventually, they can communicate with each other.'

Rory reflected on those few occasions already when he had been alone with Gary and the static – accompanied by a mumble and imagery – had built up in his ears.

That can't have been Gary though, he puzzled; *Henley said that it's ideas that are shared – not images.*

Henley seemed to have guessed what Rory was thinking. 'Who knows? Perhaps, over time, you'll be able ter speak to Gary. Har!'

Rory looked up at the Muktuk Whisperer. 'But... just now, *you* were able to speak to Gary – but you don't have an understanding with him yet.'

'Har! Nothing escapes yer, lad! Yer right, of course. But the god-child's talk is much simpler: easier symbols and notions and all that. Easier to grasp – especially fer a master Whisperer like me!'

Rory smiled and nodded. He looked at Gary, who was still performing various feats of acrobatics.

'Henley? What are the weird sac things on Gary? Does Rongomai have them too?'

Henley scratched his beard and twirled his earring. 'Every muktuk has three: one under the chin and two to port and starboard. As yer've probably guessed, they're used fer buoyancy and can keep even a heavy muktuk in the air.'

'How though?'

'We ain't got a clue exactly how it's formed, but we do know that muktuk sacs are filled with a type of helium – Helium-X it's called, or HeX, fer short – that we've never found anywhere else in the Solar System. Our best guess is that muktuks have an organ inside 'em capable of producing this special kind of helium. And the beauty of this theory is that the production of helium would lead to a very, very dense waste product. Now, what have yer noticed since coming into space?'

Rory pondered the question. He had noticed many things since coming into space: bony spaceships, town-sized alien whales and pillows with a tendency to wander off on a walk, chief among them. But he shook these thoughts away and considered the science. He became aware that he was, unconsciously, tapping his foot on the grass.

Of course!

Rory looked excitedly into Henley's face. 'Gravity! We're not floating away; it was the same on the ship.'

Henley slapped Rory on the back, half winding him. 'Har har! Rare lad! Yes, indeed we should, by all rights, be floating up into the sky – straight into space and freezing.'

'But the muktuk is so big that its gravitational pull keeps us down.'

Henley cocked his head from left to right. 'In a way… but not quite. Were yer floating about on board the *Scuabtuinne* before yer reached Rongomai?'

Rory thought. 'No.'

'"No" is right. But the reason *is* connected to the muktuks. The waste product from HeX, as I say, must be dense, despite not being all that big, necessarily. Now, if it is dense enough, then it will have its own gravitational pull, which keeps our feet' – he stamped his filthy feet – 'stuck to the ground. The crystals – or *porphuragate*, remember – seem to grow from a heavy, dense substance, which you'll probably see someday, and it's generally accepted that *that* substance *is* the waste product.'

Rory was reminded of a science lesson he once had with Mrs El-Khalil about neutron stars, which he recalled as being very dense with an incredible gravitational pull despite being much smaller than other stars.

Perhaps the muktuks are a bit like that… Rory surmised.

Suddenly, he was struck by the enormity of everything that had happened in the past several days. His entire world had been flipped on its head and, where once he had enjoyed astronomy as something that kept him grounded, even that now seemed to have been based on an arbitrary and erroneous set of laws and principles which he could no longer have faith in. A sense of panic tightened his chest and he leaned forward, running a clammy hand through his hair.

'Are yer alright, m'lad?' Henley asked, his voice not quite as rough.

Rory tried to hide the tears in his eyes. 'It's just…'

Rooory, Rooory. You seem to be enjoying yourself. But you don't deserve enjoyment. Your mum is not enjoying herself, wherever –

He met Henley's puzzled expression. Granted, the man looked like someone you wouldn't trust around children, but Rory felt comfortable in his company, as though the Muktuk Whisperer fulfilled something that, until now, had been missing in his life. For this reason, he quickly felt that rarest and most precious of sensations: trust.

'It's just that… I'm not very well – my head, you see. You should probably know that I'm not a very good person,' he said, placing his hands on his knees. 'We're chasing the Whiffetsnatcher to get my mum back, but it's my fault he got her in the first place. I… I should go.'

'Drivel, m'lad! Drivel! Yer think I en't spoken to the captain since yer found yer way into space?' Henley looked fiercely into his face. 'There en't no one that coulda stopped that man from taking yer mother. Least of all a lad. When the Whiffetsnatcher wants to take something or someone… he *always* gets his way and there en't nothing to be done about it. Believe me… I can vouch fer that.'

Henley's outburst drew Rory out of his own mind, and he regarded the Muktuk Whisperer with curiosity. A darkness had filled the big man's face, as though brought about by a painful memory. Quickly enough, it disappeared and Henley grinned once more, a little forced this time.

'Listen, m'lad,' Henley said, pouncing on Rory and taking his hands. 'Don't ever think that yer not a good person or there's something wrong with yer. Some people see children like yer as broken things – well, yer not! If a muktuk like Gary took to yer like he did, then it means yer plenty good enough. Yer still planet-minded, so if yer ever need to speak to someone – just come and find Tall-Tongued Henley!'

'See, there he is, Limmy,' came a familiar female voice.

'Henley! Get off of Rory!'

Rory and Henley turned as one to find Limmy and Mira standing not five paces away. Limmy had her hands on her hips and a very angry expression on her face; Mira had her arms folded and a blank face, and seemed quite purposely to be staring at the ground. Henley relinquished Rory's hands and hopped up.

'Why, Captain. Har! Rarely, do we have the pleasure of yer company. What brings yer down here?'

'Man overboard,' Limmy replied, shortly.

Rory realised she must be talking about him. 'I… I'm sorry, Limmy. Gary was leading me and I don't know how but I ended up here and –'

'We've been looking all over for you!' Limmy snapped.

'The muktuk calf knocked me over while I was doing maintenance,' Mira said, her words flat, her expression still fixed on the grass. 'I followed him to the entrance of the umbilical and guessed Rory must be down here.'

Henley took a step forward, and Rory was grateful for his interference. 'Blame me, if yer must, Captain,' he said, placing a hand over his heart. 'My men found the lad at the bottom of the umbilical and brought him ter me. Thought he was a stowaway. All a simple misunderstanding, yer see?'

Limmy did not look at Henley though; she only looked at Rory. 'At least you're okay... Come with *me* now, Rory.'

Limmy turned and started to traipse back towards the forest. Mira, still looking at the grass, turned as well and followed in Limmy's wake.

Rory looked to Henley – 'I better go' – and ran off after Limmy, Gary floating behind him.

'Don't forget what I said, lad!' Henley called after him. 'Yer know where ter find old Henley!'

Limmy did not respond to Rory and only turned to face him once they were several hundred yards into the forest.

'Rory, I'm sorry if I seem angry. But you *must* be careful,' Limmy said, her eyes a plea and her voice fraught with worry. 'Henley is a very, very dangerous man and this' – she looked around her – 'is a very dangerous place.'

Rory wilted under the scolding and, to his embarrassment, began to cry. He tried to hide his face from Mira whose gaze kept flicking from the forest floor to Rory's face: the force of it like surgery.

Rooory, Rooory. See, I told you: you are bad. Limmy has been good and you've let her down. She probably doesn't want you on her ship anymore.

'I'm really sorry, Limmy. I didn't mean to let you down.'

Limmy sighed. 'You *didn't* let me down. You did scare me though, kid! Come on, let's get back to the ship.'

With these words, Limmy strode off again into the forest. Mira lowered her face further still, preventing any chance of her making eye contact with Rory, and caught up with the captain. Rory tried to block out the voice inside his head by covering his ears with his hands, but an overwhelming sense of guilt threatened to engulf him.

Rooory, Rooory. She trusted you to do the right thing. I was right about you all along. You let your mother be taken and now you're not wanted here – you're a pathetic little child!

8

Minerva

Interplanetary travel, despite the speed of an adult muktuk, is a lengthy business and nearly three months passed as the *Scuabtuinne* ventured across the great expanse between Earth and Mars, piggybacking on Rongomai. In that time, Rory grew accustomed to life in space and came to understand the crew and his place on board.

He spent time with Xam at the helm, learning how the stars and the Solar System were mapped in the onboard Astronomical Cartography System (ACS), and how Xam had to communicate course alterations to Tall-Tongued Henley who, in turn, 'whispered' instructions to Rongomai. Xam, as he assured Rory early on, was indeed very much the ship's cook and delighted in talking Rory through the best way to marinade and fry meteor algae or citrus-infused insect kebab. ('The trick, little Hobster,' Xam would say as he twirled beetles pinioned on shish sticks, 'is to let their fat, squelchy bellies *absorb* the flavour of a Martian lemon by letting the shell cook first – all that moisture just *rides* down into the beetle that way.') The beetles, Xam had promised, were rich in protein but that didn't alter the fact that when you bit into their bellies, their innards spurted out like a popped pus-ridden spot. However, once Rory had strengthened his stomach to such sights, he found the beetles to be quite delicious. Xam had explained that most of the food was cultivated on Rongomai, as the muktuk – quite literally – had acres of space to use for growing all manner of vegetables, fruits and nuts, as well as pasture for certain choice livestock. It seemed that, aside from his whispering duties, Henley was also Farmer-in-Chief and responsible for ensuring the *Scuabtuinne* was maintained with enough oxygen, water and food – an arrangement that Limmy was clearly unhappy with, if her under-breath remarks were anything to go by.

Henley was not someone who Rory saw much of, as he was mindful of Limmy's displeasure at him associating with the curious man. On the few occasions they did happen to meet, Henley twirled his knife and flashed him a cheeky grin or wink, so Rory was reassured that offence had not been taken and that Henley understood the situation.

Beak, the ship's physician, was someone – or should that be *something* – else that Rory spent little time with. Beak was very much a doctor specialising in physical illness and since Rory's past encounters had mostly been with those specialising in *mental* illness, he had little cause to seek out any support – other than to attend routine physicals to monitor how he adapted to life in space; weekly sessions with therapists on Earth seemed a very distant memory now. Besides, Beak's lack of emotion suggested, in Rory's mind, that he would be unable to understand the finer details of what it was to suffer with OCD. Sometimes, Rory sat staring out of the ship's portholes, trying to imagine what relief it must be to not feel emotion at all, and found himself jealous of Beak's unique position.

Mira kept herself to herself. As she was the only other crew member of a similar age to him, she had seemed as though she would make a natural companion, so Rory had tried, in the first few weeks, to strike up a friendship. But it was clear that Mira was not remotely interested, and she came across, at all times, as dismissive and rude. She was obsessive about her work and he had little idea of what – if anything – she did for fun or entertainment, other than her tapestry, which he would have dearly liked to study in greater detail.

Limmy made it clear very early on that he was not a passenger and, consequently, was expected to contribute in whatever ways he could, which suited Rory just fine as the thought of being a real-life crew member on a spaceship was simply unbelievable. She therefore assigned him rudimentary duties that included a lot of cleaning and general support tasks for other members of the crew. It wasn't exactly what Rory had imagined, but it was a start. For Limmy's part, if she wasn't in the Dome, she was locked away in her own quarters a lot of the time, her activities a mystery; whatever she was up to, though, it seemed to occupy her mind and shorten her temper, so Rory steered clear of his social worker.

Rory's truest companion remained Gary, who grew at a respectable rate and consumed an equally respectable quantity of food. He floated about the ship quite contentedly, but it was clear that he would eventually reach a stage where he'd need more space. Limmy, off-handedly, told Rory that this was something he could think about, as a decision would have to be made on what would happen to the little space-faring whale.

The pursuit of the Whiffetsnatcher reached a dead end after little more than a month and the crew took this setback hard, Rory particularly suffering the weight of not knowing where his mother was. The objective was still to reach Widdershins first, as Limmy needed to discuss her failed mission with the Cosmic Commission, and she hoped that when they did arrive at the colony other pilots might have some information.

Deep into what must have been December – not that even the familiarity of a calendar was something to find on the ship – Limmy called the crew to the Dome for an announcement. Rory sat in a chair as Mira, Beak and Henley made their way in; Xam was at his controls, as always, and Limmy stood by her command chair, arms folded.

'Okay, guys – listen up,' Limmy began, clapping her hands. 'I'm pleased to tell you that we have entered the Martian system.' She pointed beyond the glass of the Dome and, sure enough, Rory could see a red ball growing in the distance, a few smaller darker shapes surrounding it.

'I-Is *that*… Mars?' Rory asked, gasping.

Xam chuckled. 'Sure is, Hobster!'

Rory was speechless. He was actually looking at *another world*. Up close, it appeared different to the way it did in pictures; in pictures, it was still, alone and dead, but there in front of him it was alive with the undulating patterns of dust storms, and glinting sheets of ice about its poles.

'And *that* is our destination, m'lad,' Henley added, placing a hand on Rory's shoulder and pointing to one of the black balls closer to them.

Rory's eyes settled upon a dark world that must have been one of the Martian moons.

'Minerva?'

'That's right, Rory,' Limmy said, taking control of the conversation again. 'It's time to dock in Widdershins. *And* we're back in time for Christmas.'

Xam cheered, Henley clapped and even Mira nodded a few times to indicate her approval.

'Now,' Limmy continued, 'we will move in a little closer before detaching from Rongomai. I anticipate we will be ready within a few hours, so I need all hands on deck. Xam – you just do what you do best. Mira – support Xam and be ready in case of any system malfunctions. Beak… umm –'

'I will be ready in case anyone should suffer a terrible accident,' Beak interrupted, quite matter-of-factly.

'Well… quite,' Limmy said. 'Henley – back onto Rongomai and whisper our intentions.'

'Absolutely, Captain,' Henley replied, that grin on his face and a touch of exaggeration in his voice. 'But I will be making my way back on board before we disconnect the umbilical.'

Limmy furrowed her brow. 'Why is that?'

Henley took a step forward. 'Because I have matters ter attend ter on Widdershins, Captain.'

'What matters?' Limmy demanded.

Henley smiled, moving his head from side to side. 'My matters be of no matter to you. A few *trifling* matters, is all – culiarities rather than *pe*culiarities.'

Limmy folded her arms. 'And who will maintain Rongomai in your absence? Who will whisper?'

'Har! Fear not, Captain. I have had a long and involved

conversation with Rongomai just this morning as I ate my breakfast. I can assure you that our muktuk understands what is ter come and what we need of 'im.'

Rory looked at Limmy. She frowned, perhaps concentrating hard on her decision.

'… Okay. But you had better be right about Rongomai. And keep out of trouble.'

Henley laughed his huge, hearty laugh. 'Trouble finds no companion in me, I assure yer.'

'Okay, everyone knows their job. Get to it.' The crew dispersed and Limmy turned to Rory. 'Come with me, kid.'

Rory hopped out of his chair and followed the captain away from the Dome and down several bony passages before reaching a room he had never entered: Limmy's quarters. The inside was a cosy mess of drapes, cushions and a four-poster bed on which two pillows seemed to be play-fighting. The walls – creamy calcium with those familiar blue veins – were covered in certificates and photographs, as well as maps and diagrams.

'Don't mind the mess. Let me just grab a few things,' Limmy called, pacing out of the bedroom area through an opening into, presumably, another room.

Rory walked up to the nearest wall. He read a certificate for Limmy's degree in Social Work, next to which was a photo of her wearing baggy black robes with blue trim and – what he felt to be at least – a quite ridiculous square, black hat with a tassel. Underneath that were a few more photos of her outside a building, wearing the same robes, smiling. Alone. In the background of each photo, Rory could see other young people – all laughing – in similar robes posing for pictures, but they were surrounded by what looked to be family.

Elsewhere, other certificates were plentiful: a number for 'Best Essay', 'Most Insightful Contribution to Discussion'; something about a Children in Care Council, which puzzled him; and something else reading 'Certificate of Naturalisation', with the royal coat of arms on it.

Limmy re-emerged and invited Rory to sit down at a study desk with her. Rory waited for Limmy to sit before he took his seat.

'Okay,' Limmy began, running a hand through her fiery hair and sighing. 'I'm sorry for being such a grump recently. What we're about to go through brings back… difficult memories from when I was growing up in Croydon. But I shouldn't have been so *misérable*. As a social worker, I shouldn't… let my own experiences cloud my judgement, but on this occasion, they did.'

Rory felt a familiar pang of anxiety flaring up in him.

'Oh, but don't worry: I'm going to be with you every step of the way,' Limmy added, apparently sensing Rory's concern.

'You said, "what we're about to go through,"' Rory whispered.

Limmy slapped her head. 'Idiot! Sorry. Yes. Okay. Your claim for asylum. The Chain of Migration, which is part of the Cosmic Commission, will assess you when we arrive in Widdershins.'

'*Assess* me? Like a test?' Rory replied, focusing on lining his hands up on his knees.

'Kind of. Now, I've been reading up on what they do here' – Limmy lifted a book from her desk and rifled through its pages, locating a particular passage – 'and it seems similar to what happened to me – well, in some respects. So, there will be one person who interviews you and the interview will last a few hours.'

'A few hours!' Rory couldn't believe it. His breathing came faster. His hands slipped out of alignment across his knees.

Limmy tossed her book down and held out a hand. 'Now, don't worry, Rory. I'm going to be with you for as much of it as I'm allowed. And you'll do just fine. You're a brave kid. All they'll want to do is talk to you about yourself and about why you want to come to Widdershins.'

'But I *don't* want to go to Widdershins. All I want is to find my mum!' Rory cried.

'Rory, we must consider the possibility that we… that we won't find your mum. And, whatever happens, you will have to embrace Widdershins as your new home.'

Rory made to speak but closed his mouth. He thought back to Earth and realised that Limmy was right: there was nothing left for him back in Croydon and even if he were reunited with his mother tomorrow, would he *want* to go back – knowing what he knew now about this whole other world?

'I know it's hard,' Limmy continued. 'But it can be done. I've… I've done it myself.'

Rory caught the tremor in Limmy's voice and glanced back at the photos on the wall.

'What happened to you, Limmy?'

Limmy looked up at Rory. 'I was once in your position. But I had absolutely no one. No family. And I came to the UK from a country called the Democratic Republic of the Congo – you heard of it?'

Rory nodded. 'It's in Africa. Why'd you come to the UK?'

Limmy tilted her head to the side. 'Well, a lot of bad things were happening in the Congo. A lot of violence and... and *killing*. My mother...' She swallowed hard, then smiled, eyes glistening. 'You know, I remember my mother used to take me to the marketplace and there was this woman there who sold clothes. She used to give my mother patches of material, which my mother would sew together into a skirt for me. It took her years, and' – she laughed – 'I kept getting bigger, so the skirt had to get bigger too. I could sit there for hours, just watching her sew, with the sound of rain hammering down in the metal buckets outside.

'There was talk for so long of the danger. My father would speak powerful words to my mother when they thought I was asleep. One day, some... bad men came to our village and... and my mother... she...'

Rory knitted his brow.

'Sorry, Rory. Look at me! All snotty now,' she said, managing a little chuckle. 'My father got me out, at first, but he was imprisoned and I had to work until I was a few years older than you – digging for the metal all those big companies needed for mobile phones. My father was eventually freed and he paid someone he trusted with everything he had to get me to safety. That was the last time I saw him.

'I travelled for many days. Over land in a coach. Over sea. Finally, in a lorry into the UK. The police found us – the person my father paid and me – and we were separated. I don't even remember his name now. I was taken to Croydon and there I was given clothes, and food, and a bed. I went to live with a kind family, but not before some people just like the Chain of Migration interviewed me.' Her face became dark, she turned away. '*Those* people interviewed me a lot...'

In the silence that swallowed the space between them, Rory reflected on what he had heard and he felt the anxiety inside him cooling. He tentatively reached a hand out towards Limmy and placed it on her arm. Limmy's eyes widened as she turned back to Rory.

'I hope I can be as brave as you,' Rory whispered.

The descent towards Minerva – after detaching from Rongomai – was, to Rory, unexpectedly fast. The engine that propelled the *Scuabtuinne* was clearly not composed of anything that NASA or Roscosmos currently possessed and he made a mental note to ask more questions later – so long as the ship didn't break up in the moon's atmosphere first. For now, he stood on the Bridge and watched – along with the rest of the crew – as Minerva sharpened into ever greater clarity. The moon was tiny – compared to Mars, which was fixed like a protective sibling in the sky behind it – and the surface appeared to be a compound of black continent and olive rivers. But that was not the most noticeable thing about Minerva. On the far side of the moon, a glacial structure erupted from the surface and reached all the way up into space. It had a jagged, blade-like quality and gave the moon the impression of a multi-tailed tadpole frozen mid-swim. The ruddy light of Mars infiltrated its structure, making the whole thing sparkle in a mixture of red and green.

'Minerva's mostly a mix of sedimentary and igneous rock, with onyx cliffs rearing up in great ranges – forged over aeons in a trial by stone,' Xam cheerfully explained. 'The rivers have a high concentration of algae, which is why it looks so green.

That though' – he pointed at the glacial structure – 'is the Beard.'

Rory's mouth hung open. 'W–What is it though?'

'It was once a single ocean covering all Minerva,' Limmy responded, her voice subdued. 'I forgot how beautiful it is…'

'Best guess…' Xam continued, 'at some point in Minerva's distant past, the moon aligned with both Deimos and Phobos – the other Martian moons – and the combined gravitational pull of those two worlds *ripped* the ocean from the surface of Minerva, freezing it as it reached space. Since then, the Beard has been slowly melting, which is why the moon has so many huge rivers. Seven of them, in fact: the Tears, they're called.'

As the ship skimmed the Minervan atmosphere, turbulence set in and Rory watched the crew explode into action. Switches were flicked; buttons were pressed; joysticks were shifted. Beneath the Dome, great streaks of fire flapped against the glass like flags as the heat of entry ignited the oxygen with which this world was replete. Cloud soon engulfed the *Scuabtuinne* and the turbulence, eventually, weakened.

'Coming in hot at coordinates X 30,456 and Y 78,561, Captain!' Xam yelled above the *krrraaawwwrrr* of the engine and atmosphere.

'Bring her in clean, Xam,' Limmy replied. 'I don't want any loop-the-loops or barrel rolls just because we have a guest.'

Xam turned and winked at Rory.

Rory chuckled and then drew in his breath as the cloud around the Dome parted to reveal the surface of Minerva. Though dark from orbit, up close it was an exhalation of colour: huge forests of bizarre plants winding and stretching and twirling about – as though a coral reef had been torn from Earth and relocated across space.

'Yer'll never look at fruit the same way after you've tried an acwellan apple, m'boy!' Henley growled from his position to the left of Rory. 'I was once trekkin' through the Arid Reef – what yer see before yer – when an acwellan tree started tossin' its apples at me. Big spiky things, size of yer hand, they are! Red as a drinker's cheeks they was!'

'The Arid Reef? It's… incredible,' Rory murmured, transfixed by the sight of this exotic forest.

'Reckon, they do, that these great reefs what spread across Minerva survived their dehydration when the Beard was created. Incredible, yes, but all manner of beasties in them that yer wouldn't want ter meet on a dark night. Mark me,' Henley continued, leaning towards Rory.

The Arid Reef finally gave way to the sprawling black Warren-Dominique Plains – as Henley termed them – that, in turn, raced towards a cliff in the distance, down which a tremendous green waterfall surged. As the ship drew closer to the waterfall, Rory could make out various structures situated at the top of the cliff either side of the overhang and also at the bottom of the waterfall to one side of the plunge pool.

Limmy ordered Xam to reduce speed, then stood and turned to Rory with a smile. 'Welcome to Widdershins.'

Rory could now see the whole settlement in all its detail before him. It was not what he had expected at all. In his mind's eye, he had already sculpted a cityscape of soaring glass skyscrapers, anti-gravity trains and slick steel buildings. But what he witnessed instead was something that looked very similar to the favelas of Rio de Janeiro that he had studied in Geography last year. Neighbouring the plunge pool, the bulk of Widdershins was a skeleton of buildings that seemed to have been carved from the same bony, spongy material used throughout the *Scuabtuinne*. Some of the buildings were larger than others and a narrow thoroughfare seemed to have been scored straight through the middle of it.

'Is that where everyone lives?' Rory asked, turning and catching the eye of both Henley and Limmy.

'Yes,' Henley replied. 'Volp Lane runs through it all and the different districts surround it. Each district represents the workforce for a different industry. There, for example' – he points vaguely out of the Dome window – 'is where the farmers live. And there is where yer go if yer head is sore or yer foot falls off.'

Rory nodded, unable to understand the need for segregation but he accepted it as a matter of fact. Eyes scanning upwards, he found an object that resembled a submarine sticking out of the cliff-face, though much of it was covered by some manner of vine.

'What is that?' Rory asked the room in general.

'That is the *Aeneas*,' Limmy responded. 'Remember me telling you about her?'

Rory nodded, mouth agape. The first ship to travel between worlds, and here she was.

At the top of the cliff, either side of the waterfall, two spectacular domed towers were perched with a bridge connecting them. The towers, also, appeared to be made of the white sponge and at the foot of each were several further buildings.

'And that, Rory, is where the Cosmic Commission resides,' Limmy added. 'A little more spectacular than Croydon, right?'

Xam brought the *Scuabtuinne* in over Volp Lane, pulling hard on one of his joysticks as the ship lifted across the waterfall. He steered it under the bridge that connected the two towers, twisted it to the left and brought it down in a field of turquoise grass.

Jabbing one stubby finger at a large button on his console that said OFF, and the energy of the engines seemed to wind down to a stop, much like a washing machine finishing a cycle. He turned to Rory with a grin.

'We're home!'

A short while later, Rory and the crew of the *Scuabtuinne* were in the cargo hold, into which Limmy had driven the tram three months ago (the tram itself having now been partially torn apart for scraps), and there was nothing save a blue glow illuminating faces energised with conversation. Xam chattered about the various ingredients he intended to acquire for his cooking; Henley talked about a time when he had allegedly fallen out of a spaceship and down the waterfall in Widdershins; Limmy recited various important meetings she had to soon attend; and even Mira, usually so morose, listed all the different sights she wanted to see on this, her second visit to Widdershins.

The time came to disembark and Rory watched with a thumping heart as the cargo ramp opened (after Xam kicked a few levers and cogs to get it working). A weak, red light rushed in like seawater into a cove and the smell of electricity invaded his nostrils. As the ramp came to a final stop, vegetation crunching audibly under its weight, he joined the crew in stepping down. Reaching the end of the ramp, he peered down at the thick grass outside. He lifted one foot and lowered it onto the grass, its shoots popping and snapping under his boot.

'Quite a feeling, isn't it, m'lad?' Henley barked from behind Rory.

Rory brought his other foot off the ramp, turned to Henley and nodded, a big grin on his face. He took several more steps to put some distance between himself and the ship, before contemplating his environment. The extra lightness in his limbs was immediately clear, suggesting that the gravity was not as strong as on Earth. A lungful of air confirmed the richness of oxygen in the atmosphere and the goosebumps popping up over his arms betrayed the chill. The field stretched a few hundred yards, perhaps, and a number of other ships were spread out here and there, people milling about them – one had *Skewis* emblazoned on its hull and what must have been its crew spoke with strong Scottish accents. In the near distance was a series of buildings in front of the first of the two towers Rory had seen from the Dome. The structures were quite enormous and, as he and the crew began making their way across the field, he soon realised that the material from which the buildings were constructed was carved in minute detail, offering a veritable storybook of imagery.

'They're made from the same bony, spongey stuff on the *Scuabtuinne*,' Limmy offered, leaning towards Rory, as Henley, Xam and Mira laughed about something.

'Banleuc, is what yer lookin' fer!' Henley boomed. '*That* be the name of the "bony, spongey stuff" – it's a type of calcified coral that we use as a building material.'

There was something suitably alien about the buildings, yet they retained enough of human engineering to have a certain familiarity to them as well.

'W-What are the images of?' Rory asked, narrowing his eyes to work out what the carvings were actually showing.

'A complete record of humanity's progress since Beatrix Quidnunc pioneered our first voyage into space in 1922. Back on Earth, people lock history in ter books and yer Wide Web World, or whatever yer call it, but out here... it's available fer all ter see,' Henley replied, a grin on his face.

Sure enough, as Rory craned his neck further and further, he could at last decipher images of settlements and spaceships, moons, muktuks and... monsters. As in the *Scuabtuinne*, the banleuc was veined with luminous blue and the relief imagery was glazed in something like honey, a pungent, sweet smell sweeping through the breeze.

'And here comes our welcoming party,' Henley announced.

Rory and the crew looked up to find a small entourage walking briskly over to them.

'Captain Limmy,' began a young man dressed in clothes that would not have looked out of place on a druid. 'Welcome back to Widdershins. It's been a long time.'

'Hello, Anxhela,' Limmy said, smiling as she hugged the strange man. 'It's good to see you again.'

Rory noticed Xam, beside him, tensing and grinding his teeth.

'Please. You and your crew must be tired. Do come with m– Wait a moment... Your crew manifest' – he clicked his fingers and was given some parchment by one of the people behind him, which he consulted – 'ah, yes, does not include a small *boy.*'

Rory felt everyone's eyes cutting into him and he reddened.

'No. The kid is Rory Hobble. He's from Earth and he's here to claim asylum,' Limmy responded, her tone calm.

Anxhela let the hand holding the parchment drop to his side and, with the other, pressed a finger to his lips. 'I see... Well, he will have to be assessed, of course, so the Chain of Migration can make a decision about whether he can be... accepted. Best do that now – get it over with. Follow me!'

Anxhela swept around and paced back towards the buildings, though he made for a different building from the one he had come out of.

'We better let him lead the way,' Limmy mumbled.

Rooory, Rooory. They won't want you. Then they'll make you leave. Then you'll never find your mum!

9

The Assessment

Losna House, in which the Chain of Migration was based, appeared distinctly different from the outside in comparison to the other buildings Rory had so far seen. Its banleuc walls were not carved with stories, but were instead a dank earthy discoloration, the blue veins reaching up and surfacing in knots that had the unmistakeable look of pus-filled spots. He wondered momentarily if this was what befell banleuc if it was left untreated and unkept for too long. People milled about outside, going in and out of the large doors, faces purposeful and business-like.

Anxhela led the crew inside to where the dusty light of outdoors gave way to a large and gloomy waiting area with rows of benches and rails indicating standing places for a queue system. Reception windows showed several sour-faced individuals hard at work with rolls of paper, stamps and strange-looking writing implements.

'You can all wait here,' Anxhela said, abruptly, before turning his attention to Rory. '*You* can come with me though.'

Rory looked to Limmy, who encouraged him. Xam smiled and Henley ruffled his hair. Mira sat on a bench, looking bored.

'We'll be right here, m'lad,' Henley said.

Rory caught up with Anxhela, who had already made his way over to one of the reception windows.

'Can I help you?' a large woman said from behind the glass, her voice etched with irritation.

'Claim for asylum,' Anxhela replied, rolling off his words with a disinterested tone of voice. 'Assessment required. Minor.'

'Take a ticket. Wait your turn,' the woman replied, hardly allowing Anxhela to finish. She indicated a small box on Rory's side of the reception desk, where a small pile of paper slips lay, the top one emblazoned with a glowing, blue 1.

Anxhela snatched the slip of paper before Rory had a chance and ushered him back to the crew.

'Wait here until they call your number,' Anxhela said, handing Rory his ticket. 'The rest of you can go about as you please, though Limmy: be contactable.'

With this instruction complete, Anxhela strode off, his small entourage of officials in train.

Henley and Xam patted Rory on the back or shook his shoulder, offering words of encouragement. Limmy sat forward on the bench, biting her fingers. Mira still looked bored.

'Can't be long, m'boy,' Henley growled. 'There's no one else here.'

☆

Two hours later, an officious-looking man made his way out into the reception area. 'Number one!' he called.

Limmy, Henley and Xam sat up, emerging from a half-slumber and once more encouraged Rory.

'We'll be waiting for yer,' Henley said, striking a fierce smile. 'Just be honest and yer'll do fine.'

Rory stood and made his way slowly towards the officious-looking man, taking Limmy's hand as she walked with him. His heart rate increased, so much so that he could feel the reverberations of his pulse spreading out across his chest.

'Ticket,' the man said, holding out a hand.

Rory passed the ticket over and the man studied it carefully.

'Everything seems to be in order,' he said, as though there had been considerable doubt. 'Follow me to the interview room.'

Limmy made to go with Rory, but the man held up a hand.

'What is it?' Limmy asked, looking confused.

'*Only* the boy. No guests.'

'*Guests?*' Limmy snapped. 'Just you wait one –'

'It's okay, Limmy,' Rory interrupted, placing a hand on her arm. 'I-I'll be fine.'

Limmy turned her head to focus on Rory. 'Kid, I don't want you to be on your own in there.'

The officious-looking man made a sound affecting offence. 'I'm not going to *eat* the boy, madam! Now, come along – if we're going to do this at all.'

The man marched off and Rory tagged along behind, turning once to give Limmy a weak smile. He was led down several corridors with a uniform, bony look to them, various doors to, presumably, offices lining the way. Soon enough, they reached a door with a plaque on it reading **ASSESSMENT SUITE #4**. The man coughed noisily as he opened the door, sweeping Rory inside, and loosely indicated a stool in front of an enormous desk. The desk was littered with paper – glowing, blue writing layered upon much of it – and a high-backed chair behind it visibly sank as the man settled into it with a groan. He took a gulp of something steaming from a cup, wiped his mouth with the back of his hand and leaned forward, picking up some documents. Rory looked down and placed his hands on his knees, trying to control his breathing. An image flashed into mind of him taking the cup and pouring its scalding contents over the man's hand, making him scream.

It's not you. You wouldn't do that, Rory tried to reason with himself.

'My name is Mr Johnson. You may address me as "sir" or "Mr Johnson". Today, I will be assessing your claim for asylum, verifying its authenticity and coming to a decision about how the Chain of Migration will respond to your case. Name?'

Rory looked up. 'R–Rory… Hobble –'

'Speak up.'

'I said Rory Hobble, sir.'

'Age?'

'Eleven, sir.'

'Origin.' Rory creased his brow. The man sighed. 'Where are you from?'

'Oh… Croydon… in England. Earth. Sir.'

The man wrote something down with a lazy hand.

'How did you come to Widdershins?'

'On board the *Scuabtuinne*,' Rory replied. He smiled, briefly. 'I was part of their crew.'

The man looked up from his scribbles. 'Crew? You did not hide on the ship? And address me properly.'

Rory shook his head, lining his hands up on his knees. 'They took me on board, sir.'

The man raised his eyebrows. 'I see.' And he wrote something else down, taking longer over it than Rory felt his answer had merited.

His heart skipped a beat, fear telling him now that he had made a mistake.

Rooory, Rooory. They'll all get in trouble now. After all they did for you. And you've betrayed them!

'Why have you come to Widdershins?'

Rory took a deep breath, trying to shut out the anxiety he was feeling. He was tempted to say that he had never wanted to come to Widdershins in the first place – that he would much rather be back in space chasing down the Whiffetsnatcher. He knew he could not say that, but was mindful also of Limmy advising him to tell the truth.

'I… I couldn't stay in Croydon. I would have been all alone in the flat. A-And I'd have had to have tidied it, and cooked and paid for the electricity and go to the Jobcentre to get help finding a job. No one at school could have helped me. And I had no other family. Not after the Whiffetsnatcher took Mum–'

'The *Whiffetsnatcher*?' the man said with a snort. 'The crew has been telling you our myths, it seems. There is no such thing as the Whiffetsnatcher.'

Rory was quite taken aback; he had not expected this reaction.

'But I… saw his ship, sir. Saw his muktuks. The note in my bedroom…'

'Whatever you *think* you saw: it wasn't the Whiffetsnatcher.'

Rory sank back on his stool, chin dropping.

'Now,' the man continued, 'Why have you come to Widdershins?'

Rory looked up, but the words did not come. He swallowed hard on a dry throat. 'I'm… not safe back in Croydon. I have no one,' he said, repeating himself. 'All I have is Gary and Limmy and Henley and Xam, and even Mira and Beak. And if I can't be where they are then I can't be anywhere.'

'Gary? *Another* undocumented crew member?'

'N–Not really. He's a muktuk. *My* muktuk. Just a baby.'

The man tilted his head a fraction and raised an eyebrow, almost imperceptibly.

The reality of his situation hit Rory afresh, like a chunk of meteorite puncturing a ship's hull. Perhaps Widdershins *wasn't* his home, but the *Scuabtuinne* certainly was, in many respects; it was all he had known these last few months, and its ragamuffin cosiness had grown on him.

'Okay, let's move on,' the man said, turning over the page he had been working on, and sighing loudly. 'Health. Do you have any physical disabilities or difficulties I should consider?'

Rory jerked himself out of his thoughts. 'No, sir. But I'm not much good at PE.'

'Indeed. Do you have any diagnosis of a mental health disorder?'

Rory swallowed again. 'Y–Yes, sir.'

'Speak up.'

'I said: yes, sir. I… I have OCD. I was told I had it almost two years ago.'

'Obsessive compulsive disorder – is that so?'

'Yes, sir.'

'I don't know much of it, but it's that thing where you need to have everything just so. Neatness, cleanliness and all that. Right?' He was already scribbling something down on his paper.

Rory narrowed his eyes, a little angered. 'No, sir,' he said, more firmly. 'That's not it at all.'

The man stopped writing, looked up, lay the pen down and… 'Okay, tell me then.'

Why didn't I just agree with him? Rory scolded himself.

He summoned some courage from the indignity of having his condition dismissed – not for the first time in his life – as being little more than a byword for 'perfectionism'. A curiosity. A twee trait. A quaint attention to detail. A quirk. But he knew how damaging such dismissal could be and how the stereotype so prevalent through the world he knew – or *had* known – had forced him, day after day, to retreat further into himself. He recalled Limmy's immediate understanding when he first met her in his flat back on that November evening and toughened his resolve.

'I wish OCD was just about being neat and tidy. My bedroom was never neat or tidy, though, and Mum always had a go at me for that. OCD is… well, it's *doubt*, sir. It's doubting that you're a good person and doubting that you haven't done something terrible –'

'We all doubt ourselves from time to time –'

'No! It's not like that.' He searched for the right words.

164

'You're lucky. If you ever have doubts, you probably make them go away quickly. But I don't. If I say something mean to another boy at school by mistake and he's upset, then I worry that he'll be so upset that he can't bear to live and that he'll *kill* himself –'

The man snorted, incredulously.

'It's true. I know it sounds stupid. But it's true. A-And I won't be able to get the worry out of my head. And the guilt will be in my chest.' His words were rushing from him now. 'A-And then I'm so guilty that I think that nothing else is possible except that he has killed himself. So, I'm a murderer and a really, really bad person because it's my fault. And if, just for a moment, I think it through properly and start to calm down, then m-maybe the way I remember what happened changes a-and I start to think I did stuff or said something else, when I didn't. And the doctors say that's just the way my brain works – not like other people's – and there's no cure for it. I can only manage by doing all these funny things that they told me to do, like writing a worry down and trying to write arguments against it. *That's* OCD and it seems like no one in the whole wide world knows that. Well, apart from Limmy.'

The man continued to look at Rory for a few moments, his expression hard to read, and then wrote down a few further points on his paper.

'Well then,' he finally said, 'I think I have just about all the information I need. There is just one more thing though, just to pick up on an earlier point: what would happen if you had to go back to Croydon?'

Rory opened his mouth, but the words died on his tongue. Eventually… 'I-I don't know. Sir.'

'Hmm, well, back in England, as I understand it, you would be looked after by your local authority – if you have no other family or friends. Probably go into foster care. So… you *would* be safe. Do you have anything to say to that?'

Rory felt tears in his eyes, as he sensed the situation slipping beyond his control. 'All I want to do is to find my mum. I need her to know that I didn't mean to hurt her…'

'Describe in single words, only the good things that come into your mind about your mother.'

A tear found its way down his cheek. Rory shook his head. 'Grief,' he said.

The man sighed, a note of frustration, and put down his pen again. 'And do you have any other family here in Widdershins? Someone who could look after you? *Other* than the crew of the *Scuabtuinne*?'

'Here?' Rory repeated, puzzled. 'No. I have no family here. I'm all by myself.'

A few hours later, Rory sat with his back to a mesh fence in what the man who interviewed him had called a 'holding block'. After the interview, he had been told he would have to wait here while some administration was completed and his claim processed. He wasn't told how long that would take, but he knew he had been stuck behind this fence for a long time.

He ran one finger along the rim of a small cup, long since drained of the bitter water it held. The crew of the *Scuabtuinne* would have no doubt gone off by now to attend to individual matters, unaware of what was happening to him. His first impression of Widdershins had not been positive and he hoped that the others would find something to enjoy in this alien world, even if he could not. The place felt cold and unforgiving and didn't look how he imagined a space colony might.

The intrusive thoughts were getting worse. He had gotten used to the *Scuabtuinne*, and being removed from its familiar surrounding – even with its bizarre lights and living pillows – unsettled him. His heart beat extra fast and his breathing came shallow. His hands trembled and a light sweat warmed his forehead, though otherwise he was cold.

Rooory, Rooory. They'll send you back for sure. Back to being alone on Earth. And you will be forgotten just as fast as you arrived!

Rory covered his ears and shook his head, willing the thought to go away. A tear travelled a well-worn route down his cheek as he panicked. Alone and vulnerable, the thoughts were all the stronger and he had nowhere to go and no comfort to take.

Rooory, Rooory. And don't forget you betrayed them. Telling that man that they wanted you aboard the ship. They'll be told to leave too – because of you!

'Shut up!' Rory screamed.

Rooory, Rooory. Rooory, Rooory. Rooory, Rooory.

And just as the thoughts approached a crescendo, something happened: that noise, like static, he had heard before, filled his ears, popping in his head. The static overcame the intrusive thoughts but, unlike before, it did not leave – it only grew louder and louder and then…

Perfect silence. Only… no. There was something else. Like the sound of a tidal current underwater. Smoke filled his mind and, like before, a liquid-black image – a muktuk – came into his head.

Gary? Is that… you?

The muktuk in his head flushed with colour, as though in response, and a bubbling bass sound accompanied it.

Rory jumped back against the mesh fence at the sudden activity. The bass was so close that he could practically feel it shivering down his neck, and he pulled away from the mesh fence, twisting his head back to see if there was someone behind him. But no one was there.

'Are you here?' Rory hissed. 'I can't see you.'

In his mind's eye, the muktuk became smaller, lifted itself up and an enormous black circle appeared beneath it, spinning around.

Rory bit back a response.

Can't he be clearer? he wondered.

And then a tiny humanoid appeared inside the circle.

'Whoa!' Rory yelled, jumping again. 'How did you hear me? I only thought that; I didn't *say* it.'

As Rory spoke, the little humanoid image reacted with colour, as though in response to his words.

Where are *you?*

The muktuk image in his head flickered and another image – this one of stars – flashed into Rory's mind.

He managed a chuckle, which quickly became a belly laugh as he realised what was happening.

You're speaking to me from space*!*

Rory stopped laughing. 'But how is this possible? Before… when I thought I heard noises and saw images… I just figured I was going even madder.'

The little muktuk in his head sent out a pulse, like sonar, and other humanoid images momentarily flashed up inside the circle – one of them was fairly close to the humanoid that he thought must represent him. His mind turned to Tall-Tongued Henley.

'Those are all... those are all Muktuk Whisperers, aren't they? Am I... am I one?'

A series of geometric shapes launched out from the muktuk image and encircled the little humanoid that was meant to be him.

Rory could not quite comprehend everything that Gary meant, but he could not forget that incredible scene back on Earth when he had been at the top of the church: Gary speaking to his enormous mother, looming in the cloud above Croydon. Is this how muktuks talked to each other as well?

How can you talk to me from all the way up there?

The static returned momentarily. Then the little muktuk started to pulse and the pulse appeared as a blue wave that trailed off in all directions like dust caught in the wind. The geometric shapes from the muktuk *felt* outwards and reacted to the dust before bouncing back.

Did you do the same on Earth? Is this how you knew your mum was there?

The little muktuk image lit up in colour again: this act seemed to symbolise a 'yes' response, Rory theorised. In his mind's eye, another shape appeared: uncertain, but maybe a ship – this one was a swirling mass of gold. And, this time, a grid materialised over the golden shape. The little muktuk that represented Gary drifted over so that it sat beside the golden shape, perfectly positioned on a gridline. Then four new muktuk images – all enormous – appeared above the golden shape and sat on gridlines as well; one of these enormous muktuk images pulsed and a jolt of blue flared up and fired down a gridline before hitting the little muktuk that represented Gary. The flare left behind blue dust that slowly faded along the gridline.

Rory heard the static again, scratching at the images in his head. *Gary? I think I understand. You're trying to show me how you see the universe. Don't go, though!*

And all at once, the static eclipsed Gary altogether before itself disappearing. Rory was back in the holding block. He did feel calmer and the intrusive thoughts were weaker.

He had no time to reflect on his experience with Gary before someone – a woman – walked into the holding block and unlocked a door in the mesh fence.

'How are you, young man?' the woman asked, her smile and tone suggesting the first shred of humanity Rory had witnessed in Widdershins.

'I-I'm better now, I think,' Rory replied, throwing a miserable smile back at her.

The woman ushered him out of the block and he tentatively stepped foot beyond the border of the cell.

'I'm so sorry that you were treated this way. I think it's disgusting that they do this when all you want is safety.'

Rory didn't know how to respond – he certainly couldn't disagree with her assessment, though.

'Anyway, you're free to return to your friends and go about your business.'

'You mean… just like that?' Rory asked.

'Just like that.'

'So, I'm allowed to stay here? In Widdershins.'

The woman's smile faded a little. 'Well, for the time being, yes. You have what we call "discretionary freedom" – it's… temporary. But a full decision about whether you can permanently live here will take months to come through.'

Rory lowered his head. 'Oh.'

There was an awkward silence.

'But I'm sure everything will work out for you,' the woman added, as hopefully as she could. 'Come on – let's get you back to your friends. They'll be delighted to see you.'

Out in the reception area, Henley and Xam jumped up and rushed over to Rory; Mira still sat where she had before he went in for his interview.

'What's the story, little Rory? Are you okay, dude?' Xam asked, shaking Rory by the shoulder.

''Twas an awful long time in there,' Henley agreed.

'We asked what they'd done with you but they wouldn't say!' Xam said.

'It's okay. I'm fine,' Rory replied. He looked around. 'Where's Limmy?

Xam and Henley stepped back.

'The captain was pulled away to an urgent meeting. She needs to report back on everything that's happened so far and find out… what we do next,' Xam said.

Rory was alarmed. 'You mean… But… We *are* going to find my mum, right?'

'Course we are, m'lad!' Henley urged, fiercely. Xam looked troubled. 'Nothin' could stop *me* gettin' back on the trail!' His eyes took on the same darkness Rory had seen before when he first met the Whisperer on the back of Rongomai. 'But we reckon the Whiffetsnatcher has gone where no other ship has gone before and we have no way of tracking 'im.'

Rory sighed. With each passing day, the memory of his mother seemed to drift slightly farther from his reach. It was difficult to recall her voice now and the little intricacies that made her who she was: the way she buttered her toast or always sat on the same side of the sofa. Despite every bad experience he had had with her, there were plenty of good times – times he longed for again – but the only way he could ever hope to have that was if he found her now.

'Tell you what, m'lad,' Henley said, interrupting Rory's train of thought. 'The captain will be a little while yet. Why don't yer come with me down into Widdershins. I got something that needs doin', after all.'

Xam nodded, though he seemed to look at Henley with suspicion. 'That's a good idea. I'll wait up here for Limmy. Try and enjoy yourselves – it's Christmas, after all.' He turned his head. 'Take Mira with you – she could do with stretching her legs.'

At the sound of her name, Mira looked up and scowled. 'Don't talk about me!'

Rory tried to force a smile.

I suppose it would be fun to see how Christmas is celebrated on an alien world, he decided.

But his mind was still filled with the strangeness of having spoken with Gary – spoken with an alien intelligence. He looked with renewed interest at Henley – the Muktuk Whisperer. Is this what happened to him? He still wasn't sure exactly what to make of Henley, but in this moment, he was the only person he could turn to for any hope of making sense of such madness and he could only discount Limmy's warning – whatever that was about.

As Xam walked over to Mira, Rory took a hold of Henley's arm and pulled him in closer – surprised at his own boldness. He glanced around quickly before speaking. 'Something happened. I–I don't know if it was just my imagination – no, I know that it wasn't. Gary *spoke* with me!'

Henley's grin faded. 'Gary? The god-child?'

Rory nodded.

Henley knelt and gripped Rory by the shoulders. 'Rare lad!' he hissed. 'I *knew* there was something about yer! We must go ter the temple at once!'

10

Widdershins

Henley led Rory and Mira away from Losna House to a small structure with a conical roof that sat beside the overhang of the waterfall. Spray from the waterfall's growling torrent frothed up in the breeze and settled as a fine mist over Rory's face, the water tasting metallic in his open mouth.

'That's disgusting. You don't know what's in it,' Mira said, abruptly, fixing Rory with a look of horror as Henley shook hands with an old man outside the structure and began a loud conversation.

Rory shrugged and smiled as he stuck his tongue out to catch more, just to annoy the odd girl.

Mira narrowed her eyes, crossed her arms and glowered more intensely.

'Right, m'boy – and m'girl,' Henley roared, clapping his hands as he came back over to the children. 'We can go down Eddie's elevator. Come on.'

Henley ushered the children after him; Rory trotted along

in his wake and Mira shuffled after him. They entered the structure to find that the building did not end where the cliff ended, but shot out over it with two piers: **Platform 1** and **Platform 2** marked above each. In between the piers were several rickety elevators suspended from a complicated system of cogs and pulleys by Martian slipknot. The breeze was a little stiffer inside the building and the elevators swayed gently with arthritic clicks and squeaks.

'Off we go then!' Henley announced, grinning.

'On *those* things?' Rory spluttered, horrified. 'But they look half rotten.'

The old man Henley had been talking to outside gave an incredulous grunt. 'I'll have you know, young whippersnapper, that I've been minding these for over forty years and I keep –'

Rory interrupted, blanching. 'That's how old they are!?'

The old man stumbled over his words a little. 'Well… they, uh, they're a bit older than that actually –'

'What Eddie means ter say,' Henley interrupted, 'is that he's never witnessed a death on these wonderful, safe contraptions.'

'Well, apart from the farmers in AF23… Or that sweet old lady in AF34… And that's not forgetting the fam–'

'Okay!' Henley said, clapping. 'Let's just get on. See us down safely, Eddie!'

'AF23?' Rory repeated, looking quizzically up at Henley, as he clambered onto the lift, somewhat gingerly.

'Hmm? Ah, right! I'll explain in a bit. That okay, m'lad?'

'Y-Yeah, I guess so. I just hope we don't end up like that sweet old lady he mentioned…'

After the initial terror of swaying around in a wooden elevator had passed, Rory marvelled at the spectacular view across Widdershins and the plains beyond. The settlement was not enormous, and so its distinct buildings and structures stood out against the general shabbiness of its surrounding districts. Whenever another elevator passed by, Henley would yell a hello to everyone he saw – some people seeming to recognise him ('Hullo, Henley! Haven't seen you round these parts since you was with yer last crew!' one man shouted).

Rory became aware of a noise like a giant metal bucket being filled with water.

'What is that sound!' he yelled above the roar of the waterfall.

'Look!' Henley yelled back, bending and pointing to somewhere below them.

The elevator eventually came level with it: the *Aeneas*, which Rory had seen before through the Dome as Xam brought the *Scuabtuinne* in over the colony. The waterfall cascaded over part of the old ship, which was embedded in the cliff-face with a number of metal panels missing, but the racket it created did not seem to bother the strange birdlike creatures huddled on the ship's hull – indeed, some of them *clomp clomp clomped* over to the water and took big glugs of it, their black scales twitching and shimmering. Rory asked what they were, but Henley just grinned at him, his black eyeliner catching the light like the animals' skin.

'Hey! Yer ugly gub-gub brutes! Get out of it!' Henley bellowed, sending the birds into panicked flight.

Rory watched as they took to the air, several passing frighteningly close to the elevator. Up close, they were each about the size of a goat, perhaps, the frills around their eyes petalled with a flush of yellows, reds and purples. Soon, their black bodies were mere silhouettes against the dusty sky.

'A day here is different ter yer Earth, m'lad,' Henley said pointing up at the sky.

Rory realised that the light was ruddy because Mars was so full and overwhelming that it appeared to fill most of the sky.

'A Minervan day is forty-seven hours long – much more than Earth's twenty-four – and it orbits Mars once every one-point-two Earth years –'

'One-point-one-seven Earth years actually,' Mira mumbled, arms folded – the girl slumped in one corner of the elevator.

Rory looked at Mira, suddenly curious, but turned back to Henley before he had the guts to respond to her. 'And what was that "AF" stuff about?'

'Ah! So a Minervan year is four-hundred-and-twenty-six Earth days. In Earth measures, it's been sixty-six years since Widdershins was founded, but only *fifty*-six years here on Minerva. And "AF" – that's After Foundation. The year is AF56 here.'

Rory nodded, trying to get his head round this new calendar. 'Is there day and night?'

'Not like yer used ter – about two-thirds of the Minervan day is spent with Mars in the sky – that's called "redrise" and is as close ter day as we get. The rest of the time we face in ter space and that we call "darkfall" – that's our night. As yer can see, 'tis redrise right now and the Sun lights Mars up like a Christmas Tree. Ah! Speaking of which, look!'

Rory followed Henley's finger. He was pointing into the heart of Volp Lane, where an eerie tree that resembled a skeletal

Norwegian pine stood proudly with lights at the tip of its branches.

'Lit by fungus and, at the top, more fungus: squelched and mulched in ter a star. Ha!'

The elevator shuddered to the ground, where it 'landed' with a bump and a shake in the middle of two piers much like the ones in the building at the top of the cliff. Rory, Henley and Mira stepped out and moved down **Platform 2**, past various people all dressed peculiarly in waistcoats, robes and shaggy trousers, coloured in an assortment of reds, browns and blacks.

'Right,' Henley said, clapping his hands. 'We're headed fer the Temple of the Muktuks.' He winked at Rory, then turned to Mira. 'Is there anywhere yer want ter go?'

Mira looked ahead, her eyes unfixed, and shook her head.

'Right, then – boys and girls! Let's get exploring!'

Volp Lane was a delicious feast for the senses. On either side, shops followed a crooked path further into Widdershins, separated by a tiled thoroughfare busy with people in clothes that were either reminiscent of 1940s gear Rory had once seen in the Museum of London, or utterly bizarre in design and with no point of reference: glowing neckerchiefs; shimmering wraps; and there was even a hat on one person's head that looked alive (*And well it might be*, Rory thought, considering his pillow on board the *Scuabtuinne*). Through the middle of the thoroughfare ran a series of market stalls, their holders yelling out their wares: bright fruits; nuts the size of fists; and odd, turquoise fish with legs. Above the stalls, tall poles with carved patterns hooked a series of lanterns, each lantern holding the residue of faintly glowing mushrooms, like those aboard the *Scuabtuinne* and on the Christmas Tree.

The shops themselves looked like something reminiscent of World War Two Britain: high glass windows full of wares and, again, the ornate, carved wood making up the frames. In the window of **COOK & SALTER CARTOGRAPHERS**, an explosion of beautifully hand-drawn maps promised complete familiarity with Minerva, Mars and the Solar System, while an advert stated:

SEEKING EXTRAORDINARY EXPLORERS FOR EXCEPTIONAL EXPEDITION
Ever wondered what lies beyond the RHIANDO CALDERA?
Tempted to test the JAN ICE PLAINS or the MOFFATT MOUNTAINS?
*IN THE NAME OF SCIENCE, become an EXPLORER and CARTOGRAPHER today!**
* Cook & Salter accepts no liability in the case of explorer death.

'Out here's the new frontier, m'boy. There are worlds to discover and yer can be any part of that yer want,' Henley said, clearly having noticed Rory's preoccupation with the advert.

Other shop fronts suggested similar excitement and lunacy. **ORVILLE'S OXYGEN OUTLET** promised 'the purest air this side of the Asteroid Belt', offering everything from coloured to flavoured oxygen in tanks, bottles and foil-like bags. **PLANET PET** was, quite literally, doing a roaring trade, as several customers emerged clutching cages filled with floating fluffballs that growled and snarled as viciously as any lion. **MUTLEY MOSS'S MUKTUK MEMENTOS** seemed to boast a rather large and tacky collection of cups, hats, toys and other souvenirs all based on the theme of muktuks. And **GEORDI'S GEARS AND GRIDDLES** was clearly some manner of workshop or mechanic's for spaceships and what could only be described as hot-air balloons.

Mira came to a stop. 'I'll be at Geordi's – there's a few replacement parts I need for the *Scuabtuinne*. Be back here in an hour.'

Henley saluted the retreating back of Mira and turned to Rory. 'Yer stuck with me then, lad. Yer'll have ter put up with an old fogey!'

Rory smiled. 'That's okay. I don't think Mira likes me very much anyway.'

Henley slipped an arm around Rory's shoulder. 'Oh, I don't know that yer should be takin' too much bother of that. She's the same with everyone – even Limmy. Just her way is all. She's a *fine* girl, that one – one that I'm sure a father could have been proud of.' Henley's eyes narrowed. 'Funny old cosmos, en't it? How a girl can be right there ready fer a parent's love with no parent willing to give it. And then yer can find a parent ready ter give love but with no child left ter receive it…'

Rory studied Henley's face and let the Whisperer drift into silence, shaking off the strangeness of the moment. He thought to ask more about Mira but, remembering her violent reaction to having her tapestry intruded upon back on the ship, decided that if he was to learn anything of the strange engineer, he would rather it be because she decided that he could know. He was about to turn away from Henley when his eyes settled on the Whisperer's sole earring.

'What's that on your earring – those marks?' Rory asked.

'What? Oh, this thing?' Henley replied, removing the piece of jewellery and handing it to Rory.

Rory moved it about in his hands. Engraved into it were the words, *Sugar and spice...* He frowned and looked up at Henley, returning the earring to him.

Henley grinned. 'What are little girls made of?'

Rounding another corner, and then another, Rory and Henley came to a square with a familiar building in it: another pyramid, much like the one on the back of Rongomai, though with a few key differences, such as the large entranceway through which various robed, elderly men transferred their wrinkly frames.

'This is the Temple of the Muktuks,' Henley informed Rory. 'It were built shortly after the Whisperers became a recognised group here in Widdershins.'

'B-Before – on Rongomai – you said it wasn't a religion.'

'Well we don't *worship* muktuks or the like! We don't have a holy book, or think a super muktuk came back from the dead like some bloody zombie!' Henley cackled. 'No. I said we were *devotees*. The relationship is more nuanced than worship; it's more like – what would yer understand? – it's more like... butlers attending a retired philanthropist.'

Rory didn't quite understand at all. 'You called Gary a "god-child".'

'Ah! Well noted, m'lad! True enough. It's just my weak and unimaginative way of tryin' ter describe the power of a muktuk. They are so ancient – so wise – that ter us they may as well be gods. In fact, what's ter say that Yu-Kiang of Ancient China wasn't a muktuk? Or perhaps Jonah was swallowed by Rongomai himself! With the discoveries made over the last

181

one hundred years – the *secret* discoveries, that is – we should reconsider the history of our species accordingly.'

Rory delved into his own head in the silence that followed, reinterpreting elements of history and even the modern day that had always struck him as odd.

'Anyway,' Henley said, clapping his hands. 'Enough chit-chat. Do yer want ter see what the Whisperers are about?'

The temple inside was very dark, lit only by sconces crammed with the now familiar glowing mushrooms, newer ones lumped unceremoniously over the sweet-smelling rot of their predecessors. Through the gloom, Rory's eyes acclimatised and he breathed in the musk and gentle conversation of the temple's many inhabitants. The temple appeared to consist of a single space, though Henley assured Rory that there were many secret chambers and hidden passages that only a few selected Whisperers were privileged enough to traverse. The main chamber seemed to be a fusion of stone and bookcases made of the red wood of the Ares' tendon. In each bookcase were piles of scrolls tied up with Martian slipknot.

'The records of all we know of the muktuks: their biology, the whispering, their comings and goings,' Henley informed Rory in a murmur.

After a short walk through the chamber, Henley directed Rory down a passage into a laboratory of some kind – not dissimilar from Beak's medical bay on board the *Scuabtuinne*. Flasks and vials smoked and bubbled away. Scrolls formed a sort of carpet on some of the desks. A model muktuk hung from the ceiling much like the blue whale at London's Natural

History Museum. In the corner, some bizarre egg-like objects shimmered and oozed purple gunk.

'How fare yer, lads!' Henley boomed to the several individuals who were busy with their work.

Some jumped at the unexpected sound; others furiously shushed him. One old man pottered over.

'Good to see you, Henley,' he whispered, roughly shaking Henley's hand. 'Been a while, been a while. You must have some wonderful data for us on Rongomai.'

'Plenty,' Henley growled, his smile razor sharp. 'But first, let me introduce this young man: this here is Rory. Recent catch from Earth. Planet-minded but minded ter not be. Ha!'

It was Rory's turn to have his hand shaken roughly and he could not help but smile as the old man inspected him through rheumy eyes.

'A pleasure to make your acquaintance, young 'un. My name's Bill and I'm the Chief Whisperer here at the temple. Henley's a cheeky one, but there are few finer Whisperers.'

'None finer! Anyway, tell a lad what yer do here,' Henley said.

'Ah! Well, we've dedicated our lives to learning as much of the muktuks as we can. Of all the intelligent species we've encountered so far, muktuks are the most fascinating – well, as far as I'm concerned! Aeons of memory and experience. And every time a Whisperer speaks to a muktuk, we can access that memory and experience ourselves. Just think of what we've learned – what we still *can* learn!'

'So, every time we're back here in Widdershins,' Henley said, 'I come to find Bill and give him an update on everything new that Rongomai has imparted to me.'

'And so we build our knowledge,' Bill added. 'Every Whisperer is required to do it.'

'How many Whisperers are there?' Rory asked.

Bill and Henley looked at each other, each tilting their head like birds.

'Hmm, not many, m'lad. 'Tis a rare and a *fine* gift,' Henley replied, at last, his eyes lingering on Rory for a few moments.

'As far as we can tell,' Bill continued, 'the ability to communicate with a muktuk is the province of a mind that has understood great pain and suffering. Experience – particularly bad experience – rewires the brain in ways that seem to make some people more receptive to muktuks. It's also thought that Whispering is genetic as well: if your mother or your father can do it – or someone else in your family – then you may be able to as well.'

'Can… can children do it?' Rory asked.

'Yes,' Bill replied, clicking two of his gnarled fingers. 'Though it is especially rare. The last child I knew to be capable… well, his life went down a dark path.' He seemed to catch Henley's eyes momentarily.

'Rory has the gift,' Henley said, clearing his throat, pride in his voice. 'And strongly too, I would say.'

Everyone close enough to have heard this revelation stopped what they were doing and looked at Rory, before passing on the news to those who had not heard.

'Indeed?' Bill said, his interest in Rory refreshed. 'How long have you known?'

'N-Not long… Only really today actually,' Rory responded.

'Well!' Bill continued, 'You have an excellent tutor in

Henley here. Who knows? Perhaps you will be the one to answer the Great Question.'

Rory looked to Henley, wondering what 'the Great Question' could be. But, just at that moment, a crackly sound came out of the fabric around Henley's waist. Several individuals gave him a dirty look as Henley pulled a device that resembled Limmy's radio from his belt.

'*Come in, Henley. Come in, Henley. Over,*' said Xam's voice.

Henley looked, momentarily, irritated. 'Henley here. Over.'

'*Please come to the Towers at once. Limmy's meeting has finished. Needs to speak with us urgently. We're being reassigned. Over.*'

Having collected Mira from GEORDI'S GEARS AND GRIDDLES, Rory and Henley made their way to the Towers standing so prominently over Widdershins. Rory's fears were realised when they found Limmy and Xam in a large room, both sitting in armchairs looking thoroughly despondent.

No... Please don't say we're not going after Mum, Rory pleaded with some unknown power.

'Rory,' Limmy said, managing a weak smile. She gave him a limp hug then held him at arm's length, as though seeing him for the first time. She shook her head. 'I'm sorry I wasn't there when you finished in Losna House. How was the assess–'

'Never mind that,' Rory interrupted, voice full of urgency. 'I heard Xam on Henley's radio. What's going on?'

'A lad has it. What's the verdict?' Henley snapped, seemingly more stirred than Rory.

Even Mira looked upset.

Limmy glanced from one face to the next, then to Xam, who

nodded. She sighed, running a hand through her fiery hair. 'Our assignment was always to prevent the Whiffetsnatcher from taking your mum, Rory. We pursued him, but his ship, the *Phaethon*, is in a different class to the *Scuabtuinne*; our chances of ever catching him were always... remote. He is now so far ahead of us that we couldn't even begin to guess where he is. Worse still, we have no way of locating him. The Council feels that... we should not continue. Few have ever ventured beyond the Asteroid Belt and it is considered too dangerous for us to try...'

Limmy's words petered out and Rory collapsed onto a seat, too stunned even to talk. 'B–But... my mum. What about my mum?'

Though his head was hanging, he didn't need to see her to recognise the guilt in Limmy as she swallowed on a dry throat. 'I'm so, so sorry, Rory. I argued as hard as I could. I did every–'

'What about my mum!?' Rory yelled, flashing his eyes up at everyone.

Limmy visibly jumped. Her own eyes were bleary. 'I... I'm sorry.'

'What about us?' Mira asked calmly, apparently indifferent to Rory's anguish.

Rory buried his head in his hands and the tears ran hot on his cheeks.

'We're to be given new jobs. We'll probably be split up and – R–Rory, where are you going?'

But Rory had heard enough. He jumped up and ran from the room, his head filling with familiar, poisonous thoughts.

Rooory, Rooory. Your mum has gone. She's not coming back. And it's all your fault!

11

Unscheduled Flight

Rory's Christmases, as a rule of thumb, had never been much fun. Where other children, he knew, stampeded down stairs to tear open presents or stuffed themselves with turkeys so large that shelves had to be removed from ovens in order to accommodate them, he had always spent Christmas at home with his mum – and that was rarely a good thing. There was that one Christmas where Mum had served up uncooked chicken with raw vegetables. The half-empty bottle of vodka had just been a coincidence, of course. 'Santa needed a pick-me-up when 'e came down las' nigh',' she had slurred. 'Weren't me.' Then there had been the Christmas last year when Mum forgot to get him a present and she had locked herself in the bathroom, crying and apologising through the door while chain-smoking. Rory had watched *The Snowman* on repeat while an emergency duty social worker paid them a two-hour visit following a police complaint from the neighbour. Sometimes, Rory thought of past events like these and then he would wonder why he cared so much about finding his mother. But she wasn't always like this. Things had just been bad since her drinking got out of control. It used to be that he would get out of bed on Christmas morning to find Santa's footprints leading through to a Christmas tree... never bustling with presents, exactly, but always suitably stocked with several choice gifts from Mum. 'Merry Christmas, darlin',' she would say.

Rory had never imagined he would spend a Christmas anywhere other than on Earth – indeed, who does? – but it was very much a Christmas to forget. No presents. Limited contact with Henley, who seemed to have stormed off in a rage for reasons Rory couldn't fathom. And nothing more from Gary, who didn't seem to appreciate there was any cause for seasonal greetings. He stayed with Limmy, Xam and Mira above a bar called the **ANDROMEDA ARMS** ('Minerva's first, best and worst public house', so its sign boasted), as it was all that was available at short notice. Life became little more than a tedious countdown to the Council's final judgement on how severely this little crew would be divided.

By evening on New Year's Eve, Rory lay on his little bed busily contesting with the intrusive thoughts in his head. In the corner of the room, Mira sat chewing a repulsive-looking sweet while reading a book that she had picked up on Earth. Every now and then, she made a sound that irritated Rory. *Nweee!* It resembled an involuntary rodent-like squeak. From downstairs in the bar, he could hear people laughing and singing in celebration. Limmy and Xam had themselves been downstairs for an hour or so, having finally been persuaded by both Rory and Mira that they should take the opportunity to enjoy themselves. But at that precise moment, Rory regretted the fact that he had only himself for company, Mira simply too dense a character to reach, like a neutron star spinning blithely on its own little axis.

Nweee! Mira made that squeaking noise again.

Rory huffed, turning to face her. 'Stop it! You're driving me nuts.'

Mira knitted her brow and stuck out her tongue.

Rory sighed, turning back to face the wall his bed was propped up against.

Nweee! Mira made that squeaking noise yet again.

Rory flung himself over, as dramatically as he could, and yelled, 'Stop. It. Now!'

Mira pouted, though there was a quaver in her voice when she spoke. 'Just because your mum's gone doesn't mean you can be rude to me. It's not nice.'

That was enough for Rory. He stared at Mira, believing her to be the cruellest creature in the universe, and ran through the bedroom, down the stairs – past the festivities – out onto Volp Lane and off into the lanes that led to Widdershins' various districts.

The Minervan sky was no longer dominated by Mars; instead, it was an ecstasy of stars, bluey-green nebulae and the sugary splash that was the Milky Way. Darkfall on this alien world and all the depth of the cosmos was a salutation to eternity. The turquoise mushroom lamps glowed just enough to chip away at the severest dark, but Rory still had trouble making out where he was going. He tried to ignore the cold, which gnashed at his flesh. He passed various people and strange banleuc shelters before he came to the edge of Widdershins and was suddenly faced with an ocean of seaweed grass.

A peculiar, deep warbling sound drew his attention and he turned to face a paddock adjacent to a building that looked very much like an old farmstead. Inside the paddock were creatures that looked to be a bizarre fusion of cow, seahorse and iguanodon, with two rows of three bulbous, black eyes – they were making the noise. He walked up to the paddock, leaned against its creaky wooden fence and stared at the creatures. There were about thirty of them – all of different sizes – plodding about as a herd and extending toothed tongues to snatch up blades of the seaweed grass and pull it back into their mouths to commence chewing. Towards the back of the paddock was a *large* plant – to put it mildly – that closely resembled the runner beans he remembered his school, Hurling Academy, as having grown in a small allotment. Only, the 'runner beans' on this plant were at least the size of a bus and, through their translucent flesh, he could see a row of perhaps six or seven of the strange creatures – there was no other word for it – *growing* instead of beans.

'A world where animals can grow on plants is certainly an alien one,' came a voice to Rory's left.

He jumped, turned and found himself looking up into the sad smile of Limmy, her red hair ruffling in the chilly breeze. She placed a thick blanket over his shoulders, which he accepted, gratefully though silently.

Rory looked back into the paddock. 'What are they?' His voice was little more than a whisper, but his recent troubles still weighed heavily on his mind and his tone was robbed of the excitement it might have otherwise carried.

'They're called marmoos. Here, they're farmed for the vegetables that grow on their backs. Look.'

Rory's eyes followed Limmy's outstretched finger and fell upon a particularly large marmoo: sure enough, along its leathery back was a small salad of vegetable-like growths – here a cosmic cucumber; there an astronomical avocado.

'Essentially, they're fungal growths, but they're high in vitamins, protein and potassium, and they can be harvested, then they just grow right back. Boom! It's a bit like with a muktuk – remember what it's like on the back of Rongomai? There are even species similar to marmoos that have those plants' – she pointed to the 'runner beans' – 'growing on them as well. Minervan scientists believe that muktuks and marmoos are part of the same family. Kingdom: Exoanamalia. Phylum: Minorfauna. Order: Asterataurus. And do you want to know the strangest thing about them, kid?'

Rory furrowed his brow, looking once again at Limmy with disbelief that there could be anything stranger about a creature that grew on a plant, produced vegetables on its back and looked like something from a particularly warped Pixar animation.

Limmy grinned, her eyes twinkling. 'Well, keep watching and you'll see,' she finished, cryptically.

Rory sighed, looking back again at the herd. He was beginning to get bored when he witnessed something nonsensical: one of the marmoos stretched out a multi-jointed leg in front of another marmoo whose black eyes were clouded, as though it was blind. This unfortunate marmoo tripped over the outstretched leg and fell heavily to the ground. The marmoo that had tripped it – along with several others nearby – made a deep seal-like hiccupping that sounded eerily as though...

'Are they... are they *laughing* at it?' Rory asked, feeling silly for even saying it.

But Limmy smiled. 'Yep, certainly are, kid. And watch what happens next.'

Rory looked again at the marmoos. The ones that were laughing now appeared to expel small clouds of green gas from orifices near their backside that quickly dispersed into the air. He looked again at Limmy, his mouth caught between a smirk and implacability.

'On Earth,' Limmy began, 'it's plants that oxygenate the planet, right? But here on Minerva, it's the *animals* that create oxygen – by farting, pretty much. Oxygen is a waste gas created when a Minervan animal, well, *laughs*. A sense of humour is not, apparently, limited to humans. It's... quite a remarkable discovery. Multiple species of animal on Minerva have been observed to show a sense of humour – usually slapstick.'

Rory looked back into the paddock as the blind marmoo tried to pull itself back up; his own smile withered.

'But you didn't come all the way out here to laugh, did you?' Limmy continued, her tone changing abruptly.

Rory said nothing.

'*Please* don't run off like that again, yeah? If you get lost in Widdershins then I'll struggle to find you. Remember: this is only my second time here, so most of what I know comes from reading... I knew I shouldn't have gone downstairs earlier.'

Rory sighed. 'It's fine. Don't worry 'bout me.'

'But I do worry, Rory,' Limmy responded. 'I'm...' she laughed, as though at a revelation, 'well, I'm your social worker, after all is said and done, and it's my job to worry. But more than that I care about you and I hate to see you hurting.'

Rory felt a surge of anger. Deep down, he knew Limmy would have done everything she could to challenge the Council's decision on not pursuing the Whiffetsnatcher, but he was still furious at the injustice of it all. And, on top of that, he was annoyed at himself for being angry with Limmy. And guilty. And then, of course, that voice came back.

Rooory, Rooory. After all she's done. She saved you. But you still blame her – you're disgusting!

'Shut up!' Rory yelled. 'Shut up!'

His chest heaved with each breath, aware of the silence that now fell between him and his social worker.

She'll think I meant she *should shut up*, he worried.

'Rory, I know what's in your head. And if I could see any way of us finding your mum then... then I would take it. I know what she's put you through all these years. But your mum has suffered a great deal as well. And... she doesn't deserve to be abandoned. I want you to know something.' Her voice was steady and the power of it not only drew Rory's attention, but seemed to diminish all other sound around them. 'I want you to know that I do understand what it is to lose someone you love. I told you on the *Scooby*. When you lose someone though, you should honour their memory. Be the best you can be. All I knew when I lost my mother and left my father behind was that I had to help others – just as I was helped and... just as I *wasn't* helped as well. That was my choice.

Coming to terms with what's happened is going to take time, but I'll be here for you. I'm not going anywhere. And I don't think the others are either.'

Rory listened closely to Limmy's words. 'I shouldn't have pushed her! That's the last memory I have and I don't even know if it's really what happened! She disappeared thinking I hated her – that I wanted to hurt her!'

Limmy took Rory's shoulders – her own eyes glistening. 'She disappeared *knowing* you loved her! I don't know exactly what went through her mind, or where she is now – but she *knows* you love her. How could she ever doubt it? And she would want you to be happy and to move forward. What's happened is horrible, and the uncertainty… well, I know what uncertainty feels like. It's the worst thing –'

'But there's so much I didn't say! So much I needed her to know,' Rory yelled, his tears running fast. 'But I never got that chance and now… I never will. There's stuff I could hardly figure out in my own head but that I needed her to know. So much that was bad… but so much that was good.'

'Then say it now!' Limmy urged. 'Okay, maybe she can't hear you. But say it anyway. Here' – Limmy rooted around in her waistcoat pocket, plucking out a tiny Pukka Pad and biro – 'use this.'

Rory chuckled, despite himself. 'That's not very space-y.'

Limmy laughed too. 'No. But us social workers have to make do. I always have it on me. It'll be fine. Here' – she handed the pad and biro to Rory – 'now think of a good memory and write down how it made you feel.'

Rory extended his hands gingerly towards the pad and biro – Limmy nodded encouragingly. He took it and clutched at the familiar Earth-ness of it. He cast his mind back a few years to before Mum started drinking. Back to a time when life was still tough but Mum made an adventure of it. A memory surfaced. It was his birthday and they were struggling with money, but they were referred to the food bank at a church opposite the old Castledon School and College at the far end of town. When they arrived, there were a number of other people there and loads of metal shelves filled with cans and packets. They'd queued for a little while, shown the referral voucher and Mum had said, 'It's 'is birthday today. *Seven years old*. Can you believe it?' The kindly old lady had winked conspiratorially at him and wandered off among the shelves. When she returned, she had handed over a big bag of food and a smaller bag of children's toys and books. 'Most of the food is from Waitrose and there's a great book about the planets in there too – one of them Dorling Kinders-mawotchits,' she'd said, keeping her voice low, as though to hand such treasures out was a minor crime that must be disguised at all cost. Mum had said, 'Thank you,' and they had left to explore these prizes at their leisure in the churchyard. Rory and his mother had gotten through a family-sized chocolate bar and used the other foods to imagine a feast they would never have but could well describe and laugh about.

Turning to the pad in his hand, he wrote:

mum always made the best of the worst situashuns and tryd to make sure I was happy

'What do I do now?' Rory asked.

'See those glowing things near the marmoos?' Limmy asked.

Rory looked back at the marmoo herd. 'Yes.'

'Those are photoflies – their bodies are covered in a sticky sap. Scrunch up your message and stick it to one.'

Limmy vaulted over the paddock fence and ran towards the marmoos and their attendant photoflies, yelling for Rory to follow. He smiled and, after hesitating at first, did the same. Soon, he had weird alien cows all around him and dragonfly-sized luminescent insects buzzing about his head. At Limmy's encouragement, he managed to stick his biro-written message to one of the creatures and watched as it fluttered off into the night.

'There you go!' Limmy called. 'Maybe your message will reach your mum.' Her face went hard. 'Now – another!'

Rory chuckled, scratching his head. What else to put? He remembered back a couple of years. He had gone with Mum to an appointment at the Jobcentre where she had to explain what she was doing to find a job despite being ill. They'd sat down at the curling faux-pine desk with her 'work coach' – a man named Gavin whose job it was to help Mum into work while also assessing whether she had done enough every fortnight to retain the little money she and Rory were afforded to survive. Gavin had been unhappy on that occasion, as Mum had turned down an interview with a telecommunications company based a two-hour train journey away and she was being scolded for not having taken the opportunity. 'But if I got the job I'd be worse off than I am now – with rail fares what they are,' she'd argued. However, Gavin had been quite keen to explain why Mum was wrong. 'You have to take these opportunities. You should have gone for the interview. I'm sorry, Ms Hobble, but we'll have to sanction you.' Rory knew the word 'sanction' from an early age: it meant a smaller meal, no snacks and no days out. He associated it with stomach cramps. 'No, you aren't!' Mum had railed. 'I do my best to find work, but I have to think of my son and you shouldn't make me work so far away from Rory – he's only a little boy, for God's sake!' She'd stood up to say that and many others in the Jobcentre had cheered her.

Probably why the security guards were asked to escort her and me out, Rory figured.

He clenched the biro as he scribbled:

mum new what was right and what was wrong and she fort for us both

He took the paper and, after a few failed attempts at catching an insect, managed to attach it to another photofly. He watched this one swoop about a few times before climbing towards the sky. He knew it could not possibly reach his mother, but he felt better watching the insect hurtling away as though drawn to her – just like Gary had been drawn to his muktuk mother back on Earth…

It was in this very moment that a great realisation struck him.

'Limmy!' he shouted, turning to face her. 'We *can* find my mum – there's a way. I know how!'

Limmy's smile disappeared and became an expression of surprise and intense interest. 'How?'

Rory held up a hand, as though asking her to wait a moment.

Gary? … Gary – are you there? he said inside his head, concentrating.

He waited a few moments but there was no response and definitely no static in his ears.

'What are you doing, Rory? How can we find your mum?' Limmy prompted, walking over to him.

'Sshhh. Please. Just wait a second,' Rory replied.

He took a breath, closed his eyes, and concentrated. *Gary… Please answer if you can hear me. I… I need you.*

A whole minute passed, Limmy keeping silent – though sighing once or twice – and the marmoos calling to each other.

'It's no good. I thought I had an idea…' Rory said.

Limmy smiled sadly, squeezing his shoulder. 'I know it's hard but –'

And then the static cancelled out all other noise. He could hear his own pulse in his ears. The smoke from before appeared in his mind, then the familiar image of a muktuk and the humanoid figure that represented him.

Gary! You are *there! I thought you couldn't hear me anymore.*

The muktuk image pulsed softly, as though inquisitive or perhaps reassuring.

I'm okay – and I'll see you soon. But first I need to know something. Back on Earth – where I found you – how did you know where your mum would be that time? Rory thought, concentrating hard. Involuntarily, he crossed his fingers and hoped Gary would show him what he *hoped* he would show him.

Sure enough, a huge muktuk image appeared in his mind. Then the grid that he had seen after his asylum assessment materialised and the muktuk that represented Gary moved to sit on it. The enormous muktuk pulsed and a wave of blue rushed down a gridline to meet Gary. Sure enough, the enormous muktuk moved towards Gary and they met along the grid in a blaze of blue.

Rory was thrilled: this was *exactly* what Gary had done when he was locked up after his assessment in Losna House. He knew what it meant as well: the enormous muktuk image represented Gary's mother, and the pulses firing along the gridline represented Gary *sensing* his mother.

But then the image changed again. The enormous muktuk image was joined by three other enormous muktuk images and a little golden ship. The ship and the muktuks moved away along a gridline, leaving a trail of blue dust behind. The image of Gary pulsed again, firing out a burst of light that hit and reacted with the blue dust. This reaction repeated itself but, each time, the reaction weakened as the dust gradually faded.

I understand it all! Rory thought to himself excitedly.

With a painful crackle of static, Rory's head cleared and he was back in the present moment with Limmy. He looked into her eyes, determined.

'It's Gary. Gary can lead us to her!'

Limmy looked confused. 'How, though? What just happened to you?'

'Remember back on Earth, when Gary sensed his mum at the church? He can *speak to me* – just like Rongomai speaks to Henley. And Gary's shown me how he speaks to other muktuks and how he knew where his mum would be. The muktuks – they speak to each other along a kind of grid and there's this blue dust that his mum has been trailing behind her since the Whiffetsnatcher took his ship away from Earth. *She's been leaving a trail for us to follow – like breadcrumbs.*' Rory hardly paused for breath, so desperate was he to convey what he now understood.

Limmy still looked confused, but Rory realised that the dust trail was fading and time was of the essence. He grabbed Limmy by the hand and pulled her away from the marmoo herd – startling a few of them into a clumsy canter.

'Come on! *He'll* tell you,' Rory yelled, breaking into a run and jumping awkwardly over the paddock fence.

'*Who* will tell me?' Limmy asked, bundling over the fence as well, though catching her shin and swearing in the process.

But Rory was too excited to reply.

Half an hour later, Rory and Limmy – joined now by Xam and Mira – came to a crooked little dwelling that sat a stone's throw from the Temple of the Muktuks, which loomed impressively against the night sky. Xam was a little the worse for wear after enjoying his evening a great deal and had trouble stifling his giggles. Rory knocked on the door several times before a growl came from within, by way of response. The sound of heavy boots on hard floor indicated that someone was approaching. The door was flung open.

'*What* do yer want?' Henley snapped. He was wrapped up in an orange dressing gown and had curlers in his beard. 'You lot…'

'Mr Henley,' Rory began, a confidence in his voice he had not heard in years. 'I know how to find my mother.'

Henley raised an eyebrow, his expression uncompromisingly sour. 'Is that so?' He folded his arms.

But Rory nodded, grinning. 'Gary showed me the *grid* again.

His mother – one of the muktuks pulling the *Phaethon* – has been leaving a trail along the grid *this whole time* and Gary can sense it. He still senses it... but only just. We haven't got much time.'

'Well, what do you make of it?' Limmy asked, pushing Henley for an immediate response.

Henley's expression melted into one of concentration and intrigue. 'Muktuks talk in ideas. I... I've never been shown *images* by Rongomai. Rare lad indeed' – he eyed Rory with intense interest before coming back to reality – 'and the dust yer mention, lad, sounds like a notion we Whisperers hold about how muktuks can talk across space. Perhaps what the god-child showed yer was a symbol, of sorts.'

'Yes!' Rory agreed. 'A symbol of the trail Gary's mum is leaving behind her.'

'Could a muktuk leave some kin' of trail across space?' Xam slurred, poking his head round the doorframe, perhaps curious to see Henley's home, perhaps in need of some support. 'Like a grea' big snail.' He wiggled one of his fingers.

'Nothin' physical that I can imagine...' Henley responded. 'But... muktuks have two brains – both enormous – and could it be that they're able ter leave some kind of... *mental* imprint on space itself. Again, we humble Whisperers can only guess! If that be the case though... Ha! One muktuk could follow another. It would explain how they migrate over such head-wobblin' distances!'

Henley looked more alive now. More intense. More urgent.

'So... it's possible?' Limmy asked, hesitantly.

'Aye! But not just possible; I would say *likely* – based on what we know of muktuks,' Henley said.

'Yet *you've* never known this.'

Henley fixed Limmy with a dangerous expression and, for a moment, Rory thought he might bite her or something. But the moment passed.

'No Whisperer that *I* know has ever *seen* this. Talkin' with a muktuk is tricky beyond common ability, mark me. Perhaps young Rory truly is… gifted.'

'But the trail is fading fast – Gary showed me that,' Rory interrupted.

Henley nodded, his eyes narrowing. 'Then we must leave at once.'

'Without authorisation? We can't break the rules,' Mira said, clenching her fists and stamping a foot.

'Getting authorisation from the Council is very important,' Limmy agreed. 'But, more than that, your application for asylum, Rory… Leaving Widdershins after making an application is very likely to cancel out your claim. You may not be allowed back here…'

Rory swallowed hard and lowered his head. 'I-I… understand,' he said, finally, before looking up again. 'I *have* to try and rescue Mum.'

Limmy grunted in assent, her face serious. Then she smiled. 'Well… if that trail is fading then we can't lose any more time, kid. Let's do it. Let's leave. *Now.*'

Mira shook her head; Xam whooped with delight before vomiting in the gutter; and Henley did his great barking laugh. Rory caught Limmy's eye and she winked.

'I suppose I should get in ter fitter garb,' Henley announced, untying his dressing gown cord and letting the gown fall to the ground. Fortunately, he had underwear on.

The field where the *Scuabtuinne* had landed was deserted, everyone busily engrossed in New Year's Eve festivities, and all that could be heard was the crunch and rustle of seaweed-like grass. Atop the waterfall, the banleuc Towers stood white and implacable against the cosmos, with enormous twin banners unfurled reading **HAPPY NEW YEAR!** in glowing blue. On a roost scoured into the cliff-face beside the waterfall, two of the strange, black, birdlike creatures Rory had seen earlier chittered in their sleep, only to be startled awake by the hiss of human voices and the strangled cry of Xam as he almost toppled out of the elevator. Such was Xam's bulk that the elevator swung into the cliff, sending the birdlike creatures into a frenzy of flapping and screeching as they took off into the bitter night. Xam vomited over the side, the contents of his stomach hitting one of the creatures square in the face.

'Xam, stop it!' Limmy said.

'They're a protected species!' Mira added, angrily.

Once they all reached the cliff summit, Eddie the elevator operator winked as he wished them all luck and promised that not a soul would know he had seen them anywhere near the field. Ahead of them, where they last saw it, the ship occupied an area set beyond several other craft: a dim, rotund outline against the grass and distant coral-like vegetation, but the Dome appeared to be lit...

Limmy waved for everyone to follow her and they slipped quietly across the field, Rory throwing an occasional anxious glance over his shoulder in the general direction of the Towers... but not even an exo-cricetid stirred. Faintly, on a breeze scented with something that was akin to frankincense, came song:

> *Should auld acquaintance be forgot,*
> *And never brought to mind?*
> *Should auld acquaintance be forgot,*
> *And auld lang syne!*

Must be the New Year, thought Rory.

'My res'lution is tha' I never ever never never drink tha' much again!' Xam complained.

'Shh!' said Limmy and Mira in unison.

'I-Is there meant to be light on in the Dome?' Rory asked.

'Does seem ter be peculiar, right enough,' Henley agreed.

'Maybe just Beak up to something,' Limmy suggested. The ship's doctor had remained aboard, as was its wish.

After what seemed an eternity, the crew reached the *Scuabtuinne* and, indeed, the Dome was clearly lit up in a range of colours.

'Hmm, must just be Beak... yes...' Limmy muttered, using a small remote-control device to encourage the ship's ramp to lower – 'encourage', because it got stuck halfway through its rather simple sequence and both Limmy and Henley had to leap up, grab it and use their combined weight to help bring it down, which it eventually did with an uncomfortably loud thump. They all looked about warily, as though the sound would bring all of Widdershins down upon them, but the little moon remained as it was.

They scuttled up into the hold of the ship and Xam stumbled into a crate in a particularly dark corner.

'Oww,' he complained.

'For Christ's sake, Xam!' Limmy hissed.

'If he flies this ship he's going to crash and we'll all be dead,' Mira stated, matter-of-factly.

'Aye, we'll have ter let him sober up a bit before we can leave – give him some Crater coffee,' Henley added.

Rory was preoccupied. 'Shh! Do you hear that?'

Everyone paused.

'Hey! Which one o' you took my moonshine?' Xam slurred in a deeply hurt tone.

'Shut up!' everyone barked in unison.

As their silence prevailed, the distinct beat of music filled the air.

'Is that coming from…' Henley began.

'Inside the ship,' Limmy finished, gruffly. 'Beak wouldn't be listening to music. Someone else is here.'

Limmy stomped on through the doors leading into the cargo hold, stepping over lumps of the tram that still took up so much space, and Rory, Henley and Mira jogged to keep up. Xam made his way in his own time. The music grew ever louder as the crew journeyed deeper into the ship and, when they reached the Bridge, they were greeted with quite an assault on the senses. At least fifteen people – all very much like Xam in temperament and coherence – were draped across the floor and chairs, though several were dancing too – including Mr Johnson, the man who had assessed Rory in Losna House. Beak was rolling about the deck as well, trays attached in various makeshift ways to the robot doctor with empty glasses on them. Strobe lights from what looked very much like disco balls sent a multicoloured display of light spiralling around the Bridge, catching the glass of the Dome in oily splashes. And the music was extraordinarily loud – dreamy, melodic – with an ethereal, female voice singing something about an island on a moon and being carried to lands she'd never been.

'Hey! Who's playin' my music? *Who's playin' my Enya?*' Xam demanded, marching purposefully onto the Bridge before falling flat on his face.

He picked himself up – with the aid of both Limmy and Henley – before eyeing up the crowd of strangers, who seemed, slowly, to become aware that they were no longer enjoying their former privacy.

Xam pointed dangerously at the bottles in everyone's hands. '*There's* my moonshine!' He roared, quite ferociously, and perhaps it was the dark or perhaps it was the injustice of it all, but in that moment Xam seemed very much to have the size, aggression and potency of a grizzly bear protecting its den. He charged forward and it was enough to startle each and every intruder out of their collective daze and through the hatch on the opposite side of the Bridge, with Xam in pursuit.

Rory, Limmy, Henley and Mira were left alone and stunned, with Enya continuing to play on a loop.

'Mira, fire her up!' Limmy ordered, sending the little engineer scrambling over to Xam's seat, as she herself took the captain's chair.

Workstation lights flickered into life and Henley, having unsuccessfully attempted to turn the 'disco balls' off, resorted to kicking them against a wall. Rory slumped into his seat.

Not long now, Gary. We're coming… he thought, focusing all his willpower into sending this message up into space.

'Look out there – what's he up ter now?' Henley growled, pointing beyond the windows of the Dome.

Down in the grass, illuminated by the *Scuabtuinne's* now active external lighting, Xam chased his prey with a roar that could be heard through the hull of the ship. In the distance, several searchlights suddenly burned the darkfall away and came to an intense focus on the ship.

'We've been spotted!' Rory yelled.

Henley started banging his fist on the glass of the Dome. 'Get yer backside back in 'ere, Xam!'

But Xam did not need telling – not that he could hear Henley anyway – as he broke off pursuit of the intruders and tore back towards the ship. Soon, a voice crackled through on a radio above Limmy's head.

'*I'm aboard, Captain!*' said Xam, panting and sounding far soberer now for his exercise. '*Ramp's already lifting.*'

Limmy snatched up the radio and barked into it, 'On the Bridge now, navigator!'

'*Compliance!*' Xam replied.

Shortly after, he re-entered the Bridge, wheezing terribly and with a piece of grass caught in his hair. He staggered to his chair and almost squashed the retreating Mira as he collapsed into it with a huge sigh of relief.

'No time for rest. Get us starside – chop, chop!' Limmy yelled. 'We've got patrols coming in hot. And can someone turn that *damn* music off?'

Rory looked out of the glass and, sure enough, three sets of flashing lights were snaking towards them – apparently attached to small ships – like hungry eels chasing down a fat, tasty urchin.

'What's taking so long, Xam?' Limmy called, her voice a

little more controlled now – though still battling with Enya for vocal supremacy.

'I'm trying to remember the password!' he called back, clutching his hair.

'Shakedatbooty!' Limmy, Henley and Mira responded as one.

The *Scuabtuinne* rumbled over there and grunted over here, but Xam coaxed its engines into more life than Mira had managed, much like a nurse checking that an elderly man hasn't died on her ward in the night. Henley clattered into a chair beside Rory, strapping himself in.

'Brace yerself fer the spectacle,' the Whisperer growled.

The ship lurched forward, slipped back a few hundred feet and then burst forward again, weaving its way up through the Minervan sky. Rory felt as though his skin was trying to crawl inside his skeleton, and his teeth chattered against the unevenness of the ascent. The Towers disappeared. The coral forests disappeared. The mountains disappeared. The Beard appeared.

'Three patrols – lead hailing!' Mira made herself heard above the music.

'Ignore!' Limmy commanded. 'They'll break off!'

'Woo!' Xam screamed. 'This is mad! Outer planets here we come!'

Rory stared out of the Dome as the *Scuabtuinne* surged through a layer of thin cloud and then up into the oil-dark of space. Minerva dissolved into a dark curvature beyond the glass and Mira yelled something about the patrols stopping their pursuit.

Rory felt a hand gripping his wrist.

'Yer've made me very proud, rare lad, very proud,' Henley said with a strange intensity. 'Yer leading us off the compass. Naught but a few have been there because *there*, Rory... there be *monsters*!'

Henley held his eye for one deadly moment, then slapped him playfully on the back and cackled. Rory chuckled along as best he could and leaned back into his seat.

'I said turn that music off!' Limmy yelled again.

Enya responded with her instruction to sail away, sail away, sail away...

12

Asteragradon

After the *Scuabtuinne* linked up, once more, with Rongomai the muktuk, Rory managed to make contact with Gary again and established that the dim trail left by Gary's mother did indeed lead off deeper into the Solar System. With the *Scuabtuinne* reduced to little more than a defunct satellite attached to Rongomai, the crew commenced its perilous journey.

In the days following the escape from Widdershins, Rory found himself in Henley's company on Rongomai on a few occasions. On one such, they talked about what might actually await them once they reached the Gas Giants still further from the Sun.

'Though it be a rare journey, we are not the first to venture beyond Minerva,' Henley told Rory. ''Twas brave Beatrix who led a crew on that first muktuk a hundred years ago. Ter have been among those pioneers, Rory – ah!'

Rory remembered the room with the tapestries that Limmy had shown him over a month before. Mira's wonderful images had helped to paint a vivid impression in his mind of this alternative civilisation he was slowly coming to understand.

'What did she discover out there? Did she really find... monsters?' Rory asked.

Henley smiled and folded his arms, eyes flashing between his eyeliner. 'Much is said, but none are sure of *what* she found. I wager a repeat voyage would clear up any... uncertainty.' He paused, catching Rory's eye before looking away again. 'We know that she came to Poseidon, a moon of Jupiter, the surface of which may have *aerdidomiphyte* – a moss that makes it so yer can breathe. The same is true of Gilgamesh, a satellite of Uranus, said to be nestled in its icy rings. Some say there are creatures living there that have eaten the occasional explorer who fancied himself a second Beatrix. We do know that she never went beyond the kuldrevet spawning sites between Uranus and Neptune – where the muktuks gather in their hundreds, so Rongomai has conceptualised fer me.'

Rory frowned. 'But if she – if Beatrix made that journey so long ago, someone else must have gone further by now.'

Henley clapped, raising one finger. 'Well said, m'lad! And in what would have been the 1960s on Earth, after Widdershins was founded, the Chains of Engineering, Astronomy, Physics and Chemistry jointly developed a series of exo-dirigibles –'

'Of what?'

'Dirigibles – yer know, airships – only these were suited ter interplanetary journeys. And they were sent to Phobos and Deimos, the Martian moons, first of all. But then they were sent farther.'

'Like... where?'

'Into the Asteroid Belt. Towards Jupiter. Never returned

once they reached Saturn, mind. Fuelled a lot of speculation that there really *are* creatures protecting the planet. And then there was the Whiffetsnatcher…'

Rory's ears pricked up at the mention of his mum's kidnapper, and he felt a surge of anger swell in him. 'What about him?'

'Much of his exploits fell into mythology, but he –'

'Took the children he abducted to the ends of the Solar System,' Rory finished in a mumble, suddenly remembering what Limmy told him. 'To that *planet*.'

'Haligogen. That's right… if it really exists,' Henley said, nodding once. Rory noticed one corner of his mouth twitch as though in irritation and something angry seemed to move through his eyes before suddenly disappearing. 'Utter ambergris, I should think. Not that that'd stop *some* people from doing terrible things to get the truth of it… Now, come on – I picked up some marmoo juice on Minerva; reckon Gary would *lap* it up!'

The Asteroid Belt posed little trouble for a creature of Rongomai's size and he was even joined by other, wild muktuks as he dived among the star-born rubble, cresting over icy worlds that had never felt the touch of sunlight. They passed the familiar Ceres, a dwarf planet, as well as the more recently catalogued triplet moons Orna, Eshan and Shira, all slight but striking. A few times, Rory spotted other creatures of a similar size to a muktuk. There were the petratetradophidians – colossal snakelike creatures with tiny clawed legs and big mouths that burrowed through asteroids of sufficient mass to support them. Once, he saw a school of astrochrysaora – or 'darkshifters', as Xam said they were commonly known – that resembled jellyfish but blended in almost seamlessly with the pitch black of space, so much so that when their bodies fizzled and flickered in patterns of blue, it seemed as though the darkness itself was being warped.

Gary's sense of his mother's trail remained weak, though sufficient to follow. The *Scuabtuinne* travelled on past a distant Jupiter before Rongomai steered them towards Saturn, the crew starting to feel the drop in temperature as the Sun became ever more a memory. The gas giant swallowed the rest of space with its gargantuan size.

'The trail leads into the rings,' Rory explained to Xam, who was uncertain about navigating into such a tightly clustered network of rock and ice. But Limmy gave the nod and in they went.

Saturn's rugged presence generated a thick light, banks of helium-hydrogen gas billowing above further layers of hydrogen both liquid and solid. The rings around the planet were dense and the hydrogen light pooled over rocks the size of houses, icy surfaces glistening much like the heavenly bodies inside the Asteroid Belt. Mostly, though, the rings were composed of snowflake-small particles of ice, dancing about the planet like a diamond pollination.

'Why would the Whiffetsnatcher come here?' Limmy wondered out loud.

'Captain!' Xam shouted, suddenly, pointing out of the Dome. 'Over there!'

Rory followed Xam's finger, patting Gary's head as he rumbled in the back of his throat.

'It's okay, mate,' Rory mumbled.

Some distance ahead of the ship, and beyond Rongomai, was a clearing in the rings with what appeared to be thousands – no, *millions* – of creatures shooting about in a great school. Around the edge of the school were…

'Muktuks!' Rory cried. 'But what are they doing?'

'Feeding,' Limmy explained. 'They've found a shoal of kuldrevet. I never knew they bred here…'

'Well, not many have been out this far, Captain,' said Xam.

'True… But still. Take us in slowly.'

A communicator above Xam's panel crackled. 'Rongomai is doing as he pleases,' came Henley's voice, the Whisperer currently back down on the body of the creature he so revered. 'We're going in whether we want ter or not.'

'I guess Rongomai's earned a feed,' Limmy said, her tone hesitant. 'Keep a sharp eye though, Xam. Rory, you may as well take Gary for a… float about the ship. Once muktuks start feeding they tend not to stop for a while.'

Rory plodded through the ship, impatient to be underway again, Gary puffing his little helium pouches continually to generate momentum. Now that he was alone and undistracted, the intrusive thoughts flooded back into his mind and he felt a sharp guilt for having neglected his self-admonishment for some time.

Rooory, Rooory. You stopped thinking about Mum for a while there. What a bad son you are for not thinking of her all the time. Especially after what you did!

Rory's heart flashed in a brief detonation of pain and grief.

He slipped into a familiar gloom. Gary seemed to sense his pain and nuzzled him gently in the neck. Rory smiled, sadly.

'Thanks, mate.'

Gary's crystals flashed several soothing colours.

He's grown so much, Rory realised.

Indeed, the muktuk calf was now of a size not dissimilar to Rory himself, and Limmy had said more than once that it would not be long before he was too big for the ship.

Rory rounded a corner and heard whistling nearby. He soon found the entrance to the Sick Bay, with its wooden arch chiselled with floral designs. Inside, Beak was responsible for the whistling, its plague doctor mask face eerily unmoving.

'Greetings, young man,' it said. 'Can I help you?'

Rory looked from the doctor's face to its hands, in which it held Lancelot the exo-cricetid. The hamster-like creature reclined on its back and looked curiously up at Rory, nose twitching.

'What are you doing?' Rory asked, Gary echoing his sentiment with a gentle whine.

'I am maintaining my battery,' Beak replied. Gary remembered when he'd first met Beak and how Limmy had told him that the exo-cricetid ran around inside the doctor to generate energy for its robotic host. 'Lancelot requires routine maintenance, including a full disinfection and fluids infusing vitamins, proteins, sugars and carbohydrates.'

Rory watched Beak for a while, walking into Sick Bay and taking a stool. The robot was still a mystery to him and, though his head had been flooded with questions for some time, he had never found the time to seek answers.

'Where did you come from? Who made you?' Rory asked.

'I was created on Widdershins. My maker was Dr Solean,' Beak replied, picking up a tiny brush and running it down Lancelot's belly.

'And... why were you created?' Rory continued, reaching out to Gary and patting him on the head.

'Dr Solean's aim was to create a medical bot for every spaceship and exo-dirigible in Widdershins' fleet. Widdershins is still only a small colony and training people to be doctors is time-consuming. He hoped that a bot with a database of humanity's collective medical knowledge would make for an ideal doctor. I was Prototype Seven, but Dr Solean was dissatisfied with me and had me discarded.'

'That's *terrible*. What happened to you after that?'

Beak brought a peculiar milky-blue drink to Lancelot's mouth and the little creature sipped at it with whiskery slurps.

'I was discovered, on the scrapheap, by Xam. Once he understood what I was, he saw a use for me here.'

'And...' Rory lowered his eyes – 'why was Dr Solean... dissatisfied with you?'

Beak finished feeding Lancelot, lifted his poncho and replaced the exo-cricetid in its ball. It sniffed about for a moment before re-commencing its running.

'Dr Solean found that my drive was corrupted and that I struggled to process fresh data. He also described my personality drive as a "pig's ear".'

'Pig's ear?'

'I believe he meant to imply that he had made a mistake and so I was not as he had intended. My self-analysis cycle confirms that there is much that is wrong with me.'

'Like what?'

'I lack any knowledge of many medical conditions and fail to comprehend others.' It rolled on its wheel over to a shelf and began polishing some vials.

Rory dropped his head. 'You're not the only one. Even *I* don't really understand what's wrong with *me...*'

'You refer to your obsessive compulsive disorder, do you not?' Beak said.

Rory stopped stroking Gary at the blunt mention of his condition.

'This is one such condition that I do not understand. As far as my database tells me, OCD is the illogical reaction to a false worry causing the afflicted person to carry out a routine to calm themselves down.'

'Kinda... I s'pose,' Rory muttered, scratching his head.

'But if you know that a worry is false, why does it trouble you?'

'Because...' Rory searched for the right words. 'Because it's not like there's only one voice inside your head. There's one voice saying that it's stupid to worry about it. But then there's the OCD voice that says, "What if you're wrong?".'

'Does the OCD voice carry greater agency?' Beak asked, dusting a kidney dish.

'If you mean: is it stronger, then yes. I-I... can't ignore it.'

'That sounds *weird*,' came a voice from the back of Sick Bay, behind a curtain.

'Mira?' Rory spluttered, recognising the engineer's voice.

The curtain withdrew and Mira appeared, sitting on a bed with a large, half-finished tapestry sheet.

'Why were you listening like that? That's rude,' Rory said, angrily.

Mira shrugged, her eyes empty. 'I didn't mean to. You think I did though, don't you?'

'Master Hobble? Miss Mira?' Beak interrupted. 'Something–'

'Clearly that's what you were doing. That was private stuff! Y'know, patient-doctor confidentiality,' Rory snapped. 'You're a sneaker.'

'Master Hobble? Miss Mira? I really think –'

'No, I'm not!' Mira exploded, startling Rory.

'Children! There appears to be a problem,' Beak said, firmly, pointing to the Sick Bay door.

Rory and Mira turned as one to find a sickly, greenish-yellow gas seeping in from the hallway. Gary whined and retreated backwards into the depths of Sick Bay.

'What *is* that?' Rory asked, a note of panic in his voice.

'*Bridge, this is Beak. Come in, Bridge*,' Beak said into a standalone voice transmitter. Its message was met only with silence and it tried again, but there was still silence.

'Both of you must take precautionary measures,' Beak said, wheeling its way over to a cupboard and withdrawing two face masks. 'We do not know what is in that gas, and I advise caution.'

Rory and Mira scrambled over to Beak, strapping the masks over their faces as quickly as they could. Gary cried out as he was engulfed by the gas and he dropped to the floor with a hollow *thunk*.

'Gary!' Rory yelled, running over to the muktuk. But the creature was inflating and deflating gently, suggesting he was at least still alive.

'You must get up to the Bridge and find out what is going on,' Beak called, retreating further as the gas approached.

'Come with us, Beak!' Rory pleaded, tearing himself away from Gary.

'I would not make it very far. Alas, the only face mask I have suitable for Lancelot is in the Cargo Bay. It is up to you, children.'

Mira darted forward, dragging Rory out of Sick Bay and into the hallway. The gas seemed to fill the whole ship, though it was mercifully not so thick as to make it difficult to see; instead, it was a thin mist. The *Scuabtuinne* was eerily quiet, apart from the creaking of joists and other distant outside noises, like small rocks smacking against the hull.

'I don't like this one bit,' Mira mumbled, but it was she who led Rory, occasionally directing him in which way to go.

'Have you ever seen anything like it?' Rory asked.

'Nuh-uh. If it got into the ship then it must have come from the umbilical leading down onto Rongomai – there's no other way anything could get into the ship from outside, otherwise the ship would depressurise and we'd all be dead,' Mira reasoned.

They were thrown into the wall and to the floor as the whole ship seemed to take a hit from one side.

'Now *that* wasn't good!' Rory said, pulling himself up. He offered Mira a hand but she swatted it away.

'Come on, we need to hurry,' Mira replied, racing off up the passageway.

Finally, they came to the Bridge and burst through the doors to find it dark inside, with both Limmy and Xam unconscious in their respective seats. Mira ran over to Limmy and furiously shook her, pleading with her to wake, but she did not. Rory crept towards the glass of the Dome and looked out on to a sea of what looked to be the same gas, obscuring much of Saturn and, menacingly, robbing the particles in the planet's rings of their sheen.

All was still, otherwise.

Then he heard a beeping coming from Xam's station so he ran over to find out what it was. A big red circular button flashed red and beeped – underneath the button were the words **UMBILICAL INTEGRITY**. But before he had had a chance to respond to it, the *Scuabtuinne* rocked again and the ship-end of the umbilical floated up in front of the Dome. The **UMBILICAL INTEGRITY** button stopped flashing and was replaced by a button next to it saying **DEPRESSURISATION**.

'Mira! What do I do?' Rory yelled.

Mira marched down and grabbed Xam, trying to shift his not insubstantial weight. 'You going to help me or not?' she snapped.

Rory grabbed hold of Xam as well and, together, they managed to heave him out of the chair, into which Mira confidently hopped. She flicked several switches, pressed a few more buttons and the **DEPRESSURISATION** button stopped flashing.

'I think we're safe now,' Mira said, her voice muffled behind her mask.

Rory looked up and something caught his eye outside the Dome: several wild muktuks appeared and swam towards a concentration of rocks in the distance. Suddenly, a monstrous creature shot up from a denser pocket of gas underneath the muktuks and grabbed a juvenile in its city-spanning jaws, biting it in half and swallowing a chunk in one go. Both Rory and Mira screamed.

'What the hell is *that*!?' Rory yelled.

Mira leaned forward, her breath fast and stuttering. 'It's... I think it's an asteragradon.'

'A *what*?'

'Asteragradon. Like an Earth mosasaur – you know, one of those things with a crocodile head and four big flippers – but in space. They're said to hunt muktuks.'

The asteragradon heaved its ample body fully up above the gas, with the grace of a synchronised swimmer. It was hard to tell just how big it was from this distance, but Rory guessed it to be at least as voluminous as a muktuk, if not heavier still. Six gigantic flippers propelled it through the vacuum, the membranous tissue firing with a network of golden fireworks. Its body was armoured and a line of green funnels arched across its back, gas pouring forth from them. A set of jaws made up perhaps a third of its total length and it did not seem to have any eyes.

Rory rushed to the Dome's glass, pressing himself against it and looking down over Rongomai – the muktuk was motionless, suggesting that it too had succumbed to the gas.

'We need to do something. Rongomai's just floating,' Rory said, turning to face Mira. 'If that *thing* out there sees Rongomai, then it will gobble him up!'

'What do you expect *me* to do? Get out and push?' Mira retaliated. 'Don't matter, so long as it doesn't know we're here.'

But the asteragradon's behaviour altered: it lifted its head, moving it about as though looking for something – though still, apparently, it could not see. It opened its jaws and its throat ballooned, like a frog croaking. To Rory's horror, it turned to face Rongomai and the *Scuabtuinne* before shooting off from its position and meandering towards them.

Rory backed away from the glass. 'It'll eat Rongomai for sure and then us!'

Rory ran back up to Mira and gesticulated to her, urging her to do something, *anything*. Mira didn't react well and pushed Rory away. When they next looked out of the Dome, the asteragradon was gone.

'Oh my God!' Mira squealed.

Rory scanned the heavens. 'I can't see it anywhere…'

The Dome began to darken… Any Saturnian light that had been illuminating the Bridge was extinguished. Rory looked up and saw the inside of a jaw moving over the *Scuabtuinne*.

'We're in its mouth!' Rory roared.

Mira reacted instinctively, hammering a few buttons and grabbing the control joysticks, pulling them back with ferocity – sending the ship hurtling forwards and Rory hurtling backwards. The jaw started to close and, for a moment, it looked as though the *Scuabtuinne* wouldn't make it, but it slipped between two sets of teeth and out into Saturn's rings.

'Now what?' Rory demanded, rubbing the back of his head where he had hit it against a rail.

'Now we hope that the asteragradon is bloated after its meal… I'm no pilot.'

The *Scuabtuinne* speared through several smaller chunks of rock and ice, before plummeting into a deeper patch of Saturn's rings. The asteragradon pursued hotly, Rory spotting its shadow falling over larger asteroids ahead.

'We can't keep this up and I don't know what I'm doing!'

Mira yelled in a fit of anger and frustration. 'If that monster doesn't get us then I'll crash us into a rock!'

'You're doing fine! Just –'

But Rory and Mira screamed as one and grabbed onto each other as the asteragradon rose up ahead of them and opened its jaws once more, the *Scuabtuinne* flying straight into its mouth. Rory opened his eyes and disentangled himself from Mira, who shoved him off.

'We're still alive…' Mira whispered.

'What do we do now?' Rory replied, his voice equally quiet.

He looked out of the Dome. Everything was pitch black, though the Bridge's dull lighting illuminated several strands of green saliva dribbling down the glass.

'Turn a light on,' Rory suggested.

Mira pressed a button but, instead of a light, a set of enormous windscreen wipers rubbed the saliva into the Dome's glass. She pressed the button again and then tried a different one. Suddenly, the beast's throat lit up like a cinema at the end of a film.

'Oh, wow!' Rory said, looking out.

The throat was a cavernous pink vault of glistening flesh disappearing off into a dark recess. Thick tendrils of oozing, milky-green fluid dangled from the roof like stalactites. Chunks of flesh littered the floor.

'We can't go back out of its mouth,' Mira said. 'We don't have much choice but to carry on.'

'Perhaps there'll be another way out,' Rory replied.

'Yes… once nature takes its course.'

Rory paused. 'We are *not* flying out of this thing's *bum*!'

Mira shrugged, gripping the control joysticks and pulling them back, gently.

The *Scuabtuinne* travelled on further into the creature's anatomy, like a fly in a cathedral. Eventually, the ship came to a division, the throat splitting off in two directions – in one, a tunnel carried on down into darkness; in the other a hefty flap of skin seemed to cover a second tunnel.

'Guess we don't have much choice,' Rory said.

Mira sent the ship down the open tunnel and, before long, another of the buttons on her control console flashed and beeped – this one said **EXTERNAL TEMPERATURE**.

'Something down here disagrees with the hull,' Mira muttered.

Rounding a corner, the tunnel opened into what was, essentially, a cave... a cave with a broiling, steaming lake of fluid glinting green and brown in the ship's light. The flashing, beeping button flashed and beeped all the more.

'We're in its stomach...' Rory said, half horrified and half fascinated.

'Not for long,' Mira responded, shifting some more controls, which twirled the *Scuabtuinne* around and fired it back up the way it had come. Eventually, the excited button on the console calmed itself and returned to its former dormancy.

Soon enough, they came back to the crossroads in the creature's throat and Mira hit her head back against the chair.

'We're not getting out the natural way,' Rory said, sighing with relief and folding his arms.

Mira tapped a finger on her face mask where it covered her chin, keeping quiet for a few moments before speaking. 'That blocked passage must lead to its lungs. I'm thinking that maybe it breathes like muktuks do.'

'… How do they breathe?' Rory asked, once he realised that Mira wasn't going to volunteer the information.

'How do you not know that? They need oxygen like us – but also methane – and so they dive into the atmosphere of a planet or a moon with those gases, take a big gulp, and hold their breath as they cross the stars. Their bodies absorb and use the oxygen and methane very slowly, so they can go months without taking another breath. To keep the air in their lungs, their windpipes are covered with a muscle that seals the gas in.'

'How do *you* know all that?'

'I read. Humans have known about muktuks for a hundred years, so we've learned a thing or two.'

'How does any of this help us now, though?' Rory asked, exasperated.

Mira paused. 'It doesn't.'

Rory sucked his teeth and flopped onto the floor, displacing the green mist around him and pressing the palms of his hands into the mask covering his cheeks, his breath heating his lips. As far as he could see, their situation was hopeless. His thoughts drifted back to his mum and the realisation that he had failed in his mission to rescue her. His heart raced and the guilt exploded in his head, filling every crevice of his mind like the poisonous gas back out in space, overcoming him.

Rory snapped out of his train of thought, clapped and leapt up.

'The gas! What does it use its gas for?' he asked. Mira looked blankly up at him. 'When the asteragradon attacked those muktuks, they were still moving – they hadn't been knocked out. But everyone on this ship who breathed it in is unconscious, even Gary. That's just a side effect – it's not the reason the asteragradon uses it.'

'… Maybe not,' Mira conceded.

'I don't know why it uses the gas – maybe it confuses some muktuk sense that we don't even know about – but the fact is that if it's breathed in, it will knock a person or a creature right out! Does this ship have a venting system, some way of getting rid of all this gas?'

Mira stirred. 'Yes… But it can't be done from the Bridge.'

'Okay! We need to get inside this monster's lungs,' Rory said, grinning.

Mira's expression intensified. 'I see what you're thinking.'

She flicked some switches, grabbed hold of the control joysticks and steered the *Scuabtuinne* down towards the closed windpipe.

'We need to create an opening in the muscle,' Rory said.

'On it,' Mira replied, blowing some dust off another joystick with a little targeting screen above it. She looked back at Rory. 'Hardly been used before.'

Grabbing the joystick, Mira clicked a button and the screen flashed into life in all its black-and-white glory. **WELCOME TO YOUR PENDLETON LASER 1987 (AF29) EDITION!** the targeting screen read. **DO YOU WISH TO PROGRESS TUTORIAL? Y/N** it continued.

'Looks like it's *never* been used,' Rory quipped.

Mira huffed, flicking through the screens until the viewer showed a grainy image of the muscle covering the asteragradon's windpipe. She wasted no time in firing up the laser and, outside the ship, Rory saw a thin, orange energy beam shooting off into the creature's flesh and burning an opening. The *Scuabtuinne* rocked about, perhaps as a result of the monster shuddering in discomfort.

'Careful…' Rory urged.

'I *am* being careful,' Mira snapped.

Soon enough, she had burnt a hole big enough for the ship to slip through into the windpipe. The passage was much the same as the one leading down into the stomach, only there was no temperature alert this time. They travelled on for a minute and came to a cavern with what looked like enormous roots running all over the walls, tapering off into little sacs.

'Alveoli,' Rory said, remembering his Biology class at school.

'What?' Mira replied.

'Alveoli. Where the oxygen goes before it gets into the bloodstream. Take the ship over to the nearest one. Uh, please?'

Mira did as Rory asked and brought the *Scuabtuinne* to a halt beside a cluster of alveoli.

'Okay, we need to vent the gas now,' Rory told her.

Mira jumped up and ran off without a word.

Rory settled into his usual seat on the Bridge, but not before checking Limmy and Xam for a pulse again – all was well – and then their mouths – they were both breathing, steadily. If this plan worked, the asteragradon could react badly and they would have to escape quickly, else they might be crushed or splattered on the windpipe wall.

'Rory! Come in!' Mira's voice sounded from Xam's console.

Rory scrabbled over to the communicator. 'I'm here.'

Pause. 'Okay. I've reached the flush valves down in Engineering. Once I release them, the air on board will be sucked out.'

Rory's eyes bulged. *I must have misheard that.* 'What did you say?'

'I said two things.'

'You said the air will be sucked out. It's going to be a bit difficult to survive if we can't, y'know, *breathe.*'

'There'll still be enough oxygen for a few hours... if I time this right.'

Rory cried out. '*If* you time –'

'Done it,' Mira interrupted.

All at once, red lights flashed across the Bridge and a grating alarm signalled that something noteworthy was taking place. Rory gripped the chair, his body pulled backwards with the sudden ship-wide semi-depressurisation. It felt as though the world was going to end, but the sickly gas thinned out. Suddenly, the force playing against his body disappeared and the red lights and alarm disappeared.

Once the shaking in his limbs had stopped, Rory looked beyond the Dome's windows to see the yellow-green gas drifting slowly towards the cluster of alveoli. He muttered under his breath, 'Come on, come on, come on,' urging it to find its mark. An eternity seemed to pass, but the gas reached the alveoli. A noise beyond the *Scuabtuinne* – a titanic roar – sent the asteragradon's lungs vibrating and the ship lurched back. Rory cried out, but the noise didn't stop.

'What's happening?' Mira yelled, tripping over herself as she stamped back onto the Bridge, panting as though she had just run a marathon.

'I dunno – but I think it's working!' Rory yelled back, pulling himself with some difficulty out of the navigator's seat so Mira could jump back in.

She jabbed at several buttons, grabbed at the control joysticks and spun the *Scuabtuinne* round one hundred and eighty degrees, Rory flying backwards off his feet. He picked himself up and dived into his seat, buckling himself in.

'Hold on,' Mira warned.

Dragging the control joysticks back again, Mira sent the *Scuabtuinne* rocketing up towards the monster's windpipe, the fleshy walls all around them contracting and bouncing off the hull of the ship, which continued its ascent towards the little lasered hole in the muscle. But a jerk from the asteragradon at the wrong moment threw the *Scuabtuinne* heavily into the windpipe wall – it tumbled through the hole in the muscle but crashed into the floor of the creature's throat with a skid and a splosh of gelatinous lumps, sliding along until it came to a stop teetering over the brink of the tunnel… leading down into the stomach.

'No! No! No!' Mira barked, repeatedly slamming her fists onto the control console.

Rory touched his forehead, pulling his fingers away to find blood.

'I need to reboot the system,' Mira snapped, unbuckling her seat harness, leaping up and running over to her usual position on the port side of the Bridge. 'I think we've only stalled. If I can just get us…'

The **EXTERNAL TEMPERATURE** button flashed again. Rory glanced at it, looked at Mira and then leapt across to the Dome's glass and peered down the asteragradon's throat. In the dark below, a green-brown surge of fluid came thundering up.

'It's gonna barf!' Rory yelled, swinging round to face Mira.

'Get in Xam's seat – *quick*!' the little engineer said.

Rory didn't need telling twice. He hopped in, buckled up and took hold of the control joysticks in the way he'd observed both Xam and Mira do.

Mira flicked several switches and pulled at a choke again and again.

The *Scuabtuinne* shuddered, rumbled, failed.

Shuddered, rumbled, failed.

Shuddered, rumbled –

'Hurry up!' Rory shouted. The **EXTERNAL TEMPERATURE** button flashed deliriously fast. 'We're gonna be cooked!'

Mira gave the choke one more heave and… the Bridge fizzled into life, a network of lights flickering on.

'Now! Now! Now!' Mira roared.

Rory hadn't much of an idea what he was doing, but he had watched Xam plenty of times and, besides, if Mira could do it then why couldn't he? He pulled back on the joysticks, firing the ship over the tunnel leading to the creature's stomach, and swung it viciously to port as a tidal wave of vomit erupted. The *Scuabtuinne* darted out of the way – just in time – and hurtled up the throat, into the mouth itself and towards the opening jaws.

Xam quite suddenly woke, stood up, took one look out of the Dome and passed out again.

With a whoop of excitement, Rory sent the ship screaming past the asteragradon's teeth just as a torrent of sick emptied into space like a green nebula of acid, chunks of muktuk and who knew what else. Rory and Mira cheered as one, and cheered all the more as they spotted Rongomai wending its way towards them, the gas that had sent it to sleep drifting away now. The radio crackled and a voice came through.

'*– in, Xam! Come in, Xam! Where are yer, yer overbuilt, bumbling ball of a –*'

'Henley? It's me! It's Rory!' Rory replied, ripping off his facemask at last and laughing into the console communicator.

'R-Rory?' the Muktuk Whisperer stuttered. 'What's goin' on up there?'

'It's a long story. But first, let's reconnect the umbilical, else there'll be no one left to tell you.'

13

The Tornits of Lepidus

Weeks passed in the wake of the attack by the asteragradon, but all returned to relative normality. The umbilical was successfully reattached, though doing so required Xam to wiggle into a spacesuit that made him look like a hippopotamus stuffed into a sandwich bag. No one had been permanently harmed by the gas – at least as far as Beak could tell – and even little Lancelot returned to his former furious furry ferocity, running around inside the doctor's chest.

Mira's good humour proved temporary and, before long, Rory found she had shrunk back into her own little bubble, making angry faces at him whenever he greeted her in a corridor. He wondered what he had done to upset her, but was at a loss and, of course, his anxious mind concocted all manner of reasons as to why she wanted nothing to do with him. On the more plausible end, he imagined that he may have said something spiteful to her (though he had no recollection of having done so), and on the more fantastical end he decided on one very bad day that he was somehow responsible for her left arm being irradiated and she was angry that he had hurt her so severely. As with all of his intrusive thoughts, part of him knew them to be absurd, but the more emotionally-charged side of him could not overcome the raw guilt, doubt and self-loathing.

And what did not help Rory was the sheer length of time that it took to get *anywhere* in space. The journey from Earth to Minerva had taken just over a month, which in itself had only been possible due to the near-miraculous abilities of Rongomai the muktuk. But now that they were beyond Saturn, the distance between planetary systems was immense, which gave space for his fears to fester. So, as kuldrevet breed beyond the atmosphere of planets, so too did upsetting thoughts breed within the atmosphere of Rory's mind.

As the *Scuabtuinne* and Rongomai dived deeper into the frosty reaches of the Solar System, the crew began to feel the effects. The ship itself was cold to the point where everyone wore extra layers of clothing to keep warm – the residual heat from Rongomai and the ship's *porphuragate* engine no longer sufficient to keep the temperature comfortable. Even on Rongomai, a light dusting of snow covered the creature's forests and the plains surrounding the pyramid. 'Yer think this is bad, m'lad?' Henley had said. 'Just wait till we're even farther out and the Sun is just a speck!' But Gary continued to track his mother – even all the way out here – and the crew carried on.

It was on one particularly bitter day, as the *Scuabtuinne* approached the planet Uranus, that Rory found himself in the ship's cafeteria, alone, slurping up a kuldrevet and mukchili broth. The cafeteria was tiny, consisting of little more than a large table with built-in stools (much like those he once sat on at school in the dinner hall) with an open-plan, rundown kitchen. The broth was a specialty of Xam's and he had made it the previous night for the crew – Rory, still very cold, decided that it would be perfect reheated and inside his belly.

He was sitting, minding his own business, when Mira stormed in and noisily poured herself some green juice before snatching at some fruit and dropping into a seat at the opposite end of the table to Rory.

Rory, naturally curious, could not help himself. 'Y–You alright?'

But Mira – quite dramatically, he felt – shielded her face by slamming an elbow onto the table and plunging her head into the crook of her arm.

Rory was not sure what to do, so he continued to slurp his broth, quite deliberately looking anywhere but at Mira.

'Stop looking at me!'

Rory swung his head back round to face the little engineer. 'What?'

Mira made a noise of frustration. 'You heard me!'

'Umm… no, I –'

'Yes, you did!'

Rory decided that to argue his point further would be pointless.

Footsteps approached the cafeteria and Limmy came in.

'Oh, hi kids,' she said, looking from one child to the other. 'Not disturbing a deep and fulfilling conversation, am I?'

Mira huffed. Rory grinned at Limmy, who walked into the kitchen area, grabbed a piece of fruit herself and tossed it from one hand to the other.

'Y'know,' Limmy continued, 'back on Earth, as a social

worker, I sometimes had to do something called mediation between two people who *really* couldn't see eye to eye. Mediation means that I would try and get people to be honest about their feelings and resolve any disagreements they had.'

Mira moved her head out of her arm a bit and took little bites of her fruit.

'You're the only kids on board,' Limmy added, coming over to sit at the table. 'So, you should get along.'

'Well, *he* keeps looking at me and I don't like it,' Mira snapped.

'Nuh-uh! I really didn't!' Rory retorted. 'You just came in here and got all huffy with me.'

'Okay!' Limmy said, raising her voice above the children's. 'Mira, it sounds like you were a bit upset – like I know you sometimes can be, which is fine – but why don't you say what's bothering you and maybe Rory can help.'

Mira's head dipped and, when she spoke, the words flew out of her mouth. '*Someone*-came-and-moved-my-thread!'

'What?' Rory said.

Mira bristled.

'Okay, could you say that a little slower, Mira?' Limmy asked, patiently.

'I said, someone moved my thread!'

'Your thread?' Rory repeated.

'Yes!'

Limmy ran a hand across her forehead. 'Where did you last see your thread?'

'In my room,' Mira hissed.

'Do you mean your quarters or the tapestry room?'

'The tapestry room! Why would it be in my quarters?'

'Okay, okay,' Limmy said, holding her hands up as though to placate her. 'Why don't you and Rory go look for it there?'

'I've already looked... and I'm not letting *him* in.'

'I'm sure Rory can use his Spidey senses to help though!' Limmy said, grinning. 'I've got to get up to the Bridge anyway.'

'Rory's *not* a spider!'

'I'd really like to see your tapestries again – they were cool,' Rory braved.

Limmy looked from Rory to Mira. 'How about that then? Rory help you look? Will you do that for me? I am your captain and *could* order you.'

Mira paused, then, '*Fine!*'

She got up and dragged her feet away and out of the cafeteria.

Limmy motioned to Rory, mouthing 'Go!'

Rory took one longing look at the remnants of his broth then got up and ran off out of the cafeteria and up the corridor, catching up with Mira, who had already sprung on ahead.

'Hey, not so fast!'

Mira grunted.

'Where did you last see it?'

'What?'

'The thread.'

'I don't remember, okay!?'

'... Okay.'

The pair carried on in silence for several minutes until they reached the doors barring the tapestry room. On the door was a big message reading **GO AWAY**. Mira slid the door open and marched in. Rory followed her.

He remembered the last time he'd been in the tapestry room – soon after coming aboard the *Scuabtuinne* for the first time. He had been thrilled by the sheer splendour of Mira's tapestries – work that a far older person would have been proud to call their own. Ever since being thrown out that time by Mira, he had wanted desperately to return and spend a good many hours simply reading the tapestry to absorb this secret history of humanity.

'They *really* are amazing, y'know,' Rory said, quietly, but Mira was already rummaging through a mess of materials, presumably hunting for her thread.

Rory sighed. 'Tell me what I'm looking for then, else there's no point in me being –'

'Big box. Lots of thread. Different colours.'

That's probably the best I'm gonna get from her..., he decided.

Rory sidled over to another pile of mess in a corner opposite Mira and commenced his hunt. It was very little time before he discovered a box with a heap of threads inside – the full spectrum of the rainbow.

'Found it.'

He heard movement behind him and Mira's hand briefly appeared as it snapped the box shut – Rory's fingers narrowly avoiding amputation – and pulled it away from him entirely.

'Thank you, Rory,' Rory said, sarcastically, turning to face her.

Mira made a face and stomped across to the other side of the room where a half-finished panel of tapestry lay on the wooden floor. She *thlumped* herself down, quite violently, opened the box of threads and rifled through them.

Rory got up and looked around the tapestry room – he

thought he may as well take the opportunity before Mira told him to leave. He reflected on the last time he had been here and recalled the section he had reached: '1947 – Prototype R Crashes in Roswell, New Mexico'. He looked along to the next illustration, which appeared to show a nuclear bomb and a number of muktuks swimming up into the sky. The writing above it read: '1949 – Detonation of Soviet Union's First Nuclear Missile'. He didn't quite know what was meant by 'Soviet Union', but he thought it had something to do with Russia many, many years ago.

Moving on to the next panel, the writing said: '1951 – Launch of the *Aeneas*'. The word *Aeneas* was familiar and, at last, he recalled that it was the name of that submarine-like craft buried in the cliff in the middle of Widdershins. *It was the ship that took them away from Earth all the way to Minerva…* The picture showed the *Aeneas* with crystals projecting from its stern, lit up, and, towards the front, two muktuks pulling it up from the surface of the Earth. The muktuks were both connected to the ship by umbilicals – just like with the *Scuabtuinne* and Rongomai.

The next panel along, titled: '1952 – The Colony of Widdershins is Established' showed Widdershins with only a few small buildings in it, a great number of marmoos and people moving about and pointing everywhere. A number of panels then showed various other key events, such as the establishment of the Cosmic Commission, the development of the Towers and the completion of the first interplanetary exo-dirigible. But Rory's attention was magnetised, instead, to a panel that seemed entirely out of place.

In a corner of the room, the thread-work image of a little

boy hunched and covering his head stood out against all the other images of advancement, achievement and discovery. Two figures stood behind the boy: a man and a woman. The writing above the image read: '1965 – The Clavius Scandal'. In the next image, the two figures seemed to be leaving Widdershins with a crowd behind them pointing out and away from the colony. Rory turned to Mira, eager to ask for more information, but he dared not draw attention to himself and resolved, instead, to ask Limmy or Henley later. Indeed, the next several tapestry images suggested something quite terrible happened between 1965 and 1974, involving not just this one solitary child, but others as well.

Tearing himself away, he decided to try once more to talk to Mira and risk being ejected from the room.

'H-Hey, is everything there then?' he asked, walking up behind the engineer and looking over her shoulder at the box of threads.

'Yes,' Mira said, as though the answer was the most obvious thing in the world.

Rory could not see the image Mira was working on at that moment, but he followed the tapestry backwards and was surprised to find a few panels illustrating *her* life. His eyes greedily took in as much as they could, not stopping too long over a single image, but rather flitting over several panels at once: '2010 – My Birth Day' was accompanied by an image of a man and a woman holding a baby. In the background was the outline of India with a star marking somewhere in the north with the words 'Uttar Pradesh' beside them. He skipped a few panels as his attention was drawn to '2015 – Mummy and Daddy Lost', which showed the same man and woman from the 2010 pane behind some kind of fence. On the other side of the fence, a little dark-skinned girl reached out to them.

'What are you doing!?' Mira yelled.

Rory jumped. 'I… I… umm, I just –'

Mira leapt up, like a jaguar ready to pounce. 'You're not *allowed* to look at those! Go!'

Rory was suddenly angry and stood his ground. 'Hey! All I did was try to help you. I just wanted to be friends. Why'd you have to be so *weird* all the time?'

Mira burst into tears, but carried on screaming, 'Get out!', shoving Rory back towards the door with surprising strength.

Rory's mind was filled with the memory of that final scene back home with Mum – she, too, had told him to get out. At last, he tripped and fell backwards out of the tapestry room, the door slamming shut with a fearful bang. His anger quickly subsided and the guilt took hold.

Rooory, Rooory. You've really done it now. You said mean things to her and now she's upset. What if she kills herself because of you?

Rory clutched his head, pleading with the voice to stop. Inside the tapestry room, he could hear Mira sobbing. He wanted to reach out and try to make her see that he hadn't meant to be unkind, but he knew that doing so would just upset her all over again.

I need Limmy, he thought, scrabbling to his feet and running off through the corridors towards the Bridge. All he knew was that he had to help Mira and the best person to support him to do that now would be Limmy. His mind filled with horrible images of Mira doing something terrible to herself and it was all he could do to fight back the tears.

And that's when he heard it.

The communications system throughout the ship screeched into life and Xam's voice called out, '*Everyone to the Bridge at once! This is an amber situation! Yep, not had one of those in a while. Most definitely not a drill, though – nope, nope, nope!*'

The communications system screeched offline and Rory was left in silence. *What kind of emergency could there be?* He wondered, for one alarming moment, whether the asteragradon had returned, but the ship wasn't filling up with gas like last time. A few stray pillows scurried out of bedrooms and made towards the front of the ship. The air conditioning rattled also, with the sound of creatures pitter-pattering – again towards the front of the ship. Rory took one last look behind him back in the direction of Engineering and the tapestry room, wondering whether he should go and get Mira, but decided that that would simply provoke her. So, instead, he broke into a run towards the Bridge.

Rory burst onto the Bridge, out of breath, drawing the attention of Limmy (in her captain's chair), Xam (in his navigator's seat) and Henley, who was standing beside Gary – the muktuk hovering several feet above the ground with Limmy's dressing gown draped over him.

'You okay, kid?' Limmy asked, her breath crystallising in the cold air.

Rory shook his head. 'I upset Mira and she's crying in the tapestry room but it was an accident and I never meant to do it it's just that I wanted to see her pictures and now I think she may kill –'

'Whoa, whoa, whoa!' Limmy said, holding her hands out. 'Mira's upset?'

'Yes! What if she does –'

'She gets upset quite a lot,' Xam interrupted. 'Sometimes she does cry.'

Rory looked from Xam back to Limmy.

'I know how this sounds,' the captain continued, 'but the best thing we can do is leave her be for a while, so she can calm herself down. She can jump between moods very quickly – as you know.'

Rory felt that knot of guilt in his chest loosen a little. As with any attempt to seek reassurance, he was far happier to rely on the opinion of *anyone* other than himself. He couldn't trust his own inner voice, after all, but the rational voice of someone else was usually strong enough to subdue his OCD… at least for a while.

'Come on, m'lad – grab a chair and take a gander at what we've found,' Henley growled, patting his usual seat.

'O-Okay.'

Rory took the proffered chair, scratched Gary on the head and took a deep breath. Everyone else turned back to face out of the Dome – its glass frosted on the inside. There, in front of them, was the gas giant Uranus: a startling marble, still, in the indifference of space – only a faded turquoise in colour, quiet and temperate. Cold.

'It's so… lonely,' Rory muttered, leaning forwards.

'In Greek myth, Uranus was born out of Gaea, who was born out of Chaos,' Henley remarked. 'With only Gaea fer company, he must have been lonely, yes.'

'Why are we at amber alert?' Rory asked.

'Technically, we're not,' Limmy interrupted, 'because *someone* hasn't made the mushrooms yellow.'

From the way she was glaring at Henley, Rory could tell whose job that was supposed to have been.

Henley growled. 'We all know yer put us on an amber alert. Why'd I have ter change the colours…?'

But he obediently slumped away towards the first of four large mushroom lights on the Bridge, squirting a strange black ink over the first, which turned its dull blue glow to a heavy amber.

'Why are we on amber alert anyway?' Rory queried. 'That's like: not bad enough to be red, but something's wrong, right?'

Limmy pointed out of the Dome. '*That's* why we're on amber.'

Rory looked out of the glass again and watched as the *Scuabtuinne* descended into what seemed to be a field of ice and rock.

'We're in…'

'The planet's rings, yes,' Limmy finished Rory's sentence. 'But that is not the reason for the amber alert. Tell me, Mr Space Brain – how many moons does Uranus have?'

Rory thought about it, ignoring Henley's rather loud curse as he dropped a vial of ink beside the fourth mushroom. 'Twenty… Twenty-five– No! Twenty-seven.'

'And our survey says: *eh-eh*!' Limmy replied. 'Conventionally, yes, but if you look over there…' She pointed to an object half-hidden in shadow, though the glittering from its surface set it out against the dark. '…you will see the thirty-third moon – all the other newbies are all over the shop.'

Rory continued to look. Uranus's reflected light streamed

across the sea of its rings in front of the object, illuminating a glimmering, oily palette of ice, but only a raggedly uneven crescent of the thirty-third moon was lit. There was something menacing about it, slunk back in the shadow.

'What is its name?' Rory asked.

'Lepidus,' Limmy replied. 'Each of Uranus's moons are named after a character in Shakespeare or Alexander Pope. This brooding little guy is Lepidus, of Shakespeare's *Julius Caesar* and *Antony and Cleopatra*. I can't say Shakespeare ever did it for me, kid, so I couldn't tell you much about old Leppy.'

Henley sighed, turned on his heel as he 'ambered' another mushroom, and quoted:

'I must not think there are
Evils enow to darken all his goodness:
His faults in him seem as the spots of heaven,
More fiery by night's blackness; hereditary,
Rather than purchased; what he cannot change,
Than what he chooses.'

Xam clapped. 'Dude! That was *deep*. Who said it?'

'Shakespeare, you prat!' Henley snapped.

Xam ducked his head. 'Oh, right...'

'I still don't see why we're on amber alert,' Rory said, bringing the subject back to its point.

Limmy drew a breath. 'Well –'

'There are stories,' Henley interrupted, 'so it goes, of *creatures* that live on some of Uranus's yonder moons, Lepidus among 'em. Creatures that will eat any careless traveller who happens upon the Uranian system. These creatures are called tornits.'

Rory was alarmed. 'B–But how would anyone know if only the Whiffetsnatcher has been out this far before?'

"Cos –'

"Cos the Whiffetsnatcher brought many stories back with him to Widdershins,' Limmy said, interrupting Henley this time. 'And one of them was of the various species he encountered out in the cold recesses of the Solar System. Tornits were among the more fantastical and the story spread and was exaggerated over time.'

'It's said that the Whiffetsnatcher made a deal with the tornits,' Xam added, in a hushed voice. 'That if *he* and his crew were granted safe passage, then the tornits could capture and consume *any* person who ever followed him. Shady geezer, eh?'

Rory looked back out of the Dome at Lepidus, its icy surface still glittering in the dark. He imagined all manner of horrors ready to burst forth from the cold shadow.

'Why are we here then?' he asked.

Limmy sniffed. 'Henley will tell you that.'

Henley poured ink over the final mushroom, the colour of it promptly blurring from blue to amber. 'Rongomai needs ter take another deep breath – he's low on air.'

'And Lepidus is the one moon that has air?' Rory asked.

'Lepidus and a few others – though the stories speak of tornits on all the moons with air,' Henley added, apparently guessing his thinking.

'Rongomai can just take a big breath from the upper atmosphere, right?' Rory suggested. 'No need to land on Lepidus and then no need to fear these… tornits.'

Henley crossed the Bridge and gave Gary a playful scratch

on the head. 'Yer'd think that, m'lad, but there's one thing we haven't mentioned about the tornits yet –' He stopped talking and his eyes darted about, looking all over the ceiling. 'Shh! D'yer hear that?'

Everyone listened, silent.

Limmy sighed. 'There's nothing, Henley. Stop trying to –'

This time, they all heard it: the sound of thudding on the hull.

'There!' Rory shouted, pointing out of the Dome, as a dark shape crossed a pane of glass.

A thick crackle slipped from the radio above Xam's head, making everyone jump. '*Limmy!*' came Mira's voice.

'Mira?' Limmy mumbled, before leaping off her chair and snatching up the radio. 'Mira! Mira, are you there?'

'*Limmy, help!*'

'Mira! Hold on! Where are you!?'

Mira's next response was a scream. Rory clapped a hand over his mouth. There was a deep, energetic snorting sound and then the radio cut off entirely.

Silence.

'What. The. Hell. Was. That…' Xam muttered.

'Our cue!' Henley roared, drawing his knife before leaping past Gary and taking to the corridors of the ship.

Rory shook himself out of what seemed a nightmare. 'I'm coming too!'

Gary screeched and shot after him.

'Rory, no!' Limmy cried, trying to grab him.

But he was gone.

The ship seemed altogether darker now that he knew there was *something else* on board. He caught up with Henley at a crossroads of corridors, and the big Whisperer swatted his knife at Rory, as though instructing him to keep quiet.

The Muktuk Whisperer leaned in close. 'There are monsters abroad!'

'You mean "aboard",' Rory whispered back.

'No – *abroad*. Means that– Never mind, get back!'

Henley ushered Rory into a dark recess, as huge shadows scrabbled across the banleuc passage up ahead. Peeking around the corner, Rory saw them: three creatures, each at least seven feet tall, covered in thick white hair, limbed like a human but with clawed and elongated hands and feet. Their faces were bald and glistening, limp strands of translucent hair hanging down from a head that seemed to inflate and deflate like a frog's throat pouch. Each creature had two eyes, burning golden above a snout-like nose and mouth stretching across its face. One turned its head and, in place of an ear, it had a fleshy opening like a bed of worms.

Rory pulled himself back into the recess and, recovering from the horror of seeing these things, found his nostrils flooded with a thick, rotting stink that was reminiscent of the boys' urinals at school. He looked up into Henley's face, who widened his eyes as though in warning. All he could hear now was the snorts and grunts of these creatures, interlaced with noises as though of someone vomiting everywhere.

'They're pirates, m'boy,' Henley whispered. 'Boardin' ships that pass near their worlds. They can survive exposure in space. If they've got Mira, then they may leave.'

Together, Rory and Henley listened carefully, the tornits still only just around the corner. Eventually, their heavy, muffled footsteps indicated that they were moving off down another passage.

'We have to follow them! We have to find Mira!' Rory hissed.

'I know, m'lad. Let's go – *but*... keep quiet and hang back.'

They crept along the corridor in the wake of the tornits. Rory could hear his heart thundering so loud in his chest that he thought it would give them away. But they were not seen or heard and soon came to the staircase leading up to the umbilical. There, at the foot of the stairs, were five tornits in a circle, surrounding something squirming on the floor. Rory thought it must be Mira and was about to burst forward when Henley grabbed him around the midriff with one thick arm. He pulled him with force behind a crate and grabbed him by the jaw.

'Don't even *think* about it,' he bit out, eyes glowing almost as madly as the tornits'. 'That isn't Mira anyway. Look.'

Rory felt Henley's hand loosen, his jaw aching even from a few seconds of pressure. He peeked out from behind the crate and watched the tornits more closely. They were, indeed, hulking over something that was definitely not human, trying to prevent it from escaping, it seemed. At last, some light caught it and Rory saw that it was one of the alien pillows, desperately attempting an escape. He looked back at Henley, who shook his head. Rory took a deep breath and looked again. One of the tornits lifted the pillow up by a couple of legs, so it was flailing in the air, unable to call out, as pillows – terrestrial or otherwise – do not have mouths. A second tornit stretched out one multi-jointed finger and a claw grew from the tip. It then stabbed the pillow once, making it scrabble all the more, fluid seeping out of it. Then another Tornit did the same. Then another, until the pillow was dripping what must have been its blood.

'Don't watch, m'boy,' Henley said.

Though Rory was compelled by the ghastly sight, he did eventually look away as the tornits start to rip chunks off the pillow and eat it. His first thought was of Mira.

And then a *thud thud thudding* from behind them signalled another tornit approaching. Henley dragged Rory deeper into the shadows of the crate just in time, as the tornit flew past.

'Let me go!'

Mira.

Henley gripped Rory, but he managed to look out from behind the crate. A tornit lifted her up by the arm and leaned in towards her face. Mira continued to kick and scream; the tornit opened its mouth and vomited a clear gelatinous fluid over Mira's face, the little engineer swallowing the stuff deeply.

'No!' Rory shouted, shaking off Henley and leaping out towards Mira.

The tornits turned as one – some still stuffing chunks of pillow into their blood-soaked mouths – and locked their collective gaze on Rory. He stopped mid-run, the terror of the situation overcoming his urgency to rescue Mira. For her part, the engineer had gone limp and the substance on her face had hardened. The tornit that had vomited into her face stuffed her into a marsupial-like pouch on its distended belly. Rory felt Henley's hands closing over his shoulder.

'Stupid lad! We en't gettin' out of this one. Don't look.'

Rory clenched his eyes shut, his ears filling with the snuffle and snort of the revolting creatures as they loomed over him. But, as he expected the first of them to grab him, a familiar war cry echoed up the passage from behind him. Static filled his ears and an image fell into sharp focus inside his mind: a small muktuk and a humanoid. He opened his eyes as Gary – Limmy's leopard-print dressing gown streaming from his back like a cape – burst past him and bowled straight into two tornits, sending them flying. The other tornits were on him like dogs on a chicken bone, though, and Rory reached out a hand, convinced that the not-so-little muktuk would suffer the same fate as the pillow. Gary's crystals began to pulse. The tornits grabbed him with their vile claws. The crystals pulsed faster and faster and faster and… a brilliant flash of light erupted from them with almost physical intensity. The tornits all cried out with hideous snorts and throaty screeches, before scaling the walls and sliding down the umbilical.

Rory ran over to hug Gary, laughing for his life. But then his laughter subsided as he realised that Mira was gone too.

'Mira!' he screamed, until his voice was hoarse.

Gary whined, almost sadly.

'*Liberate tutemet ex inferis…*' Henley muttered, looking up into the light.

Back on the Bridge, Limmy and Xam both wrapped themselves around Rory, scolding him for being stupid enough to follow Henley, while simultaneously comforting him about the loss of Mira. Henley drew their attention to something beyond the Dome. Sure enough, Rory saw them: seven tornits leaping from icy rock to icy rock, heading towards Lepidus.

'What are we waiting for?' Rory demanded. 'Let's go!'

He flung himself in his chair, buckled up and looked around at Limmy, Xam and Henley, who stood, glancing from one to the other.

Limmy stepped forward, a tear streaming her cheek. 'Rory… If we follow them, I can't guarantee that Mira will still be alive when we reach her – and we may very well be killed trying.'

'I know!' Rory said, finding his voice choked and his own eyes watering. 'But if she dies, it's *my* fault. I was the one who upset her. That's why she stayed in the tapestry room. If she'd come to the Bridge with me, she… She wouldn't have been caught.'

'Rory, there's no way I would abandon her,' Limmy said, setting her expression grimly. 'Don't get me wrong. I just want you – everybody – to know what we're up against.'

Both Xam and Henley nodded as one, affirming their own determination to rescue Mira.

'Everyone to their station then,' Limmy commanded, sinking into the captain's chair. 'Let's go monster hunting.'

14

In the Lair of Fleek

The descent into the atmosphere of Lepidus revealed a dark, silent world, contorted with igneous rock gnawing through thick tors of perfect snow. The *Scuabtuinne* settled into a craggy clearing in between several biceps of basalt, long solidified after some prehistoric pyroclastic disaster. The legs of the ship crunched into the ground, the tremors of which sent pulses of dusty snow billowing out into the moon's darkness, like a secret being extinguished.

Rory joined Limmy and a number of Henley's muktuk crew – or should that be 'followers'? – in the cargo hold.

'You have to let me go!' Rory yelled, not for the first time.

But Limmy, tied up in a thick coat, thermal trousers and intimidating boots, was urgency personified. 'Kid, I'm not arguing. When your captain gives you an order – you obey!' she snapped. 'Now, get back on the Bridge with Xam and Henley.'

The cargo ramp juddered open, pressing into the rock with

a crack and a crick, like arthritic joints expelling trapped air. A savage chill flooded in, stealing Rory's breath and racing up his neck into his ears and nose.

Limmy faced the group of men and women behind her – all of them attendants of Rongomai, quickly brought onto the ship before it disconnected from the huge muktuk. 'We're not leaving without Mira. But watch yourselves out there. Death is waiting. Stick together and we'll be okay.'

Rory watched, helplessly, as Limmy led her team out into the snow and soon the dark consumed them, leaving only their torches waving about before they, too, disappeared. The ramp closed with a finality that made him gasp.

I've gotta see what's happening, he decided, before racing back through the ship to the Bridge.

'Hey, Hobster!' Xam said by way of welcome. 'Hang in there, dude…'

Rory glanced briefly at Henley, who stood beside his chair with an expression on his face that could have probably ignited this whole chilly world. Gary floated beside Henley, emitting a low bass whirring noise, as though he was concentrating on something. Making his way to the windows of the Dome, Rory peered through, wrapping arms about himself to try and keep warm. Outside, Lepidus was so dark that even the brilliant white of the snow could not contest it.

They had followed the tornits to this point, watching them jump into the atmosphere of the moon near here. Unfortunately, this location on Lepidus faced away from Uranus, and so the sky was an overcast mess of iron grey, with shards of starry space pocking the cloudbanks here and there.

'How can they breathe out there?' Rory asked, quietly.

'The moon – like Uranus – mostly has hydrogen, helium and fart for air. That's what my scans tell me,' Xam replied, pressing several buttons and flicking a few switches.

'Okay, but how can they breathe?'

'Well, little guy, Lepidus also has these big bubbles of oxygen and nitrogen that drift across the planet. If you run from one to the other – holding your breath when you're outside a bubble – then you can breathe.'

'How can you tell where an air bubble is?'

Xam pointed out of the Dome.

Rory had trouble seeing them, at first, but as his eyes adapted further to the dark, he could make out large pink bubbles – each perhaps the size of a house – drifting along, almost like traffic.

'Why are they pink?' Rory asked, turning to face the navigator.

'Readings indicate they're spores that produce the oxygen,' Xam added, smiling. 'Pretty, huh?'

A few minutes later, the radio above Xam crackled for attention. The navigator grabbed it and spoke. 'This is Xam. Is that you, Captain? Over.'

Crrr. '*This is Limmy. Over.*' Her voice sounded distant and fractured.

'Please confirm location, Captain. Over.'

Crrr. '*Hard to say, but we've descended into a crcrccccrrrrrrrr caldera, I think. You should see these rocks cccrrrrrccrcrrrcrrrccc creeps. Over.*'

Rory listened intently and when he looked back, he saw Henley concentrating too.

'Captain, any sign of those ugly baboon monster things? Over.'

Crrr. Crrr.

'Captain?'

Crrr. '*Read you. Nothing as yet, big man. Clear channel. Will call in when ccccrrrrrrrrrccrrrrrrrr. Over.*'

'What was that?' Henley asked, looking to Xam.

'I think she'll call in when there's something that needs calling in,' Xam replied. Sighing, he closed his eyes and leaned back against his headrest.

Rory walked back up from the windows to his own seat and settled into it, rubbing his hands on Gary's crystals for warmth before he did so.

'She were a fool ter leave me behind,' Henley piped up, a few minutes into the collective silence. 'Takin' *my* people like that.'

Rory looked at Henley in surprise.

'She's still *their* captain,' Xam replied, coolly.

'They're attendants upon the great Rongomai,' Henley retorted, opening his arms aggressively. 'And 'tis *I* who whispers ter Rongomai.'

Xam twisted in his seat, so he faced Henley head on. 'Yet *you* answer to Limmy, despite all that,' Xam said, bristling. 'You signed up to be part of this symbiont crew.'

'Symbiont crew?' Rory interrupted.

Xam didn't take his eyes off Henley, but responded to Rory. 'Each pairing of ship and muktuk for a specific mission is called a "symbiont expedition". You've got the crew on the ship, and the attendants and Whisperer on the muktuk – together they become a symbiont crew for however long the mission lasts. *Most* Whisperers understand that the ship's captain is the boss.'

Henley growled. 'But what our navigator neglects to mention is that there be an unspoken agreement between captain and Whisperer: the muktuk attendants are for the *Whisperer* ter command –'

'Except in emergency situations – like this,' Xam interrupted, placing emphasis on each word he spoke.

Henley barked and waved his hand. 'But ter leave me here is a deliberate insult. As though, on a moon full of monsters, I am the one ter fear.'

Xam reclined. 'Your reputation precedes you, Tall-Tongued Henley. What can I say?'

Rory puzzled over these words and Henley made to retort, but the radio crackled into life once more.

Crrr. '*Come in! We've crrrrrrrrrcccccrrr what appears to be an entrance to ccccrrrccrcrrccrr.*'

Xam picked up the radio. 'Captain, please repeat. You've found an "entrance"? Over.'

Crrr. Crrr.

Xam looked from Rory to Henley, his eyes wet with worry. 'Captain, do you copy? Over.'

Crrr. '*… have now entered ccccrrrrrrrcccrrrrr. There's no sign of movement but– Wait, what's that? I think there's something up ah–*'.

And the radio cut out entirely, as though it had been turned off at Limmy's end. Xam looked at his own radio with a dumbfounded expression, shook it, tapped it… but nothing.

'What happened?' Henley demanded.

Xam turned the radio over in his hands, then replaced it above him. 'It's completely dead. Can't say why but we now have no way of communicating with them…'

Silence. Rory looked out of the Dome into the black and

white of shadow and snow. *What's going on out there?* he wondered.

'This is exactly why I should have led them!' Henley snapped at Xam, shaking Rory out of his thoughts. 'Who knows what danger she's led 'em inter?'

'The captain will look out for them,' Xam replied, impatiently.

'She can't even protect herself – let alone her crew!'

Xam pulled himself up from his chair – with some difficulty – and strode towards Henley. 'It's not her fault Mira was taken.'

Henley moved down to the glass, pointing outside. 'We don't know what's out there! Well, apart from *monsters*. Limmy's on a fool's errand.'

Xam followed Henley down and pushed his finger into the Whisperer's chest. 'You calling her a fool?'

'What if I am?'

The two continued yelling at each other, oblivious to all else. Rory sighed and looked at Gary, whose rows of eyes suggested intense disappointment with the supposed adults in the room. All at once, Rory's ears were filled with static and then the muktuk image and the humanoid image were there in his mind, both inside a large black circle. The image sort of *zoomed* out like unpinching an image on a smartphone screen and Rory could see the dust trail left by Gary's mother: it was ever so faint. The image faded. Rory looked at Gary again and nodded.

He knew what he had to do.

Taking a final glance at Xam and Henley – the former was waving frantically and the latter was slamming one fist into the palm of his hand – he saw his opportunity. Rory got up from his seat, slowly, and tiptoed towards the door. One more look at Xam and Henley – no change – and he dashed into the corridor.

In the cargo bay, Rory located a side room with lots of gear – spacesuits, helmets, gloves – and found the tinfoil thermal suits. Most were way too big for him, but fortunately there was one that might fit a smallish woman, so he pulled the silvery onesie on as quickly as he could. The inside was like an explosion in a cotton wool packing factory, which he imagined would serve him well in a few minutes.

Pulling on a balaclava-goggle combo, he turned at the sound of a bump and something crashing to the ground: Gary had floated into the cargo bay with Limmy's dressing gown covering his face and had bumped into a mop and bucket. Rory smiled, despite himself.

'Come here,' he said, shuffling over to the muktuk as he tried to adapt to his new clothing.

He lifted the dressing gown off Gary's head and rested it instead along the muktuk's back. A deep, appreciative whirring stirred in Gary that he could feel just as much as he could hear it.

'You've got to stay here,' Rory instructed, his voice muffled through the balaclava. 'You're the only way I'll make it back to the ship: my mind to your mind, like two Vulcans. Radios are useless and it's too dark to see very well.'

The helium pouch under Gary's throat inflated and then deflated slowly, as though the creature was sighing.

'Don't be like that,' Rory said. 'I'll be back before you know it, 'kay?'

Patting Gary on the head, he turned and made his way over to the cargo bay ramp, where he pressed the button to release it. Once again, Lepidus opened its chilly maw, only this time Rory did not feel the Arctic air and – waiting for the first pink oxygen bubble to appear – he staggered down the ramp and out into the snow. His heart hammered against his ribs for fear of what would come next. Only once did he look back at the ship, after he had walked perhaps three-hundred yards, shuffling from pink bubble to pink bubble, and he could make out both Xam and Henley waving furiously at him, presumably to try and draw him back. But it was too late. He faced ahead and resolved to go as far as it took to find Mira, Limmy and the others and bring them back safely.

He had been walking for some time now – it was hard to work out exactly how long, but his legs were weary from the strain of dragging the boots through the snow in a great, crunchy heave. Moving from one oxygen bubble to the next was relatively straightforward, and the longest he'd had to hold his breath was forty seconds – *long enough, though*, he thought. Behind his foil balaclava, he could feel the sting of sweat dripping into his eyes; but he didn't think overheating would be a problem on a world as cold and bleak as Lepidus. For a companion he had only his torch, which dimly illuminated snow-filled pockets out of the darkness. Sinister rock formations rose and crashed to his left and right, hiding who knew what. The loneliness was acute. He considered himself stupid for not having grabbed a radio on his way out of the ship; the thought of hearing Henley or Xam's voice right about then was a comfort he could not enjoy.

Eventually, his torch illuminated something out of place up ahead, lying on the snow with a small drift already settled on it. He paused momentarily, his pulse quickening. Cautiously, he moved forward, stepping out of an oxygen bubble. The shape in the snow revealed itself to be the shredded remains of a foil coat – just like the one he was wearing – and across the slash marks was a red splatter...

Blood.

He looked up, conscious again of the fact that he was all alone. In the distance, he heard what sounded like the echo of a snort.

It's just your imagination, he told himself. *But I've got to find Mira quick.* The jacket was way too big to have been Limmy's, but if something had happened to the crew then there was no telling what could be happening to the little engineer at that moment.

Shortly after, having stepped into another oxygen bubble, Rory felt his path gently incline and he saw an increasing amount of rock-face to his left. *Must be a mountain path*, he thought, *or something...*

And that's when he heard a hideous, strangled howl, streaming through the air, flooding his body. The hairs on the back of his neck rose despite the stuffiness of the foil jacket. His mind's eye cast back to the *Scuabtuinne*... the stinking, vile beasts – the tornits – grunting and snorting. He moved forward, nervously, his torch throwing its light like a pendulum – left then right, right then left – burning up the darkness, Rory all the time poised as though, any moment, the torch would startle a tornit.

Rounding a corner on the path, Rory *felt* as much as he heard a snort in the rocks above him. He swung the torch up to see what was there, caught a glimpse of *something* and, with a yell, stepped backwards and slipped, the snow betraying his balance. The torch flew from his hand. Suddenly, he was sliding down the snow as though it were a chute and starting to choke after being ripped from the safety of the oxygen bubble. Gathering speed – and with a sharp pain leaping up into his right leg – his body punched through both snow and ice and he crashed upon some rock.

His head swam. It had all happened so quickly that his brain struggled now to keep up with the various messages his body was sending. His leg… still hurt, but he could move his toes. His back… sore. His ears… ringing. But he could breathe again.

Looking up, he saw a hole in the dark ceiling of a cavern, snow drifting in like flour through a sieve. He pulled himself to his elbows and took stock of his surroundings. The cavern was dark and his eyes took a few minutes to adjust. In spite of the gloom, he made out the loose form of shapes here and there: more igneous rock, similar to the rock on the moon's surface. Also, the air was touched with pink spores, flitting about like dandelion seeds, giving him oxygen. All was silent and he was thankful at least that the chilling snorts had stopped.

He allowed himself a few more minutes before pulling his body up, leg heavy with pain, but mobile at least. Testing it with varying degrees of pressure, he lived up to his name and hobbled on. Now that he had no torch, he could only guide himself by touch and the echo of his footfalls bouncing off rock – the different types of sound suggesting whether rocks were closer or farther away. The spores provided only the faintest illumination.

He worried he would never find Mira, that this venture had been pointless and might even result in his own death as well as hers – if she wasn't dead already. His heart thudded a mile a minute, though all was quiet around him.

The cavern system closed into tunnels, which he struggled through, before opening up once more into another cavern. This one, however, held a lake, illuminated from the bottom by glowing eel-like creatures, their ambient blue light winding through the water and throwing aurorae over the cavern ceiling. It would have been a quite beautiful sight under any other circumstance, but on a moon possibly swarming with hungry, hairy monsters his appreciation of natural wonder was, understandably, diminished.

He stepped down a path towards the lake and his ears pricked up: a faint whimpering somewhere off in the gloom. He stopped in his tracks and pulled off his balaclava-goggle combo – all the better to hear. There it was again… Definitely a sound – not a snort though; something far more delicate.

Rory paced on, his breath collecting in mist. He stopped every few steps to listen out for the whimpering again. He passed the lake, rounded a corner and heard the sound again – far louder this time. It seemed to be coming from ahead of him, down in a hollow. He descended, the dark consuming him once again now he was out of sight of the luminous eels. In the hollow, he found a cave entrance, to the right of which sat a huge boulder that looked almost to have been placed there by some deliberate force.

The whimpering came once again, and it was clear that its source was inside the cave. Rory tried to settle his nerves.

You can do this – just go in there, he urged himself.

He stepped forward and entered the cave. At the back, glowing pink mushrooms were arranged around what looked like a chair, set at a table. Lit by the fungal glow, a figure was curled up to the left of the chair. As Rory's eyes adapted, he realised who it was.

'Mira!' he hissed, rushing forwards to hug her.

He felt her hug him back, her arms shaking violently – probably just as much from fear as from the cold.

'Y-You c-came for m-me...' Mira murmured, teeth chattering – the *thing* that the tornit had vomited over her face back on the ship was now gone.

Rory smiled, sadly. 'You're freezing. Here – wear my onesie.' With difficulty, he pulled his onesie off and helped Mira into it, the little engineer silently accepting the warmth it bestowed.

'I th-thought y-you'd all l-left me.'

Rory fought back his tears, wrapping his arms about himself; he had thick clothing on under the onesie, but he could feel the cold coursing through him like anaesthetic. 'Of course not! W-What happened after... after those *things* took you?'

Mira's teeth continued to chatter. 'Th-they took me through s-space. One of them v-vomited something into m-my stomach – but it k-kept air in my l-lungs. Its p-pouch thing sw-swallowed me and I was w-warm and I could hear its insides b-beating and p-pulsing. It was dis-disgusting. Its *s-smell*!'

'I thought they were g-gonna eat you. And w-what's with that ch-chair?'

'Not yet. But they brought me here and there was an-another one who didn't l-look like the others... That ch-chair...' Something in Mira's face changed. 'We n-need to go. Now. L-Look around you. It's g-game over, Rory! Game over!'

Rory looked. He hadn't noticed, but the floor was littered with bones. Most of them looked as though they might belong to the eels from the lake, but others had an unnervingly human quality to them.

'It'll be b-back soon,' Mira whispered.

'What will?' Rory asked.

'Come on, l-let's go,' Mira instructed.

Her body stopped shivering and she got up, pulling Rory with her towards the mouth of the cave. But a shape fell across it and the children stopped in their tracks. Rory watched in horror as a tall, gangly figure stepped into the cave, tossing something heavy to the floor and pulling the boulder from outside the cave across the entrance. The 'something heavy' on the floor moved about and *started to talk.*

'Please! Please don't!'

It must be one of Rongomai's attendants! Rory realised.

The gangly figure stooped, picked up the man on the floor and trudged towards the mushroom-lit chair. It flumped into the chair, slammed the man on the table, reached down beside the chair and lifted up a large blade.

'That's the s-second one,' Mira said, matter-of-factly, as the man pleaded. 'You might w-want to look away, Rory.'

Mira turned her head and Rory copied her. Behind him, he heard the blade *thwacking* into the table, followed by a scream and then a mulchy, crunching sound. The procedure was repeated twice more before the screaming stopped.

Rory's hands shook. His skin tingled. His head swam.

This can't be happening, he told himself.

All at once, he was painfully aware of the danger he and Mira faced; in his own mind, he thought it to be his fault. Slowly, he turned to face the monster in its chair. The mushroom light plucked it from the shadow well enough for him to mark its features. There were similarities to the tornits, but this creature was completely bald, like a new-born rat with wrinkled, pink skin. Its eyes were globular and its mouth wide. Blood dribbled down its chin and stray hairs erupted from random patches of flesh like the spokes on a bicycle wheel.

'Keep qu-quiet,' Mira whispered. 'Stay in the sh-shadow and he won't know you're here.'

'Oh, but that's where you're wrong,' the creature said in English, with a voice like its nose was pinched and gravel was stuck in its throat. It stared with inquisitive, bulbous eyes at them both.

'Do I surprise you?' it continued. 'Your language is not so challenging for my race.'

Rory and Mira looked at each other. Mira made to speak, but Rory held up a hand, swallowing hard.

'Are you g-going to eat us?' Rory asked, finally starting to control his shivering.

The creature settled back in its chair. 'I'm quite full, thank you. Besides, I am far more interested in your company. For now. Your mind is much like the girl's. Frayed. *Interesting.* Now, step forward. Both of you.'

Rory looked at Mira, who nodded. He took her gloved hand and, to his surprise, she didn't pull away. Together, they stepped forward and forward again, the creature urging them on until they were a mere six feet from it. What was left of the crewman remained on the table, along with the knife.

The creature seemed to guess at the children's discomfort. 'Don't think too badly of me. I must make do with bitter *sllk-sllks* from the lake. So, when a juicy warm-blood, like you, comes along I can't resist.'

'But he was a person!' Rory countered.

The creature eyed Rory with renewed interest, its mouth curving in what for all the world looked like a smile. 'You warm-bloods eat other warm-bloods on your water world, yet you judge *me* for eating a warm-blood here...'

'Th-That's different,' Rory replied, his heart racing again. 'They're just a-animals. They're stupid.'

The creature leaned forward, the mushroom light catching the blood on its chin in glistening spools. 'So too are *you*. *I* am what you call a tornit. You're a long way from home and a long way down the food chain.' It made a heaving, chuckling noise deep in its throat. 'But you are both too interesting to eat, so you are my guests. It's been a long, long time since I spoke to anyone...'

'Please,' Rory said, 'All we want is to go back to our ship.'

The creature rose, its face reduced to something puckered and cold. 'And you will not, so long as I say so.' It stretched long, bony arms, covered in sallow flesh, and got up from behind the table, lifting the body of the crewman and carrying it over to a corner where it slung the corpse.

Rory looked the creature up and down. 'What... *are* you?'

The creature turned its head. 'I told you already: I am a tornit.'

'But what is a tornit and why do you look different from the others?'

The tornit returned to its chair and sat down. 'Tornits are an ancient species. We are planet-hoppers. Once we lived closer to the Sun, but our species broke into two: the warm and the cold. The warm remained behind and forced the cold farther and farther out. We are their descendants, after they settled on the moons that orbit this planet. But that was long ago and now there are just the tornits of Lepidus remaining.'

'And... and who are you?'

'*I* am Fleek,' the creature said, laying a hand on its chest. 'I am the Eldest here and I control all other tornits with a flash of my mind.'

'With a flash of your mind?'

'Yes. They are wretched, with their heavy, hairy bodies and their snorts and grunts. They are the inevitable result of *any* creature that is denied warmth. Though it may sound immodest, I am all the intelligence left of the tornit race, and I wield it as you warm-bloods might a weapon or a fork.' Fleek closed its eyes, baring its teeth as though in contempt. 'Ah, yes! I can feel every last one of them now. Shuffling and slavering through the snow and the rock and the ice. Ripping up *sllk-sllks* from the lake, cramming them into their unquenchable mouths. Every brain in this universe has its own electricity.

When I sensed the electricity of your muktuks, and then of you, I sent the tornits after you.'

Mira stepped forward. 'After… me?'

Fleek stared at her. 'Yes. Yours is the most intricate mind I have sensed in a long time.'

'In a long time?' Rory repeated. 'Who else comes this far out? *What* else comes this far out?'

Fleek turned its gaze upon Rory. 'There have only ever been two other warm-bloods from your water world who have come to me. One I sensed recently; the other I sense now, although… his mind is changed.'

'The Whiffetsnatcher. Do you mean the Whiffetsnatcher?' Rory asked, his voice growing excited.

Fleek leaned back in its chair. 'Ah! That is how you warm-bloods label him… Yes, I see. He first came to me when I was stronger. My tornits were ready to eat him, but I spoke with him and his electricity was like nothing I've known before. He had a crew with him on his ship and one of the crew also, I remember, had a worthy mind.'

Rory hardly knew where to begin; his questions were so numerous. 'You said you sensed one of them recently and one of them now…'

'Your Whiffetsnatcher stopped here with an… *offering* as part of our arrangement – not for the first time.' Fleek extended a hand towards another corner of its cave. 'He has told me that on your water world your ancients used to make sacrifices to the gods for a safe voyage.'

Rory's heart missed a beat. *What offering?* he thought. He felt Mira's hand grab and tighten on his, as though pulling him back, but Rory dragged his hand free and strode over to the

shadows. Part of him expected to find his mother there, but…
there were only bones: broken and child-sized. He recoiled.
But something shone dimly in amongst those bones. He bent
down to pick it up. It was an earring on which were engraved
the words, *All things nice…* He frowned and dropped it.

Fleek made a deep sound like a cruel chuckle. 'Of course,
you fear him. When you give a thing a monster's name you
help build the monster. But he is like you other warm-bloods
– just a higher mind with higher ambitions. Clavius Hobble is
the best of you.'

Rory's heart sunk into his guts. 'W–What did you say?'

Fleek extended an arm, idly flexing its claws. 'I said Clavius
Hobble was the best of you. He didn't know barriers. He
sought only to –'

'*Hobble?* That was – *is* the Whiffetsnatcher's name?' Rory
interrupted, pacing back to the table and placing his hands on
it.

Fleek looked up, eyes narrowing. 'Yes.'

'What does he look like?'

'Much like any other warm-blood. Except his skin is looser
than yours, he is taller and he is bald.'

It must be a coincidence. Surely… Rory thought, the horror
of Fleek's revelation gaining strength in his mind, nonetheless.
He recalled Limmy talking about the myth of Haligogen many
months ago and how it was said that the Whiffetsnatcher took
children.

'Did he ever mention… Did Clavius Hobble ever talk about
Haligogen?'

Again, that cruel chuckle came from deep within Fleek. 'It
was *I* who told him about that world.'

'What is it? Where is it?'

'I think that's enough questions from you for now,' Fleek replied, its eyes flashing, its mouth snapping and its fists slamming on the table, sending splatters of flesh and blood into the air. Rory and Mira jumped. 'Remember: this is *my* domain and you are *my* guests.'

'Guests should be treated well,' Mira muttered, defiantly.

Fleek turned to her. 'I haven't eaten you, have I?'

'What do you want from us?' Rory demanded, his voice filled with urgency.

'I've told you already: *her*' – it indicated Mira – 'electricity is uncommon. When you are as lonely as me you reach out to intelligence... wherever you find it.'

'Why her and not me?'

'Your mind... is closed,' Fleek said, leaning back in its chair and closing its eyes. 'I can *feel* the chaos and the battle raging inside your head, though. It is like a rock and you will not let me in – I wonder what you keep there... Hers, though' – again, it indicated Mira – 'is calm and inviting. It welcomes me.'

'I don't welcome you!' Mira snapped.

Fleek opened its eyes and looked at her with an approximation of a smile. 'Oh, but *your mind* does! Much like the tornits. I can reach inside your head quite easily. A little tug here, a little push there and I can alter you. For example...'

Mira's breathing quickened. 'Wh-what are you doing? Stop it!'

'Mira?' Rory said, grabbing her. 'What is it?'

'I'm back in India. Naan? Pita? No, no, no!'

Rory grabbed Mira's arms as she started flailing at unseen

adversaries. 'Stop it!' Rory yelled at Fleek. All of a sudden, Mira stopped screaming, her arms falling to her sides, but she panted as though she had run a race.

'That is just a hint of what I can do with an open mind. But I do not wish to harm anyone. I am perfectly civilised, despite appearances.' In a slow and tired manner, Fleek heaved itself to its feet once more. 'You warm-bloods offer something that few other sentient species do – even the muktuks, despite the things they have seen – and that is: *story*. Your lives are filled with story and experience, while my destiny is to eke out the centuries here in this damp cave, surrounded by the ruckus of those monsters beyond. Your stories are a prize, and do not think that I will so easily surrender that. As time goes by, you will see the benefits of being my guests here on Lepidus. But there will be time for further talk later. Now, I must rest.'

Fleek padded away deeper into its cave and, in the dim light of the glowing mushrooms, Rory watched as it clambered up the rock and into a cleft. He was reminded of an old catacomb – only one in which a corpse had crawled back into its place of rest. He looked at Mira, who returned his gaze with eyes that seemed to say, *Let's just keep quiet a while…*

Sure enough, not five minutes had soon passed before Fleek was completely still.

'D'you think he's asleep?' Rory whispered.

'Maybe,' Mira mumbled, glancing at the boulder covering the cave entrance. 'I'm so… tired.'

Without a moment's pause, Mira rolled over and buried her head into the hood of Rory's onesie. Rory opened his mouth to speak, but thought better of it. He scooted up to the nearest wall and leaned back into it, the cold filling his torso. His teeth chattered again and he wrapped his arms around himself. His leg still hurt from his fall and he realised just how tired he was as well. Perhaps resting his eyes couldn't hurt…

When he woke, the cave was still dark; the boulder still covered the mouth, Mira was still asleep and Fleek was still in its wall-tomb-bed-thing. He rubbed his eyes, to draw some life into them. Once he was, again, sufficiently aware of the grim reality of his current predicament, Rory reflected on that name: *Clavius Hobble.* He could have laughed at the absurdity of it all. But it was no joke: the Whiffetsnatcher could be a relative of his. But who? He had never known his dad, who had been killed when he was very young – it was only ever him and Mum. But a man with – what had Fleek said? – a bald head. Mum was still quite young herself. He'd never known his grandparents either: Grandma had died when Mum was still a teenager – he knew that much – but by the time he was old enough to ask about a grandfather, Mum's mind had already started to slip away. The Whiffetsnatcher might have his name then, but he didn't have an identity. And then another thought: *what if Fleek was lying? He got inside Mira's head; what if he's lying and he* can *get inside my head?* That was an altogether unpleasant yet plausible consideration. The last thing he needed was another monster in his mind.

Rory looked across at Mira – still asleep – and yet another thought came to him: her tapestry – there was a section – what was it? – ah, yes! – 'The Clavius Scandal'. 1960-something or other… He remembered the image Mira had captured of two people walking away from Widdershins. He couldn't think what it meant, but perhaps Fleek wasn't lying. If Rory had questions before, he was overflowing with them now. However, as desperately as he wanted them answered, he knew that time was short. He tried reaching out, inside his head, to Gary, but the little muktuk was nowhere to be sensed.

'Mira!' he hissed.

No response.

'Mira!' he hissed again.

No response.

'Wake up, Mira!' he hissed one final time, shaking the engineer's shoulder.

Mira's shoulder snapped away from Rory's hand. 'Leave me alone!'

Not now. Don't get into a sulk now... he pleaded.

'We have to get out of here. We have to find Limmy and the others and get out of here *now*.'

Mira rolled over to face him. 'There's a rock in the way. It's impossible!' Her voice was urgent and frustrated.

'Shh! I have an idea. But... you need to tell me what it was like... him getting inside your head.'

She turned away from Rory again. 'Don't want to.'

Rory tried to control his own growing frustration. 'Mira, if you don't, then we're going to be stuck here forever!'

A moment's pause... then she turned back to face Rory. 'It... it felt like I was sharing my mind with someone – some*thing* – else, and it could control what I was seeing in my head.'

'Okay, that's good! Well, not good – you know what I mean,' Rory replied. 'But how did he get inside your head? Could you feel any way of fighting it?'

Mira's eyes dropped. 'It was like... my mind was tucked

away behind the branches of a willow tree... but there was a big gap in the branches and he walked through. I don't know... it's hard to describe...'

Rory looked up and over at Fleek, still unmoved. He smiled weakly. 'It's okay. I've got an idea.'

Several more hours – or so Rory guessed – passed, he and Mira both dozing on and off. By this stage, the reek of death in the cave had reached such a level that it brought tears to his eyes and thirst had forced the children to risk slurping up small puddles of fluid from pools in the rock. The fluid seemed to be water, but had a slight taste of iron to it as well. From beyond the cave came the occasional snort, grunt or squeal of what could only have been other tornits, jostling about in the dark of the Lepidean cavern system. Not once was there a sound that resembled a human voice.

Eventually, Fleek stirred – its limbs pressing out beyond its 'bed' – and the creature clambered down the rock and shuffled towards its grim dining table.

'Where are you, my dear warm-bloods,' it called in its rasping, nasal voice, head tipping from right to left. 'Ah! There you are – right where I left you.'

'Where else can we go?' Mira said, pouting, as she pulled herself to her feet. 'Let us go...'

Fleek wagged one long, clawed finger. 'Now, we don't want to go through that again. But if you do as I want then... slowly... you will be rewarded with more freedoms.'

'I'm hungry. I need to eat,' Mira snapped.

Fleek's expression grew unpleasant – its approximation of

anger, perhaps – and Rory stepped forward, seeing his opportunity.

'*You* must be hungry too, right? You hardly, er, touched your dinner earlier,' he said.

Fleek brought its gaze upon Rory. 'You warm-bloods may not be the most appetising meal, but you're far better than the *sllk-sllks* from the lake.'

'So, you'll eat?' Rory asked. He tried to ignore Mira's alarmed expression. 'Who knows? Maybe the next one will taste better.'

Fleek turned its eyes away and pressed one claw to its mouth, as though in thought. 'I suppose it couldn't hurt to try... Yes, I'll have one of the tornits bring another warm-blood to me.' It looked at Rory with something close to suspicion. 'Though... I do not see why you would encourage me... What are you plotting?'

'Nothing,' Rory replied, carefully. 'It's just... Mira's hungry and... you might share with her' – Rory actively pushed Mira away from him now as her expression moved from alarm to horror – 'some of the food. We'll... eat our own... in desperate circumstances.'

Fleek still looked suspicious. 'Why not try *sllk-sllk*?'

Rory quickly came up with an excuse. 'Err... Mira isn't a pescatarian.'

Fleek narrowed its eyes, then closed them and leaned back. A few moments later, it opened its eyes again. 'There. Food is coming.'

Rory managed a smile. 'And while we're waiting, I have a proposal.'

Fleek looked down at him, something like a smile splitting its face. 'Oh, and what is that?'

Play it cool, Rory…, he told himself.

'Before you slept, you said you wouldn't answer any more of my questions.'

'Indeed.'

'Well… if you let me ask *my* questions, then I'll… let you inside my head,' Rory said. Fleek's fingers danced over the table-top. 'We're not leaving – like you said – so what's the harm in giving me my answers? At least I'll know… A-And you get a second mind to explore.'

Fleek stood abruptly and paced up and down, clearly wrestling with the idea and perhaps working out whether this – if not the meal – was, in fact, a trick. Rory looked at Mira, whose face was a picture of fury. He tried mouthing some reassuring words to her, but she folded her arms and frowned still further.

Fleek eventually turned back to the children. 'Let me counter: you get *one* question, you allow me into your mind and, if you go back on your offer, I get to eat *you*. You look far more appetising than the one I had earlier.'

Rory shook his head, his heart racing. 'No. Five questions… But the rest stands.'

Fleek wagged a lazy claw. 'Three questions then. That is my final counter. And… be careful, lest you anger me and I gobble you up anyway.'

Rory paused, then… 'Deal.'

Fleek took its seat at the dining table again. 'Splendid. Now, how do you propose to open your mind to me?' Rory felt a piercing pain in his head, as though someone was digging a nail into his skull. 'See – you resist at every turn! But I can help you.'

All of a sudden, the cave fell away and Rory was back in his flat on Earth. He drew a sharp breath and took in his surroundings. The windows looked out on to a night sky. The kitchen was overrun with dirty pots, pans and plates, as it always was. The sofas were stained and torn in places with a coffee table covered in cigarette ends. There was a sweet, sickly smell that pervaded the flat, apparently with no obvious source. His mum was nowhere to be seen.

Knock, knock.

Rory turned his attention to the front door. 'Who's there?'

But there was no answer. Rory walked tentatively towards the door and rested his eye over the peephole. However, all he could see was grey.

Knock, knock.

The knocking made him jump. 'I said who is it?'

'It's only little old me,' came a nasal voice. 'Won't you let me in? We have a deal.'

'How is this possible?' Rory called, looking around at his flat again. 'How are we back on Earth?'

'Your water world? Do you honestly think we've travelled there? No. Though I cannot get into your mind, a few images are so strong that you project them. *This* place was the strongest, so I'm using it to help you understand.'

'U–Understand what?'

'That your mind is only ever as strong as its experience. What trials have you put it through? What pain?'

'You have no idea,' Rory mumbled, but then, a little louder… 'And if I let you through that door…'

'Then you will have let me into one part of your mind. I don't know what lies beyond. I don't know how big this

277

place is, or how many parts it has. I do know that there is one location in it that is more important to you than any other – perhaps a safe place. Once you let me in there, then I will have full access to your mind… and' – a hint of amusement entered Fleek's voice – 'you can ask your questions.'

Rory instinctively looked towards the hallway, leading to his bedroom. *If I could choose one safe place here, then it would be in my bed… And I'll still be safe so long as I don't let him in there…*

'Okay, I'll let you in!' Rory called again. 'But… if I let you in then I get to ask my first question.'

The silence behind the front door was long, but then… 'I agree.'

Rory sucked in a breath, wondering momentarily if, in this illusion, it really was air he was breathing. There was no sign of Mira either and no suggestion that she was elsewhere in the flat, out of sight; if she was, she was keeping very quiet. He stepped nervously towards the door, unlocked it and lifted the catch. A few moments later, the door opened, slowly, and there stood Fleek. In the moonlight, the monster's flesh radiated with a greyish glow that perfectly caught the shadow in every fold of its wrinkled skin. With a single movement, Fleek stepped inside the flat, ducking its head as it did so. It looked around and sniffed the air.

'This is a warm-blood's cave?' Fleek ventured.

Rory screwed up his brow, before understanding. 'Yes… but our homes are built – sometimes high into the sky.'

'So many bizarre items, some not so bizarre…' Fleek muttered, continuing to look around as it moved further into the flat.

Rory took a step back and tried to keep calm by controlling

his breathing enough that his heart rate slowed. For his plan to work, he needed to keep perfect control of himself... for now.

'Let me ask my question then...' Rory said, more as a tentative statement than anything else.

Fleek stopped, lifting a claw from the top of the sofa and looking across at Rory, who had circled back towards the TV. 'As you wish. I am no breaker of deals.'

'Promise to answer truthfully?'

Fleek's mouth curled and it placed a claw across its chest. 'Cross my heart and hope to die. Yes, I sense a memory of yours where you say that to another warm-blood... Mrs El-Khalil. Its meaning is correct here.'

If he senses memories of my teachers then he is definitely inside my head, Rory realised, doing his utmost not to run out of the flat and away from this creature.

He had given as much thought as time allowed to what he should ask and had decided that, more than anything, the most important thing was finding the Whiffetsnatcher.

'Okay... Where *exactly* is the planet Haligogen?'

Fleek commenced a languorous walk around the sofa towards Rory. 'Well, that depends on how you view space. For a muktuk, Haligogen is beyond the end of its pilgrimage. For me, Haligogen is beyond my reach of thought. For the Sun, Haligogen is almost beyond light...' The tornit paused in its riddle, frustrating Rory. 'But for you, Haligogen is beyond understanding. No? Not enough? Well then, how about this: it sits beyond the planet you call Neptune, but before Pluto. It is twinned with a burning, salt-tailed moon.' Fleek scurried the last few steps around the sofa, past the TV and coffee table, sending Rory back towards the kitchen. 'Now that I have answered your second question –'

'Wait – what!?' Rory interrupted. 'That was my *first* question!' He tried to keep his cool and, for a moment, the flat around him trembled.

'What was that?' Fleek asked, a hint of nervousness in its voice, as it looked around.

Rory shook his head. 'Don't change the subject! That was my *first*!'

Fleek turned its attention back to Rory. 'No,' it snapped. 'Your first was when you asked if I promised to answer truthfully. Really, I shouldn't have allowed you your second just yet' – its mouth curled again – 'but I felt generous.'

Rory span around, ran past the kitchen, down the hallway and into his bedroom, slamming the door behind him. Throwing himself on his bed, he tried to calm himself using deep breaths, waiting for the inevitable knock. This was the only place in his home he had ever felt remotely safe. His little pair of binoculars sat on the table beside his bed and the night sky was alive with stars.

'Thought I told you not to come back,' came an ominous voice from across the room.

Rory looked over to see a figure emerge from the shadows.

'M-Mum?' he managed, hardly believing what he was seeing.

'Look what you did to me, Rory!' she spat, parting strands of hair to reveal a nasty gash on her head. 'It's that *weirdness* in yer – makes yer mental.' She pulled a packet of cigarettes and a lighter out of her dressing gown pocket, lit one and replaced the packet and lighter. She kept her eyes on Rory as she inhaled deeply. 'What yer staring at?' One of her eyes narrowed.

Rory swallowed hard, a tear running down his cheek. 'I've missed you so much, Mum. I'm so sorry for what I did.' He got up to give her a hug, but his mum held up a hand, smiling cruelly.

'Don't be stupid, Rory. Yer know I'm not *actually* here. But yer know who I *really* am. This room represents the deepest part of your mind and yer've never been alone here.'

Rory stopped and retreated across his bed, hardly daring to believe he was face to face with...

'Need a clue?' his 'mum' asked. 'Roooory? Roooory? What if your plan fails? What if you enrage Fleek and put Mira in danger? Mira will die because of you!'

Rory crawled into the corner of his bed, banging his head against the wall, trying to keep calm. *This is all part of your plan – don't listen to it! It's just your OCD – it's not real!*

And then came the *knock, knock* on the bedroom door.

'Little pig, little pig, let me in... That was a fable your mother once told you. It seems appropriate here.'

Rory looked at his mum, still drawing on her cigarette, now sitting cross-legged on her bed. 'What if yer let it in and it doesn't hold its word? What if yer plan doesn't work? You need me for yer plan. But why would I co-operate?'

Rory's eyes flashed and he regained his focus. 'If you don't help me now you'll have to share my head with that monster for the rest of my life. If Fleek is in here with us then you're not so special anymore. Who knows? Maybe Fleek will find a way to destroy you. Every time you make me sick with fear, doubt and worry, you give me a choice: stand and fight or run away.

Well, now it's *your* turn. This room is the deepest part of my mind. If you want to stay here, you'd *better* fight.'

Mum's face contorted more and more as Rory spoke. She stubbed the cigarette out on her hand without a wince. 'Don't you dare...'

But Rory dashed for the door, just as his mum leapt forward as well, screaming in fury. He ripped the door open and threw his mother off him as Fleek stepped inside, gently closing the door behind it.

The tornit's eyes darted from Rory to his mother, both of whom stared at Fleek, waiting for the monster to speak. 'What is this?'

Rory's mother scurried onto her bed, the shadows swallowing her.

Fleek pointed. 'What is *this*?'

'The deepest part of my mind,' Rory replied, urging himself to stay calm, just for a moment longer. 'I've upheld my end of the deal; now, you need to uphold yours.' Fleek tried to speak again, but Rory interrupted, raising his voice. He had battled over which of the two questions remaining he needed to have answered more desperately. There were so many things he wanted to know, but he realised that Fleek would not be able to answer most of them. However, if Fleek was right and the creature had spoken at length with Clavius Hobble then he would surely know something about him – perhaps even who he really was. But there was another question, more urgent...

'Where are Limmy and the rest of the crew being held?'

Fleek's mouth folded, as though in bitter disappointment. 'You could have asked me anything and you chose that... Fine. It doesn't matter. You're not going anywhere. They are all in a cavern guarded by my tornits through an underwater passage in the lake you would have passed as you reached my cave.' Fleek rushed through its answer, impatient. 'Now, your mind belongs to *me*.'

'Oh no, it doesn't!' 'Mum' screamed, leaping off of her bed and throwing herself into Fleek.

Rory clenched his eyes and let the OCD flood his mind. His heart raced. His breath shortened. And when he opened his eyes, he saw that his mother, despite her smaller frame, seemed to have strengthened, gripping Fleek's forearms and wrestling the monster to its knees.

'What is this horror?' Fleek squealed at Rory. 'What is this nightmare?'

Rory looked deep into the tornit's eyes, a tear running from his own but a victorious smile finding his lips. 'My life.'

He picked up his binoculars and hurled them through the bedroom window. Leaping up onto the bin that served for a bedside cabinet, he turned back once more to face the creature screaming up at his mother.

'Fleeek? Fleeek? What if the stress is too much for the children? What if they both die? Then you'll be all alone again!'

Rory looked out of the window, assured himself that what was happening was all just in his head and leapt out, the sound of Fleek's tormented voice screaming still ringing in his ears as he hurtled towards the ground.

15

A Change of Command

Rory's eyes snapped open at the sound of the tornit screaming, and he found it writhing around on the floor, clutching its head, eyes closed. He turned towards the mouth of the cave, where Mira was on her knees watching the huge stone being rolled away. One of the – *what would you call them?* – normal or 'grunt' tornits stood beyond the boulder, clasping its head with one hand – something approaching shock on its face – one of the crewmen over its shoulder, unconscious... maybe dead.

Rory had seconds to readjust and focus on his next move.

'Mira!' he yelled. 'Get outta the way!'

The tornit tossed the crewman to the ground and staggered into the cave but, instead of attacking either of the children, it ran straight over to Fleek, snorting and gurgling in a language incomprehensible to the human ear. Finally, it collapsed to its knees.

'Run!' Rory screamed, leaping forwards and yanking Mira

up onto her feet. 'Fleek is projecting its pain to the other tornits.'

At the mouth of the cave, Rory checked the crewman, but the man's vacant eyes stared lifelessly up at him and he had to look away. Mira turned in the other direction, but Rory took her hand and urged her on. They headed back up the slope, down which Rory had originally come before finding Fleek's cave, and soon reached the cavern with the lake, illuminated by the *sllk-sllks*.

'I hope you don't mind water,' Rory said, guiding Mira to the edge of the lake.

'No, I'm a strong swimmer. You won't keep up. Why?'

'Because there's an opening under the water that leads back into another cavern where Limmy and the others are being kept.'

Mira shrugged off the onesie Rory had given her, sucked in a lungful of air between chattering teeth, and dived expertly into the water, gliding down into the lake like a lithe seal. Rory took a deep breath, dived in after her and his ears were immediately closed off to everything but the dull, pressurised weight of water. It was all he could do not to open his mouth in shock as the icy water drove into his skin. His heart thumped, but he calmed himself. The *sllk-sllks* were everywhere, wriggling about in all directions, their blue lights rearranging shadows against rock and weed alike. Mira wasn't lying: she powered through the water towards a large and very obvious tunnel, through which she swam. Rory followed her, his anxiety growing in tandem with the darkness and his lungs beginning to burn as he panicked about how long he could hold his breath. Fortunately, a few stray *sllk-sllks* slithered through the tunnel as well, their light leading the children quickly upwards, where they broke the surface of a pool, each gasping for pink spore air.

They looked around. Above their heads, a high, stalactite-riddled ceiling hung, mushrooms illuminating the rock with a mauve glow. Mira swam over to the side of the pool and hoisted herself out, extending a hand to Rory and helping him up as well. Their teeth chattered against the razor chill and Rory worried that if they were too cold for too long they would die.

'C-Come on, let's get m-m-moving: that will h-help us w-warm up,' he managed.

Mira simply nodded, her jaw firmly clenched, though she was unable to prevent her lips from wobbling.

The children walked through the cavern, with no sign of tornits – thankfully – but also no sign of Limmy or anyone else. After a short while, however, they felt a breeze and, turning into a separate section of cavern, found Limmy and the muktuk attendants huddled together on the floor.

'L-Limmy!' Mira yelled, flinging herself upon her captain.

'Mira!' Limmy squealed back, planting kisses on the girl's head. 'Thank goodness you're alive! But look at you – you're soaking wet and freezing cold!' She hugged Mira tight and looked up. 'Rory? Why are you here? Where's Xam?'

But Rory returned Limmy's alert gaze, seeing the captain in a new light. Did she know about Clavius Hobble? Had she kept anything from him? By now, every other member of the crew was wobbling to his or her feet, muttering to each other.

'Come on, g-guys!' Rory called. 'W-We need to get out of here w-while w-we still can!'

'We can't leave the others behind!' one woman shouted, desperately.

'Yes, those monsters took two of our people,' a man added.

A general yell of agreement wentr up.

'They're… they're d-dead,' Rory replied, hugging himself. 'Me and Mira, w-we…' He recalled the death of that first man and screwed his eyes shut. 'We saw it.'

There was more mumbling among the crewmen.

'Then there is nothing we can do,' said the man who spoke before. 'For a muktuk attendant not to be buried on the back of their muktuk though…' He made a strange sign with his fingers over his face, like a prayer.

'Is there a way out?' Limmy asked, Mira helping her to her feet.

'There was a b-breeze back in the main passage,' Rory replied. He clasped a hand to his head, feeling a sudden stab of pain. A familiar static filled his ears and he realised…

Gary knows where we are…

'What is it, Rory?' Limmy asked.

Rory looked at her. 'I know where to go.'

He dashed out into the passage and looked in one direction, then the other. Up one way, the breeze was strong; down from where he and Mira had come, there was the growing echo of a snort and a trampling of feet.

The tornits are coming…, he realised.

He turned back to the crew. 'Follow me! Quick!'

Rory, despite his exhaustion, broke into something of a run and led the others up the passage. Collectively, they resembled a flock of penguins waddling away to escape a pursuing polar bear. Soon, they came to a section of the passage where the roof had caved in: heavy boulders and rock were stacked up in front of them, impeding their progress. The breeze was fierce and not so oxygen-rich anymore, and Rory could see specks of starlight through small gaps in the rock.

'What do we do now!' the crewmen shouted, crowding about the rock, hammering at it with fists.

Rory looked back into the passage as a large group of tornits approached, crawling over floor, wall and ceiling alike, their golden animal eyes glinting against the light of the occasional mushroom.

'Look away, children…' Limmy muttered, throwing herself in front of Rory and Mira.

But as the monsters accelerated towards the group, the ceiling above them collapsed in a deafening explosion of rock, snow and ice. The hum of engines filled Rory's ears and the glow of porphuragate penetrated the cloud of dusty snow. As it cleared, he was presented with a view of the *Scuabtuinne*, settling down, with its ramp extended. The crewmen cheered as one, hugging each other and patting Rory on the shoulder.

'Please do come aboard,' came the voice of Beak, the physician wobbling on its wheel at the top of the ramp with Gary floating at its side. 'I must assess each and every one of you.'

Rory grabbed Mira's hand and, together, they ran up the ramp with all the crew hot on their heels. But when they looked back, Limmy hadn't moved.

'Come on!' Mira yelled.

Limmy looked up. 'I don't deserve to be rescued…'

'Come on!' Rory barked, echoing the little engineer.

'Yes, come *on*!' Xam's voice echoed through a speaker system in the cargo hold.

Limmy snapped out of whatever was preoccupying her mind and ran up the ramp to join her crew. As the *Scuabtuinne* took off, Rory's last view of Lepidus was one of bitter darkness, pinched out of sight as the ramp juddered shut.

Once the *Scuabtuinne* had left the appalling moon behind, the whole crew convened on the Bridge to discuss what should happen next – everyone who had been out in the cold wrapped in a foil blanket, save Limmy, who stubbornly refused one. Rory slumped into his usual seat, gripping his own blanket tight around him, with Gary cooing soothingly at his side, though even the little muktuk could not tear him from his thoughts. Xam sat cross-armed in his navigator's seat, his breath condensing against the screens at his panel, and Mira stared absently into the distance in another chair. Limmy was perched on some steps nearer the glass of the Dome, her back to everyone else. The muktuk attendants, however, noisily clamoured around Henley, as they might have done a prophet, thanking him for their rescue.

'How are yer?' Henley said to Rory, at last pulling away from his adoring followers. 'And *you*, Rory, doing such a stupid thing as leaving the ship on yer own!'

'I'm sorry, Henley,' Rory replied, absently.

'Hmm… Well, if yer hadn't then yer wouldn't have found Mira or my attendants,' Henley added, backing down. And then his voice became fierce again. 'But we're lucky to have escaped that moon with our lives. And that's no thanks ter our captain.' Henley sighed. 'That little excursion killed a lot of time – *and* two of my people! How far behind are we, Rory? Yer spoken ter Gary yet?'

He hadn't. He looked at the muktuk. The familiar static had been building in his ears ever since coming back aboard and it was clear that Gary wished to convey something of importance, but Rory was utterly terrified that it would be bad news. However, he couldn't put it off forever.

Rory closed his eyes, allowing the static to fill his ears and, as before, he felt the presence of the little muktuk in his mind. There were two images: one representing Gary and the other representing him. They revolved around each other but, other than that, neither of them moved. There was no trail visible, as there had been before…

Rory opened his eyes and wiped away a tear or two. He looked up at Henley and shook his head. Henley sighed, nodded and then clapped a comforting hand on the boy's shoulder.

'Listen up, everyone,' came Limmy's shaky voice. She had moved over to the captain's chair, one hand on the arm, her face gritted with sombre resolution. 'Today's losses were a tragedy –'

'Wouldn't have happened if I'd been leadin' 'em!' Henley growled. 'And they can't even be buried on the back of Rongomai.'

All of his attendants yelled in anger and resentment.

Limmy met Henley's gaze. 'There was nothing I could do,' she said through chattering teeth. 'And this journey has gone on too long now. As of this moment, we are heading back to Widdershins.'

Rory's mouth fell open in disbelief. 'No…' he mumbled.

'*What?*' Henley barked. 'And have their deaths mean *nothing*? Brave souls both. No, no, no. We carry on.'

'Rory?' Limmy called, looking past the Muktuk Whisperer. 'Can Gary sense his mother?'

Rory dipped his head, closed his eyes and opened them again. He looked up to find everyone on the Bridge looking at him. 'No.'

Limmy held one arm out towards Rory, then looked at Henley and said, 'There you go.'

'But I do know where Haligogen is,' Rory added and, once again, drew the attention of everyone on the Bridge. Some people gasped; others mumbled among themselves.

'How do yer know that, m'lad?' Henley asked, his tone almost suspicious. 'Has Gary told yer somethin'?'

Rory shook his head, looking briefly to Mira and back again. 'On Lepidus, when I found Mira, she was with this… monster. A tornit… but it wasn't like the others. It spoke. And it had a name: Fleek.'

Again, people spoke among themselves. Even Xam was transfixed. Limmy's expression was querulous and Henley urged his followers to calm.

'And… what did this *Fleek* say?' Henley asked, quietly.

'He told me where to find Haligogen. He told me that it's beyond Neptune, but before Pluto. He also said that it's twinned with a burning, salt-tailed moon…'

Henley's eyes flashed. 'Vejovis…' he muttered.

'What?' Rory replied.

'Vejovis,' Henley repeated, louder this time. 'Some of the myths call it that. It burns with a cloud of sodium…'

'He also told me something else,' Rory interrupted, quietening the Bridge again. 'He said that... he said that the Whiffetsnatcher... that his real name was... Clavius *Hobble*.'

At this, several heads dropped – not least of all the heads of Henley, Limmy and Xam.

'Oh! Just like you, Rory,' Mira said, innocently.

Rory nodded, looking down. 'Yeah... just like me... You all knew, didn't you?'

Henley made to speak, but Limmy paced across the Bridge and knelt down in front of Rory. She tried to take his hands but he snatched them away. Inside, he could feel the surge of blood through his veins and his cheeks growing hot, despite the cold.

'Rory...' Limmy began, slowly, her breath forming a vapour. 'Yes, some of us did know. Did Fleek tell you anything else?'

Rory shook his head.

'Okay... The Whiffetsnatcher is... well, he's your grandfather. *Your* mother is *his* daughter,' Limmy continued. 'But I don't know what he wants with her and why he's travelling to Haligogen.'

'How do you know who he is, though?' Rory snapped, tears springing afresh to his eyes.

Henley stepped forward. 'Clavius, yer grandfather, were the first human *born* in space – he's famous. He was – *is* – a gifted engineer and was so from a young age.'

'But he's also famous for other reasons,' Limmy interrupted. 'You see, Rory, Clavius Hobble was born with a severe disability that prevented him from walking. His parents... well, they *abused* him, and Widdershins – by all accounts – was a very different place back in what *you* would call the 1950s.

'There were fears that something about Minerva was affecting babies inside the womb. Hurting them somehow. Over twenty per cent of children were born with either a physical disability, or went on to develop mental health problems. The Chain of Health, Medicine and Exo-botany and the Chain of Exo-biology did research on it for the Cosmic Commission, but… they decided that these children had no place in the colony. It was easier to pretend it wasn't happening. Someone called Dr Cillian Caulder' – there was an uncomfortable shuffling of hands around the Bridge – 'built a home called Caulder Place where all these children with disabilities went to live – including your grandfather. But your grandfather stood up for the other children throughout his childhood and even invented something to help himself walk.

'In what was 1972 back on Earth, there was the Caulder Place Scandal where it was discovered that Dr Caulder had directed experiments on the children to try and find out why they were born the way they were. But he never asked for permission from their parents and did these experiments against the children's wishes. Clavius fought for justice and was a key reason the Chain of Social Beneficence was founded, which ensures that vulnerable children are protected. Despite that, Dr Caulder was not banished from the colony and was kept on, just transferred to different projects.'

'Yer grandfather couldn't take that,' Henley said, joining the conversation again. 'He determined that he would explore the farthest reaches of the Solar System – to prove that a disability needn't hold anyone back. Was something no one had even dared attempt since Beatrix. He couldn't have been more than twenty-five years old when he finished construction of the *Phaethon* with his team. Left Widdershins shortly after…'

'And after *that* is where history and myth blur,' Limmy finished.

'What do you mean?' asked Rory, his head still bowed.

'That's where the stories come in,' Xam added, from his navigator's seat. 'Haligogen. Tornits. The Pry.' Xam's voice came nearer, suggesting he had gotten up from his chair. 'In 1984, Clavius returned to Widdershins and told *everyone* about his adventures. But he was laughed at. Ridiculed. He said that the planet Haligogen could *heal* people. When the excitement of his return wore off, no one gave him time of day. I think he's meant to have met… well, she would be your grandma, little Hobster… at that time.'

Rory felt even more confused. He remembered having spoken to Limmy when he first came into space about Haligogen; she, too, had told him it was rumoured to have the power of healing people. 'My grandma died on Earth. She… she had a heart attack. And Mum never said anything about not being born on Earth – she'd have probably mentioned something like that!'

'I don't know, m'boy,' Henley said, sighing. Rory looked up at him and something in the Muktuk Whisperer's face darkened. 'But I *do* know that, over twenty years ago, children started going missing after Clavius went rogue. His ship would appear in the Minervan sky and children would disappear. A lot of parents were *destroyed* by the loss of their children… And that's when we first knew of those *hateful* creatures, the Pry. I'm sorry, Rory, but I don't know anything more about where yer mum features in this tale.'

Henley managed a weak smile and something in Rory softened.

'I do,' came Limmy's quiet voice. Rory turned his attention upon her, frowning, and something hardened once again. She lowered her head. 'And I've known since I first met you on Earth. The *Scuabtuinne's* mission was always a bit of a mystery – even to me. All I knew, back on Earth, was that I had to protect you and your mother, Rory. I knew then who the Whiffetsnatcher really was and I knew that he was interested in your mother. But it was only when we reached Widdershins and I spoke to the Council that I found out the truth. And perhaps you want to hear what I have to say next in private, Rory.' She raised her head, eyes meeting Rory's.

'No. Tell me now,' Rory replied, through tears.

Limmy nodded. 'Very well. Your mother was born in 1988 to Clavius and Monica Hobble. From a young age, it was clear to her parents that she suffered from some kind of mental health condition. Clavius became what he, as a child, had hated: a parent who could not look past his own child's disability. He told Monica he would take Joyce to Haligogen to try and "cure" her. But Monica couldn't bear to be parted from her daughter and told Clavius to leave. Clavius tried to abduct your mother multiple times, but not before abducting other children from Widdershins and maybe even children from Earth – we don't know for sure. His name was almost forgotten and he became known simply as the Whiffetsnatcher. The Pry would foretell his arrival, as they were sent ahead as scouts to find the children and pinpoint them – where the Pry come from and what they are, we don't know either.

'Widdershins grew so fearful and the community blamed

Monica and Joyce for drawing the Whiffetsnatcher *to* the colony. So… they turned on them. They were banished from Widdershins and forced to live in hiding on Earth. In Croydon. And it worked. The abductions on Minerva stopped and, a generation later, the Whiffetsnatcher is little more than a story now.'

Rory's cheeks were red with heat and slick with tears. 'Why didn't you tell me any of this sooner!? I trusted you, Limmy!'

Limmy's face contracted, as though in pain. 'I–I'm sorry, Rory. Taking you off Earth, introducing you to all of… *this*… I thought that for you to know the full truth *too* early would be devastating. What with your OCD, I… I was worried what the effect would be. And I… er' – Limmy too was tearful – 'I decided that you should not know. Not yet. I never meant for you to find out like *this* and I was always going to tell you.' She made to take Rory's hand again, but Rory yanked it away.

Rooory, Rooory. The trail has gone dry. People have died. And it's all your fault!

'Shut up!' Rory yelled, wrapping his arms about his head. He felt Gary nuzzle him.

'Leave him be, Limmy,' he heard Henley say in a dangerous tone. 'Yer've done enough.'

'*I've* done enough?' Limmy snapped. 'I'm the only one here taking responsibility for difficult decisions! I don't see *you* doing that, Henley. But *this*… This has gone far enough! Don't touch me!'

'Okay, okay – sorry,' came Xam's wounded voice.

'Xam!' Limmy's voice was farther away now. 'Get back in your seat. We're turning around. We've lost two people already. We're *not* losing anyone else. We're going back to

Minerva. We have children on board and their welfare is paramount. I was a fool for going along with any of this in the first place.'

There came a general clamour from Rongomai's attendants.

'We cannot go back now,' Henley growled. 'The deaths of my two men – of Curry and Stevenson – will count fer *nothing*!'

'And what of *our* lives?' Limmy retorted. 'I am responsible for the deaths of those men and I am sorry – truly I am. I failed as a captain. I failed as a leader. But I will *not* make another wrong decision.'

'And how yer goin' ter go back… if I don't *tell* Rongomai we're *goin'* back?' Henley positively spat.

Rory uncovered his face and looked up to find Limmy, in her captain's chair, glaring up at Henley, who stood with his shoulders and legs set apart, facing her.

'I am your captain,' Limmy said, through clenched teeth, emphasising each word. 'And, as such, you will do as I say.'

'No. I will not.'

Limmy looked both shocked and afraid. 'Henley, this is a symbiont expedition! The *Scuabtuinne* will be stranded without Rongomai. Article 2 of the Code of Spacefaring clearly st–'

'Don't quote the Code ter me,' Henley snapped. 'This expedition was not sanctioned by the Commission and we are *well* past being bound by their rules.'

'But you *offered* Rongomai as the muktuk for my ship, all those months and months ago. Your reputation preceded you: angry, pig-headed, a man who struggled with orders, *tall-tongued* – you told me that you being part of this mission was a *punishment* from the Council. But, on Widdershins, the

Council told me the truth: that you had volunteered – *pleaded* to be part of this symbiont expedition! Why, Henley? What is it you want? Were you after a ship this whole time? Did you think that I would be a pushover? Some silly little girl who couldn't stand her ground. Well, *I'm* the captain. So you can damn well do as you're told!'

Henley's face twisted in anger. 'Yer don't know the first thing about me. Yer don't know the first thing about leading. And yer *ain't* getting my acquiescence.'

Limmy leapt up out of her chair. Behind her, Xam did the same and the muktuk attendants closed around Henley.

'Stop it!' Mira yelled.

But the adults did not seem to pay attention.

'Henley, this is your last chance: I want you to take your attendants and go back down to Rongomai. We are turning around.'

'No chance,' Henley practically whispered, eyes squinting.

Rory's mind was filled with images of the crew fighting each other. Broken bones. Blood. Cries of pain. He squeezed his eyes shut and tried to control his breathing.

Rooory, Rooory. They're arguing because of you. They're going to hurt each other – just you wait and see. Soon, there will be killing!

'Mira's right,' he said, jumping up from his seat and setting himself in between Limmy and Henley. 'Please… stop it. I don't want anyone to be hurt because of me.'

'Too late, lad,' Henley told him. 'We've gone past that – but it weren't yer fault. If Limmy hadn't taken my attendants with her, then they wouldn't be dead.'

Limmy appeared to be fighting back tears. 'Henley, please, we must go back!'

'We must not!' he roared. 'The god-child may have lost the trail, but Rongomai may yet sniff out the sodium moon of Vejovis! Come on, men! Off the map we go!'

Henley turned to leave the Bridge, the attendants cheering behind him. But Xam plodded forward with a few determined steps, grabbed Henley, pulled him back – Limmy and Rory both yelled at him to stop – and punched him square in the jaw. The Muktuk Whisperer grunted, slamming into to the floor with a *thwack*. Various attendants rounded on Xam, but the big navigator raised his fists and they retreated. Limmy pulled him away and told him to sit back in his chair and leave the situation to her.

Rory looked down at Henley, who spat out a globule of blood and looked fiercely up into the boy's eyes.

'Yer know I'm right,' he whispered. 'If yer ever want ter see yer mum again, then we *must* go on!'

The words swirled about in Rory's mind and, for a split second, there was only him and the Whisperer, everything around them reduced to background noise. The moment ended and the muktuk attendants picked Henley up off of the floor, shuffling out of the Bridge. Soon, there was only Rory, Limmy, Xam and Mira left.

'Xam, you have the Bridge,' Limmy mumbled. 'I can no longer captain this ship.'

And with that, Limmy also left the Bridge.

Rory, Xam and Mira looked from one to the other. Finally, Rory swallowed a knot and ran after his social worker.

Rory found Limmy in her quarters, standing at her porthole window, looking out into space. He knocked at her door, but she did not answer and he felt uncomfortable invading her privacy; however, he was worried.

'Hi, Limmy…' Rory said.

He waited a moment, but Limmy did not answer, so he moved cautiously across the room towards her. Settling at her side, he looked out of the window too. Together, they kept a contented silence.

'They're beautiful, aren't they?' Limmy said, after a while.

Rory looked up at her sad, gentle face. 'What are, Limmy?'

She smiled down at him. 'Oh, the stars. Y'know, I remember when I came to England and that first night I was in my foster parents' home. All the way over on my journey, I'd looked at the stars each night because they… they never changed. And, in that little bedroom, on that little street in Croydon, I looked out of the window that first night and I could hardly see the stars for all the light pollution. That's when I knew I was truly in a strange and alien place. Being up here, though… I feel like I'm home again.'

Rory sensed that Limmy wanted to talk.

Perhaps it makes her feel better, like with me, he mused.

'Limmy? How did you end up as cap– How did you end up in space? You must have been special when you were a child.'

Limmy continued to look out of the window, smiling. 'Oh, I'm nothing special, kid. Never was. I learned about all *this*' – she held her hands out – 'because of my foster parents. Eliza and Gideon Thorne… They were a funny old couple – loved 'em to bits, of course – but they *were* odd. Descendants, they told me, of some of the original members of the Gammaguild and they were a contact point for Widdershins on Earth. Didn't believe a word of it, of course, but thought they were telling wonderful stories at the time. Then, when they actually took me, one night, to see their spaceship... well, that's when everything changed. That night, I saw the Congo from space. It looked so big compared to England... but I realised how small it really was.'

She lowered her eyes. 'My foster parents told me that our society – y'know, back on Earth – didn't expect much of children in care but that expectation was wrong and I was destined for something more. At school, I was picked on for not having a *real* mum and dad, and they knew I had a social worker too. It was difficult enough being an African girl with a French accent! I guess being an outsider made it easier when I enrolled for Command Training. I met others like me and all of us had different goals: some just wanted to leave the planet behind, get as far into space as possible and never look back; but others, like me, weren't quite ready for that. I'd been given this opportunity, but it didn't feel right to leave behind so many other kids who were in care and who weren't being given the same chances as me. That's why I applied to university to become a social worker; I wanted to make a difference. Besides, because I'd decided to stay on Earth, I needed a cover if I was to be an agent for Widdershins.'

'Did you know much about Widdershins at the time?' Rory asked.

'Only what my foster parents told me. They made it sound... idyllic. And when I asked why they were still on Earth, if Widdershins really was all that, they simply said, "Oh, well, we can't be dealing with all that space stuff at our age!

The stars are for the next generation," and that was enough for me. It never sat easily with me that Widdershins should stay hidden, but... I came to accept it.

'By the time I earned my command, I was already carrying out jobs for Widdershins, and when I qualified as a social worker, I was well placed in a local authority to link up with other sleeper agents.'

Rory looked back out of the window. 'How did you come to... how did you come to captain the *Scuabtuinne*?'

Limmy chuckled. 'This old heap of junk? It was a present from my foster parents. They passed it on to me. Xam was in care – like me – and he was my first recruit. He would go back and forth to Minerva and, one day, he brought Beak along, telling me, "Any great ship needs a proper crew and Sick Bay can't be empty!".'

'What about Mira? How did she come aboard?'

Limmy's smile faded. 'She was... never meant to. Mira was looked after by my foster parents after I left home. I kept on going back to them, of course, and that's how I got to know Mira. But then my foster parents died and... Mira couldn't bear to be with another family, so I took her aboard the *Scuabtuinne*. She fell in love with engineering and was a natural, so she filled the role and spent hours reading and reading about Widdershins and our secret history.'

Rory paused to consider all his social worker had said. 'So... this crew only exists because of *you*. It's like a family.'

'A family I'm not fit to lead,' Limmy said, sighing and moving away from the window to settle on her bed. 'Those two muktuk attendants... Curry and Stevenson... trusted me with their lives and I... I failed them.'

Rory cast his mind back to his encounter with Fleek and the brutality of the tornits. 'There was nothing you could have done, though. You heard what Henley said: this is farther out than almost anyone has ever been and there *are* monsters here.'

The mention of Henley made Limmy flinch and she scowled. 'Henley... Henley is a dangerous man. I don't know what his game is, but he *is* up to something.' She looked up and directly into Rory's eye. 'Don't trust that man, kid.'

Silence fell between them but was soon punctuated by the sound of the ship heaving and buckling. Rory looked around the room, as though expecting to see the walls and ceiling cave in.

'That'll be us underway,' Limmy said. 'You should get back up to the Bridge. Xam and Mira may need a hand.'

With that, Limmy turned her back on Rory and drew her legs up into a foetal position. Rory realised that he was not going to get anything more from her and so, with a final glance over his shoulder, left Limmy to her privacy.

As he made his way back up the corridors towards the Bridge, he heard a familiar static reach his ears, increasing in volume until it felt like it had filled his entire head. His vision dripped away as well and he experienced the sensation of falling. But before the impact of hitting the ground, he found himself standing, alone, in a huge, open space – completely white, with no objects or horizon. Then, all at once, a vast, complicated network of turquoise lines flew into focus – like an artist's impression of the brain's neural pathways. It was like a far more involved and exquisite version of the network Gary had shown him before. And at the thought of Gary, Rory's head rang with the little muktuk's squeal. But the squeal was not a single, simple animal call; it tapered off into a series of bass-toned whirring noises, punctuated with dolphin-like squeaks and chirrups. Rory listened, spellbound, to what could only be communication. Its complexity far exceeded anything he had heard from Gary up until that point, but he was sure that it was Gary, nonetheless, reaching out to him. But why?

Suddenly, part of the turquoise network flared up, like a node and, farther off and deeper into the network, Rory spotted another node lighting up, as though in response. And then, with a rumble like thunder, the network collapsed in on itself. A pain like the worst kind of burn exploded inside Rory's head and his vision was transported back to the *Scuabtuinne*, where he screamed in the corridor, thrashing about on the floor. Above him, the very air itself seemed to dissolve before splitting around a shape that materialised out of nothing. Before Rory realised what was happening, he found himself looking up into the eyes of Gary, the muktuk squealing and looping the loop as though in celebration. The pain in his head cut off, like a tap being turned off.

'What…' Rory panted, 'did you just do, Gary?'

16

Not Down in Any Map

The days rolled out in long drawls of frost as the *Scuabtuinne* travelled still farther from the Sun. The Uranian and then the Neptunian systems withered into memory as Rongomai – under Henley's influence – led the crew into deeper, darker mystery and danger. They passed muktuk pods, decimated schools of kuldrevit and stranger creatures still: the eel-like stellaeurypharynx; something that looked like a fleshy ball that lived in a shell of ice – Xam called it a glacieremita; and something that no one had seen before that resembled a cross between a snowflake and an octopus. Rory was confident, however, that Xam's description of it as 'that tentacley-ice-cream-dude' was unlikely to catch on.

The temperature aboard the *Scuabtuinne* had dropped below zero degrees and there it stayed, leaving the banleuc corridors covered in a permanent frost and the glass of the Dome sparkling with ice. Everyone was dressed, at all times, in thick, furry clothing with hot water bottles lining pockets. Even so, the cold was difficult to bear and the heat given off by the porphuragate engines left only Engineering and the surrounding quarters with anything that faintly resembled heat.

After his bizarre experience with Gary, Rory had – with a slight pang of guilt – travelled down the umbilical to meet with Henley, who had been delighted to see him.

'I've never heard of the like,' the Whisperer had told Rory, twisting his beard and scratching at his eyeliner. 'Yer a rare lad and the god-child is a rare god-child. Indeed.'

Rory hadn't been entirely confident Henley believed everything he was saying; besides, the Whisperer had appeared distracted.

'Henley?'

'Yes, m'boy?'

'Limmy,' he had lowered his head, 'thinks you're... well, that you have other reasons for wanting to carry on with our journey.'

The words had hung like a question in the air, inviting a response but also, as Rory remembered, challenging Henley not to respond. Henley had looked back curiously at Rory, before breaking into a grin.

'Listen well, lad,' he'd started, dropping a lazy arm around Rory's shoulders. 'I've known yer fer some time now and I've come ter think of yer in a... well, in a *fatherly* way. And what kind of a father would I be if I didn't help yer ter get yer mother back, eh? I want to find the Whiffetsnatcher and yer mother just as much as you. Yer the closest I got ter family – 'part from my attendants and Rongomai, of course... Oh, and I know yer fond of Limmy and I'm sorry fer upsetting yer but

– as admirable as she is – she *is* still young and it's in her nature ter be cautious. We *can't* have caution now at this crucial hour!'

He had scratched Rory's head and Rory had felt a little better.

'How *did* you end up as part of this symbiont crew? Anyone can see that' – he had suddenly become self-conscious – 'well that you and Limmy don't like each other. She said that you pleaded to be part of the mission.'

Henley's smile had seemed bitter. 'There are… stories about me, lad. I used ter be part of symbiont crews with *different* missions to this one. There are some that would say that my attendants and I have been *demoted*. But when I heard about Limmy's mission – ter protect yer mother from the Whiffetsnatcher – I jumped at the chance.' He'd started toying with his engraved earring then, eyes narrowing, and something had struck Rory momentarily, though he hadn't been able to place what it was. 'Limmy knew I had a reputation and – again, young as she is – she made a snap judgement about me.' He'd laughed, loud and almost forced. 'But what's important is that yer know me and yer *know* I can be trusted, eh?'

Standing on the Bridge, looking out of the Dome, Rory reflected on Henley's words and wondered whether Limmy and Henley could ever see eye to eye. His social worker had been, largely, absent from her captain's duties, stating that with Henley making the decisions about where to send Rongomai with his whispers, her role was mostly useless and, at least on the *Scuabtuinne*, Xam was the only person who was really needed on the Bridge. But a grave request from Xam for everyone to come to the Bridge changed all that. So, Rory found himself gazing out of the Dome at a shifting cloud of gas with Xam, Limmy, Mira and even Beak all in attendance too.

'What are we looking at, Xam?' Limmy asked, leaning forward in the captain's chair. 'I don't see much... except cloud.'

Xam held up a single finger and grabbed at the radio-like device above him as a scratchy noise and a voice came through.

'*... there?*'

'I'm here,' Xam spoke coolly into the radio. 'We're all on the Bridge now, Henley. What is it? Over.'

The radio crackled, then... '*Watch.*'

Rory turned from the radio and patted Gary's head, the not-so-little muktuk floating beside him. From below the lower half of the Dome, Rongomai drifted up, its mountainous crystals flickering through a hundred shades of purple. The *Scuabtuinne* groaned as the umbilical shifted its position like a disturbed sleeper.

'*Venting now, over!*' the radio crackled.

Rory and the rest of the crew looked out of the Dome, eyes scanning for the slightest sign of activity. At first, nothing happened and everyone looked to each other, as though for confirmation of some missed spectacle. But then, close enough to Rongomai to make the muktuk noticeably flinch, a huge, blue flame blazed into life. Rory gasped, and everyone else on the Bridge made a similar noise of surprise. However, the flame did not fizzle out, but commenced a journey along an invisible line, much like the fuse on a stick of dynamite.

'Xam, find out what the hell he's doing!' Limmy yelled.

Xam flapped about for the radio and, grabbing it, shouted, 'What is that, dude!? Err, over!'

The radio responded with Henley's jagged laugh. '*That, big boy, is our compass to Haligogen and that vile Whiffetsnatcher! Over.*'

Rory looked to Limmy, whose frown suggested she did not know what Henley meant. Xam raised his eyebrows and Mira shrugged.

'I do not feel equipped to be here,' Beak interjected. 'Permission to –'

'Shut it, Beaky,' Limmy said, her tone firm. She hopped up and stepped towards her navigator, opening out a hand. 'Xam, give that to me.'

Xam slapped the radio into Limmy's palm and settled back into his seat.

'Henley, explain. Over.'

'*Ah! Captain! Good ter have yer back! Enjoying the show?*'

'I'd be enjoying it far more if I knew what it was and I knew that it didn't threaten my ship. Over.'

'*Yer mark that gas cloud ahead of us? Well, yer can't see it but here begins a trail of oxygen-enriched sodium particles that runs on in ter that cloud and twists and turns off before finally reaching…*'

Rory's eyes widened. 'Vejovis! The moon around Haligogen with a sodium tail!'

'*Ah! Rare lad!*' the radio practically roared, loud enough to make Gary squeak, perhaps in fright. '*I whispered soft ter Rongomai, told him ter vent a little HeX*' – Rory recalled HeX as being the Helium X element that the muktuks used to inflate their pouches – '*Just enough ter react and…*'

'The reaction will burn all the way through the gas and lead us to Haligogen,' Limmy said aloud, working it out for herself.

'*Precisely. That cloud is vast – easy ter get lost or ter miss something – but Vejovis leaves a crumb trail fer us ter follow. When Rory told us about what that Fleek creature gave as Haligogen's position, I whispered to Rongomai. It took a while fer me ter understand the ideas that Rongomai put in my head, but I got there. He showed me a field of sodium out here between Neptune and Pluto. He didn't know what it was, but I worked it out – it was the salt burning from Vejovis, like blood dripping from a deep cut,'* Henley barked. *'Now, we best be chasing that spark or we'll lose it. Over.'*

Rongomai lurched forward, making the *Scuabtuinne* scream and grate in excruciation, and it was sufficient to toss Xam onto his workstation, throwing his hands around like a frenzied pianist. The ship itself fired forward and returned to its habitual position with very little of its symbiont muktuk visible from the Dome. The gas soon enveloped them but, through the green and brown gases, the flare of the HeX/sodium reaction scattered a ghostly blue light out into the surrounding cloud, flashing like lightning. For many hours, they travelled on through the gas in silence and anticipation.

Eventually, Rongomai and the *Scuabtuinne* broke through the cloud and came into a clearing where the stars were once more visible. But not only the stars…

'I-Is that…?' Rory almost whispered, standing up.

The rest of the crew stirred from a collective slumber and leaned in closer towards the Dome as though this might improve the view.

'Must be,' Limmy muttered.

Beyond the Dome, a dark planet perched quite unassumingly in the eerie gloom. Visible beneath a thick cloud dominating much of the atmosphere, the surface looked ashy.

'*We found her,*' the radio crackled. '*At last we found her! We found Haligogen!*'

Rory felt his heart skip a few beats, hardly believing that, after all these months, he was now only a matter of hours from seeing his mum again. But a familiar stab of anxiety shrivelled any sense of growing excitement, and his thoughts turned from happiness to revulsion. He quickly realised that part of him did not want to find his mum. All those times when she had raised her voice, mocked him, forgotten to feed him... all of that suddenly charged him with a need for justice. But it competed with the familiar voice that urged him to consider just how despicable a person he was for having such thoughts.

'Rory? You okay, kid?' Limmy said. She seemed to have been trying to get his attention for a while.

Rory blinked his eyes a few times. 'Yeah, I'm fine.'

Limmy's eyes lingered on him as though to say, 'Oh no you aren't. But I'm here for you.'

'Here comes the spark again!' Xam announced, pointing to the blue flare as it fizzled through space on its trajectory to Vejovis.

Haligogen's sole satellite hung above the planet, small and unimposing, yet startlingly white with a wispy tail hanging off of it like liquid nitrogen.

Rory became aware of Gary's crystals flashing in a disco of pinks, purples, greens and blues. And then the static returned, dialling up in intensity so fast that he yelled with the shock of it. Again, he was dimly aware of a sense of falling as his vision was taken over by pure, uninterrupted whiteness. The turquoise grid jumped into focus, as it had before, and a node pulsed into a single, large black sphere with another, smaller sphere next to it. Within the larger sphere, Rory watched as a golden shape appeared, with four muktuks beside it.

Haligogen and Vejovis… And the Whiffetsnatcher is down there on the planet, Rory realised.

Suddenly, the smaller node representing Vejovis shattered, collided with Haligogen, and then the planet, along with the golden ship and the four muktuks, crumbled into oblivion. Rory was confused and Gary's subsequent noises did nothing to clarify what he had seen.

'Rory! Wake up!' came a voice.

Rory opened his eyes, his forehead sweating despite the Bridge's freezing temperature, and he looked up into the faces of Limmy, Xam, Beak and even Mira.

'Mr Hobble,' Beak declared. 'Has not expired.'

'Course he hasn't!' Xam replied, wiping his forehead. 'The little Hobster wouldn't miss this.'

Limmy and Xam lifted him to his feet and eased him into his chair. Rory noticed that Gary was missing.

'Where's…' he began.

Limmy looked at Xam, then back at Rory. 'Oh, yeah…' She pointed beyond the Dome.

Out in space, Rory could see a little glowing blob seemingly teleporting further and further towards Haligogen, appearing and disappearing like a stone skipping across a lake.

'Did you know he could do that?' Limmy asked.

Rory thought back to the incident outside Limmy's room after they escaped Lepidus. 'Not exactly, but I think I knew something was diff–'

He stopped speaking as the *Scuabtuinne* groaned once again

and Rongomai commenced its movement towards the planet as well.

The radio above Xam sparked into Henley's voice. '*What were that coming out of the ship? 'Twere skimming the heavens. Over.*'

Xam, eyes still fixed to a point beyond the Dome, absently pulled the radio to his mouth. 'That was Gary. He… *teleported* off the Bridge and out into space. Now he's jumping towards Haligogen faster than an exo-cricetid with a firework up its backside.'

'*Can it be?*' replied Henley, his voice quiet and full of awe. '*The Great Question…*'

Limmy snatched at the radio above her own head. 'What are you talking about now?'

But Rory's eyes widened. He remembered back to when he was in Widdershins with Henley and the conversation they had had with Bill, Chief Muktuk Whisperer, in the Temple of the Muktuks.

'You said that one day I might answer it,' Rory called out to Henley – Limmy and Xam looking at him curiously. 'But you never told me what it was…'

The radios above both captain and navigator scratched and scraped with static before Henley's voice returned. '*Aye, m'lad. That I never did. The Great Question concerns an… irregularity with the muktuks and the way they travel. In the year that you would call 1951, Rory, the* Aeneas *launched from Earth ter establish a colony on Minerva.*' Rory recalled that the *Aeneas* was the first interplanetary ship built by the Gammaguild. '*Well, yer ever wonder why that miserable submarine ended up stuck fast in the waterfall above Widdershins? Huh? It* materialised *there.*'

'That's just a crackpot story that no one believes,' Limmy interrupted.

The radio fizzled. '*The* Aeneas *made it from Earth to Minerva in less than a minute. It was documented* –'

'Poorly detailed accounts probably made by some planet-minded loon with the space-bends,' Limmy countered.

'*How else d'yer explain the god-child travelling at the moment then?*' Henley growled. Rory looked back out of the Dome at Gary, who continued to flicker across space in movement that did look for all the world like mini-teleportation. '*The Great Question was how the* Aeneas *managed to travel so far, so fast. We Whisperers held that it must have been something to do with the muktuks – something we didn't know about them. We theorised that they could travel great distances in a way that we didn't yet understand, but ter us t'would look like teleportation.*'

'Whatever he's doing,' Xam began, 'he seems in a big rush to get to that planet!'

Rory rubbed at a spot on his head where a dull ache throbbed, intermittently. '*He's* down there… Gary showed me.'

Limmy turned to face him. 'You mean…'

Rory nodded. 'Gary sensed his mum. Which means my… *my* mum is there too.'

'*Don't worry, lad!*' Henley barked through the radio. '*We've cornered the Whiffetsnatcher now and he's not getting away this time.*'

The *Scuabtuinne* lurched on, dragged by Rongomai, towards Haligogen. The mysterious planet loomed ever larger beyond the Dome, its atmosphere a choking mass of grey storms. Tens of thousands of miles away, yet still a large presence in the heavens, the salt moon Vejovis sat – a white watcher, bleeding sodium into the void.

Entering Haligogen's upper atmosphere, Gary finally dematerialised and did not reappear. Rongomai sank towards the planet as well and the *Scuabtuinne* fell into a nightmarish prison of cloud above and below, brown tornadoes clad in lightning connecting different layers of the storm. Rory stared in awe at the sight, so alien and dramatic. The ship shuddered more and more as it drove deeper towards the surface.

'Readings show that the atmosphere is one hundred and fifty miles thick – mainly carbon dioxide, carbon monoxide and...' Xam yelled above the turbulence, 'something else. I don't know what but... nothing that's ever been recorded before.'

'What do you mean? A new element?' Limmy asked, her voice clipped, eyes trained intently on the sight beyond the Dome.

'I'm just not sure,' Xam replied. 'Whatever it is it's too much for the *Scuabtuinne's* computers to handle.'

'Xam, a tuna sandwich would be too much for the *Scuabtuinne's* computers to handle – probably just a malfunction. Mira – how's the ship holding up? This storm is intense.'

'Hull losing integrity,' Mira reported, matter-of-factly.

Limmy turned to face her. 'Will we make it?'

Mira shrugged. 'I don't know!' she responded, almost accusingly.

But the juddering sensation suddenly stopped and the ship sailed through a final layer of cloud, revealing the planet's surface. Haligogen appeared as a rocky contortion of ashy

315

mountain and canyon. The darkness had an almost solid quality to it and would have been complete were it not for the livid light of Vejovis shining through the cloud, throwing a silvery sheen over everything it touched.

'Why would anyone want to come *here*?' Xam muttered, clearly unimpressed.

Rory gasped, pointing out of the Dome. 'Look! Over there!'

Everyone focused on the object of Rory's attention. Some way up ahead, four adult muktuks floated about, each still attached by umbilical to a golden object, which looked to have landed.

'It's the *Phaethon*,' Limmy announced. 'He really is here.'

'And look again!' Rory yelled, jumping to his feet.

In the distance, the small, glowing form of Gary materialised in among the four adult muktuks, who all circled him, crystals running through a spectrum of purples, pinks and turquoises. One approached Gary, opened its mouth, and extended a tentacle, Gary reciprocating.

Just like back on Earth above the church, Rory recalled.

'He found his mum again, kid,' Limmy said, softly. 'Now it's your turn.'

'Hey! What's happening to the *Phaethon*?' Xam spoke up, drawing everyone's attention back to the Whiffetsnatcher's ship.

Rory looked back at the golden menace to see a build-up of electricity forming into a ball within the grasp of two ominous-looking pincers.

'Uh-oh. That doesn't look good...' Xam muttered.

Sure enough, the ball of electricity reached a white intensity and a huge arc of lightning fired out, tearing into Rongomai.

The muktuk's squeal was audible and seemed to echo out over the surface of Haligogen. Immediately, the gigantic creature swerved from its course towards a range of mountains. On the Bridge of the *Scuabtuinne*, alarms echoed the animal's distress, Henley's voice ripping through the radio in a series of panicked updates and Limmy yelling instructions to both Xam and Mira. Rory clung on to the arms of his chair as Rongomai's descent wrenched the ship along with it.

'Release the umbilical now!' Limmy screamed.

'Can't! It's jammed!' Xam responded.

'Porphuragate drive failing!' Mira added.

Rongomai fell through a mountain, shearing the peak off in a whirlwind of rock and dust. It twisted to the side, dragging the *Scuabtuinne* with it like a sinking ship sucking a lifeboat down in the aftermath of its demise. The side of another mountain loomed large and Rory prepared himself for the inevitable collision, but it didn't come. Instead, a rending, grating roar – as though of metal being chewed into unnatural shape – drove through the ship.

'Umbilical detached!' Xam yelled. 'Top hatch sealed!'

The release did not come in time. The *Scuabtuinne* scraped along a small, jagged peak and hurtled towards the surface.

'Porphuragate drive failed,' Mira announced.

'Hold on to something!' Limmy screamed.

Rory buckled into his seat and gripped the arms. The ashy surface loomed closer and closer and then… a noise like thunder as the ship collided with the planet in a cloud of ash. He felt the ship spinning, sliding and rolling all at once before, with a tumultuous wheeze, the *Scuabtuinne* came to a stop. In the dim emergency lighting, Rory could only see his breath misting in little red clouds. Around him, the rest of the crew moaned and groaned, but at least everyone was moving. Limmy rubbed at a cut on her head, a trickle of blood running down her forehead; Mira crawled over her own workstation, blinking furiously; Xam massaged himself, complaining of an acute pain in his backside.

The Bridge door nearest Mira opened and in rolled Beak. 'Please state the nature of your medical emergency,' the doctor said, turning first to the little engineer, who swatted at him to go away.

Beak rolled over to first Limmy, then Xam, establishing from both that they had no immediate need of help.

'And you, Master Hobble?' Beak asked.

Rory looked up into the plague doctor mask and realised something. His heartbeat was steady. His lungs were no longer searing with anxiety. His forehead wasn't scrunched up. And his mind was clear, like the air after a thunderstorm. It was a sensation he hadn't felt in years and, despite being on a strange planet at the end of the Solar System, it was the most alien experience yet.

'I'm… absolutely fine. In fact, I feel good.'

Limmy, her attention clearly piqued, looked Rory up and down. 'What do you mean, kid?'

'I mean, those horrible thoughts are gone. That voice isn't there. I don't feel scared anymore.'

Limmy looked at Xam, then at Mira and back to Rory. 'Just like the legends describe…'

'Radio's dead, Captain,' Xam said, smacking the device above his head. 'No way to contact Henley. Guess that's one blessing!'

'I don't much care for him, but I'm still responsible for the muktuk attendants,' Limmy replied, her face determined. 'We need to reach them.'

Rory looked out of the Dome for the first time since the crash landing and spotted something in the distance along the igneous plains.

'What's that?'

Everyone's gaze followed his outstretched finger. Perhaps a quarter of a mile away was what could only be described as a house, looking much the same as any respectable, two- or three-bed property back in South London might, complete with front garden. Surrounding the house was a smooth-surfaced, transparent dome that seemed to be filled with artificial light – completely unlike the one enclosing the *Scuabtuinne's* Bridge.

'Well… that's unexpected,' Xam quipped.

Rory bored a hole through the building with his eyes and came to a conclusion driven by absolute certainty.

'My mum's in there.'

Limmy assessed him. 'Why do you say that?'

Rory continued to study the house. 'I… I don't know, but I know I'm right.' Suddenly, he turned to his social worker. 'I have to go there. I have to see her.'

Limmy kept her eyes on Rory, assessing further. 'I'm going with you, kid. If your mum's in there then we can expect the Whiffetsnatcher to be close by.' She turned to her navigator. 'Xam, I want you, Mira and Beak to make contact with Henley. Rongomai went down hard and there could be a lot of casualties. But we must help. We must help.'

☆

Twenty minutes later the crew was in the cargo bay, everyone geared up in thermal spacesuits – different from the ones used on Lepidus where the atmosphere had had oxygen – that made them look like a cross between a deep-sea diver and a praying mantis; nevertheless, the suits were surprisingly flexible and Mira assured them that they would offer protection, despite the fact that they were on a world that registered one hundred and fifty degrees below zero. Even Beak wore a specialist suit to prevent his cogs freezing or Lancelot, the exo-cricetid, turning into a furry Cornetto.

'According to calculations,' Xam said, speaking into the communications system that linked everyone's suit. 'Rongomai's body is two miles to the north of our position.'

'Rongomai's… body?' Rory repeated, looking up into Xam's face through his transparent helmet.

Xam lowered his eyes. 'Yes… I'm afraid the muktuk's not showing any life signs, little Hobster.'

Everyone was quiet for a moment.

'Then how are we getting off this planet?' Mira demanded.

'We'll have to cross that bridge when we come to it,' Limmy said, her tone firm. 'For now, let's concentrate on our respective missions. Still no word from Henley, Xam?'

'No, Captain, not even a growl…'

'Keep trying and keep in touch,' Limmy commanded, walking over to the big button that opened the hatch and stamping on it.

The hatch opened without fuss this time, but the blast of wind Rory expected to feel did not roll into the cargo bay; instead, the air was utterly still. Once the hatch touched the planet's ashy surface, the crew walked forward, stepping over debris that had mostly been chipped away from the tram still sitting in ruin behind them, and out onto Haligogen. The gravity felt a fair bit weaker than on Earth or even on Minerva, and so movement was easy. Each footstep left a defined print on the surface, ash shooting up in the collision with each boot and drifting serenely skyward where the violent storm raged on, only the occasional crack of thunder breaking the silence.

Clearing the ship, Rory and the rest of the crew looked back towards the mountain range where Rongomai's shattered visage lay strangled by rock and ash – a vast cloud still spilling through the atmosphere in lazy harmonics. Its crystals were clear and empty, and its pouches hung saggy like the skin on a grandparent.

Xam swore. 'Could anyone have survived that?'

'I don't know,' Limmy answered. 'But we have to find out.'

Rory turned away from Rongomai, looking back at the house instead, unaware of its own incongruity on this alien world. He took a step towards it.

'Do you really think your mum is in there?' Mira asked.

Rory turned to the engineer, her face expressionless, and nodded.

Mira nodded also. 'Every day, it's harder for me to remember *my* mum,' she replied, before turning and heading off in the other direction.

Rory watched her catch up with Xam and Beak, who were looking at him.

'Good luck out there, Hobster!' Xam said, giving Rory a thumbs up.

'I, too, wish you good luck, Master Hobble,' Beak added in its posh, English tone.

And with that, Xam, Mira and Beak turned their backs and began their journey to Rongomai.

Limmy walked over to Rory and clapped him on the shoulder. 'C'mon, kid. Let's go find your mum.'

The house grew nearer and nearer, as Rory and Limmy hopped towards it, and the features became clearer. A lawn with a row of evergreens; a bright red front door; windows in the Victorian style; a red-tiled roof and chimney. In that moment, on the verge of achieving what he had set out to do so many months ago, a new thought came into Rory's untroubled mind. It was a thought informed by his recollection of all those times when he went hungry, when he was yelled at and that one occasion he was slapped in the face. He questioned whether he wanted to rescue a person – someone he should have been able to trust – who had brought so much misery into his life. Perhaps this journey was only ever about his guilt for a crime he now realised, in the clarity afforded by this planet, he had not committed. Though the memory had been warped before, he recalled perfectly in that moment that he had not pushed his mother over but rather, instead, he had pulled her hands from his shoulders.

Reaching the dome around the house, Rory and Limmy examined the structure, looking it up and down.

'Looks almost… plastic,' Limmy noted.

Rory stretched out a hand to lay it upon the dome but his hand went straight through the surface, as though he had dipped it in water. He looked at Limmy, who copied him and, together, they took tentative steps through the dome until they were stood at the foot of a path leading up to the front door – a big **426** in metal lettering above a knocker. Sunlight seemed to fall over both house and garden, though from no obvious source, and Rory looked at the grass wrapping round the side of the building, stretching perhaps to a rear garden.

'Do you want to knock?' Limmy asked.

Rory looked again at the front door. Taking a deep breath, he walked along the tiled path and, lifting the knocker, he banged it one, two, three times.

Silence.

He knocked again.

Silence, still.

Knocking it, louder this time, he waited for a response, but nothing came.

'Perhaps we should check around the back,' Limmy suggested.

Rory turned to her and nodded, confused as to why the house was seemingly empty. He walked with Limmy around the side of the house until the rear garden came into view.

His breath left his body.

There, on the lawn, pruning a lily bush, Rory saw his mum. She was dressed in very ordinary clothing, as might befit a summer day, and had no helmet on. Without a second thought, he disengaged the lock on his own helmet and removed it. Limmy protested as he did so, but with the first lungful of air, he found his decision vindicated and took a step towards his mum, disturbing the grass and a few stray twigs. His mum stopped what she was doing, turned and dropped the garden scissors she was holding. Her hands rushed to her mouth as she sucked in her breath. Tears filled her eyes and she stood up.

'Rory, is that really you?'

Rory felt the tears in his own eyes. 'Hello, Mum.'

17

A Life That Cannot Be

She had changed. Her face was not so pale and the frown marks around her eyes were no longer there, not even a trace of them etched into her skin. Her hair was combed and washed, running down to her shoulders instead of knotted in greasy strands. Her hands did not shake and, as she drew them away from her mouth, she held them loosely in front of her dress. But above all else, it was her eyes that marked her so differently from the mother he'd last seen at home all those months ago: they shone with an awareness that had previously been absent and Rory found traces of the love there that he had not felt in so long.

All of a sudden, his mum rushed over to Rory, slid down onto her knees and wrapped her arms around him, weeping uncontrollably. 'Oh my God, I've missed yer so much! I didn't know what 'ad happened and if I could 'ave come lookin' for you, I woulda done.'

Rory didn't know how to react. He glanced up at Limmy,

who finished removing her own helmet and beamed at him. So, he turned back and wrapped his arms around her, slowly, hardly believing that such a change in his mother should have occurred. But then he remembered the changes he himself had felt since coming to Haligogen and the mystery lost its aura.

His mum pulled back, eyes red and nose running. 'Oh dear, look at the state o' me!' She rubbed her face with the back of one hand and took Rory's hand with her other. 'Come inside, let me get you somethin' to eat and drink. Yes. You must be 'ungry. You too – what was it? Lintel? Lemsip? No! *Limmy* – that was it!'

Limmy smiled. 'That would be nice. How about it, kid?'

Rory looked up at his social worker and nodded, letting himself be led on.

Mum smiled. 'Wonderful. Come on, we can go through the back door. I've got shortbread biscuits – believe it or not – and plenty o' tea. Lovely house, ent it, Rory? Very posh.'

They walked into a kitchen-diner in the style of a country house and both Rory and Limmy took a chair each at a dining table, Mum ushering them in before busying herself about the kitchen itself. They set their helmets on the floor beside them.

'You can't be comfortable in them heavy things,' Mum said.

'Oh, the suits?' Limmy replied, making a show of looking herself up and down. 'Outside of the… well, away from this house, it's very cold and there's no air. *Incroyable!*' She laughed, as though the pressure of humour had been building up, and she shook her head as she did it. 'Truth be told, this is all very strange. I mean, we're on a remote planet with no breathable atmosphere, yet we're in a perfectly respectable suburban house inside some kind of bubble thing. Do you know what's going on, Ms Hobble?'

Mum finished making a pot of tea and brought it over on a tray with three china cups and a small plate of biscuits. She took a seat and began pouring the tea, raising her eyes to Rory only and ignoring Limmy's question as though she hadn't heard it.

'Rory, I'm so sorry I yelled at yer… back 'ome. After *he* took me, I thought I'd never see yer again.' She stopped the tea-pouring and leaned in, offering Rory her hands, but he lowered his eyes. 'So much of it's a blur an' I don't exactly know how it all 'appened, but – and this will sound barmy – my *dad* took me, right outta our home. He said he… he said he wanted ter make it up ter me – ter make everythin' better. Said that this planet could make things right. It's got some… *power*, this planet does. An' truth be told, I feel better in myself than I've felt in a long time.'

'How long have you been here?' Limmy asked, quietly.

Mum turned to the social worker, as though she had forgotten she was there. She withdrew her hands from Rory and poured the tea again, placing a cup in front of everyone.

'Honestly, I dunno. I've got no clock, no phone, no internet – not that I'd expect any of that on another planet! But… it's been a while, 'cos he's come and gone a few times. Sometimes, he'll come and stay with me for a few days. Said he wants to get to know me. Keeps apologisin'. I wouldn't have believed half the stuff he told me 'less I'd seen all… *this* with my own eyes. Rory, all I asked for was for 'im to take me back to yer. He'd get angry when I asked for that and disappear for ages, before comin' back and apologisin' all over. He's been gone a while this time, but I expect he'll come back.' Her eyes widened, as though in realisation of something terrible. 'Oh, Rory, I don't know what he'll do if he finds yer here. I can't bear it, but yer must go!'

'We're here now,' Limmy said. 'And you can come with us. We're not leaving you behind. Right, Rory?'

But Rory's eyes remained downturned. He had listened attentively to all his mum had said, but now, at the crucial moment, the thought returned – the same thought that had come to him as he walked over to this house.

'Rory?' Limmy said again, gently.

'I-I don't know,' he replied. 'I don't know anymore.'

There was a grave silence.

'We've come all this way, Rory. I know that you've gone through so much but, deep down, your mum loves you and I don't want you to do anything that you later –'

Rory looked up. Mum held up a hand, nodding once to Limmy. 'Rory, I know what I've put yer through. And I understand why yer hesitant. But I've changed. All this time spent away from yer – it was the kick up the backside I needed. But like I said, since comin' here I've felt better in myself.'

'But it's all a lie,' Rory replied, his voice full of despair. 'You *haven't* changed; this planet changed you! As soon as we leave, you'll be back to your old self. And I don't want to go through that again!'

Mum made to speak, her eyes wet, but this time Limmy was the one to hold up a hand. 'I think Rory needs to get it off his chest. Let him say what he needs to say.'

Rory looked from his mum to Limmy, who nodded and managed a weak smile. He turned back to Mum and channelled all his concentration. 'Every time I woke up – back home, I was scared of what you'd do. If I said or did the smallest thing wrong then you might have yelled at me – or you just yelled at me anyway. I got worried that you'd forget to do dinner and I'd go hungry again. I got worried that you wouldn't pay the bills and we'd have to sleep in the park. I got worried that Curtis and Sean in my class would keep being nasty to me 'cos they knew about you. And… and I got worried that when I came home from school you might be… that you might have… '

But Rory couldn't say it, though Mum's tears suggested she knew what he had been trying to say. 'Oh, God, Rory… I can't… I can't change things that 'ave 'appened. An' I *do* try. But I know that I hurt yer. It's just that so much happens in my head and… and it's difficult, y'know?'

'Underneath it all,' began Limmy, speaking quietly to Rory, 'your mum doesn't want to hurt you. Even grown-ups struggle, kid. But you have this chance. She does seem different–'

'Yeah, but that's only because of *this* place!' Rory snapped.

'For the moment, maybe, yes,' Limmy replied, calmly. 'But if, underneath it all, she had always *wanted* to hurt you and if everything she ever did wrong was because she *chose* to, then this planet wouldn't have been able to hide that. It's removed the trouble from your mum's mind – your mind too – and, beneath all that, is a place where she loves you very much. It's a place that exists in her that I think was always there.'

'And what happens when we leave here?' Rory replied, snivelling.

'Then you both try and find a way back to feeling like this that doesn't involve being a billion miles from home. I'm not saying that's easy, but it is possible. Let your heart guide you – sometimes it only whispers, so you must listen closely.'

Rory looked up again at Limmy, who smiled warmly back at him, and then looked at Mum, who also smiled, wiping a tear or two away with the back of one hand and reaching out to her son with the other. He thought about reaching out to her – all he needed to do was accept her hand, but something still held him back. His mind filled with a montage of all those times he'd been in pain, hungry or afraid and, in that moment, they eclipsed the good. A feeling swelled in his chest like magma.

'No!' he cried, before he could swallow the anger. 'It's too late for any of that. I *don't* love you!'

The light drained from Mum's eyes and, slowly, she withdrew her hand.

'That wasn't very nice now, was it?' The voice was a man's and came from the back door. Rory, Mum and Limmy looked towards its source. The figure was tall, pale and bald. His eyes glimmered with animal cunning and large, dry lips sat perfectly still, set within a patch of grey stubble. He wore a spacesuit quite unlike anything the *Scuabtuinne* could boast: it was skin-tight and resembled a leathery suit of rusty armour. There was no sign of a helmet.

'Y-You're back…' Mum said, her voice faltering.

The man took a step forward and, instantaneously, Rory, Mum and Limmy rose from their chairs.

'Who are you?' Rory asked, trying to keep the fear from his voice. He knew there was only one man it could be, but he needed to hear it.

'My name is Clavius Hobble, though many people call me the Whiffetsnatcher. And am I to take it that you are Rory?'

Rory nodded.

The Whiffetsnatcher placed his hands behind his back and moved forward, almost lazily. 'I seem to recall leaving you a very specific instruction, back in your bedroom, yet here you are all the same.'

Mum stepped in front of Rory, who was nearest to the Whiffetsnatcher. 'Please just let 'em go. They only came looking for me, but I'll stay.'

The Whiffetsnatcher stopped and looked up at Mum. His shoulders were a little hunched and he craned his neck towards her. 'I have no intention of harming... your son. He is family, after all. All I wanted was to bring you somewhere where you could be at peace – where I could protect you from all the pain on that sorry little dying planet –'

'I'm sorry,' Limmy interrupted, stepping in front of Rory as well, 'but where have you been all your daughter's life? You've torn her from her own child and taken her to this lonely, bitter world, like she's your possession. How dare you even consider yourself her father?'

The Whiffetsnatcher eyed Limmy with cool intensity. 'I don't expect you to understand, but everything I've done has been for my daughter.'

'Like abducting children?' Limmy said, her voice agitated. 'Doing who knows what with them. You're a predator, Clavius, and it's not safe to be anywhere near you.'

'I was trying to help those children!' the Whiffetsnatcher snapped. 'I never meant them any harm.'

'And how many did you take?' Limmy retorted, with just as much anger. 'How many children did you take from their parents?'

'Only ever the ones who needed help.'

Limmy didn't respond this time and, in the silence that followed, the Whiffetsnatcher sighed.

'Have you ever heard of the Minervaphage?'

'Yes,' Limmy replied. 'It was the name given to the condition on Minerva that left some babies born with…'

'*Defects*,' the Whiffetsnatcher spat. 'Yes, like myself. Imagine my parents' disappointment: I was the first space-born human and I came out of the womb with twisted, useless legs. The whole colony of Widdershins was terrified that every baby would be born like me, but many weren't. Those that *were* born different were said to have the Minervaphage, which was just some made-up word for a problem no one understood. To this day, it's not understood.

'Anyone born different was shunned. My own parents physically abused me for years because I wasn't *right*. When news of that got out, they were made to leave the colony. Even still, all children like me were kept in a home called Caulder Place, as though we were a dirty secret. I exposed the mistreatment of children there – got the whole place closed down and Dr Cillian Caulder himself disgraced. *And* I was the first person to journey beyond the Asteroid Belt to the ends of the Solar System itself. No one believed me when I returned and told them about Haligogen. But look at me – look at me walking on legs that are no longer crippled! *That* is the power of this planet.'

'But what about the children?' Limmy replied, bringing the conversation back to its original point. 'How were you helping them by snatching them from their families?'

The Whiffetsnatcher stepped forward again, hands still

clenched behind his back. 'Once I knew what this planet could do, I realised that it could offer those children a future free of their physical or mental impairment.'

'You took them here…' Limmy said.

'Yes. On Widdershins, their parents despised them. I offered them a chance.'

'But you didn't offer them a chance, did you? You didn't stop to think that taking those children might not be what they wanted or needed,' Limmy replied, her voice low and trembling.

'In time, I was sure they would understand.'

'And what about those children on Earth?' Limmy continued.

'I had to take them for… other reasons,' the Whiffetsnatcher mumbled.

'W-Where are the children now?' Rory asked, his voice quiet.

The Whiffetsnatcher looked at Rory, standing in between his mother and Limmy. 'They are here, on Haligogen. This is… their world now.'

'I haven't seen any other children,' Rory said.

'That's because yer wouldn't recognise 'em as children,' Mum interrupted.

The Whiffetsnatcher sighed, heavily, as though preparing to drop a great weight. 'No. My plan didn't work out as I thought it would. The planet *did* change those children, but not as I had imagined it would.'

'Oh my God,' Limmy gasped. 'They're… they're the Pry, aren't they?'

The Whiffetsnatcher said nothing, his silence answer enough.

Rory thought back to his pursuit on Earth – those grim little creatures with wrinkly flesh and an unspeakable despair in their eyes. His breath came short and he looked up at the Whiffetsnatcher with renewed horror.

'Why did you keep doing it?' Limmy demanded, her voice rising.

'Each time, I thought that, perhaps, I had worked out what was going wrong. I tried it with children from your dying world and I had the same result.' His expression hardened and he looked off as though into the distance. 'Oh, at first it was successful and every child I brought here was given the chance that unfeeling genetics had robbed them of. Limbs were repaired and minds were reshaped. They laughed and they played in a new childhood… for a time. But it didn't last. I held their hands as they changed. As their skin wrinkled. As their eyes darkened. As their bodies were transmogrified before my eyes. They no longer needed food. They no longer needed water. Even something so simple as air became superfluous. And when I took them off the planet's surface, the changes remained and the essence of who they were was lost forever. They had become husks of the children they had once been and not a day went by when I didn't weep for what I had done to them. They did not survive what I did, but rather they persisted in spite of it. Their obedience to me became a parody of love for a parent. I was the creator of a new species and it mocked the boundary between life and death.

'You're hearing me now and you think me a monster. Good. Perhaps that is what I deserve. But monsters do not start off as such. Monsters are the subtle threading together of anguished experience and desperate misery – and both my anguish and my misery were compelling.' At this, he clutched his forehead and frowned, as though in revelation. 'But wait... *am* I such a monster? Or rather, have I simply held a mirror up to not one but *two* worlds incapable of accepting those among them they deem lesser? I reached out for the possibility of conformity..., and wouldn't all parents do likewise who have looked upon their children and wept for what could have been – even in those dark and lonely moments?' He turned his cold gaze upon his daughter. 'I did it for *you*, Joyce. I had to find out what went wrong and correct it, before I could safely bring you here. And I *did* work it out. In a way. For whatever reason, this planet will change an adult without corrupting them as it did with the children. So long as an adult remains on Haligogen, the change will last...'

Rory listened intently and wondered whether Mum might have done the same to change him, had she been in the Whiffetsnatcher's place. He tensed, wondering if, beneath his spacesuit, his skin had started to wrinkle. Would he, too, become another soulless member of the Pry?

The Whiffetsnatcher took a step towards his daughter, but she retreated, stumbling into a chair.

'Why didn't yer tell me before? Yer told me about my mother, about being born in space and them people hiding me on Earth – but yer didn't mention what yer did before.'

'I only ever wanted you to be happy,' the Whiffetsnatcher continued. 'You were born with the Minervaphage too and I've spent my life trying to make it right.'

Rory was suddenly aware of another presence – this one

behind him – and he turned to see who it was. In the archway separating the kitchen-diner from a hallway was Tall-Tongued Henley. His face was bloody and he had on the same kind of spacesuit that Rory and Limmy did. In one hand, he held his helmet; his knife hung in a sheath at his side.

'But there's nothin' yer can do ter make it right, Clavius!' the Muktuk Whisperer hissed.

'*You?*' the Whiffetsnatcher grunted. 'You should be dead!'

'Rongomai and a great many of my attendants *are* dead, but it'd take a lot more than a lightning bolt from the *Phaethon* ter kill *me*.'

'Henley, where are Xam, Mira and Beak?' Limmy asked, turning to face the Whisperer.

'I thought they were with you, *Captain*,' Henley replied, not removing his eyes from the Whiffetsnatcher. He didn't expand.

Rory exchanged a glance with Limmy, who looked worried. Henley was different, as though something dangerous had always been lurking beneath the surface but was only now making itself completely visible.

The Muktuk Whisperer stepped purposefully into the kitchen-diner, approaching the Whiffetsnatcher in increments, talking as he went. 'I've waited a long time fer this moment, Clavius. Limmy's mission gave me the perfect opportunity, though. Ter return ter Haligogen and look in ter yer eyes. And now that I do, I see fear.'

'What's going on, Henley?' Limmy demanded, her voice bold, though still a little shaky.

'I know yer wondered why I shoulda volunteered myself and Rongomai fer this symbiont crew, all those months ago. It was always ter try and find Clavius here. Yer see, I've been hoping ter be… *reunited* with him fer decades now.'

'Reunited?' Rory said.

'Aye, m'lad. I were part of yer grandfather's first expedition ter Haligogen! Oh, we were a fine young crew aboard that golden ship of his, and what wonders did we find,' Henley said, his voice full of energy and a hint of madness.

Rory remembersed Fleek's words, when he had been trapped in the creature's cave: *there have only ever been two other warm-bloods from your water world who have come to me. One I sensed recently; the other I sense now, though… their mind is changed.* He realised now that the tornit had meant Henley – he'd known the Whisperer was aboard the *Scuabtuinne.*

The Whiffetsnatcher's head dropped. 'Henley, don't…'

'When we returned ter Widdershins – and after we'd become the laughing stock of the colony – I distanced myself from Clavius. Settled down with a good woman and we had a child. Yer didn't like that, did yer, Clavius? I moved on with my life, but yer own family weren't what yer hoped it would be.' Henley took several steps forward and grabbed the Whiffetsnatcher by the throat, ramming him into the wall; Rory, Mum and Limmy cried out. 'Is that why yer did it? Is it?'

'Did what, Henley?' Limmy asked, her voice now full of fear.

Henley's shoulders shook. His voice choked. 'She were only four. Maybe she weren't like the other children but she were *loved*. And he *took* her – right out of her bed as she slept!'

Something in the room changed. Rory could hardly breathe and he thought back to all those times he had been with Henley – he had always sensed, more in what *wasn't* said, that something had been amiss. Henley had kept this truth hidden the whole time. Beside him, Mum started to cry. Limmy pressed a hand on Rory's shoulder, her other covering her mouth. Suddenly, it all made sense to him: Henley had been the driving force all along and even when Limmy had decided that they should go back, it was *he* who had urged them on.

'I'm sorry, Henley,' the Whiffetsnatcher wheezed, struggling with the Whisperer's grip.

'What'd yer do with her!?' Henley roared — a primal, ferocious demand.

'Please, Henley…' the Whiffetsnatcher gasped. 'I didn't mean for…'

'Didn't mean fer what!?'

'I didn't mean for it to be *her* who was chosen. She was already changed by then and… Fleek would not let me pass otherwise.'

Rory could hear his heartbeat in his ears as he sank to the floor, the horror of the Whiffetsnatcher's confession registering. He recalled in that moment, reading the engraving on Henley's earring in Widdershins months ago; it had said, *Sugar and spice…* And then, in the cave with Fleek, another earring among the bones that had said, *All things nice…*

What are little girls made of? the old rhyme came to him.

Henley's daughter.

The world sounded distant and seemed to move in slow motion. Limmy fell to her knees by his side, trying to lift him. As Henley screamed wretchedly, the Whiffetsnatcher struggled with him, managing to bring a knee up into the Whisperer's chest before grabbing a chopping board from the kitchen counter and clubbing him over the head with it. Henley fell to the floor with a spatter of blood, and the Whiffetsnatcher turned tail, throwing open the backdoor and running out into the garden. The strange, artificial light in the bubble that surrounded the house was failing and Rory could see directly up into the sky of Haligogen where the furious orange cloudbanks parted, revealing the moon, Vejovis. His vision was obscured as Mum appeared in front of him, her desperate words lost in an echo. A hand gripped her ankle and she was dragged backwards by Henley, his face a mess of blood and tears. Henley rose from the kitchen floor, and grabbed Mum by the shoulder, throwing her out into the back garden, where she fell to the ground in a heap. Henley followed, his hand moving down to remove the knife from its sheath. He seemed to yell something, as the Whiffetsnatcher, at the bottom of the lawn, stopped and turned back. Rory watched as Mum stood, her head turning slowly to look back at her son. Momentarily, Rory made eye contact with her and she smiled, a single tear rolling down her cheek. 'I love you, Rory,' she seemed to mouth. No sooner were the words out of her mouth than Henley had plunged the knife into her chest. Her expression was one of surprise, before the life faded from her eyes.

18

The Great Question Answered

'We have to go, *now*!' Limmy screamed at Rory, dragging him to his feet and grabbing their helmets.

Rory obeyed, mechanically, his brain hardly able to process what he had just seen. Limmy dragged him through the house – the way Henley would have entered – and they crashed out into the front garden.

The reality of Mum's death hit Rory and he cried out, pleading with Limmy to go back. Limmy turned, held each of Rory's shoulders and looked him in the eye.

'I'm so sorry, Rory. But she's gone. We *have* to get out of here now, before either Henley or the Whiffetsnatcher comes after us. Now, put on your helmet!'

Rory's hands shook as he struggled to secure the helmet back over his head, but he did so and Limmy gave him an encouraging nod. Once Limmy's helmet was also secured, the pair stepped outside the bubble, back into the ashy waste of

Haligogen. Rory gave the house one final glance and bit down on the agony he felt.

Up ahead of them, set against a backdrop of mountains and the remains of Rongomai, was the *Scuabtuinne*, but there was still no sign of Xam, Mira or Beak. Limmy tried hailing them through her suit's comms system, but there was no response.

All of a sudden, the scorched landscape around them lit up in a brilliant assault of white. Both Rory and Limmy came to a stop and looked behind them. In the sky, the clouds tore apart as though blasted by an unseen force: the sodium tail of the moon, Vejovis, had erupted in a silent ball of fire, astonishingly bright, forcing both Rory and Limmy to shield their eyes.

'Oh God...' Limmy muttered through the comms. 'The sodium was still reacting with the HeX that Henley vented. I think... I think that whole moon is covered in salt!'

Rory glanced at Limmy. 'But if the sodium and the HeX are still reacting, that means...'

Limmy looked at him, her expression one of alarm.

At that moment, Gary materialised in front of Rory, making him jump with the suddenness of it. The creature shot out an intricate range of noises and its crystals pulsated in a complex array of purple, pink and turquoise. All at once, Rory's ears filled with static and his vision faded. In his mind's eye, he could see himself, Limmy and Gary, as well as something that he took to be the *Scuabtuinne*. Further away were three other figures that he thought must be the missing members of the crew. A huge circle appeared and enveloped all of the images and then his mind's eye panned out to where a second smaller circle appeared next to the huge one. The smaller circle broke apart and fell upon the huge circle, breaking it apart as well.

After the events had played out in his mind's eye, there was nothing left.

I think I understand what you're telling me, Gary.

Rory's vision and hearing returned; Limmy shook him, but he ignored her and simply stared at Gary, whose crystals were no longer pulsing quite so manically.

'What is it, Rory? Did the muktuk speak to you again?' Limmy asked, urgently.

Rory swallowed hard. 'Yeah. Xam, Mira and Beak – they're alive... I think they're still near those mountains. But...'

Limmy waited, before prompting. 'Yes?'

'We need to get off this planet as soon as possible.'

They both looked towards the sky again where Vejovis' white surface was fissuring with fiery wounds.

The moon is breaking up, Rory realised. *And it will take Haligogen with it when it blows.*

Rory's attention was pulled back to the surface of the planet by Gary, who, through a series of teleportations, had travelled independently back to the *Scuabtuinne* and materialised on the Bridge, the muktuk performing loop-the-loops behind the glass of the Dome.

'Come on!' Limmy said. 'We need to get back to the ship as well. We'll fire the old girl up yet and find the others. Then we'll get out of this hellhole.'

Several minutes later, Rory and Limmy joined Gary on the Bridge. Limmy – seated where Xam would normally be – shouted instructions to Rory, who stood at Mira's position, pressing buttons and reading screens that all indicated the

Scuabtuinne was in a less than satisfactory condition. For one moment, he wondered how the little engineer would react if she could see him standing there, touching her things; he managed a weak smile at the thought of it. No sooner was the smile on his face than his heart sank at the memory of his mum's death and he felt awful for finding anything amusing so soon after the tragedy.

'Okay, kid. I'm gonna try turning it on. Tell me if anything comes up on any of the screens in front of you.'

'Okay,' Rory replied, quietly.

The ship juddered and there came a sound as though of a loud machine starting up from panels beside Rory, as well as from behind him and beneath him. Faint, ice-blue lights flickered across buttons in front of him but, all too quickly, the brief show of life subsided. Limmy tried it at least four more times, swearing more spectacularly with each failed attempt. Eventually, she slammed both her fists down on the arms of Xam's chair and held her head in her hands. But Rory looked intently at the screens and buttons in front of him, trying to piece together the nuggets of information that the (briefly) lit buttons had given him.

'I think there's something wrong with the porphuragate drive,' Rory said, after a while.

Limmy lifted her head and craned her neck to look at him. 'Why'd you say that?'

'One of the buttons that kept lighting up… it said **"DRIVE DE-SCINTILLATED"**.' But Limmy looked blankly at him. '"Scintillate" is the word used to describe the flashing in a diamond. So, I think the button meant that something is wrong with the porphuragate itself.'

Limmy's eyes glinted and a smile spread across her face. 'The porphuragate needs to be charged – that's what that button means! Well done, Rory. But... there's no way to charge it without Rongomai.'

Both Rory and Limmy's attention was taken now by Gary, who flitted about the Bridge as though nervous. 'We don't need Rongomai!' Rory said, nodding.

There was the sound of an almighty crack, as though the world had split in half. Gary squealed and Rory and Limmy looked up and out of the Dome at the sky, where Vejovis glowed with an ominous red and orange. There was a flash and, in eerie silence, part of the moon broke clean and commenced a slow tumble away into space. A matter of moments later, a blast pulverised all of the cloud in the sky and struck the surface of Haligogen, sending up a sea of ash; the *Scuabtuinne* groaned and buckled – for a moment, Rory thought it would be torn apart, but it withstood the assault. However, in the near distance, the house that the Whiffetsnatcher had built was torn away in a whirl of brick, glass and wood.

'We don't have much time!' Limmy mumbled.

Rory raced into Engineering to find Gary already waiting for him. He had only been here a handful of times before and it was as he remembered: a bronze web of pipes, wheels and dials on a platform built around a huge collection of crystals that jutted out of the ship and into space – some manner of foam sealing Engineering off from depressurisation. Last time he'd seen them, the crystals had been glowing a steady blue, humming with the electricity that powered them. But now, the crystals were miserably translucent, like a half-melted glacier.

How do we charge them? Rory asked, inside his head.

In response, Gary rumbled a few times and drifted over to a large, charred cable – a series of thousands of copper-like wires all bound together – half-connected to some kind of huge dynamo that looked uncannily as though it had been plucked straight from the nineteenth century. The muktuk turned to Rory and flashed its crystals.

You think we can get that *thing working? Are you kidding?* Rory responded.

A stutter of static in his ears and Rory had the image of him and Gary in his own head celebrating some great triumph: he cheered and Gary spun around.

Okay, okay. But how?

In response, Gary opened his usually firmly sealed mouth and extended that little tentacle he had first revealed at the top of the church roof back on Earth. As before, a ghostly lightning storm seemed to swirl inside it, developing in intensity as Gary sent the tentacle out towards the charred cable. Making contact, the tentacle built to a terrific, white glow, which arced out and into the cable itself. The cable screeched with the impact of the lightning and an electric current fired up towards the crystals of the porphuragate drive. At first, the crystals only fluttered with a dull, prismatic blue but, soon enough, they ignited a cyan fire, humming with energy that made the hairs on Rory's arms stand on end. Gary finally detached his tentacle from the cable, and drew it back into his mouth.

Nice going, mate! Rory said, inside his head, smiling at the muktuk.

A radio crackled into life from one corner of Engineering. *'Kid, I don't know how you and that crazy muktuk did it but we've got power again. Quick, get back up to the Bridge and let's go find the others!'*

Rory didn't need telling twice and he broke off in a sprint back through the ship.

Rory found Gary already there beneath the Dome, shooting from one side of the Bridge to the other as though in a panic. Limmy was still in Xam's seat, hands moving from button to lever to joystick at about half the speed Xam was capable of.

He took a sharp breath as his eyes travelled up to look beyond the Dome. Filling the sky of Haligogen, the moon Vejovis was an impossible spectacle, cloaked in a ring of fire.

'Try not to look, kid,' Limmy said. 'Just focus on the task! Get back to Mira's station and buckle up!'

Rory did as he was commanded and clipped the seatbelts into place just as the *Scuabtuinne* lifted out of its trench in a ballooning of ash that covered most of the Dome before clearing. The ship swivelled awkwardly to starboard, holding its position only when the corpse of Rongomai and the mountain range heaved into view. In the distance, Rory saw three figures running towards them over jagged rocks and tors.

'Hey! Is that…'

'Must be, kid.'

Then Rory spotted more figures behind Xam, Mira and Beak, closing in on them. 'Limmy, are those…'

'The Pry, yes. Hold tight – I'm not much good with these controls.'

The *Scuabtuinne* blasted over the plains, its shadow burnt ominously across the ashy surface by the inferno-hooded moon plummeting from the heavens. The colour of the mountains, up ahead, intensified, as did the titanic body of Rongomai. The figures of Xam, Mira and Beak shone and the glass of their helmets shot off shards of blinding light. Behind them, the Pry seemed to cry out, arms thrown up over their faces. Rory looked at them with revised feelings as a great sadness flooded him, knowing now what they were. Their fate on this terrible world was clear to him, but he had an idea.

'Limmy, the Pry… if they're left here, they'll die,' Rory said, quietly and with deliberation.

Limmy's head dropped and she sighed, audibly. 'I know. And it… pains me. What the Whiffetsnatcher did to them was appalling.'

Rory took a deep breath, unsure how his social worker would respond to what he had to say. 'Okay, I don't think we can leave them here. If there's any possibility for them to go back to being normal then we have to try. But if we leave them on this planet then we'll never know. I've lost so much here – this is a chance to try and do something good. They're just… kids, like me.'

The ship flew in low, close now to the remaining crew outside.

Limmy nodded, twisting her neck and flashing a smile at him. 'The welfare of the child is paramount… I'm listening to any ideas you have!'

Rory smiled and nodded. 'Right. Once Xam, Mira and Beak

346

are on board, they run up through the cargo bay and lock the door behind them. The Pry will follow them on to the ship and then we just lift the cargo bay ramp. They're trapped in there – but safe – and we escape.'

Limmy smiled again. 'I like it. Alright, let's do this!' She turned to face out of the Dome again and yanked the radio down from above her. 'Xam! Do you read me? It's Limmy! Over!'

The radio crackled, but then a voice responded, interspersed with heavy pants. '*Captain! We're… glad to see you! God… I'm… tired! If this… is… exer… cise… I… do not… want… to ever… do it… again!*'

'*Keep… going, Xam!*' chimed in Mira, panting as well.

'*Indeed, you are not yet approaching cardiac arrest,*' Beak added in a perfectly calm voice, unhelpfully.

'Xam, did you make it to Rongomai? Are there any survivors? Over.'

Xam tried to respond, but struggled so much so that Mira took over. '*We didn't see anyone… Captain. But… we did think… we saw Henley… pass us at one point… But that must have… been our… imagination. Over.*'

Rory felt a pang of hurt and anger at the mention of the Whisperer's name.

Limmy sighed. 'No, that wasn't your imagination. We'll fill you in later. Xam, I'm gonna drop the cargo bay ramp. Listen carefully: once you're all on board, keep going through the cargo bay and lock the door behind you. We're gonna have passengers. Over,' Limmy said, laying out her instruction in a serious voice.

'*Pass… engers?*' panted Xam.

'No time to explain!' Limmy said, urgently. 'Dropping the ramp now. Let's hope the darn thing doesn't jam. Over.'

From outside the ship came a dull *thunk* as the ramp slammed into the ground. Rory watched as Xam, Mira and Beak reached the ship and disappeared from sight, under the Bridge, to where he knew the ramp would be waiting. Behind them, the Pry seemed to have gotten over the shock of Vejovis's blinding light and were staggering on towards the ship, soon lost to sight beneath the Bridge as well.

'Xam! Update, please!' Limmy yelled into the radio.

'*We're all on… board, Captain,*' Xam responded. '*Door to… the cargo… bay closed. But… the Pry… followed us… Over.*'

'That's fine, Xam. Get up to the Bridge ASAP, all of you. Over and out,' Limmy commanded.

Rory and Limmy's attention was drawn towards the sky, where a shockwave of flame erupted, followed several seconds later by a noise like a thousand cracks of thunder. Beneath them, the planet itself rumbled. Gary whined and his crystals flickered weakly.

'The moon… it's entered the upper atmosphere of Haligogen. We need to get out of here now,' Limmy said, her voice dangerously low.

Rory looked out at the planet's surface and saw no more Pry. 'I-I think the Pry are all on board. But what about Rongomai's attendants? What if some of them are still alive?'

Limmy's shoulders dropped and she shook her head. 'We simply don't have time to search for them now. We don't even know if any of them are alive. It breaks my heart, but… we have to go.'

A brief silence between them was broken only when Limmy

pressed the button on her panel for closing the cargo bay ramp, muttering something about hoping it actually closed properly for once. She pulled on a joystick and the *Scuabtuinne* spun around, nose pointing towards the sky. Vejovis loomed to port with a promise of death and catastrophe.

'Engine looking good, kid?' Limmy asked.

Rory checked the various dials and buttons in front of him. 'It looks okay, yes. I think...'

At that moment, Xam, Mira and Beak tumbled onto the Bridge – Xam and Mira with helmets removed and faces drenched in sweat. Xam called a greeting to Rory and high-fived Limmy, who hopped out of the navigator's seat and into the captain's chair. Rory stepped smartly away from Mira's station, waiting for a volley of abuse, but instead she nodded to him and even offered a 'Thank you'. Rory dashed over to his usual seat and Beak rolled to a stop beside him.

'Did you find your mother, Master Hobble?' Beak asked, casually.

At this unexpected question, Limmy, Xam and Mira all turned to face Rory, whose face crumpled. 'Yeah, we found her, Beak...'

'I'll bring you up to speed later, guys. All you need to know right now is that *this*' – Limmy swept an arm around the Bridge – 'is all of us.'

Xam and Mira looked sadly at Rory, who lowered his eyes under their gaze.

Outside, another tsunami of fire tore across the sky – but this one was far closer than the last, and torrents of ash and rock leapt up from the surface of the planet. The *Scuabtuinne* rolled to starboard and a great tearing sound suggested a rupture of the ship on its port side. Everyone's attention snapped back to the impending disaster.

'Get us out of here, Xam! *Now, now, now!*' Limmy screamed.

Xam didn't need a second invitation. 'Hold on to your stomachs, guys!'

The *Scuabtuinne* burst forward and up through the sky. Out of the starboard side of the Dome, Rory saw several mountain peaks collapse and Rongomai's body shifted position. A flash of light, so sudden and blinding, penetrated the Bridge making everyone groan and shield their eyes. As it subsided, Rory looked out of the port side of the Dome to see a column of fire exploding over a distant point where Vejovis had finally smashed into Haligogen. It was absolutely silent, but another shockwave approached, wrenching up the very tectonics of the dying planet.

'Xam…' Limmy said, her voice almost a warning.

'I know, Captain. I know.'

As the shockwave neared them in a deluge of rock and fire, the ship started to shake, then to rattle and then to scream in an agony of metal.

'We're gonna try and crest it like a wave!' Xam yelled above the deafening noise.

Rory watched out of the port side of the Dome as the shockwave gathered momentum and he clung on to his seatbelt as the *Scuabtuinne* lifted above island-sized rocks. Everyone screamed in unison as the ship entered a maelstrom of smaller rock, narrowly avoiding chunks that would have swatted it like a fly. Fire curled around the Dome and rock bounced off the glass in jabs and punches, cracking it here and there.

'We're gonna make it! We're gonna make it!' Limmy yelled.

And the *Scuabtuinne* stopped rattling, the fire disappeared and the rocks softened to a calmer rain of fist-sized projectiles. Everyone on the Bridge held a collective breath, as though any moment something terrible would happen, but it did not. The ship surged on and the green cloud surrounding Haligogen came into sharper focus.

Xam chuckled and turned his head. 'We actually did it! We actually –'

But before Xam could finish his sentence, Rory, Limmy and Mira pointed, as one, out of the Dome and cried a warning as one final crag of rock hurtled towards them. Xam could not respond in time and the ship roared again in a screeching of metal – conduits on the Bridge blowing in a flourish of sparks – and the *Scuabtuinne* spun around and around. On the Bridge, Gary squealed and somersaulted about, bouncing off the Dome and the floor. Beak slid across the floor and toppled against the arcade machine terminals beside Mira. Eventually, the ship's rotations slowed and, finally, stopped, bringing it round to face Haligogen.

'Direct hit! And the engine's failing!' Mira yelled, touching her forehead where a nasty cut bled over an eyebrow.

'Look at the planet,' Rory said.

Haligogen was now a charred mess with what remained of Vejovis eating into it, like a crispy orange being stuffed into a coconut and ignited with a blowtorch.

'She's gonna blow…' Xam added, his voice quiet.

The realisation hit everyone: they weren't going to make it out alive.

After a few moments of silence, Limmy unbuckled her belt

and rose out of the captain's chair. 'I'm sorry, guys. This is a real bummer. It's been the biggest honour of my life to serve as your capt–'

'Wait!' Rory said, surprising himself.

That familiar static filled his ears – faster each time now – and all the physical world fell away so that he was once more on that white, astral plane, his ears filled with perfect silence. But this time was different: there were no little figures representing him or a muktuk or a planet; instead, Gary himself occupied this place with him. The muktuk emitted a deep and soothing noise, floating over to Rory as it did so.

Thanks, mate. Is this… is this 'cos you know it's the end?

Gary's whirring bass moved up a frequency and it turned to face into what could have been the distance, only this white place had no sense of depth. All at once, something approached, hurtling towards them and coming to such an abrupt stop in front of him that Rory cried out. It was Haligogen, with Vejovis tearing it apart.

I know. We both lost our mums to that planet…

But Gary's face looked upwards and Rory watched as several objects – one faintly glinting gold – lifted up from the planet and fired off into nothingness. Rory wondered what it meant, but shook his head: what difference did it make now? However, the muktuk seemed to sense Rory's surrender and made several squeaks, before turning to face the empty white behind Rory. Rory turned around and found the turquoise network he had seen before flicker into life. A little way along one strand of the network was a node with a small planet spinning around on it. It looked like…

Neptune… What's Gary showing me?

Almost instinctively, Rory reached out towards the icy world with one hand and felt himself being pulled along the network until the planet spun around both him and Gary. He looked up at the muktuk, who bounced up and down, mid-air, and squeaked some more. Rory chuckled, despite himself, and looked up and along the network again. In the distance was another world – this one itself a weak turquoise with rings and moons: Uranus. Rory reached out to it, just as he had with Neptune, and once again felt himself dragged along the network. But as Uranus approached, he was reminded of the ordeal on its moon, Lepidus, and he swatted at it, sending him further on along the network. Gary squeaked with greater enthusiasm still, as they passed first Saturn, then Jupiter and then the Asteroid Belt. Approaching the Martian system, Rory held up a hand to try and stop. His movement along the network ceased abruptly.

Look, Gary! There's Mars – and there's Minerva…

Gary squeaked and squeaked, as though desperately willing someone to get the right answer in a game of charades. Rory looked at the muktuk and scrunched his forehead.

But… What do you want me to do?

Gary squeaked and squeaked – more urgently. Rory looked from the muktuk back to Minerva, lifted one tentative hand, and then reached out to hold the moon in the palm of his hand. Gary looped-the-loop and his crystals pulsed white, with a revving noise that came from him in waves. Rory understood at last, as the turquoise network fell away and the white flickered out, bringing him back to the Bridge of the *Scuabtuinne*, where Limmy, Xam, Mira and Beak crowded over him as he lay on the floor.

353

They all spoke at once, asking him what had happened – whether he was alright. He batted away their hands, eyes unfocused, and he pulled himself up. Beyond the Dome, Haligogen finally exploded in silent trauma, sending out a bombardment of rock that seemed to rain Hell itself upon the ship. In front of the Dome, Gary floated, his crystals just as brilliant as they had been on that white plane, his squeaks just as insistent.

It's the Great Question, isn't it, mate? It's what Henley spoke about back in that temple in Widdershins. Muktuks can travel far – real far.

Snapping out of his trance, Rory leapt forwards to try and reach Gary before the shockwave from Haligogen destroyed the ship. He threw a hand out to the muktuk as the hull of the *Scuabtuinne* buckled inward.

'Now, Gary!'

The muktuk exploded into a ball of light and the ship whirled away from Haligogen, entering some kind of plasma tunnel in space, which materialised in front of them. A force like a hurricane smacked into Rory and the rest of the crew; together, they screamed as the *Scuabtuinne* was catapulted at unimaginable speed. The light streaming from Gary intensified until it burst altogether, sending the muktuk flying into one side of the Bridge and Rory into another side. Looking out of the Dome, he watched as the ship thundered towards black ground and olive rivers, multicoloured tangles of coral-like plants on the horizon. He smiled with the realisation of where they were and, as the *Scuabtuinne* crashed into Minerva's igneous soil, he lost consciousness.

☆

The bed was soft under his weight and his head was held soothingly by a pillow that moved a little – for one moment he wondered whether the pillow had been trained to do this as a form of alien massage, and a smile spread across his face. As he opened his eyes, he found Limmy, Xam, Mira and Beak all rushing to him, just as they did on the *Scuabtuinne*. But he knew he couldn't be on the ship anymore – not if the high, white ceiling was anything to go by.

'W-Where am I?' he said, his dry throat making him cough.

Limmy helped him with a cup of metallic water and he settled back into his bed.

'In answer to your question,' Limmy replied, smiling, 'you are on Minerva, in Widdershins, snuggled up in a bed in the Lacnod Infirmary and it is four hours past redrise.'

'You've been out cold for two days, little Hobster,' Xam chuckled, enthusiastically.

'We have been most concerned for your wellbeing, Master Hobble,' said Beak.

'*I* was sure you'd be fine, though,' Mira added, haughtily.

Memories of what happened on the Bridge of the *Scuabtuinne* returned and Rory cast his gaze about looking for...

'Gary! Where's Gary? Is he okay?'

Limmy held her hands up. 'He's just fine. Don't worry. Look.'

Rory followed Limmy's outstretched finger, which indicated the bed next to him. Gary lay on the bed, a cover over his lower half and his crystals pulsing gently. Rory looked back at Limmy, still worried.

'When we crashed, Gary was knocked out cold – as were

you – and his crystals were only flashing weakly. But he's okay now. Just needs to rest,' Limmy said.

Rory rubbed his head, aware now of a dull ache behind his ears.

'W-What happened, though? How did we get here?'

'We got lucky,' Xam replied. 'Crashed a couple of miles outside of Widdershins and a patrol picked us up. I think the whole colony saw us arrive! Ha!'

'It seems,' added Beak, 'that a tunnel opened in the sky, Master Hobble, out of which we came.'

Rory looked from one face to the next, Xam's clearly suppressing what must have been an urgent need to explode with excitement.

'W-What about the Pry?' Rory asked, remembering the *Scuabtuinne*'s cargo.

Limmy managed a weak smile. 'Well, when we crashed, the cargo bay ramp tore away and most of the Pry ran off, kid. The patrol that found us reckon the Pry headed straight for the Arid Reef – y'know, the forest here on Minerva. But… a number of Pry didn't make it and we… saw their bodies in the cargo bay.'

Everyone fell quiet.

'But we did save a lot of 'em, Hobster,' Xam said, cutting through the silence. 'No idea what they're up to now, but we got a lot of 'em to safety.'

'And that's all on you, kid. You saved them,' Limmy said, smiling.

'And now we're famous!' Xam added, Limmy elbowing him and Mira dramatically holding a finger to her lips.

Rory frowned. 'Famous?'

Limmy sighed. 'I was gonna let you rest up first, but…

yes. Oh, well it is quite exciting. Apparently, the whole of Widdershins is talking about us, y'know, after seeing the hole open in the sky and our little ship flying through.'

'And then we went, "Nyyyaaarrrgh! Smash!" and the ship *boomed* as it hit the surface and everyone heard it!' Xam added, bouncing a little.

'There're crowds *everywhere* now,' Mira said, with a tone of distaste.

'It would seem the Temple of the Muktuks is particularly celebratory, Master Hobble,' Beak noted. 'You may be in for some questions from them on the nature of your bond with the muktuk calf you designate "Gary".'

'Oh! Talking of being questioned,' Limmy said, holding up a finger. She rooted around in a pocket of her waistcoat and pulled out a folded slip of paper. Unfolding it, she handed it to Rory, who took note of the glowing blue ink. He looked up at Limmy, questioningly. 'Read it! Read it!'

Rory scanned the parchment. There was a seal at the top with complicated crest and the words 'Chain of Migration'. He swallowed hard, remembering back to his assessment all those months ago with that cold man.

Dear Mr Hobble,

I am writing to inform you that, following your assessment for an asylum claim in Widdershins, the Chain of Migration has reached a decision.

You will be pleased to learn that your application has been successful and you have been granted leave to remain until you are 17.5 years old, at which point you will need to make an application for further leave. You will now need to register for identification and provide details of an address. We have been advised that your advocate, Limmy Oshunwale, will assist you with these tasks.

Should you or your advocate have any queries in the interim, please come directly to our offices to book an appointment.

Yours sincerely,

Mr Theodore Johnson
Assessment Officer
Department of Assessments
Chain of Migration

─────────

Rory looked up at Limmy, mouth hanging open. 'D–Does this mean… I don't have to go back to Earth?'

Limmy beamed at him. Xam beamed at him. Even Mira allowed a small beam to break across her face. Beak could not beam at anyone.

Rory chuckled to himself. 'You hear that, Gary? I'm an alien like you now!' But his laughter trickled out.

Rooory, Rooory. So happy, yet Mum is dead. Dead, dead, dead. And you turned her away at the end so she died thinking you didn't love her – you're a terrible person!

Limmy waved Xam, Mira and Beak out of the ward and settled down on the bed beside Rory. 'I've… brought the others up to speed with everything that happened on Haligogen. Do you… want to talk? You know I'm here for you.'

Rory felt the tears on his cheeks. 'I... I turned her away... when she wanted to make things right... She died thinking that I didn't love her.'

Limmy took in a breath, as though to steady herself. 'I don't believe that, Rory. I saw her face, at the end, and she knew how much you loved her. Your reaction to what she was promising was perfectly natural, kid. The Whiffetsnatcher said it was all a trick of that planet, but who's to say? Only time could have given her the opportunity to show you if she had truly changed, but you were both robbed of that chance – and that is not your fault, nor is it your mum's. Your mum hurt you a lot and, at the end of the day, you are still just a child and the responsibility to regain your trust would have been hers and hers alone. I know that you're going to be fighting this in your head for a long time to come, because that's what your OCD does to you. You may get memories that aren't even real. But you did nothing wrong and I am extremely proud of you, Rory Hobble, extremely proud.'

Rory felt a little better, though the tears did not stop. 'I *did* love her, Limmy. I promise you I did.'

'I know, Rory. But you don't need to prove that to anyone – least of all to yourself.'

Rory drew in a deep, shuddering breath and rubbed his face. With Limmy's reassurance, the thoughts weakened, but they were never far and would always come back.

'What happens now, Limmy?'

Limmy smiled and stood, ambling over to a window. 'Come here.'

Rory looked blankly at her for one moment, before removing the sheet covering his lower body, hopping out of the bed and walking over to the window as well. It took him a moment to realise that the Lacnod Infirmary must have been in one of the two Towers he recalled as sitting atop the waterfall in Widdershins. Far below, the colony itself bustled with life and he could see the Temple of the Muktuks – its pyramidal shape standing out against all the other buildings and structures. Beyond Widdershins was an ashy plain and, beyond that, part of the Arid Reef sat still and colourful in fossilised calm. The sky was alight with the enormity of Mars and one of the planet's two traditional moons pottered along in a shadowy orbit.

'What is it, Limmy?'

Limmy smiled at Rory and the Martian light caught her face, flooding her dark cheeks with red as though of dawn. 'Out there lies our next adventure. I don't know where it is, or what it looks like yet, but I know it's there. Perhaps it's at a quarter past darkfall, or twenty-five to redrise. Perhaps it's right here on Minerva or up there, slightly to the left of *that* star' – she said, pointing at an indiscriminate bulb in the heavens – 'but so long as we all remain together – you, me, Gary, Xam, Mira and Beak – then we can't stray too far wrong.'

Rory smiled and put an arm around his social worker. 'I'll be waiting for your signal.'

Behind them, Gary cooed in an unstressed sleep, crystals cultivating a palette of pink, purple and turquoise, mind unravelling a universe without limits.

It was almost time to wake.

Information for parents and teachers about OCD from OCD Action

ABOUT OCD ACTION

OCD Action is the national UK charity providing support and information to people affected by obsessive compulsive disorder (OCD) and related conditions (body dysmorphic disorder (BDD), trichotillomania and dermatillomania). OCD Action's support extends to parents and other family members, friends, carers and professionals.

Support and information is provided via a range of support services, including a phone and email helpline, a network of Skype/Zoom/phone support groups, independent, local support groups, an e-helpline for young people and peer-support forums. OCD Action works to raise awareness of the disorder amongst the public and front-line healthcare workers, and campaigns for better access to quality treatment.

INFORMATION FOR PARENTS

OCD can affect anyone at any age. It's not uncommon for OCD to develop during childhood/early teens, and though this can be incredibly difficult for the young person and their family to deal with, it's important to remember that OCD is a treatable condition and there is lots of help available.

If you are concerned that your child may have OCD, here are some helpful steps that you can take to support them.

Understand the impact that OCD is having on them

It is important that you try to understand and appreciate the impact that OCD is having on your child. Compulsions can be both mental and physical, so although you may be able to see some of the behaviours they are carrying out to try and relieve anxiety, there may be other compulsions that they are carrying out that are less 'obvious'; these can be equally draining and time consuming. It is also important to remember that before the compulsion comes the obsession. Obsessions are typically distressing intrusive thoughts, feelings, urges or images and can cause high levels of anxiety.

Allow your child the space to explain how they are feeling and why they feel the need to carry out their compulsion – this will help them to feel less isolated and less ashamed of their condition.

Appreciate that they can't 'just stop'

OCD is a debilitating disorder. It makes people do things that they don't want to do and have thoughts that they do not want to have. They cannot just stop. It is important to show that you recognise this and that you acknowledge how hard it can be. The symptoms may seem irrational to you, but the fear for the person with OCD is very real.

Support the person, but not the OCD

It is common for people living with OCD to try and involve others in their rituals and to seek reassurance from loved ones that nothing bad is going to happen. Although compulsions may temporarily relieve someone's anxiety, ultimately, they feed into the OCD and cause the cycle of obsessions and compulsions to become stronger. It is human nature for parents to want to help their child feel as happy as possible, and sometimes compulsions are unavoidable, but be mindful of 'sneaky compulsions' and, where possible, try to avoid facilitating the OCD.

Offer hope and support

Sometimes people with OCD find it very hard to see the light at the end of the tunnel. The reality is that most people with OCD will benefit from treatment and be able to get their life back on track. There are lots of inspiring stories on the OCD Youth website that you can share with them to help offer hope. There is also a video for young people available at www.ocdisnotme.com. Accepting help can be difficult, especially as OCD treatment can feel really scary at times, but seeing other young people fight the condition can be really inspiring and a good motivator to accept help.

Show the alternative

When you are in the midst of OCD it can be hard to imagine life without it. It can be helpful for you to talk to your child about what things would be like without OCD. Help them to visualise what they could be doing or what you could be doing together. Setting small goals and having something to work towards can be helpful.

Seek treatment

The first step to seeking treatment is to visit a GP who can refer you and your child on to a mental health professional for an assessment and diagnosis. From there, treatment for OCD can be offered. There are two recommended treatments for OCD, cognitive behavioural therapy (CBT) and medication. CBT for OCD should always include *exposure and response prevention* (ERP).

Remember that having OCD is no one's fault

It can be really challenging to learn that your child has OCD but remember that this cruel condition can affect anyone. The cause of OCD is largely unknown, and it is no one's fault that your child has OCD – the important thing to focus on is getting better and living a life free from the condition.

Seek support for yourself

Seeking treatment for OCD and living with someone with the condition can be really challenging. If your child has OCD, it's important to remember to look after yourself too. OCD Action offers a range of support services for parents. You can call or email the Helpline and speak to trained volunteers who can listen, provide support and offer information.

support@ocdaction.org.uk
0300 636 5478

OCD Action also offers online support groups specifically for parents, which you can access from the comfort of your home. The groups offer a safe, supportive and non-judgemental space for you to chat to other parents in similar situations. For each group, a private Facebook group is available, so you can keep in touch with other parents in between sessions.

The OCD Action forum also has a specific section for family members and friends. This 24-hour peer-support network is available 365 days a year for you to chat to other people in similar situations.

Should I tell my child's school?

It is your choice whether or not you tell your child's school about their OCD. It is worth keeping in mind that telling your child's school about the problems that they are facing can be beneficial. The school will be able to provide more tailored support for your child if they are aware of the difficulties they are experiencing. It is important that your child feels involved in making the decision about whether or not to tell the school, as they may have some concerns about this. Breaking down these concerns and talking to them about the benefits of notifying the school can be helpful.

Once OCD treatment begins, it can be beneficial for the young person's teacher to liaise regularly with the Child and Adolescent Mental Health Service (CAMHS) or equivalent service that your child is receiving care under. This liaison can facilitate a greater understanding of how the child's symptoms are presenting in school and also provide an opportunity for school staff to identify, implement and monitor potentially helpful strategies.

If your child feels comfortable, it might also be useful to provide the school with some information about OCD. OCD Action can provide you with information resources that you can share with your school.

Information about OCD Youth

OCD Action has an OCD Youth service for young people aged 14–25. OCD Youth is run by young people with OCD, for other young people. As part of the service, an e-helpline and peer-support forums are available. Their youth specific website hosts a range of insightful and inspiring blog posts and support information.

Website: www.ocdyouth.org

OCD is a debilitating disorder and can impact any area of a person's life. For children and adolescents, OCD could have an impact, often quite significant, on school life. Below you can find some tips for supporting a young person with OCD through their education.

Spotting signs and symptoms

OCD affects everybody differently, but there are some common signs and symptoms that might indicate a young person is potentially struggling with OCD during school hours. They include (but are not limited to):

NB: showing these symptoms does not necessarily indicate mental health difficulties. Only a mental health professional can make a diagnosis.

Signs to look out for	What could be happening if the young person has OCD
Seeming distracted or difficulty concentrating	Performing mental rituals or worrying about something related to OCD
Being overly tired	Up late at night performing rituals or being mentally exhausted from worrying
Having particularly messy work	Feeling the need to rewrite work because it isn't/doesn't feel 'right'
Frequent or prolonged toilet visits	Completing cleaning or checking rituals
Inability to handle objects, touch certain things or sit in certain places	Fearing becoming contaminated
Excessive questioning, confessing or seeking reassurance	Worrying that something bad has happened/will happen
Repeated lateness	Being delayed by rituals
Arranging items on a desk or needing things to be a certain way	Carrying out ordering or symmetry rituals
Repetitive behaviours such as getting up and down from a desk or opening and closing the door	Feeling the need to perform these rituals to stop something bad from happening
Reduction in grades or decline in school performance	Becoming overwhelmed by obsessions and rituals, leading to falling behind at school

If I know a young person has OCD or a related condition, how can I help?

Working in conjunction with treatment providers

- If the young person is currently under the care of a mental health provider, it can be helpful for you to be in regular contact with them, providing the young person and their family are happy with this. The mental health professional working with the young person can help you to set out reasonable adjustments that compliment any treatment that is being undertaken. Working towards similar goals using consistent strategies to manage the OCD symptoms will be more effective for the young person both in school and at home.

- If the school has a Special Education Needs Coordinator (SENCO) or staff trained in mental health first aid and wellbeing, work with them to identify what support can be offered to help the young person at school.

- With the family and young person's permission, request an Education, Health and Care plan (EHC) for the young person from their local authority. EHC's help to set out any additional needs the young person may have in school.

Raise awareness of OCD in your school

With the young person's consent, you may wish to organise a mental health awareness/OCD session in school to help educate students and members of staff about the condition. Although understanding of OCD has improved in recent years, there are still many misconceptions surrounding the condition that can lead those living with OCD feeling embarrassed, ashamed, or sometimes even unaware of their condition.

Raising awareness of OCD can help school peers be more understanding, consider their language, and it may help others who are struggling in silence.

Making reasonable adjustments at school

If a young person confides in you about their OCD, you may consider making some adjustments in the classroom to help them through the school day. Where possible, these adjustments should be made in conjunction with the young person's mental health providers, to assure that adjustments are consistent with any treatment being offered. Adjustments will vary depending on the young person's individual circumstances, but you may consider some of the following:

- Short breaks during lessons.

- Having a specific desk/equipment for the young person to use. For example, having their own lab coat in a science lesson.

- Understanding if the young person finds certain subjects challenging. For example, they may not be able to say certain words, phrases or numbers when asked to as that may trigger their anxiety.

- Consider extending deadlines or decreasing the amount of homework given if the young person is falling behind or struggling to meet deadlines.

- If the young person becomes highly anxious in the classroom as a result of their OCD, it may be helpful to recognise this and what may trigger this anxiety. Depending on what stage they are at in their treatment, options are to help them 'sit out' their anxiety, discuss it, or take a planned break.

• Allowing extra time or support during exams.

A challenge for teachers is finding the balance between helping the young person 'face their fears' whilst at the same time not causing the young person to become overwhelmed.

Support outside of the classroom

• Be aware that any circumstances that differentiate a young person from their peers may lead to bullying. Awareness talks could help to educate peers on this.

• If a young person confides in you about their OCD, give them the space to talk and be listened to. This condition can make people feel isolated and ashamed, so having a space to speak about their worries can make a big difference.

• Living with OCD can rob people of their confidence and lead to them being withdrawn. It can be helpful for school staff to highlight the young person's strengths outside of OCD – for example, excelling in a certain hobby, or a particularly note-worthy personality trait such as being understanding and kind.

• Be mindful not to punish behaviours that they cannot control. OCD is challenging for both the person living with the condition, but also those close to that person. It can be difficult to watch someone carry out behaviours that might seem irrational, pointless or sometimes even disruptive. Be mindful that those living with the condition cannot simply 'snap out of it'. Having a good understanding of OCD can help you differentiate between OCD behaviours and 'regular' day to day difficulties.

- Maintain effective communication with the young person's family to ensure you are all working together to put the best strategies in place to help.

- Understand that co-morbidity is common with OCD and other mental health conditions, such as depression, attention deficit hyperactivity disorder (ADHD), autism and Tourette's.

- It is important to be mindful that for some young people symptoms are much worse at home than at school. Teachers need to understand that children and their families may be affected significantly by OCD in the home. Where possible, be aware of the pressures the young person is experiencing and the potential impact they can have on school performance, even if no intervention is currently necessary in school.

Reach out to OCD Action

It is important to remember that you can only do so much to support a young person living with OCD. If you aren't sure how to help, or if you are finding the situation challenging, then there are people who can help. OCD Action's Helpline welcomes calls from school staff and can provide information, support, or a listening ear when you need it.

support@ocdaction.org.uk
0300 636 5478

Acknowledgements

I'm not sure whether people ever read the Acknowledgements, so I guess that means I can say whatever I want because no one's looking.

Bum. Fart. Bogeys.

Oh, but then again I suppose the people who have a *reasonable* expectation of being mentioned might read the Acknowledgements so they can say, 'Oh! Oh! Look, I'm there!' I'd hate to disappoint them, so let the acknowledging commence!

I'd like to thank my wife, Johanna, and daughters, Freya and Eleanor, for their unceasing love and support over the years. Each of you gives my life meaning.

This book would not have been published without the generosity of the 248 supporters who pledged for it while it was crowdfunding, so I will always be indebted to all of you for backing me and I really hope it was worth the wait.

The team at Unbound has been absolutely fantastic and I owe my thanks to so many of you, but I do wish to pick out a few in particular: Xander Cansell was the one who gave me a contract; John Mitchinson has been clear that he is proud to have published this book; Andrew and Craig in Editorial have always been lightning quick to get back to me; and Mark Ecob and his team did a spectacular job with the cover design. However, I must give a very special mention to Anna Simpson, Head of Editorial, who has been an absolute joy to liaise with and continues to be exceptional in her support. Unbound is more than just a publisher though. It has spawned a community of authors who are particularly active through Facebook and who have always been enormously supportive. I'm not sure what I'd do without you all.

My two editors, Hal Duncan and Philip Purser-Hallard, also have my thanks, as their warm words were very encouraging and they each gave me important suggestions that improved the book.

Next, I'd like to thank everyone at OCD Action who has supported me over the years. But my biggest thanks go to Olivia Bamber. Olivia has been an absolutely crucial part of this project and I would need many pages to list everything she has done to help me. I am absolutely certain, however, that had she not been involved then this book would not have been published.

A shout out to the Leaving Care service in Croydon Council who remain a wonderful work family and an inspirational set of people.

I'd like to thank the OCD community – especially on Twitter – which has taken me in as one of its own and shown enormous belief in what I am doing. In particular, Dr Jo Edge has been an incredible source of support – were it not for her help, I may not have been published.

Finally, I'd like to thank you, dear reader, for buying this book and giving it a go. I hope you enjoyed it!

Unbound is the world's first crowdfunding publisher, established in 2011.

We believe that wonderful things can happen when you clear a path for people who share a passion. That's why we've built a platform that brings together readers and authors to crowdfund books they believe in – and give fresh ideas that don't fit the traditional mould the chance they deserve.

This book is in your hands because readers made it possible. Everyone who pledged their support is listed at the front of the book and below. Join them by visiting unbound.com and supporting a book today.

Neil Ackerman
Richard Adam
David Adams
Karen Adams
Zoe Adams
Femi Afelumo
Ruby Ahmed
Nazia Ali
Jess Allen

Lulu Allison
Gina Antchandie
Matt Arsenault
Natalie Ashcroft
Joanne Askew
Tim Atkinson
Chris Baier
Lily Bailey
Ina Bajrami

Olivia Bamber
Jacqui Banton
Kirsten Barnicot
Zena Barrie
Chris Beckett
Catherine Benfield
Ashleigh Bennett
Kelly Best
Letitia Betteridge
Elizabeth Biggs
Stephen Blascak
Jade Bloomfield
Hannah Bond
Stephanie Bretherton
Hannah Brice
Dan Brotzel, Martin Jenkins & Alex Woolf
Erica Buist
Jacqui Castle
Jamie Chipperfield
Mathew Clayton
Lynsey Cobden
Jason Cobley
Steph Coen
Paulette Comrie
Tamsen Courtenay
Chris Cusack
Amanda de Grey
Sarah Dobson
Jessica Duchen
Rhianne Elleston Pascall
Abi England
Seb Falk
Justin Fischedick
Matilda Fitzmaurice
Evan Foster
G.E. Gallas
Richard Gilmour
Ayisha Govindasamy
Susan Grace
Claire Grant
Josephine Greenland
Daniel Gretton-Doidge
Geoffrey Gudgion
Hannah Gyebi-Ababio
Claire Handscombe

Tamara Hanley
Eleanor Harris
Lianne Harrison
Daniel Head
Jeanette Heidenberg
Emily Hodgkinson
Paul Holbrook
Stephen Hosking
Jen Hughes
Robin Hummel-Fuller
Rebecca Jackson
Laura Johnson
Dulcie Jones
Sam Jones
Dan Kieran
Patrick Kincaid
Shona Kinsella
Allie Klionsky
Linda Knowles
Helene Kreysa
Jamie Kwon
Ian Lavis
David Lawrie
Chris Limb
Marcia Lindsay
Victoria Locke
Deborah J. Long
Lindsay McDowall
Ana McFarlane
Aleisha McKenzie
James McMahon
Shirley Medcalf
Aaron Millican
Mary Monro
Joy Morris
Chelsea Moss
Glyn Myers
Rhel ná DecVandé
Sandy Natarajan
Carlo Navato
Fride Nilsen
Helena Nordberg
Stephen Nyasamo
Peter O'Brien
John-Michael O'Sullivan
Gideon Obeng

Louise Owen
Benjamin Owsley
Maxwell Owusu-Brempong
Lucia Partridge
Justin Pollard
Giuseppe Porcaro
Catherine Pretty
Ritesh Rathod
Reni Ravi
Zelda Rhiando
Adrian Robbins
Jessica Romanowski
Jessica Scalzo
Deborah Schauffler
Nicki Shaw
AnneMarie Silbiger
Ian Skewis
Lianne Slavin
Rebecca Smith

Janice Staines
Karen Tay
Clare Toner
Peter Tucker
Billy Turford
Giulia Ubezio
Zsuzsanna Ujhelyi
Barbara Valentini
Maggie Vine
Danielle Walker
Karen Walker
Tom Ward
Edward Whatley
Nadine White
Louise Wilkin
Hal Williams
Joan Williams-Payne
Joshua Winning
Laura Wood